T0127716

# JJ Kapock

## Early Life

John Gary

authorHOUSE®

*AuthorHouse™*
*1663 Liberty Drive*
*Bloomington, IN 47403*
*www.authorhouse.com*
*Phone: 1 (800) 839-8640*



*Published by AuthorHouse 05/29/2018*

*ISBN: 978-1-5462-4031-0 (sc)*
*ISBN: 978-1-5462-4029-7 (hc)*
*ISBN: 978-1-5462-4030-3 (e)*

*Library of Congress Control Number: 2018905201*

*Print information available on the last page.*



*This book is printed on acid-free paper.*

# Contents

# Chapter 1

IT'S EARLY SPRING. BASEBALL SEASON is upon us. JJ Kapok, our hero, is ready to get the ball and glove out of the closet.

It's a beautiful day. He calls Tommy, Jimmy, and Billy and asks them if they want to meet on the school field and get a game going. They are all ready and willing. "Okay, see you there at noon. Call some other guys. Let's get as many as possible."

At noontime, JJ says, "Hey, what do you guys think about the Orioles this year?"

Tommy says, "Oh, they probably will finish last again."

Jimmy says, "I don't know. The new catcher, Gus something, is supposed to be a home run hitter, and their pitching is pretty good."

Billy says, "Yeah, but nobody is going to beat the Yankees. Mantle, Marris, Yogi. These guys are really good. I don't think anybody can beat them. They're going to win it all again this year."

JJ says, "I hope that you're wrong. I like those guys, but I can't stand the owner. He's a real asshole. Besides, he has so much money that he keeps buying up all the great players. That's not right. They need to do something about that or that asshole will keep winning every year."

"Money talks, and New York has plenty of it."

"Did you hear the latest Yogi joke? 'If you keep missing the ball, you'll strike out every time,' and he does it with a straight face. He is really funny."

"You ready to play?"

"Let's wait a little longer. We only have twelve guys. Are we expecting a couple more?"

"Yeah, here come two more."

"That's enough. That gives us seven on each team. If any more show up, we'll just add them on."

It's perfect weather, but after seven innings everyone is ready to call it a day. Who cares what the score is? It's been great to play. Its 5:00 p.m. and starting to get dark.

"Hey, let's go down to Pop's Place and get a Pepsi. As soon as those street lights come on, our moms will be looking for us."

"Yeah, I can't wait 'til they change the clocks so we can get some more daylight."

"Yeah, but my butt is tired and my mom's cooking chicken. So that Pepsi sounds real good right now."

"Okay, tomorrow, same time."

"Yeah, sounds good. Maybe we'll keep score tomorrow."

As they all hop on their bikes and head for home, the street lights come on. Pepsi first. Then they listen for Mom calling. "JJ, where are you. You know that you're supposed to be home before the street lights come on."

Just made it.

Mom says, "You're late. Where have you been? Go wash your hands. Your chicken's getting' cold. Your dad has already gone to work, so what's left on the table is yours. Don't make a pig of yourself or you'll have a belly ache. Did you wash your hands? They still look dirty. You'll make yourself sick."

"Geez, Mom. Calm down. I just got in the door. And I still love you. Those other girls are pretty. But you're the only one who cares about me."

"Yeah, well don't tell your father. He might get jealous. And what about that girl that lives around the bend?"

"Yeah, I love her too, but she doesn't know it. I'm going to marry her when I finish school. By then we will both know about the 'Birds and the Bees.'"

"Somehow, I think you both know about the 'Birds and the Bees.' You better behave yourself."

"Mom, I'm only ten years old. But she's nice. Her grandmother lets me fish off her pier, and she always asks me how many fish I caught that day. She's a nice lady. And you should see her aunt. She's beautiful. She's only 4' 10", but she is all woman. I think she's about twenty-one. And if Julie gets her looks, she is going to be perfect. She's already taller than the aunt."

"Boy, for a ten-year-old you notice things that you shouldn't be looking at."

"Mom, it doesn't hurt to look. Besides, give me a few years and I'll become an expert at girl watching."

"In a few years, Julie will have you wrapped around her finger. And she will slap you alongside of your head if she catches you girl watching."

"In a few years, if she looks as good as her aunt, I'll have the girl that all the other guys are watching."

"You really have all this stuff figured out. I can't imagine what you will be thinking about when you're thirteen?"

"Don't worry Mom, I'll still love you. And I'll make sure that Julie doesn't catch me girl watching. Any more chicken?"

"No! You ate six pieces. You must have a hollow leg. Where are you putting all that food?"

"I'm a growing boy. I have to get ready for baseball season. We're playing again tomorrow. I hope we have enough guys to have two full teams."

"You watch those street lights and I'll have more chicken for you when you get home."

# Chapter 2

SUNDAY NOONTIME, IT IS A beautiful day. JJ and friends gather at the baseball field. This time they have seventeen players, so one volunteers to be the umpire. Just as they were ready to start, the GI Public Bus stops, and Martin, a black boy from Freetown, gets off.

"Hey, can I play?"

JJ knew Martin from a Food Bank project that his Boy Scouts troupe did in Freetown. Freetown is an all-black community with a mix of hard-working people and single-family moms. It had high crime problems, but the working people and the good moms had formed a Community Watch group and were working with the police to clean up the community. The county Parks and Rec department had asked the Boy Scouts troupe to help. The first project was the food drive to help the very poor families. It was a big help. Many of the young boys wanted to join the Boy Scouts. But the white parents objected to mixing white and blacks. So our troupe sponsored an all-black boy Scout troupe. The first in the county. And some believe it was the first in the state.

JJ was the pack leader sponsor for the new troupe, and Parks and Rec had ask him to start a baseball team that would play six games during the summer against the black boys. He was having problems, because many of the white moms didn't want their boys going into Freetown. So JJ asks his Scout Master what he thought he should do. The Scout Master said that he would make some phone calls to see if he could help. He also suggested that JJ talk to some of the fathers to see if they would act as coaches for the teams. One of the fathers was married to a black woman, and he said "yes" and that he would use his pick-up truck to help. JJ asked him if he would help convince some of the other fathers to help. Nine of fifteen fathers said yes, and they told their wives. Next thing you know, all the mothers became supporters. They made cupcakes and iced tea for every game. They became friends with the black moms. They even invited some of them over to their house for backyard cookouts. Wow, that was unheard of, to actually have black friends.

"Yeah, sure. Did you bring a glove?"

"No, I didn't know you guys were playing."

"That's okay. We'll put you on the other team and you can use mine when we're up."

"Hey. Wait a minute, JJ. I don't want to play with no nigger."

"What? You know Martin. He's our friend from the Freetown Food Drive."

"I don't give a damn. I don't want to play with some nigger."

"Why? You afraid that he will be better than you? I'll bet you a buck that he gets more hits than you."

"You're full of shit. I'll play circles around him."

"Well, okay then. Get your ass out in the field. We came here to play baseball!"

Martin played well, but Joe was one of the best players on the field. He was big for his age and he could really hit.

It was getting late and the street lights were about to come on. The last GI Public Bus would be coming soon. Martin and everybody else there knew that Martin had to catch that last bus before dark. For a black boy to be in an all-white community after dark was *not safe*. As they waited for the bus, some very bad white guys drove by and yelled, "You better get your black ass out of here before we get back." Joe heard them just as the bus blew by the bus stop and didn't stop to pick up Martin.

"What do we do now? Those guys will be back. They'll beat the hell out of me!"

"I don't know, but I'll stay with you. Let's go to Pop's Place and I'll call my father. Hop on my bike. Let's get out of here."

Just as they began to leave, the bad boys pulled in front of them, blocking their exit.

"I thought that I told you to get your black ass out of Beachwood!"

"I tried, but the bus just passed me without stopping."

"I guess the bus driver didn't want any niggers on his bus, so we are goin' to teach you a lesson."

JJ knew that real trouble was brewing. "Hey guys, wait a minute. We were going to Pop's Place, which is right on the border. I was going to call my father to see if he would take him home."

"Shut up, fat boy, or we'll kick your ass too."

"You guys aren't from Beachwood. What do you care if he stays here a little longer?"

"Didn't I tell you to shut up?"

By now one of the bad guys was standing next to JJ. Within a blink of an eye, JJ turned quickly and punched him squarely in the nose. Blood squirted everywhere, and he went down light a sack of potatoes. The second guy swung hard, hitting JJ on the side of his head, directing it at his ear. It knocked him sideways, stunned.

Martin, who was a small guy, swung with all his might, striking the guy squarely in his testicles. The guy was rolling on the ground and throwing up whatever was in his stomach. He was in real pain. As Martin turned to face the driver, he was struck on the top of his head with a police-style Billy club, splitting the skin and knocking him to the ground. By now, some of the older boys from Beachwood who had been playing football saw what was happening and yelled to JJ.

"JJ, do you need some help?"

JJ, was still stunned, and his ear was ringing so bad that he couldn't hear them. The football players started running towards the car.

The driver was helping his buddy off the ground as he yelled to JJ.

"Now I'm coming for you, fat boy."

JJ couldn't hear him, but he knew what was coming.

"I'm coming for your nigger-loving ass."

Suddenly the driver was struck in the back by a large rock. It seems that Joe had come back just in time. As the driver turned toward Joe, he was tackled from behind by one of the football players. The driver was a big guy, 6' 3" tall, maybe 260 lbs. Two more football players jumped on top of him, and they beat the hell out of him. Mr. Bloody Nose and his buddy were now retreating to the car, leaving the driver to fend for himself.

"Hold up, hold up," screamed JJ.

"What, you want us to stop? We're just beginning to have some fun!"

"Yeah, yeah, I know you are, but we got to get Martin to the hospital. Any of you have a car?"

"Yeah, I do, but I think that we ought to take him to the fire hall. It's just down the street, and they can take care of him."

The bad guys are now back in their car.

One of the football players yelled to them, "I know you guys. You're from Sunrise Beach. I guess we'll have to pay you a visit and kick the shit out of one of your twelve-year-olds."

The driver, who was badly beaten up, said, "I'll be back, you bastards."

"That wouldn't be smart. If you come back to Beachwood, you will leave with four flat tires and a flattened nose," replied one of the football players.

"Come on guys, we need to get him to the fire hall. Hey, after they're finished with him, can one of you take him home? He lives in Freetown."

"Oh, he won't be going home, they'll take him to the hospital. He'll need stitches for that head."

"Will one of you call his mother?"

"The fire hall will do that. They will need her permission to transport him. He'll be okay. You've done your job as a friend."

"I don't really know him that well. We just met last month in Freetown."

"Well, I think that you just made a new friend for life."

As they leave the area, JJ turns to Joe. "Why did you come back?"

"I didn't want to see you get your ass kicked for some black guy."

"Okay, so now he's some black guy, not a nigger?"

"Black guy, nigger, what's the difference?"

"Come on, Joe; you like Martin. Admit it."

"He is a good ballplayer."

"Come on Joe, the color of his skin doesn't make him a bad guy. Look at those assholes from Sunrise Beach. They're white. They hurt him bad, just because he's black. He didn't do anything to them. They are the bad guys."

"You're right, but don't tell my father that I helped a nigger. He'll kill me!"

"But why?"

"I don't know. He says that they're all lazy and don't want to work. He says that they all carry knives and will cut you and think nothing of it."

"I don't understand that. Your father is a good person, and he works with blacks all day at the housing project."

"Yeah, I know he does, but he don't call them niggers because they work. As a matter of fact, he calls them his buddies."

"Boy, I really don't understand that. Come on, let's get on our bikes and get home. I know that I'm going to hear it from my mom."

"Me too. She gave me a bad time yesterday 'cause I was a little late, but I think she'll be okay when I tell her what happened."

"You're going to tell her that you came back to save Martin, a black boy?"

"*Hell no*! I'm going to tell her that I came back to save your ass. She loves you, and when she sees that ear of yours, she'll believe me."

"You little chicken shit. You like Martin. You should tell your mother the truth."

"I am. If I hadn't thrown that rock, your head would have been next for that Billy club. And yes, I do like Martin. Tell me something, where do you think a black guy gets a name like Martin? They are generally Sambo or something like that."

"Sambo? That's from a children's book. I don't know, but I'll bet he is named after that preacher from down South. You know the one who is always stirring up trouble about black people having to sit in the back of the bus. Black people really like him. But those Southern cops sure don't. They are constantly locking him up, but somehow he keeps getting out, and he comes back for more."

"What's he crazy?"

"I don't think so. I think he really believes that stuff he is shoutin' about. I listened to him on TV the other night. I couldn't understand much of what he was saying, 'cause he's always yelling at the top of his lungs, and I can't understand very much of their words. I think that they speak English. But I could tell that he really believes whatever he is saying. But the cops locked him up again. He locked arms with a bunch of other preachers and walked down the center of the street blocking traffic again. That's all it took. The cops locked him up again. A couple days later he's out on the street doing all again. Maybe he is crazy."

"Well, I'll see ya in school tomorrow. You better put somethin' on that ear."

"Ah, you can bet that my mother will have something to fix it."

It's dark as JJ walks through the door.

"Hi, Mom. I'm home!"

"Where you been, boy? I told you not to be late. I had to put the chicken in the refrigerator. What in the world happened to your ear? Let me make an ice pack so you can hold against it to help the swelling come down."

"Boy, it hurts, and it's still ringing."

"What happened?"

As JJ was explaining the events, he kept dozing off.

"Don't fall asleep. When you hit your head like that, you got to stay awake for at least two hours to make sure you didn't do brain damage."

"What happened to Martin?"

"I don't know, and I don't have his phone number. Ray, the football player, said that they would take him to the hospital. Ray volunteers at the fire hall, so I think that he knows what they do."

"I'll call the fire hall, see what I can find out."

"Thanks, Mom. Boy, this ear hurts."

"Ray was right. They stopped the bleeding and took him to the hospital. He wanted me to bring you up there, but I told him that I didn't drive, so guess what? Mr. Robbie is coming here to look at your ear. So stay awake."

About twenty minutes later, Robbie and Earl were knocking on the door. Robbie opened his medical case and looked at JJ's ear.

"Mrs. Kapock, I don't see any damage. Do you want me to take him to the hospital so that a doctor can take a look at it?"

"Not if you think he's okay. Me and his dad will take him to the base tomorrow. You know that his dad is retired navy, so we get our medical care at the base."

"Okay, I'll put some topical cream on the ear and give you some pain pills. He'll need them as the night moves on."

"I need them now, this hurts. Do you think that this ringing will stop?"

"No, that will be with you for a while, but the pills will help. And it's okay to sleep now. I don't see any signs of a brain bleed."

"Thanks, Mr. Robbie. Thanks, Earl."

"You're welcome. Next time, duck quicker!"

# Chapter 3

THE MAIN ROAD THROUGH BEACHWOOD ends at the Stoney Creek, which is a small inlet off of the Chesapeake Bay.

The community refers to it as the Wharf, which is a large bulk-headed area that has been back filled with stone and CR-6 filler. It is large enough to park 15 or more cars, and is used as the community Swimming Area. At the end of the wharf the water depth is about 10 feet. And the bulkhead projects about 75 feet into the creek. So you can also swim off the sides of the wharf.

The wharf can handle large numbers of community swimmers. The only problem is that people come down to the wharf in their cars with coolers filled with beer.

They get drunk and they throw their empty beer bottles in the water. These bottles often break and many of the swimmers have received serious cuts.

Several time a year, JJ and some of the boys in the community would wait until low tide and they would walk the entire swimming area picking up broken glass and trash. The efforts are limited; as the water gets deeper, they cannot see the bottom and unable to find the broken glass. The County Government was suppose to hire Marine Contractors to clear this area twice a year, but whenever the Budgets were tight, this was one of the areas where they made cuts.

The American Red Cross would give swimming lessons there twice a month, but several times their instructors sliced their feet or ankles on broken Beer Bottles and they stopped the lessons until the County Certified that it was safe to swim.

During the summer months this area was often over-crowded and the danger of someone getting hurt was great.

It also attracted drunks, who would start fights and bring weapons. Often the police were called, and often people were hurt.

It's a beautiful day and people of all ages are arriving at the Wharf to spend the day swimming. Many of the young ladies, ages 12 to 19 were wearing two piece bathing suits, and exposing lots of flesh and body parts. Some of the 14 year olds had breast that were too large for their young bodies. If you had to guess their age you would guess 18 to 20.

The young boys their age loved it. The problem was the older boys and young men 18 to 30; they took advantage of the young girls, who liked the older boys looking at them, and feeling their breast. Some of these girls would take their tops off to impress the older boys, and some of the young men would reach into the bottoms with their hands and they would stay there for a while. Often there was open sex on the beach area. At times there were more bathing suits on the beach than there were on bodies. Many of these girls had great bodies and they knew it, but their minds were not mature enough to handle the young men. The results were, a lot of un-intended babies. Many of those 14-year-old girls had to quit school before they were 16.

JJ and Tommy had a group of girls from school who they played with, as friends. They got a lot of "free feels" and the girls loved it, but they were not pursuing sex with them. Because they all knew each other from school, the girls felt safe with them, and they like the guys playing with their bodies. They would play water games and JJ and Tommy would grab them by the butt and push them off the wharf into the water. Often when they would come up out of the water, their tops would come off and they would laugh and joke about who had the best nipples; but this was all in fun. The older boys would actually pull the girls tops up and play with their breast. JJ and Tommy were always getting into fights trying to defend the girls. Often they both got beat up by the older boys. JJ actually became friends with the police officer who patrolled the wharf, and he made sure that the older boys knew that he was friends with the cops.... But sometimes that didn't help.

One day when he was playing with Molly, a nice looking young lady, who he was tossing over the side and then helping her up the ladder so he could get a good view of her 36Cs ; Ted a grown man(23) came over to her. He had a 6" hunting knife that he was showing to everyone. He appeared to be drunk. As JJ was helping Molly up the ladder, Ted pushed him away

"get out of here kid, I'm taking miss big tits for myself"

JJ charged at Ted, trying to push him over the side, but Ted deflected JJ and cut him across the back of his shoulder with the knife. Blood shot out and Tommy tried to help JJ but Ted was a fully grown man and he just pushed them aside.

As Molly step onto the wharf from the ladder, Ted grabbed her by the strap holding the top of her bathing suit. Ted took the knife and cut all the straps, removing the top completely, and he threw it in the water. Molly was completely exposed and JJ was laying on the ground bleeding. By now other people were gathering around and yelling at Ted to stop. Ted forced Molly to his car. Tommy ran to the pay-phone and was calling the police. Ted cut the bottom of Molly and he was going to rape her, but there were too many people around, so he closed the door and drove off. It was just beginning to get dark and everyone was concerned about Molly. Ted drove out of the community and no one knew where he went. The Police and Medical people arrived very quickly and took JJ to the Hospital; he was in a lot of pain; the cut was about 3" long and was deep. JJ was clearly shakened and he kept asking about Molly.

Ted was out of control. He knew that he was in trouble but he didn't seem to care. He drove to a dead end road in the woods. Molly is sobbing and begging him not to hurt her. "Shut up bitch" Don't make me beat you. Have you even been fucked before? Molly had had sex with some younger boys, but never a full grown man, and Ted was very large. "Don't give me any back talk... you do exactly what I tell you to do and you will be okay" Get in that back seat....still sobbing, Molly moved to the back seat". Have you ever sucked a mans dick"? No, I've never had a man before". But you have been fucked before"? Yes, but I've never seen someone that large". Well, you're going to put it in your mouth first. When it gets hard, you're going to put it in you". No please, I've never had a man before; and I can't take something that large". Shut up and start sucking. Molly does as she is told. Ted removes his penis, and inserts into Molly. it is so large that she begins to scream. That excites Ted and he continues to push harder. Molly is now screaming in pure pain. A couple riding their bikes past the road heard the screams and went to investigate. As they approached the car they could determine what was going on. The woman rode back to the main road and went to a gas station to call the police. The man who was as big as Ted, confronted him. Ted attempted to stab him. But the man also had a knife that he carried for protection while riding at night. Ted decide to run. He pushed Molly out of the car and pulled away. The man didn't have anything to give Molly to cover up with, but when his wife returned, she took off her blouse and gave it to Molly. The police and medical people were there in a matter of minutes. They transported Molly to the Hospital

The Police were in pursuit of Ted. He was travelling at high rates of speed and was out of control. He ran a stop sign and was struck in the rear drivers side of the car. It spun him around and he was now going in the opposition direction. He past the police car and was heading back towards town; his right tire slipped off the road; he lost control of the car and flew directly into the woods where the rape took place; he struck a tree, and that quick, Ted was dead.

Back at the Hospital the Doctors were treating JJ's cut. It was deep and bad. They attempted to clean it, but the knife was old, rusted, and dirty. They think that they got the wound clean, but they can't be sure. JJ will be okay, but Molly is emotionally and mentally damaged. Ted had cut her nipple with the knife. They think that they will heal okay, but mentally she is a mess. Ted was so large that he did serious damage to Molly. She is torn so badly that she can't walk. They are keeping her overnight and will decide treatment after she heals some.

This is a day that no one in Beachwood will forget. The police and the community will study what needs to be done to make the Swimming Area safe for the citizens

As for JJ, Tommy, Molly and her girl friends the swimming hole will never be the same. It will be impossible to go there and not have memories of that day.

# Chapter 4

Several years have passed. JJ and his friends have developed a great relationship with the boys from Freetown. They now play ten games a summer, alternating fields. Yes, that right, the white parents take their children into Freetown. The white parents have made many friends with the black parents. They actually go to each other's houses for outdoor cookouts, and at the end of the season they hold a banquet, one year at the Freetown Community Center, the next year at the Beachwood Fire Hall. The black parents started it because they wanted to show the white parents that they love and care for their children in the same manner and that they try to live normal happy lives. And boy, could they cook. What a feast. No one left the table hungry, and they all took carry-out home with them. This was probably the only white friends they had, and vice versa, but they grew to care for each other and looked forward to the banquet each year.

Think about it: this all started because some white boy punched another white boy in the nose while trying to protect a black boy from being beaten by some white bullies, and some red neck white football players came to their rescue. Look at the lifelong friendships that have because some kids wanted to play baseball together.

JJ is fourteen years old now and stands 5' 10" tall, weighing about 180 lbs., with cold black hair and a smile and personality that everyone liked. The guys that he traveled with were playing "matchmakers" with him and Julie. You know, the girl around the corner with the great-grandmother that all the kids loved, the *hot* aunt that all the guys would die for, and the great fishing spot! Well, they really didn't need to encourage JJ very much, because Julie, who was a dancer, tap dancing, ballet, and modern jazz, had developed into a beautiful young lady, stealing a page from her hot aunt. Julie was 5' 2" tall and very well put together. Nice breasts that you simply couldn't miss when she wore a sweater, great legs when she wore a skirt, and while she was a little shy, she had a great smile and a personality that matched JJ's perfectly. And she lived next door to the grandmother who had the great fishing pier. So while JJ loved baseball and golf, fishing was becoming much more interesting to him. Everyone knew that JJ wasn't real interested in the fish in River Creek, but he sure did like Grannie's granddaughter.

JJ had met Julie's mother and father on one of his trips to the fishing pier. They were both hardworking blue-collar people who moved from the city to the waterfront community of Beachwood. Julie's father was building a house next to Grannie's with the help of some of his friends. It was nearly completed, and he worked on it every day after coming home from his regular job. Julie had two younger brothers, Roy Jr. and Walter Charles. They were very young, but they worked with their father to help build the house, and both of them knew a lot about construction, as did Julie. They were a traditional blue-collar family with great values.

Beachwood was a tough neighborhood. It had five local bars, three small community stores, and the local volunteer fire station. It had a community swimming pier and boat ramps for boating on River Creek. At the entrance of the community was the area junior high school that serviced its population of about a thousand families and about three other surrounding communities. The people had very strong law-and-order values, even though many of the boys got in trouble with the local police. Many of the guys did not finish high school. They quit school, got a job in construction, bought a car, and started their own life.

It's now May 1957. Eisenhower had just been re-elected president, and Beachwood was almost totally Democrats, so they were not happy about the election results. It was still the local talk at all the Bars. JJ's parents were Democrats all their lives, and they supported Stevenson. Of course, they never worked in his campaign, never contributed a penny to the campaign, and knew nothing about him, but he had a "D" behind his name, and if the Democrats ran a jackass for president, they would vote for him. The school held a mock election, and while JJ was very interested in US history and fascinated with the election, he followed his parents' example and did not get involved. Eisenhower won 60/40 and the community was stunned. Since the community was 75 percent Democrat, how could Eisenhower win? During the real election, people were putting up signs "I like Ike," and the blue-collar red necks of Beachwood were tearing them down. The poll workers were all wearing Stevenson buttons and handing out his ligature because they were being paid to do so. When the polls closed and the votes were counted at Beachwood, Eisenhower won 60/40. Local Democrats demanded a recount, but no matter how many times they counted those votes, Eisenhower won 60/40.

This was JJ's first real look at politics. He couldn't understand why everyone was so upset. So he waited for his father to come home from work, and as they were eating dinner, he asked his father, "Dad, did you vote for Eisenhower?"

"*Hell no*! I'm a Democrat. I never vote for a Republican. They are for big business and rich people. Democrats are for the little guy, the working class people."

"But Dad, you served under Eisenhower during the war. Didn't you think that he was a smart guy?"

"He was a great general, but he's been a bad president. He gives everything to GM, Chrysler, Ford, US Steel, and all the other big companies, anything they want, but he doesn't give the little guy *shit*!"

JJ didn't think that this was good dinner conversation, so he changed the subject.

"Well, other than that, how the car running?"

"It's got one plug that is misfiring, but that's an easy fix. I'll change it Friday."

"Do you mind if I be excused? I want to go to the store before it closes."

"The store doesn't close for three hours. You can go. Say hello to Julie!"

JJ knew that Julie's father was active in the local Democrat Club, so he thought that he would get another opinion. Besides, it gave him an excuse to go to Julie's house.

"Hi, Mr. Roy. What are you doing to the car?"

"Just changing the oil. How are you doing?"

"I'm okay, but everyone seems to still be talking about the election, and I can't figure it out."

"What can't you figure out?"

"How did Eisenhower win? Who did you vote for, Mr. Roy?"

"I'm a Democrat, but I vote for the person, not the party. Eisenhower was a great general and has been an okay president. Stevenson couldn't beat him the first time, so I don't know why the party didn't pick someone else to run against him."

"So you voted for Eisenhower?"

"Oh, I didn't say that. No one knows who you vote for when you go into that booth, and I don't tell them, but as far as my friends at the Democrats Club are concerned, I voted for Stevenson. That way, I don't have to listen to all that bullshit. Does that answer your question?"

"I think so."

"Julie's down on the beach. That's who you really came to talk to."

"Thanks, Mr. Roy. I guess while I'm here, I'll ask her if she is going to Teen Club Friday night?"

"Yes, she's going to Teen Club, but I know that you want to ask her yourself."

"Thanks again, Mr. Roy."

"Ya hootie there." That was a personal joke between Julie and JJ. "Your dad told me that you were down here, so I thought I'd come down and ask you if you are going to Teen Club Friday night?"

"Yes, I intend to, but let me ask you something. Are you going to come over and ask me to dance, or are you going to hang in the dark corner with your buddies."

"And make me hunt you down every time there is a 'Ladies' Choice'?"

"Well, yeah, I want to dance with you, but you know it's good for my ego when you come looking for me, and it gives the guys something to talk about besides cars and movie stars."

"What do they say?"

"I can't tell you that, some of it would make you blush, and some of it is XXX rated."

"Well then, don't tell me. I don't need to hear the dirty talk from that bunch."

"Oh, it's not all dirty, unless you think that it's dirty because they like you in a sweater and your poodle skirt."

"Is that all you guys think about?"

"No, just most of the time. We talk about cars, school, and, like I said, movie stars."

"Speaking of stars, do you know that the girls think that you look like Elvis, that dark black hair and that combed-back duck style haircut?"

JJ responding in his best Elvis voice, "Well, thank you very much. Do you think that I should have someone announce, 'Elvis has entered the building' whenever I come in?"

"No, I don't think so. That's a little too much role-playing."

"I don't think that the guys think that I look like Elvis, but that's because they all want to be like Elvis."

"Why?"

"Are you kidding, he drives the women crazy, pulling on his clothes and screaming."

"So what, do you think that you have to be like Elvis to have girls like you? Can't you just be yourself?"

"No, you don't have to look like Elvis, but it sure doesn't hurt. But besides his looks, I really like his voice. Have you ever thought about all the different kind of songs that he sings? When you get past that silly 'Hound Dog' song, he sings a wide range of songs, from gospel to rockabilly to love songs. He really does have a great voice. I like 'Peace in the Valley.' Did you know that Ed Sullivan wouldn't let him sing any songs that implied religion in them?"

"No, I didn't know that. Why?"

"I don't know, but I heard that Colonel Parker told them that if they wanted Elvis back, they had to remove that restriction, that Elvis was mad when he found out about it."

"You sure know a lot about Elvis."

"Not really, I like all the singers, Pat Boone, Buddy Holly, Jerry Lee Lewis, The Big Bopper, and I really like Jonny Cash and his all-black outfits. All these guys are good, but our parents think that we should like Sinatra or Perry Como. I think they are good. I love Sinatra when he sings 'New York, New York' or 'My Way.' But I think Elvis is one of a kind. He's the king. There'll never be another Elvis."

"Is that important?"

"I don't know, but life is supposed to be fun, and Elvis is fun. When he starts swinging those hips and moving around, those girls start screaming, and everybody starts moving to the music. That's fun. It gives people a break from all the bad stuff going on in the world, and that can't be all bad."

"No, I guess not, but why does he do all that jumping around?"

"I guess it's just part of the show. His mother asked him that same question, and he told her that he just can't help it. He loves the music, and it makes him want to move. I think it neat."

"I think that it's funny!"

"That's good. He makes life fun and you enjoy it, but the reporters make it dirty. They call him Elvis the Pelvis."

"What does that mean?"

"You know. He's moving around like he's having sex. Moving his pelvis."

"Is that what it looks like when you're having sex?"

"I don't know. Want to have some sex and find out?"

"*No*! and if you start talking like that, I'll push you off the end of the pier," and with that she gave him a little shove as a joke, but JJ's foot got caught on one the ropes that was tying up a boat with, and off he went. Remember—it's early May. As he come up from under the water, he says, "Damn, girl, now look at what you've done. God, this water is damn cold, and I'm soaked!"

"Oh, I'm sorry. I was only playing with you. I didn't mean for you to fall in. Come out of there and take your clothes off. No, I mean ... I don't know what I mean. Come up to the house and I'll get you a blanket."

"What the hell am I going to tell my mother?"

"I'll call her and tell her what happened."

"What are you going to tell her, that you tossed a 180-pound man into the water?"

As they got to the top of the hill, near the house, Roy, Julie's father started laughing.

"What the hell happened to you, boy?"

As JJ began telling the story, Roy began laughing harder and louder.

"You just got your first lesson about messing with a woman. You never win, and you aren't even married yet!"

"I don't think that it's very funny, Mr. Roy."

"It's funnier than hell. She was only playing, and look at you. I can't wait to see you when she really means it!"

Julie comes out of the house with a blanket.

"Here, put this around you as you walk home. You can bring it back later."

"Hell, boy, get in the car, I'll take you home. I want to see your mother's reaction!"

"Very funny, Mr. Roy. If I wasn't so cold, I'd walk home, but I'll take the ride."

"JJ, I'm sorry. I didn't mean for you to fall in."

"*Yes*, she did!"

"Oh, Daddy, stop that. You're going to make him mad at me."

"He's not mad. His ego is a little wounded, and his clothes are a little wet, but he'll get over it. I'll bet that his mom will laugh as hard as I did when she hears this story. A little 90-pound girl tossed her big 180-pound superstar into River Creek."

"I'm glad that you are getting a good laugh. I still don't think it's so damn funny!"

"Oh, maybe he is mad? Come on, get in the car."

"See you at Teen Club."

"Yeah, if I don't get sick and die from this. Then maybe you won't think that it's so funny."

"I think that he is mad. Come on get in the car. I'm glad you know how to swim, because she doesn't. You might have drowned!"

"Very funny, very funny!"

"By the way, I did vote for Ike."

# Chapter 5

It's the Thursday before Teen Club, and JJ has caught the GI Public Bus to go to Cromwell Township. Cromwell was about two square blocks of commercial retail stores. One was a clothing store that catered to teenage dress styles. JJ had bought a pair of dark blue pegged pants with a gray stripe tailored into the side seam of each leg at this store last month. For those of you who don't know what pegged pants are, the tailor makes the cuff of the pants two inches smaller in circumference than the pants legs themselves. This makes the pants tapper in at the bottom of the leg. It also makes it hard as hell to get your foot through the bottom hole. To a teenager, these pants were the cat's meow. You were Mr. Cool Guy.

Now he wanted to buy an Elvis jacket. Everyone wanted an Elvis jacket, but they were $45, which was a lot of money, more than most teenagers could afford. JJ worked part time at a golf course and did odd jobs for people in the community. He almost always had money, but $45 was a lot of money, even to JJ. But he was determined to be the first in his crowd to have an Elvis jacket. As he walked into the store, the salesman remembered him from last month.

"Mr. JJ, how are you doing? Good to see you again. The salesman worked on commission and he knew a sucker when he saw one, so he was laying it on thick."

"What can I do for you today, Mr. JJ?"

"Well, Sol, everyone says that I look like Elvis, so I think that I want to dress like him. I want buy one those Elvis jackets like you have in the window."

"Oh yes, Mr. JJ, they are beautiful. Silver gray with sparkles. The sleeves are tapered like your pants with button closure. The collar is extra wide and tall so you can wear it up, just like Elvis does."

"Do you have it in my size? I think I need a thirty-six."

"Oh, yes Mr. JJ, I'm sure that I have one that will fit you. We just got our shipment in; you know that we have a waiting list for this shipment, but you know that I will take care of you. You are my special customer. Let's try one on. Yes, that fits perfectly. You look great."

"Do you think that I can wear this with my blue pants?"

"Oh yes, Mr. JJ, the gray stripe is a perfect match with the jacket."

"Good enough. Wrap it up. I'll take it."

"Very good, Mr. JJ. What else can I do for you?"

"That's it."

"What about a pair of silver-rimmed sunglasses?"

"No, I don't think so."

"I'll make you a special deal. How about a pair of shoes with Cuban heels?"

"No, I don't think that I have enough money."

"Oh Mr. JJ, your credit is good with me. I'll let you pay me $10 a month!"

"I don't know."

"How about a silk scarf with 'Taking Care of Business' written on it?"

"I don't know."

"Look the shoes are $30. The sunglasses are $20, and the scarf is $10. That's $105. I'll knock off $15, making it $90 total. You pay me what you can today, and I'll put the balance on credit."

"So, if I give you $60 today, I'll own you $30, and I can pay that off over time."

"Yes, Mr. JJ. That would be perfect. I want you walking out of here looking exactly like Elvis. Can I take a picture of you and pin it on the jacket in the store window?"

"Sure, you got a deal."

# Chapter 6

It's Friday night, and JJ is getting ready for the big dance at Teen Club. He would normally go early and help set up the tables and chairs at the fire hall, but tonight he was dressing kind of special, and he wasn't going to take the chance of damaging his new clothes. Besides, he wanted to be a little late so that he could make his grand entrance.

Okay, get this picture. Dark blue pegged pants with a gray stripe down both legs, with 2.5-inch Cuban-heeled shoes that are so pointy that it makes his feet look four inches longer. A gold satin dress shirt with flared wide collar, a blue satin tie (the guys didn't wear ties, but this was special), a gold tie tack with a diamond, and of course the *Elvis jacket*, with a silk pocket scarf with "Taking Care of Business" printed on it. Silver-rimmed sunglasses even though it was nighttime. He thought about a gold chain necklace but thought that might be overkill. Combine this with his cold black hair, combed back in a duck style, and now you have a fourteen-year-old Elvis.

JJ had worked all this out with Mr. Robbie and Earl—when he was about to enter the fire hall, they were going to play Elvis's theme song, and Earl was going to announce, "Elvis is in the Building." He really did look like Elvis. JJ knew that all his buddies were going to laugh and make fun of him, but he didn't care. Life is supposed to be fun, and he was making it fun. He planned to walk directly to Julie and ask her to dance. He had asked Earl to play "Loving You," a slow dance. He had no idea how everyone was going to react, so he didn't know what to expect. Teen Club started at 7:30 p.m., so he thought that an 8:15 p.m. entrance would work.

It was 7:30 p.m. and the fire hall was already filling up, and like usual all the girls were on one side, which was well lit, and all the boys were filling up the corner that was darker, with less lighting. The music had started, and several people were dancing, mostly girls dancing with girls (that was acceptable), because most of the boys wouldn't ask the girls to dance. JJ was very nervous and not certain what to expect. Mr. Robbie and Earl had done a good job keeping this a secret, so no one was expecting Elvis.

It's now 8:10 p.m. and Mr. Robbie has been watching for JJ. As JJ's father was pulling up to the door, he asked JJ, "Is this a dress-up night or something? I've never seen you wear a tie to Teen Club."

"No, not really, but I spent all this money on these clothes, so I thought that I'd wear them. I don't think that I could go to school looking like this."

JJ's father had only seen Elvis one time, on *The Ed Sullivan Show*, so he didn't know that JJ was an Elvis lookalike.

"Well, you look pretty sharp, son. I hope the girls will like your new digs, or at least one girl that I know of."

"Thanks, Dad. I'll walk home after Teen Club closes at 11:00 p.m."

As JJ gets out of the car, Mr. Robbie gives Earl the signal, and everyone begins to hear Elvis theme song begin. Everyone is looking at each other, and you hear some of them say, "What's going on?"

As JJ walks through the door, Earl announces, "Elvis is in the Building." Because of the sunglasses, most of them don't realize that it is JJ. You can hear some of the girls say, "Who is that?"

"I don't know, but he is *hot*! He sure looks like Elvis."

JJ wasted no time. He walked directly to Julie and said, "May I have this dance, young lady?"

Julie knew that it was JJ as soon as he opened his mouth. Trying not to laugh, she replied, "Well, of course, Mr. Presley. I would be honored."

By now, the guys in the corner knew who it was and started shouting, "Elvis, are you going to sing for us?"

JJ wasn't expecting that. The girls picked up on what was going on, and they began, "Oh, yes, Elvis, you've got to sing for us."

Earl had started the record "Loving You," and JJ had Julie on the dance floor, but the crowd kept shouting, "Sing, sing, sing."

JJ kept giving his buddies the high sign to stop, but they were having too much fun to stop. The girls began cutting in on the dance. Both Julie and JJ didn't know what to do, so they just went with the flow.

When the song ended, all the girls ran up to JJ.

"Can I have your autograph? Are you going to sing for us? I love your jacket! Those pants are really cool. I love those sunglasses. Can I get a pair?" They were having a great time carrying the whole thing on, and the guys were all over in the corner laughing. They started yelling, "Sing, sing, sing."

"I'm going to kill you guys if you don't shut up."

That just made it worse. They started again, "Sing, sing, sing," and we want Elvis to sing for us. Then the girls started, "Elvis, please sing for us. Sing for us, sing for us, sing for us."

Now Mr. Robbie and Earl joined in. "Come on, Elvis, sing for us." Mr. Robbie knew that JJ could sing. He had heard him sing in the school glee club at the Rotary Club luncheon.

JJ reluctantly consented to sing, so Earl turned off the record player and announced, "By popular demand and many requests, here's Elvis."

JJ got up and sang "Blue Moon." He sounded exactly like Elvis. He was so good that the hecklers shut up, and the place went silent. Everyone was stunned at the talent that JJ showed. He even wiggled his Pelvis. The girls all screamed. The boys all laughed, and it was a big hit with everyone. When JJ finished, in his best Elvis voice, he said, "Thank you very much, thank you very much. I'm sorry to say I have another engagement, so until the next time, peace to you all."

JJ walked out of the building and took off the sunglasses and the tie. Meanwhile, Earl announced, "Elvis has left the building." All the girls sighed and laughed.

As JJ was ready to go back into the building, a car with six big guys from Sunrise Beach pulled up.

"Hey, *asshole*! I told you we'd be back. Only this time we're going to kick the shit out of some these nice cars."

JJ ran back into the building, but he was too late. You could hear headlights popping and fenders banging.

"Mr. Robbie, there's a bunch of badasses from Sunrise Beach outside banging up our cars."

"Okay, JJ, you guys stay in here. I'm calling the cops."

Without thinking, Earl, who was a very big man in his early thirties, ran out the door, intending to stop them. By now the guys knew that there was something happening. They heard the noise but didn't know what it was. They raised one of the fire engine doors. The fire engines were parked outside the doors, so most of the view was obstructed.

"Hey, those bastards just busted my headlight!"

"What?"

"There's a bunch of guys out there busting up our cars."

"What?"

"You heard me. They are busting up our cars."

JJ jumped in front of the door. "Don't go out there!" he yelled at the top of his voice. Mr. Robbie has called the cops.

"Hell, by the time they get here, my car will be ready for the junkyard."

"Hey, they got Earl down on the ground and they're hitting him with baseball bats."

All the guys ran toward Earl. There must have been twenty of them. They pulled the guys off of Earl and began beating on them. There must have been three Beachwood boys for each Sunrise boy, but the Sunrise boys had clubs and baseball bats. Several of the Beachwood boys were badly injured but managed to take the bats away from the bad guys. They began beating on the bad boy driver. Just then, a lonely police officer pulled up. He saw what was going on and called for backup. Mr. Robbie turned on the firehouse siren, which they use to call the volunteer firemen. People were coming from everywhere. Three more police cars arrived. There was mass confusion. Earl, who was badly hurt, was now on his feet and swinging at anything and everyone. He didn't know where he was and didn't know who the enemy was. A police officer approached him, and he struck the officer in the face. The police didn't know who the good guys were and who the bad guys were. By now the volunteer firemen were arriving. They separated the Beachwood boys from the bad guys and made them sit on the ground. This helped the police sort out the Sunrise Beach boys. They put handcuffs on them and put them in the police cars. Now things seemed to be settling down. JJ ran over to Earl, who was badly beaten and still out of his mind. JJ shouted to the police officer who was trying to put handcuffs on Earl. "Hey, he's one of us."

The police officer turned quickly. "Shut up kid. I don't care who he is. He just assaulted a police officer."

"But can't you see that he's hurt? He didn't know who you were. He was just protecting himself."

"I told you to shut up kid."

As they were entering the door of the fire hall, Earl, who could barely walk, spun around and yelled, "Get your damn hands off me." With that, the police pulled out his Billy stick and was about to strike Earl. JJ grabbed the stick and knocked it out of the officer's hand. The officer pushed Earl through the door and turned and grabbed JJ by the sleeve of his Elvis jacket. He swung at JJ so hard that he hit the wall and busted his nose. Blood went everywhere, including on the Elvis jacket. He tore the sleeve of the jacket and blood was on the satin shirt.

"No, no," shouted Mr. Robbie. "He's one of the good guys. He was trying to help that guy," he said, pointing to Earl. "He's our captain and driver."

"How was I supposed to know that?"

"That's what I was trying to tell you, you asshole," yelled JJ.

"Didn't I tell you to shut up, kid?"

"Yeah, and look what it got you. You arrested two of the wrong people. You busted my nose and ruined my new jacket."

"You're a smart ass, aren't you, kid?"

"Maybe so, but at least I'm not a bully like you."

"Mr. Robbie was trying to help, Officer. He's one of the best boys in the community. He's never in trouble and always trying to help people. He's a pack leader in our Boy Scout troupe."

"All right, all right. What's your name, boy?"

"JJ Kapock."

"Kapock, isn't your father one of our reserve officers?"

"Yes he is, and he wouldn't throw people around like you do! Look what you've done to my nose. And look at my jacket. It can't be fixed."

"Boy, you really are a smart ass. I'll bet your father would be real proud of your behavior and smart mouth."

"Yeah, well, I guess your police chief would be real proud of how you handled things."

"You don't let up, do you? I'm going to talk to your father."

"Go ahead. I'll bet that when he hears my side of the story, he'll support me."

"I've had enough of you. Mr. Robbie, we're going to take these guys to the police station. I going to release Earl. Since he hit me, I'm not going take any action. But I think that you need to take him to the hospital. We'll take these bums there after we get all our information. Your boys really did a number on most of them. And they really did a number on several of those cars."

"Yeah, they even busted up one of our fire trucks that we use for small brush fires."

It's now past 11:00 p.m. and everyone has left.

"JJ, over here. I asked my mother to wait and take you home."

"Thanks, Julie. I could use a little help right now. Thanks, Mrs. Conners."

"Get in, JJ. You sure are a mess."

"Yes, Mama. I wasn't expecting the night to end like this. My dad is working night shift, so he won't be home. I don't know what I'm going to tell my mother."

"Do you want me to come in and talk to your mother?"

"Would you do that? She's going to be upset when she sees my face and my clothes."

"Sure, I'm surprised that the policeman didn't have someone take you to the hospital!"

"That guy was a jerk! Some of the firemen cleaned up my face, and it really burned, and you can see how sore it is. That wall was just cinder block with some paint on it. It really scraped me up."

"Well, we're here. I'm going to come in with you. Your mother is probably wondering who's car is in her driveway. Julie, are you coming in?"

"Yes."

"We can't stay long. Your brother is home alone."

"Hi, Mrs. Kapok. I'm Julie's mother. We met at the fire hall on Community Day."

"Oh, yes. I know who you are—and your beautiful daughter. Is something wrong?"

"Yes, I asked JJ to wait outside for a few minutes because I didn't want you to be alarmed. There was some trouble at the Teen Club tonight, and some of the boys got into a fight with some boys from Sunrise Beach. The police were called, and they arrested some of the boys. JJ wasn't directly involved in the fighting, but in his efforts to help Mr. Robbie and Mr. Earl, he had a problem with one of the policemen. He threw JJ up against the wall and scratched his face up. He tore some of his clothes and got blood on them. He and JJ had some words, and we left. Julie asked me to bring JJ home."

"Thank you, Julie, and thank you, Mrs. Connors. Let's let him in so I can see if he needs anything."

"We're going to leave. My two boys are home alone, and I've been gone for almost an hour."

"Thank you again for helping, JJ. Come on in here, boy. Let me take a look at your face. My goodness, look at your clothes. I don't think that I'll be able to get all that blood out! Thanks again, Mrs. Connors."

"Good night, Julie."

"Good night, JJ."

# Chapter 7

It's early Fall and some of the older boys who live in Beachwood have lost their summer jobs. Money is tight and the police suspect that they are doing some things that could put them in jail.

There have been several house robberies and 5 of the guys from Beachwood are prime suspects.

The police have asked Mr. Robbie to help them gather information. Mr. Robbie has asked JJ if he has heard any talk about what is going on? JJ has heard nothing, but Julie heard some of the older girls talking. They were bragging that because their boyfriends are so broke, "all they have been doing is having sex in the back seat of the car, because they don't have money for gas….. so they don't go anywhere". These girls are a little older than Julie & JJ, so they really don't know them well. JJ knows one of the guys, and he has been in trouble with the Law before. JJ knows this guy by the nickname "Lucky" and JJ believes that Lucky could be one of the guys committing the crimes, and he knows the guy hangs out at Johnny's Bar where Mr. Roy goes for beer.

JJ doesn't know how he should handle this because he knows that one of the homes that was robbed was a friend of Mr. Roy. He thinks that Mr. Roy might take things into his own hands, and confront Lucky. So, JJ decides to talk with Mr. Johnny who owns the bar and get his opinion as to what he should do?

Mr. Jonny knows Lucky, and he agrees with JJ. He suggest that he, JJ, should have the Police Captain stop by the bar to talk to Mr.

Johnny......Mr. Johnny will let the police believe that he heard the information in the Bar. This is a good plan.

That night the Police Captain went to talk with Mr. Johnny.... while he was there Lucky and two of his friends came into the bar. They saw Mr. Johnny and the Police Captain talking but they didn't think that the conversation was about them. But the Captain thought that it was strange that these three guys didn't have money to take their girls out, but they were in the bar spending money on beer and playing shuffle board?

As the Police Captain was leaving, he stops at the shuffle board table:

Hi, guys, how you doing?

Lucky knows the Captain: We're doing okay...things are a little slow right now at work, but at least we got a couple days in this week.

That's good news....let me buy you a beer.....Johnny, give these guy a beer, on me! And I'll see you later.

After the Captain leaves, Johnny could hear the three talking, but he couldn't understand what they were saying. The three finished the beers and left the bar.

It was clear that they were planning something.

That night JJ was at Julie's house when Mr. Roy came in and said, " Did you know that a couple of your buddies got shot tonight?"

What! What happened?

Well somebody has been hitting Mr. Sander's gas tank; two or three times a week. His driveway sits back off the road and you can't see the cars, or his pick-up truck from the street. So he rigged it with an alarm that turned on a light in his house if anyone messed with the gas cap. Well, around 7:30pm the light came on. Mr. Sanders got his shot gun and went out the back door.....when he came around the side of his truck, there were two guys with a gas can and a hose, stealing gas. He turn on a flashlight and told them to stop. They both ran...he shot the one in the back of the leg: the other one didn't do so well: he shot him in the back and blew out his left lung: he's in the hospital and they don't expect him to live; the other one is in the hospital and they think that he will recover but may end up walking with a limp.

You want to hear the crazy part; the police arrested Mr. Sanders for shooting them....they are on his property, stealing his gas, and he's the one that gets locked up.

Why does he get arrested?

They said that his life wasn't in danger and therefore he had no right to use deadly force to stop them.

Well, what was he supposed to do?

Let them run, and call the police.....

What do you think will happen to him?

I don't think that any jury will find him guilty......but he will have a trial and need to hire a lawyer, and all that stuff cost him money...just because these assholes were stealing his gas.....and the worse part....they can sue him for shooting them, and they will collect money for being crooks...

That sounds crazy; doesn't he have a right to protect his property?

Yea, and he will win that part; but he doesn't have the right to shoot them!!

That's not right; all that for a few gallons of gasoline; What will happen to them for stealing the gas?

The one who got shot in the leg is a minor; so I don't think that much will happen to him. The other one is 18, so if he lives he will end up in jail.

Geez! All that mess for a few gallons of gasoline. Now the one is going to have problems walking for the rest of his life; and the other one, if he lives, will be missing part of his lung. I hope that send a message to the bad guys, that there is a price to pay for doing the wrong thing.

Later that week, the names of the two guys is made public, and JJ finds out that one of them is the guy named, Lucky. He's the one who lost the lung. He is still alive but in very bad condition. JJ doesn't really know the other guy.

Lucky has been in trouble before and everyone is talking about how much jail time Lucky will receive.

At the Fire Station everyone is talking about the "Gas Robbery". Most of the guys know Lucky because he did some volunteer work. Most think of him as a "Bad Dude", not someone that they would hang with, but they are going to visit him at the hospital.

Darrin, the other person involved with Lucky, has had his hearing in Juvenile Court, and was found guilty. Sentenced to three years in jail. One year in Juvenile Detention until he turns 18 years old, and the other two years are suspended and given Probation.

The Police have impounded Luckys' car and he won't get it back.

Lucky has improved enough that he can stand trial, but he is still in the Hospital.

Luckys' girlfriend is telling everyone that Lucky will sue Mr. Sanders for $500,000 for shooting him. Most people believe that he will win the suit.

It's now April and the trial for Lucky' is starting. It isn't expected to last very long since they were caught in the act and it is expected Lucky will plead "Guilty" to the charges.

"All stand": the court is now in session. The case before us is the State of Maryland vs Charles L. McGaron, the Honorable James D. Pitcher presiding; Please be seated.

The States Attorney presented the charges. Luckys attorney introduce himself and the judge ask him how his client pleads?

Everyone was surprised when Lucky pleaded "Not Guilty"

The trial lasted about 4 hours. The States Attorney called Mr. Saunders and the Police Dept. and Lucky's attorney cross examined them, and then called Darrin and Lucky to give their side of the story. Darrin and Lucky both stated that Mr. Saunders did not give them any warning; he turned the flashlight on and began firing. They seemed to think that this was very important and they wanted in the record. No one could tell if this had any effect on the Judges thinking. The Judge closed the case for the day and would start the next day at 9 am. He would render his verdict.

The next morning the Judge made an opening statement and proceeded to find Lucky "Guilty as Charged". Sentenced him to 3 years in jail, he dismissed 1 ½ years and placed him in the County

Detention Center. No one felt as though they won. Lucky has permeant damage, and will always have problems breathing. Mr. Sanders still faces a Civil Law Suit by both Lucky and Darrin. The States Attorney felt that the sentence was very "Light", and so did the Police Dept.

Most of the people of Beachwood felt that the Court System was not strong and did not send the message that they wanted sent to Lucky's friends. They felt that the community was still going to have problems with petty crime. To make matters worse, a month later Lucky was awarded $ 250,000 in his Civil Suit against Mr. Saunders, and Darrin was awarded free Medical Care for his leg for his entire life. No one could believe the Court Verdict, and Lucky rubbed it in their faces by buying a brand new car to drive through the community.

# Chapter 8

JJ's PARENTS' HOUSE SAT ON a hilly three-acre site that had water across the front and swamp-type cat tail on the one side. The water was fairly clean, with a muddy bottom. After one of the major hurricanes, an old wood-plank rowboat washed up onto their property. JJ tried for weeks to find the owner. He even ran a small ad in the local newspaper. No one claimed it. It was in bad condition and needed a lot of work, but to a poor boy like JJ he thought that God had sent him a pot of gold. He bought a pair of saw horses, a paint scraper, a propane torch, some sandpaper, brass screws, and lead filler. JJ's father had an old 12-horsepower outboard motor that he bought over ten years ago. It didn't run and looked like it belonged in the junkyard, but it was free. JJ got Tommy and Jimmy to help him turn the boat upside down and place it on the sawhorses. They tormented him about trying to fix the old, rundown boat. But JJ lived on the water and didn't have a boat. He knew that he couldn't afford to buy one, so this was the answer to his prayers.

That weekend, the weather was perfect. He decided to start his project. There were at least eight layers of paint on this wood, so he couldn't scrape it without using the blowtorch. He would heat it up until it bubbled up, and then he would scrape it while it was still hot. The fumes from the paint were making him sick, but he wasn't going to give up. Finally, he ran out of propane. This was a good excuse to stop. After all, he had been working six hours on this baby and had cleared a spot about 2 feet by 2 feet on the bottom. He thought, *At this rate, I ought to be able to finish this baby by*

*November*. By then the water in the creek would be frozen. But he wasn't giving up, so he called his father at work and asked him if he would pick up three bottles of propane and a plastic tarp to cover his bare wood on the bottom. He asked his dad if he would check the price of an electric belt sander and an electric drill. His dad asked him what he was doing. So he told him of his plan. He also asked his father if he knew of a place that could fix the outboard motor. Dad told him that he bought the motor at Sears and that they would have a repair shop that could do it. JJ knew that he couldn't afford to do that, but he wanted to plant the seed in his dad's head that the motor needed to be fixed. JJ's father could fix almost any kind of gasoline motor.

Now, if he could figure out how to get his father to do it, he would have solved one of the big problems. He knew that this project was going to make him broke. He had already spent $60 for materials, and he only had 2 feet of an 18-foot boat done.

A bottle of propane cost $1.19, and he was going to need forty bottles at the rate he was going. This project was beginning to look a lot bigger than he thought.

He heard the horn blow and he knew that his father was home. His father was bringing the propane and the tarp around front.

"JJ, let me see this project that you've got yourself into. My God, boy, that thing must have a dozen layers of paint on it. You'll be in college by the time you get this done."

"No, Dad, but I do have to come up with a better plan."

"Well, I checked the price of the belt sander. It's $29. The drill is anywhere between $8 and $20, depending on what you need."

"Wow! Those tools are expensive. I don't have that kind of money now, but I'm going to caddy for Mr. Wagner and Mr. Poe tomorrow. That's generally good for $6 to $8, and depending on how busy the golf course is, I might be able to pick up another double in the afternoon. The days are getting longer, so you generally can get two rounds in if you start early, and those guys always start early. They tell me that their wives won't fix them any lunch if they are too late. It sounds like Mom telling me to be home before the street light comes on."

"Yeah, it never stops. Women have their rules, but I don't think that it's lunch that they are worried about!"

"What do you mean, Dad?"

"Never mind, son. You will understand as you get a little older. You know, I think that I have an electric drill in the shed. If you can find it, you can have it."

"Dad, I don't think that I will live long enough to find it in that shed! But I'll look—and thanks."

"You know, I'll bet you that Mr. Roy has a belt sander. He must have needed one while he was building that house."

"Yeah, I'll bet that he does. Maybe he will let me use it?"

"Yeah, and it'll give you another reason to go around to Julie's house!"

"Dad, you guys have got to lighten up. We're just friends. Can you see if they have any boat paint at the PX on base? It's a navy base; they must paint boat bottoms."

"You know that you have to use copper paint on the bottom."

"What is copper paint?"

"It's like primer paint for raw wood, but on the bottom of the boat. It fights the salt water and gives you a good surface for your final coat."

"I'll bet it's expensive."

"It really is, but you only have to use it on the bottom and about 4" to 6" up the sides, where the water line is."

"How much do you think I need?"

"I don't know, but I think that a gallon will do it."

"How much do you think it cost?"

"I don't know, but I'll go by the PX in the next couple of days and find out. You won't be needing it soon. You got a lot of prep work to do first."

"Boy, you're not kidding. This is a much bigger job than I thought. Maybe I can get a Tom Sawyer project going? Do you think that Tommy and Jimmy are dumb enough to fall for that stunt?"

"No, son. Even as dumb as they are, I don't think that they will fall for that one."

"I'm going to walk around to see if Mr. Roy is home. He gets home early from his day job, and if he's not working on his house, I know that I can find him at Johnny's Bar, having a beer."

"Somehow, I think that if he's not home, you'll call Johnny's Bar and ask him if you can wait there until he gets home."

"For God's sake, will you lighten up? Okay, so she's beautiful. So what?"

"So what? When she wears one of those sweaters, you can't put two sentences together. She's got your eyes looking at her chest, and your ears can't hear what she's saying."

"Dad, we're just friends. Geez, I'm going to see if Mr. Roy is home. Will you tell Mom where I'm going?"

"I'll tell her, but that's the first place she calls when you're not home and she needs something."

"Okay, Dad. I got it. I'm in love! Didn't you like girls when you were fourteen?"

"I started sooner than that. I had a girlfriend when I was ten years old."

"Ten? What did you know about girls when you were ten years old?"

"Nothing. Hell, I'm forty years old, and I still don't know anything about girls, and I suspect that when I'm sixty years old I still won't know anything. Son, if you can figure out women, you will own the world!"

"Thanks for the wise words, Dad. I'm leaving. I've got twenty-six years to get where you are now, and that's nowhere, so I guess working on this boat isn't as difficult as I thought. It certainly isn't as difficult as women."

"No, it isn't, son. And after you put all that time and effort into it, what do you have? A thing of beauty, a sore back, and a lot of fun memories."

"Goodbye, Dad. This has been a great talk. And all I wanted was three cans of propane and a tarp. By the way, what do I owe you?"

"The products are free. The words of wisdom are priceless."

As JJ started around to Julie's house, he began smiling. *That really was a great talk. I didn't know he had all that talking in him. He's actually funny. I enjoyed that. Hell, I didn't think I had all that talking in me. Now if I can just get him to fix that motor!*

Arriving at Julie's house, JJ sees the two brothers outside. *That's a sign that Mr. Roy isn't home. I don't see his car.*

"Hey, junior, is your dad home?"

"Don't call me junior, you big smart ass."

"Hey, you little squirt. I'll bounce you on your head."

"Ha, you gotta catch me first, and as slow as you are, Dumbo, that'll never happen."

"Where's your father?"

"I don't know. Go ask my sister. That's who you really came to see."

"Give me a break. Is everybody going to yank my chain about Julie? Even this little piss ass is on my case, knocking on the door."

"Hi, Mrs. Connors."

"Hi, JJ, come on in. Julie's in her room. I'll call her."

"Actually, Mrs. Connors, I'm looking for Mr. Roy."

"Sure you are, JJ. Come on into the living room. I'll get Julie. I think Mr. Roy is still at Johnny's. I'll call him to see when he thinks he'll be home."

"You want me to wait in the living room? That's where the TV is. I think that the *Mickey Mouse Club* is on."

"Oh, I don't watch that anymore, Mrs. Connors. I'm little too old for that now."

"I guess you are, but I still remember you when you were that nice little fat boy sitting on my pier."

"Mom! That's not nice to say to JJ. Besides, I'm sure that we can find something to watch. Maybe the *Buddy Dean Show*."

"Yes, you always like dancing. Take JJ into the living room. You can sit on one of those chairs that your father brought that is a chair and a half wide."

Julie looked at JJ and said, "Well, don't just stand there. Come join me on one of our new chairs."

Everything happened so fast that JJ looked like a deer that was caught in your headlight. Just standing there like a dummy. Julie grabs his hand. "Come on, it's only twenty feet. You're a big boy. You can make it."

As they sat down in the chair, JJ started thinking about what his father had just told him—"When you see her you can't even put two sentences together."

*But I wasn't even looking at her tits. I didn't even see her coming. Is she wearing one of those sweaters? God, even her mother doesn't believe that I came here to see Mr. Roy.*

As she bent over to adjust the TV, all you could see was those beautiful legs, which went all the way up to that beautiful ass. She was wearing shorts, and JJ knew that her mother would be coming back into the room. *I have to be careful. I don't want to get caught staring at her body.*

"JJ, Mr. Roy said that he will be about thirty minutes. You can either wait here or you can go up to Johnny's and he'll beat you at another game of shuffleboard."

"He knows that I can't beat him, I don't think anybody can."

"You know that he has been the bar champion for three years in a row. As long as he's not drinking heavy, nobody can beat him."

"Good, you know that you can't beat him, so you should stay here with me. Besides, I'm better looking."

"That certainly was humble and modest, Julie."

"Oh, Mom, you know what I mean, and besides, JJ and I don't get to talk very often."

"I'm sure he would rather stay here and talk with you, but knowing your father, thirty minutes could turn into two hours."

"JJ doesn't have any other plans. He can wait. Can't you?"

"Yeah, if your mother doesn't mind me being here."

"You're welcome to stay up 'til 10:00 p.m."

"There, that's settled. Mom, we're going down to the pier. I want to show JJ the new light that Dad just installed."

"Okay, but turn the light on."

"If I do that, you will be watching everything we do."

"That's what mothers are supposed to do."

"Can't you take a night off from being a mother?"

"No, I can't do that. Being a mother is a full-time job, with lots of responsibilities. You'll find that out soon enough. Besides, if I'm not watching you, you can bet that your brothers will be."

"Can't you bring them in the house so they won't be a pest?"

"That's what brothers are supposed to be, a real pain in the butt to their older sister."

"Well, they don't have to take their job so seriously. You would think that they are being paid for it."

"How do you know they're not?"

"How are JJ and I supposed to get to know each other?"

"You seem to be doing just fine, but if you keep talking, your father will be home and you will have lost all that time."

"Come on, JJ. let's get out of here."

"How will I know when your father gets home?"

"Are you kidding? They will know every move we make."

"Go on, JJ. I'll call you when Mr. Roy gets home, or I'll send one of the brothers to find you."

As they began walking down the hill to the pier, Julie waited until they came upon a very dark spot. She stopped. "Here this will do just fine."

"What do you mean? Fine for what?"

"Come on, JJ, kiss me. You've wanted to do it for over a year now."

"How do you know that?"

"That's what girls do. They let you chase them until they catch you. You were caught that night at Teen Club, when you did that Elvis act. Mr. Robbie is good friends with my grandmother. She told her how you planned all that, and the girls knew it. They knew that you didn't do it for them. And who did you come directly to when you walked through that door? Me. My heart was beating so hard I could barely keep it in my chest. I thought that you were going to ask me to go steady while we were dancing, but the girls kept cutting in. And then the fight started and ruined the whole night."

"Will you?"

"Will I what?"

"You know, go steady with me?"

"Not unless you kiss me, stupid."

"That's a yes?"

"Sealed with a kiss."

"We better get down to that pier light or the watchdogs will be coming after us."

"Sounds like a plan to me. Do you think that your mother told your father to stay at the bar for a little while?"

"I sure do. We women stick together. And my parents think that you're the nicest boy in Beachwood."

"Have your parents and friends been heckling you like my parents and the guys?"

"I don't know about your buddies, but my girlfriends never let up. All they talk about is 'What does JJ think about this, and what does JJ think about that, and did he like your Poodle Skirt, did he like your sweater?' I didn't know the answers to a lot of the questions, because they never leave us alone enough to talk, so I had to make up a lot of the answers. And my parents kept asking me when you were coming over."

"Boy, if you heard my parents, you would think that I was here all the time. And the guys were always asking me detailed questions, like, 'Does she French kiss, what's her bra size?' and I didn't know the answers to that."

"Thirty-four B, but don't you tell any of them that. They'll find out soon enough about the French kissing, but it's none of their business what my bra size is. And the girls, they don't ask those questions, because they assume they know the answer to the kissing stuff, and they figure that you've been in my bra, because all of them have let their boyfriends into their bras. And some have done more."

"You're kidding!"

"No, I would kid about that. And just because we are going steady doesn't mean that you have the keys to my bra."

"Why not?"

"Because I have different valves than my girlfriends. I don't judge the ones who allow bra play, but the others are going to get themselves into trouble. I'll bet that by the end of the year, one of them will be pregnant. One of them actually has her mother buying her birth control pills. The mother says that she is going have sex no matter what she tells her, but she doesn't want to be raising any new babies. And she is older than most of us. I think that once school is out she is going to get married."

"How old is she?"

"She'll be eighteen, and she has a bad home life. I think that her father sneaks into her room at night and does things to her."

"Her father? What does he do?"

"I don't know, JJ. She doesn't talk about it in detail. All she talks about is getting out of that house."

"Where's her mother?"

"I don't know! I'm not there. Boy, that really got your attention."

"That's awful. You're supposed to trust your parents. When can I get the keys?"

"Keys to what?"

"Your bra. I've been wanting to see those boobs ever since I saw you in one of those dance outfits that you wear. You know, that red one. That's pretty sexy. And when you dance, they bounce around."

"You mean my Indian outfit, the one where I wear the feather on my head."

"Yeah, and it has that trim all around the right places."

"Is that all you do, just look at my boobs?"

"No, but it does make me wonder what's under there."

"The second Tuesday of next?"

"What?"

"That's when I'll give you the keys."

"Really? That's great. I guess we really are going steady."

"Julie, your father is home."

"That was perfect timing. What do you want to see my father about?"

"Oh, I want to see if he has a belt sander that I could use to repair my boat?"

"You really did come around to see him? I thought that you were making up an excuse to see me."

"Well, yes and yes. I really did want to ask your father about the sander, and it did give me a chance to see you."

"That's good. I wouldn't want to be second fiddle to a belt sander."

"Hi, Mr. Roy. I thought that you were going to be a half hour, so I waited."

"Half an hour. I told her that I was going to be a couple of hours, because we had just started a shuffleboard set—you know, three games. What do you want?"

"I told you that we girls stick together," Julie pipes in.

"Yes, you do. I'm repairing my boat, and I was wondering if you have a belt sander that I could use?"

"Yeah, I have a couple of them. They are in the basement. Julie knows where they are. There's also a whole box of sandpaper belts. All grades. You can have them. Let me know if you need more. I can get more from work."

"Wow! Thanks, Mr. Roy. You just saved me a ton of money."

"You're welcome. You can buy me a beer the next time you come into Johnny's."

"Heck, I'll buy you two!"

"Come into the house and I'll give you the keys to the basement door. Julie can show you where they are."

"How come you didn't build stairs down to the basement from the inside?"

"I didn't want to take up the floor space. And no one really uses the basement for anything but junk."

"And tools!"

"Yeah, and tools, but mostly junk. It'll take her a little while to find them because of all the junk. Here, Julie. Here are the keys."

"Thanks again, Mr. Roy. When do you need it back?"

"I don't need it right now, so bring it back when you're done with it. If I need it, I'll tell Julie. You two are always talking on the phone. She'll let you know."

JJ and Julie head to the basement.

"The lightswitch is hard to find. He put it in before he installed the furnace. There it is. Watch your head. The ceiling is low, and he built all these racks that hang from the floor joists. We have to talk low. They can hear every word through these air ducts. Besides, I'm not interesting in talking. They interrupted our kissing."

"Boy, I made out well tonight. I got my sander and sandpaper, I got my girl, and I'm getting my keys to your bra. I'm doing okay."

"Remember—the second Tuesday of next week."

"Yeah, what does that mean? There aren't two Tuesdays in a week."

"No, kidding."

# Chapter 9

A WEEK HAD PASSED SINCE THE fight at the Teen Club. Mr. Kapock didn't notice that JJ's face was cut and swollen, so JJ didn't need to explain anything to his dad. His mother knew the story because she heard it from Mrs. Conners. JJ was working on his boat project when he heard his father's car pull up. Just as he looked up, his father was approaching him.

"I need to talk to you. Guess who paid me a visit at work today? The police officer that you gave a blast of shit at the Teen Club!"

"Dad, you would have done the same thing."

"Not hardly! Haven't I taught you to respect the law?"

"Yes, and I did. I was only trying to help."

"My ass! According to the officer, you knocked his club out of his hand and interfered with an arrest."

"That's only partly true. He was going to hit Mr. Earl. You know, Mr. Earl, he's the captain at the fire station and drives the fire truck. Mr. Earl was beat up bad by the guys from Sunrise Beach. He was in a daze. He didn't know where he was or what he was doing. This guy had him in handcuffs when he tried to push him through the door. Earl turned quickly, and this guy pulled out his club and was going to hit Mr. Earl. I was trying to stop him from hitting the wrong guy."

"Why were you involved?"

"He was going to hurt the wrong person. You always tell me that when you know you are right, speak up. That's what I was trying to do when this jerk grabbed me by the arm and threw me against the wall, busted my face, and tore my new coat. If it hadn't been for Mr. Robbie, he would have hit me. He was really out of control."

"You should have stayed out of it, let the adults handle it."

"It was nothing but confusion. The cops didn't know who were the bad guys and who were the good guys. If he had hit Mr. Earl, he would have been in big trouble."

"You don't hit the captain of the fire department. What if he had hit the captain of the police department?"

"He is the captain. He heard the call on the radio in his personal car, and he responded to help his troops."

"You mean that he's a captain and he used such poor judgment?"

"He's not accustomed to being hit in the face! Did you see Mr. Earl hit him in the face?"

"No, but you could clearly see that Mr. Earl was hurt and didn't know where he was. Those guys hit him with baseball bats and kicked him while he was down on the ground."

"Where were you while that was happening?"

"I was trying to help the other cops separate the Sunrise boys from the Beachwood boys. I was getting our guys to calm down and sit on the ground. In fact, after this *captain* banged me up and Mr. Robbie came to my rescue, the other offices told this jerk that I was helping them. By then the jerk had already done his damage. He asks me my name, and when I told him, he told me he knew you. He told me that he was going to tell you how bad I was. But I thought that after the other officers told him that I helped them, that he would realize that he made a mistake. Police officers can make mistakes. That why I didn't come running to you complaining."

"Yes, they can. That's why you're going to tell the captain that you're sorry."

"What?"

"You heard me!"

"*No*, I'm not going to do that."

"What?"

"You heard me, Dad. You know that I don't disobey you, but

you tell me to stick to my guns when I know that I'm right. And in this case, I'm right. His own officers would confirm that."

"You were wrong for sticking your nose into his arrest."

"Oh, I should let him hurt Mr. Earl, simply because he hadn't bothered to find out who he was before he hit him with a club. For God's sake, Dad, he should be telling me that he's sorry. He busted up my face and ruined over a $100 of my clothes. Ask Mom; she tried to wash the blood out of my satin shirt and my jacket."

"You mean that your mother knew about this?"

"Yes, Mrs. Connors brought me home and told Mom what happened. If you don't believe me, talk to Mrs. Connors or Mr. Robbie."

"It doesn't matter. You're going to tell the captain that you're sorry."

"*No*, I'm not going to do that. It goes against everything that you taught me to believe in. It goes against my Boy Scout oath to always tell the truth."

"You either do it or you're on restriction until you do. You come home from school and you stay in the house. No baseball, no friends. You think about that. You'll change your mind."

"No, I won't. I'll stay here until I'm eighteen years old, but I'm not telling Mr. Jerk Captain that I'm sorry. I really can't believe that you are doing this."

Mr. Kapock goes into the house, and JJ, with tears in his eyes, returns to working on his boat.

"Did you know that he got into a confrontation with the police captain," Mr. Kapock asked his wife.

"I didn't know that it was the captain, but I was told what happened."

"I put him on restriction. He's not the leave the property until he tells the captain that he was wrong. And I expect you to enforce it."

"Wait a minute, John. This ain't the navy. You don't give me orders, and you can't restrict me, unless you want to go to work in dirty clothes and damned hungry. And if I know JJ, he believes in what is right, and in this case he is right and you are wrong. I spoke to Mr. Robbie, and he said that JJ was the most help of anyone there. He said that he got all the Beachwood boys calmed down. And they were really mad. All their cars had been smashed up, and several of them were hurt. He said that JJ stopped the police from hurting Mr. Earl."

"Yeah, and that's where he was wrong. He had no business getting involved in that arrest and confronting the captain."

"Well according to Mr. Robbie, JJ was the hero of the night, and for that, you want to punish him? Two wrongs don't make a right! The captain was wrong, and I think that your reaction is wrong. The boy did something that he believed was right, something that you taught him. His Scout Master called and said that everyone is talking about it, and they are going to give him a Good Citizenship Merit Badge. He should be good and confused by now. Everyone is telling him that he did good, and the person who taught him right from wrong is telling him that he did something bad! I'm certain that he will never agree that he was wrong. This is going to be a very long restriction. He'll probably be old enough to join the navy by the time he gets his freedom back."

"What do you think I should do? He shouldn't have talked to the captain like that. And I'm told that he used some very raw words!"

"If you really think that you need to do anything, you should tell him that you thought that his choice of words was very bad but that you understand that he was trying to help—and that *you* are going to talk to the captain and tell him that you're sorry that this happened, that the community is going to give him an award, and that, in his acceptance speech, you have asked JJ to say that he thinks that the police department did a great job handling the problem. That way everybody wins."

"How did you get to be so smart? I'll think about that. When are they giving him this award?"

"I don't know yet."

"I guess I'm pretty smart for a ninth-grade education. The award will be in approximately two weeks, provided that JJ can get off restriction. In the meantime, you can at least let him use the phone so that he can talk to Julie."

"What did you think of Mrs. Connors?"

"I think that she is a very nice person and her daughter is really beautiful."

"I saw the mother in Pop's store the other day, and you sure can tell where the daughter gets those nice little breasts!"

"Honestly, John, will you ever get that dirty sailor mind cleaned up?"

"What? The woman has big tits."

"You can't even handle my little tits. What would you do with all that?"

"I don't know. Let's go in the bedroom and I'll practice a little more."

"You don't need any practice. That horny navy brain never stops thinking about anything but sex, but I guess once a month is good for a man your age."

"Thanks, I'll try to increase it to twice a month."

"Okay, enough sex talk. Sit down and eat your dinner. I guess I should have cooked some oysters!"

# Chapter 10

It's been a week since JJ was placed on restriction by his father, and JJ is holding firm on his refusal to speak to the police captain. Every day, he comes home from school and goes to work on his boat. He has made some real progress. He has the entire bottom scraped and sanded. The belt sander has really helped. His lack of knowledge has made him do some things over. For a while each night he would put the cover on his work, which looked perfect, but when he came back the next day, he found that the grain of the wood had risen due to the moisture in the night air. He wasn't speaking to his father, so he couldn't ask him for advice. So when he saw Julie at school, he asked her to ask her father for suggestions. The next day, as he was getting ready to start working on the boat, Mr. Roy pulled into the driveway.

Hi, JJ. Julie tells me that you are having some problems with your project? Can I take a look at it?

"Yeah, sure. I'm doing okay, but each day I have to redo some my work before I can start again. The wood grain grows whiskers overnight, even with the cover on it."

"Yeah, some of the nighttime moisture is still getting in. You could try another plastic cover, but you could put a coat of primer on the parts that you have finished, but you have to let it dry before you do any more sanding."

"I thought that I had to paint it all at the same time or I would get overlapping of the paint."

"For your final paint coat, that's true, but this is just the primer coat. If you get some overlapping, the final coat will cover most of that up. Besides, this is the bottom of the boat. I don't think that the fish in River Creek are going to tell anyone that you have paint overlaps. How's the sander working?"

"It's great, and it sure works quicker."

"Did you father tell you that you have to use copper paint on the bottom?"

"Yeah, but I don't know how much it cost? And being on restriction, I haven't been able to work any side jobs."

"It cost about $50 per gallon, but I have some half-full cans at work. We started a job, opened a can, didn't need it all, and when we started the next job someone opened a new can. There might be enough to do your bottom. And Joey's father uses the same stuff at the housing project. We ought to be able to get you enough for your boat bottom."

"You're kidding! That would be great, Mr. Roy. That would save me a lot of money."

"What are you going to name your boat?"

"Name it?"

"Yeah, all boats have a name. Generally after a woman."

"Why a woman?"

"Because they cost so damn much!"

"This boat is definitely a female. I've already got a $150 in her already."

"I think that *Julie* would be a good name. She has already cost me a fortune, and she only a daughter. Pity the poor bastard that marries her."

With that, JJ's father pulls into the driveway.

"I'm going up to Johnny's. I'll see if I can get that paint for you. See you later."

"Thanks, Mr. Roy."

As Roy passes John in the driveway, Roy says to John, "That's a really nice boy you got there. He is something special."

"Thanks, Roy. His mother has done a great job raising him."

"Oh, I think that you had something to do with it. He is really a good person."

"Yeah, we think so too."

"I'm going to see if I can get him some copper paint for his project. We use it all the time at work."

"That's really nice of you."

"As I said, he's really a special kid. See you later."

As John enters the house, he calls to his wife, "Boo, I'm home. Did you know that Roy was here?"

"I didn't talk to him, but I saw his car."

"He apparently came to talk to JJ."

"Yeah, since you two aren't talking, he asked Julie if she could ask her father about a problem he was having with the wood after it was sanded."

"Well, I think that I've got that problem solved."

"I went to talk to the captain, and he said that he was sorry, that he realized that he did some things wrong, and that JJ was only trying to help."

"Now, where did you get that brilliant idea from? Now what are you going to do?"

"Let me finish. He's concerned that JJ may harbor bad feeling towards the police. I told him that he liked the other police officers but referred to him as a jerk!"

"That wasn't too smart."

"Yes, it was. He was falling all over himself wanting to know what to do to fix that I told him about the award that JJ was going to receive and what I was going to ask JJ to do. He said that he thought that that was a great idea and that he was going to take it a step further, that he was going to give JJ a 'police citation' and that he would present the citation himself to JJ. Maybe that would remove the 'jerk' title."

"Sounds like you two had a good conversation."

"And I just got promoted to sergeant in the police reserve."

"I didn't think that they had ranks in the reserve unit."

"They do, but they are only in force if there is no full-time officer at the scene."

"Maybe I was wrong; two wrongs *do* make one right."

"No, you were right. But now I have to fix things with my son."

"Yes, you do, and you can start with buying him the paint

he needs to finish his boat. He doesn't care what color it is, so I thought that you could get some of that ugly navy gray. I saw some at the PX when we were there last week."

"Damn, boo, that's going to cost over $100."

"That's the price you pay in life for making dumb decisions. Besides, you were going to buy it for him anyway!"

"Do you think I should buy it before or after I tell him that he's off restriction?"

"I think that you should tell him about the conversation that you had with the captain. It'll show him that you can admit to mistakes and how to handle fixing them. And tell him that you are proud of him for sticking to his guns."

"You know, I really am. I didn't know what to say when he talked back to me. When he was little, I would simply stand him in the corner. Now that he's almost grow up, I can't do that anymore. It's not easy being a father."

"It never is, but as long as you do the things that you taught him and you respect the things that are important to him, like his Boy Scout oath, I think that you will do just fine."

Just as John was finishing his conversation with his wife, JJ came into the house.

"Sit down. I want to talk to you."

"Oh, you're talking to me again?"

"Don't get smart. Just sit down and listen. As of now, you're off restriction. But I do want you to do something for me. I stopped by to talk to Mr. Robbie, and I talked to the police captain. Apparently, I overreacted. I was upset that you talked back to an adult, much less a police officer. I should have had these talks before taking action. But when you talked back to me, it confirmed that you were talking back to adults. The captain admitted that he did not handle things in a proper manner. He said that it was like a zoo there, nothing but confusion. All he knew about Earl is that he punched him in the face. He didn't know that Earl had been beaten by the Sunrise boys. He thought that Earl was one of them and that you guys had jumped on Earl. When Robbie came to defend you, you wouldn't shut up. He had already torn your jacket and bloodied your face. So now he realizes that you were very mad. He said that's why he didn't arrest you for interfering. He said that he was taking the cuffs off of Earl while Robbie was trying to calm you down, and all he could hear from you was 'You tore my jacket, jerk." That's when he asked you your name. He said that he considered not saying anything to me. But he is a father too and thought that I should know. But all I heard was that you called a police officer a stupid jerk. I think that you will admit that your language was pretty bad. But we all say things in the heat of the moment that we regret."

"I don't regret it, Dad. He was wrong and he hurt me and destroyed my clothes!"

"Yes, I know that, but can you understand his actions?"

"Yes, I do."

"Here's what I need you to do. The community is giving you a Good Citizenship Award next week."

"They are?"

"Yes, and in your acceptance speech, I want you to say that the police department did a great job responding to a bad situation. Can you do that?"

"Well, yes. They did do a good job—all except Mr. Jerk Face!"

"Well, guess what Mr. Jerk Face is going to do. He is going to give you a police citation for your help in calming everyone down."

"He is?"

"And he is going to present it to you personally, with a check for $100 to replace your clothes. All the officers pitched in to raise the money."

"Holly cow, Dad! This has become a great day. Mr. Roy is getting me some copper paint, I'm getting money to replace my jacket and shirt, and I'm off restriction!"

"Is that a yes?"

"What do you mean?"

"That you will make a public statement that the police did a good job."

"Oh, yes. It's the truth, and I don't have any problem telling the truth!"

"No you don't, son. And one more thing: I'm very proud of you for sticking to your guns. But could you be a little easier on me next time? You know, dads make mistakes—just like Jerk Faces."

JJ has tears running down his face. "You got it, Dad. Next time I'll just tell you to go to hell."

"No, that's what you did this time. Think of something nicer."

"Okay, Dad, you got a deal. I love you. Now is it okay to go around to Julie's house?"

"Yes, son, you have your freedom back. And JJ, it has turned out to be a great day!"

As JJ left the house, John heard his wife crying in the other room.

"What are you crying about?"

"I held it back as long as I could. I didn't think you were ever going to stop talking. That was beautiful. You don't get many chances in life to have that kind of talk with your son. Before you know it, he will be all grown up, and you will wonder where all those years went. You may be a dirty old sailor, but that was beautiful. I didn't think that you had that in you."

"Speaking of something in you. Are you interested?"

"For God's sake, John, I try to pay you a compliment and all you can think about is sex."

"Yeah, I think that's a good way to end a great day."

"How about some dinner and some TV instead?"

As JJ begins his walk to Julie's house, he's thinking, *I'm free. I thought that I was going to be there forever. I think that I'll stop around Johnny's Bar and tell Mr. Roy the good news. Then I'll go to his house to see Julie.*

"Hey, Mr. Roy, guess what. I'm off restriction. I'm free again."

"What happened?"

"Oh, it's a long story. I'll tell you later. I want to go tell Julie."

"She's not home yet. This is the night that she teaches dance lessons. Her mother will pick her up in about half an hour. You can buy me that beer that you owe me."

"Okay, Mr. Jonny, one Rolling Rock please?"

"You aren't old enough to buy beer!"

"I know that. You know that I don't drink beer. I can't stand the taste of it. It's for Mr. Roy."

"Well, put the money over there where he sits—75 cents. Do you want a Pepsi?"

"Yes, sir."

"Well put another 25 cents there. You trying to beat him at shuffleboard?"

"You know that nobody can beat him."

"Tell you what, if you can beat him in a set, the beer and the soda are free."

"Okay, Mr. Johnny. You sure don't make tough bets, do you? A fourteen-year-old kid against the bar champion for a buck. Are you going to give me Las Vegas odds?"

"I'll spot you fifteen points a game."

"I don't know what that means, but I've got an hour to kill, so I'll give it a try."

"Hey, kid, we've been trying to beat him for years. If you do it, we'll buy you a six-pack of Pepsi."

"Set it up, JJ. I'll let you go first."

"Okay, here goes nothing."

JJ lost the first two games, which meant that he lost the set.

"Hey, Tom, I'll bet you a six-pack that you can't beat the kid, and I'll spot you fifteen points a game!"

"Mr. Roy, I was only playing to kill time until Julie gets home."

"Relax, JJ. Her mother is going to stop here to pick up a six-pack to take home. So win this for your future mother-in-law. And she'll give you a ride to the house."

"Set them up, Tom."

"Okay, kid. I hope that I don't hurt your ego!"

JJ beat Tom in the third game just as Mrs. Connors walked in. Roy walked up to Tom. Okay, Tom, pay up. The kid has a heavy date."

Roy takes the six-pack and hands it to his wife. "Here, this is compliments of you future son-in-law. He's free tonight and wants to work on that future stuff. Give him a ride to the house so he can BS with Julie."

"Come on, JJ. I don't know what that was all about, but I'm sure that you can explain it to me on the way home."

JJ gets into the car.

"JJ, what are you doing out?"

"I'll explain it all to you when we get to the house."

"Well, it sounds like you have all kinds of explaining to do, especially that future son-in-law stuff. And how did you get this beer," asked Mrs. Connors.

"Can I tell you when we get to the house?"

"Sure, but remember you only have until 10:00 p.m."

"Yeah, I know, and it'll take every minute to do so!"

# Chapter 11

IT'S APPROACHING THE END OF the school year, and JJ has nearly completed his boat. It's all navy gray except the copper bottom. Mr. Roy tells JJ that he needs to put a coat of paint over the copper or he's going to blind all the fish in River Creek. JJ didn't catch the joke, but he asked Mr. Roy, "What color do you think I should paint it?"

"I've got some light blue paint that we used to paint the bottom of the community swimming pool. I don't know if you can use it over copper, but I don't see why you couldn't. I'll call the paint store and ask them?"

"I didn't think that I had to paint over the copper."

"I don't think that you have to, but you don't want to blind the fish, do you?"

JJ still didn't catch the joke.

"Do you think that the blue will go with the gray?"

"What, are you going to enter this boat in a beauty pagan? The blue will look good."

"Okay, I got it this far. One more coat isn't going to hurt. Besides, I still don't have the motor running yet."

"God damn, JJ. This is supposed to be your project, not mine!"

"Oh, I wasn't asking you to do it Mr. Roy. I'll get it done soon."

"No, I know that you weren't expecting it, but I got a guy at work who I can get to fix it, but you will have to pay for the parts. I have no idea what that will cost, but it couldn't be much. It's just a simple 12-horsepower motor."

"What do we need to do?"

"Let's you and I toss it in the back of my pick-up truck and I'll take it to work tomorrow. I don't know how long it will take him, but I'll get it back as soon as possible."

Again, as JJ and Roy were loading the motor into the pick-up truck, JJ's father pulled into the driveway.

"Where you going with that motor?"

"Mr. Roy's got a guy at work that can fix it."

"I can fix it. I've just been trying to figure out what I needed." Looking at Roy, John asks him, "Can you get me a 55-gallon drum? I'll need to fill it with water and put the motor in it. You know that it's a water-cooled engine, so if I can put it in the drum and get it started, I won't burn it up. Besides, it's been sitting so long that I think that I'm going to take the head off and clean up the pistons. I can do all that right here and you don't have to haul it back and forth."

"JJ, it sounds like your dad has a better plan than mine. Let's lean it against the wall and I'll bring the drum tomorrow. If you need help getting it into the drum. I'm sure that three of us can do it."

"Thanks, Roy. I was thinking about this thing and the only thing that I didn't have was that drum."

"Hell, that's no problem. We end up crushing them in our compactor and selling the scrap metal so this one will live a little longer before it makes it to the scrapyard. JJ, we just might get this boat in the water."

"Thanks, Mr. Roy. Thanks, Dad. We're getting closer to the water."

By now JJ is getting excited. He can see that the boat will be in the water soon. The next day at school, in his gym class, he was talking to some of his friends about the boat when one of the other classmates spoke up. "You have a boat?"

"Well, not yet, but I should have it the water in a couple weeks."

"Where do you live?"

"I live in Beachwood. Where do you live?"

"I live in Wellington."

"Woo!" said the other guys. Wellington was a very upscale

community. You certainly had to be upper-middle class to wealthy to live there. Not many guys knew Justin because he was a little shy, and Beachwood Junior High was very blue collar and didn't meet Wellington standards. But JJ was the type of guy who everyone liked. He could fit in with any group. But even JJ was a little nervous about making friends with someone from Wellington. However, it was very clear that Justin was looking for a friend. He felt like a misfit in this crowd of rednecks. Justin was about 5' 5" tall and weighed about 150 lbs. He was all muscle, and you could tell that he worked out with weights. The coach was about to pair up the guys for some wrestling. JJ stood about four inches taller than Justin and outweighed him by at least 25 lbs. All the other guys paired up with other buddies. JJ could have paired up with anybody. They all wanted to take on JJ. Before JJ could say anything, Justin said, "Do you want to match up?" JJ is thinking, *I'll kill this guy in a matchup.*

"Sure, but I'm not very good at wrestling. I prefer baseball or basketball."

"That's okay. You can see that no one here wants to pair up with me. How about giving me a chance?"

"Let's go at it!"

The whistle blew, and Justin had JJ on the matt within seconds. All the other guys looked at Justin and said, "Where the hell did you learn that stuff?"

Justin's face was beet red. He looked at JJ and said, "My parents had me in private school and they had a wrestling team. I was the captain of the team."

"Damn, with those moves you must have won every match."

"No, actually, we lost all but one. Hey about your boat, I have a little fourteen-foot boat that my parents gave me last year. When you get your boat in the water, let's meet up."

"Okay, that sounds good, but I don't know much about the waterfronts."

"I know all the coves and communities on our side, and I know where the swimming pier is in Beachwood, so we could meet there."

Justin was excited about making a friend at school, and he knew that JJ was very popular, while he was not. He just wanted to be one of the guys, but his parents kept him so sheltered that he didn't know how to make friends. But he and JJ bonded, and Justin was busting his buttons to tell his mother that he made a new friend at school.

"Mom, guess what? I finally made a real friend at school. And it doesn't seem to bother him that I'm from Wellington. I think that he is one of the most popular guys in class."

"That's nice, dear. Go wash up and get ready for dinner. Your father will be home and you can tell us all about him."

As they sat down for dinner, Justin turned to his twin brother, who looked nothing like him, and said Andy, "Guess who I made friends with today at school. JJ Kapok."

Andy, who had no friends and didn't care, responded, "You mean that guy who looks like Elvis Presley?"

"Yeah, that's him."

"Mom, you should see this guy. He looks like a mobster. Cold black hair, combed back like a duck's butt."

"Justin, that doesn't sound like someone you want to become friends with."

"You going to judge this guy based on what Andy says? He doesn't have any friends."

"And didn't have any friends at the other school. Andy should live in a cave. As long as you send him food he'd be happy."

"Maybe so, but I'd rather do that than be associated with some hood from Beachwood."

"Beachwood! Is that where he lives? Ask Mr. Casey, Justin's father."

"Yes, sir. And he's a nice guy. None of the guys have even talked to me all school year. And we got talking about boats, and he wrestled with me in gym class. Now all the guys are talking to me."

"Did you beat him?"

"Yeah, he's four inches taller than me and outweighs me, but

I took him down in ten seconds. But I felt a little bad. I didn't tell him that I was the wrestling champ at Brook Dale School."

Mr. Casey laughed. "That was a little unfair."

"Yeah, but I don't plan to tell him. All the other guys laughed at him. They had never seen him taken down. But it didn't seem to bother him. He looked at the other guys and laughed. 'Any of you brave souls want to take him on?' It was great. Finally, all these guys looked at me like a real person."

"JJ will be putting his boat in the water in a couple of weeks, and we're going to meet up down at the Beachwood Swimming Pier."

"I don't mind you making friends with Elvis ... I mean JJ ... but I don't want you hanging around Beachwood."

"Mom, we're just going to show off our boats. I won't go into Beachwood. Those guys would never accept someone from Wellington. That's what I think is neat about JJ he likes everybody. He's a pack leader in his Boy Scout troupe."

"He's in the Boy Scouts? Asked Mr. Casey. That's positive. You'll have to have him over and introduce him to your mother and me."

"He doesn't have any way to get here. That's what neat about him having his own boat. He could pull up to the pier."

The Caseys had a 150-foot pier, with a boat lift for Justin's boat. They owned a 65-foot Yacht, and Justin's older brother, who was married and lived in a Rancher style house on the same property. Had a 21-foot Chris Craft Speedboat. Justin's boat was a 14-foot all-mahogany version of a Chris Craft. It had a 50-horsepower outboard motor with a 20-gallon hose-connected fuel tank. And this baby was fast! No one in Beachwood would be able to afford to buy a boat like this, much less a fourteen-year-old boy. JJ was in for a big surprise.

Mr. Roy delivered the 55-gallon drum and helped JJ and his father put the motor in it and secured it with a 2 x 4 wood frame. The Kapok's had a well-water system, so it was going to take some time to fill the 55-gallon drum. In the meantime, Mr. Kapok removed the cover of the motor and removed the head. The inside was black with fuel deposits and was a mess. Mr. Roy asked him if he wanted him to take the carburetor to his guy at work. It needed to be rebuilt, and they agreed that the guy could do a better job working in a shop. John removed the two pistons and again Roy suggested taking them to the shop and let then soak in engine cleaner. They worked well together as a team, and they were determined to get this engine running. By the end of the week, they had all the parts cleaned up, the carburetor rebuilt, and a new head gasket. They were ready to start the engine.

This motor had a pull-type starter, similar to a lawnmower. Everyone was nervous about what was going to happen when they tried to start it. They decided to let JJ have the first pull. He pulled it with all his strength. It just sputtered. He tried it again, and nothing happened: John took one of the spark plugs out, poured a little gasoline into the piston hole, and replaced the spark plug. JJ tried again. This time it sputtered a little and began running perfectly.

With this kind of motor, you had to mix the oil with the gasoline before putting it in the tank. Since John had not used this engine for several years, he put too much oil in the gasoline and it was pumping out dark gray fumes. They slowed it down to an idle and let it run for awhile. They shut it down and poured about a quart of pure gasoline in this three-gallon tank. They started it back up and let it run for about an hour. By now it was running pretty smoothly. They decided that they would put the boat in the water and check it for leaks. Tommy and Jimmy had come down to help launch the boat. They had brought some Pepsi in a thin jar. They knew that JJ wasn't going to let them hit his baby with a Pepsi bottle. This boat weighed a ton. It was all hardwood planks. It took all of them to get it in the water. Everyone was expecting it to fill up with water and sink. They waited and they waited. Not a single leak. JJ had done a great job. They decided they were all too exhausted to put the motor on it and take it out. It was beginning to get dark. Noontime tomorrow was the time for the trial run.

"What did you name her, JJ?" Everyone knew the answer, but it wasn't painted on the boat.

"Well, even though you scared me with the cost of Julie, I decided to name her *Julie* anyway."

"Mr. Roy handed him a plastic bag. Solid brass letters, spelling Julie. Somehow I thought that you might come to that conclusion, so I purchased these as my gift to your new boat."

"All of you guys made this happen. Thank you very much. I'll put these letters on tomorrow before we take her out."

The next day it rained all day. JJ still worked to put the letters on, but they decided to wait until the next day to take Julie out for her first run. The next day was beautiful, and everybody was there at noontime. JJ insisted that the real Julie wait on her pier. He was going to pick her up and bring her back to his house.

They placed the motor on the back of the boat and started it up. It ran perfectly. The boat was so heavy that the 12-horsepower motor was working very hard to push Julie through the water. A good estimate would be that at top speed, *Julie* would do about 5 knots, approximately 6 to 7 mph. But JJ didn't care how fast it was. He finally had his own boat. When he pulled up to Julie's pier, one couldn't say who was happier.

"Come aboard, my lady. This craft is named in Your Honor. And there are a group of friends waiting around the bend to greet you."

Julie was wearing shorts and one of her famous sweaters. She was simply beautiful and beaming with happiness.

"'Tis my honor to enter your lovely craft and to meet your friends who await me."

JJ steered the boat back home. When they got to his house, you would have thought that the *Queen Elizabeth* was docking. Everyone was cheering, and smiles were everywhere. Yes, all of JJ's work and all the support and help that he received were being enjoyed by everyone. Another great day.

# Chapter 12

It is near the end of school year. *Julie*, the boat, has been launched. The weather is getting nice. Plans are being made for the freshman Prom. People are playing golf now, which means caddy money, and JJ has turned his attention toward buying a car. He's one and half years from getting his driver's license. It'll take him some time to save enough money to buy a car, but he will do it. His father told him that if he earned enough money to buy the car, he would pay the auto insurance. Auto insurance for a teenager is very expensive, and most insurance companies will not insure a teenager, but because his father is retired navy, he can get a rider on his father's policy.

JJ hasn't seen Justin to tell him that his boat is in the water, but today is gym class, and Justin will be there.

"Hey, Justin, guess what? I got my boat in the water. My dad fixed the motor, and it's running good! I had it out over the weekend, but I didn't know how to find your house from the water."

"My house is easy to find. From the Beachwood swimming pier, you go up toward the Big Rocks, and we're the second cove on your left. But my mother doesn't allow me to go out on a school night, so we'll have to wait until Friday after school."

"That sounds good. How will I find you?"

"I'll meet you at the swimming pier at five thirty. What does your boat look like?"

"It's navy gray with a light blue bottom."

"You mean that it's painted?" Justin had never seen a painted boat!

"Well, yeah, it's an old wood plank rowboat. What's yours?"

"Mine's a natural wood with varnish. It's small but fun. It's not like my brother David's. He has a 21-foot Chris Craft with an onboard motor. It is really fast."

"Does he go fishing in it, on the bay?"

"Oh my God, *no*. He won't let you walk on the deck with your shoes on, even if they are rubber boating shoes. If you scratched his finish, he'd throw you overboard!"

"What does he do in it?"

"He just runs up the creek and goes out into the bay."

"Then what?"

"What does he do in his boat?"

Justin didn't understand the question. "Well, he comes back!"

"He doesn't fish or crab, or even swim off of it?"

"No, it's a speedboat!"

"Hey, class is about to start. If I don't see you again, I'll meet you at the pier at five thirty Friday."

Class ended, and JJ and Tommy were walking down the hall when JJ asked Tommy, "Have you ever heard of somebody having a boat that you can't fish or swim off of?"

"No. Who the hell would have a boat like that?"

"Justin's older brother. He says that it is a speedboat."

"So what? Does that mean that you can't do anything else with it?"

"I don't know, but it sure sounds like it."

"I think that Justin is weird. I don't know what you see in him?"

"He's okay. He just comes from the other side of the creek."

"Yeah, I know, Wellington. I guess they don't know what boats are for."

"I'm meeting him Friday at the swimming pier. Do you want to come?"

"Yeah, I guess so. What time?"

"I'm going to meet him at the pier at five thirty. So why don't you meet me at my house around five."

"Okay. What are we going to do?"

"Nothing really, just meet and talk about boats and cars."

"Yeah, I never hear him talk about girls. That's why I think he is weird."

"No, no, he likes girls. He told me the other day that he was concerned because he doesn't have a date for the prom. Do you know anybody that would go with him?"

"I just told you that I think that he's weird, and now you want me to find him a date?"

"Yeah, you can help out here. What about your sister? She's a year younger, but unlike you, she's nice looking."

"I don't know if my mother would let her go, and I'm not going to ask either one of them."

"Do you mind if I ask?"

"Hell, no. I don't care, but I think you're crazy. What are you, in love with a guy or something?"

"Cut it out. Don't you believe in helping friends?"

"Yeah, but I don't have any weirdo friends."

"At least go with me when I ask your mother."

"I'll go, but don't get mad if I laugh."

"Come on, Tommy. A little help here!"

"Okay. Are you going to stop after school?"

"Yeah, that's the plan. If your mother says yes, it's going to take me a little time to convince your sister."

The school bell rings, and it's the end of the day. JJ and Tommy walk to Tommy's house. He lives about nine long blocks from the school.

"Hi, JJ. What brings you here?"

"Well, Mrs. Dunn, I need your help with something."

"You need my help?"

"Yes, Mamma. You see, I have this friend that I'm trying to help. He needs a date for the prom, and I was wondering if I could talk to Connie and see if she would go with him."

"Aren't you sweet. You know, that's how I met Mr. Dunn, only it was our junior prom. He was very shy. And one of my girlfriends told me that he wanted to ask me to go but couldn't get up the nerve to ask, so she and I worked out a plan that we would talk about it while he was standing around with us. And it worked."

"What did you do?"

"We got talking, and she said to me, 'Connie, who are you going to the prom with?' And I responded, 'I don't have a date yet.' So she turned to Tommy, Mr. Dunn, and said, 'Tommy, do you have a date for the prom?' He said no, and she said, 'Neither does Connie. You two should go together!' Mr. Dunn looked at me and said, 'Would you like to do that?' I said yes, and we've been dancing together ever since."

"That's a great story, Mrs. Dunn."

"Have you asked Connie if she wants to go?"

"No, but don't all girls like to go to proms?"

"Yes, most do. Does she know your friend?"

"She met him, but he's kind of shy, like Mr. Dunn."

"Oh, Mr. Dunn isn't shy anymore. After hanging out with me and my girlfriends, he came out of that shell, and if anything, I have to calm him down all the time."

"What's your friend's name?"

"Justin. He's short. But he's a little taller than Connie."

"Do you think that he would want to take her? You know that she's younger than you, and that could be a problem."

"Yeah, I know. Actually, Justin is a year older than me, but Connie is pretty, and he's okay looking."

"He's a weirdo," pipes in Tommy.

"No, he is not. He's a very nice person. He lives in Wellington. Tommy, I thought that you were going to help."

"When is the prom? You know that girls need time to buy a gown."

"If she will do it, I'll help pay for the gown."

"That won't be necessary. I'm sure that her father will pay for it."

"Geez, that's great. It's the third week in June."

"That's not far away."

"I know but I haven't talked to Connie yet, so I don't know if she'll do it."

"She's in her room. Let's find out. Connie, can you come down here?"

"Yes, Mom. I'll be right there. What's up?"

"JJ has something that he wants to ask you."

"JJ wants to talk to me? You never talk to me. I'm too young for you. You're a freshman snob."

"No, I'm not. I like you a lot, and we just don't get a chance to talk."

"Why would you want to talk to me when you have Julie hanging on your arm all the time?"

"Julie is my steady, and she is my date to the prom. And that's what I want to talk to you about. One of my friends is looking for a date to the prom, and I was wondering if you would like to go with him."

"Someone wants to take me to the prom? Can I go, Mom? Who is this guy? Do I know him? What's he look like?"

"Slow down, Connie. Give JJ a chance to answer you. And yes, you can go if you want to."

"Mom, every girl wants to go to the prom! All my girlfriends will be jealous. Who is this guy?"

"It's Justin from over in Wellington."

"You mean that good-looking redhead guy? Oh yes. I love you, JJ. Mom, I'm going to need a gown."

"I know, dear, but we have three weeks to find one."

"JJ, are you sure that he wants to take me?"

"Well, no, Connie, I didn't know if you would go."

"Are you kidding? Every girl I know wants to go to the prom, and he's a hunk. Wait 'til you see him, Mom. He's built like a football player, with beautiful red hair, beautiful teeth. Oh yes, JJ. You better make it happen now that you got me all excited."

"I'll call him tonight at home. Do you have a picture that I can show him, just in case he doesn't remember you?"

"Oh yes. I hope that he does remember me."

With that Tommy piped in again, "I doubt it. This guy isn't really into girls. He's weird."

"Thanks, Tommy. You've been a lot of help."

"I'll get you a picture, JJ."

"JJ, this is a nice thing that you're doing. I think that you are going to make two people really happy."

"Thanks, Mrs. Dunn. I hope that you are right. Tommy has been anything but encouraging. I thought Connie would say no, but I'm glad that she didn't."

"Here the picture. It was taken at Christmas, so it's fairly new. I hope that he likes it."

"I have to get home. I'll call you as soon as I know something. Thanks, Mrs. Dunn."

"You're welcome, JJ."

"Thanks, JJ. I can't wait to hear from you."

# Chapter 13

It's Tuesday. JJ and several of his friends were excused from school to appear in court for the case against the six guys from Sunrise Beach. They were not certain if they were going to be called upon, but the state attorney wanted them there in case the judge needed to hear from them. Mr. Robbie, Earl, four police officers, and the police captain were all there.

The judge listened for several hours. Both the prosecutor and the defense attorneys made their closing statement. The judge adjourned for one hour. He said they he would return with his verdict. There was no doubt that they were going to be found guilty. Two of the boys were seventeen years old and could be treated as adults. The other four were all sixteen years old but were still facing jail time. As the judge returned, the bailiff announced, "All rise."

The judge stated, "Please be seated." Everyone sat down except JJ. The judge looked at him kind of puzzled.

"Can I help you, young man?"

"Yes, Your Honor. As a victim, may I address the court?"

"It's highly unusual at this point in the trial, but if the attorneys don't object, I'll hear what you have to say. Hearing no objections. State your name for the court."

"JJ Kapok from Beachwood community."

"What is it that you want to say? I already have my verdict, and I'm ready to proceed."

"Yes, Your Honor. Please excuse me. I'm a little nervous. I've never been in a courtroom before."

"Let's hope that this is the last time in your life, but please proceed. Relax."

"Your Honor, we know what these guys did was very bad. They hurt a lot of people and did a lot of damage, but they are young, like we are, and we hate to see their lives destroyed, so before you find them guilty and throw the book at them, can we make a suggestion?"

"Let me get this straight. You've never been in court before. You don't know my verdict yet, and you want to make a proposal to me as to how to handle this case?"

"Geez, Your Honor, when you say it like that, you scare me. Since we were the ones hurt, I thought that you would want to hear from us."

"Frankly, young man, I have to rule by the law, no matter what you think. But I know that it takes courage to speak up, so I do want to hear what you have to say."

"Thank you, Your Honor, but now you have scared me."

"Come on Mr. Kapok. No one is going to do anything to you, so relax and say what you have to say."

"Well, Your Honor, two of these guys are seventeen years old. One wants to join the army, and the other wants to join the navy. I don't know why they would want them, but if they do. Maybe the service can straighten them out. My father is a retired navy man, and he signed up when he was seventeen years old. He's fought in two wars, and I think that he has served his country well. Maybe we can turn a bad thing into a good thing by letting them sign up. Maybe they help someone instead of hurting them. The other four guys are just a little older than us. We'd like to beat them up again, but instead of hurting each other, maybe we could do it in baseball or basketball."

"You want me to let these guys off with no punishment?"

"Oh no, Your Honor. We're just trying to figure out a way to do it without destroying their lives and their future."

"Well, out of mouths of babes. Gentlemen, do you hear this? Go on, Mr. Kapok, how do you propose to do that?"

"Allow the two older ones to join up and make them take their pay and pay for the actual damage to the property. And we have a baseball field that sits on school property. Parks and Rec is going to supply us with the topsoil and the grass seed. And this is a big field. After the work is done, it has to be watered twice a day. As punishment, make these guys repair our ball field. And they can get part-time jobs and pay back some of the damages. I work, and I'm saving to buy my first car, so they can work and payback for the bad things they have done."

"I see that some of your friends are here. Let me see if they agree with you. You there, the one with the cast on your arm, do you agree with him?"

"Reluctantly, yes, Your Honor. They broke my arm. I missed the entire basketball season, and I may miss part of the baseball season. But I think nothing is gained by putting them in jail. Make them join the Police Boys Club and maybe help others."

"You there, the one with the crutches. Do you go along with this idea?"

"Well, I didn't at first—they broke my ankle, and like Don, I missed the entire basketball season, and the doctors don't know if I'm going to be able to play football again, and that makes me mad. I didn't do anything to these guys, but I don't think that JJ's idea is so bad. They still have to pay a price, and if they don't, you can always yank them back in here."

"Gentlemen, I can't believe what I have just heard. I don't know what is in the drinking water at that Beachwood school, but they sure are instilling good values into these young people. Maybe I've been on the bench too long. This proposal is far too liberal for me. But when you consider that it is coming from the victims, it sure makes you stop and rethink things. Okay, thank you, boys. Please sit down.

"Will the defendants rise? You young men have truly broken the law. You have hurt people, as you have heard. You have destroyed property. You have struck police officers, and you nearly killed Mr. Earl Faber. I find you guilty of all the charges, and frankly, I *was ready* to throw the book at you. But what I've heard in my courtroom today is something that I have never experienced, and it gives me hope that there are still a lot of really good young people out there.

"Our country is in better condition than I realized. Captain, I know that you would like to see a harsher penalty, but I'm going to accept Mr. Kapok's proposal, exactly as he presented it, and let me tell you, guys, I don't want to see you in my courtroom for a long time. And if I do, you will serve a long stay in the county jail. This case is completed."

"JJ, you are full of surprises!"

"Thank you, Captain. I hope this works. I know that the army recruiter said that he would accept Bow if the judge would let him enlist. The navy guy hasn't decided."

"Hey, we get our baseball field fixed and we don't have to do all the work, so I guess we had a little motive to let them off the hook! Captain, I hope that when we next meet, it is on friendlier terms."

"Me too, JJ."

"Come on, guys. We got a day off from school. Let's get out of here and enjoy what is left of it."

Mr. Robbie dropped two of the boys off at their houses, and he took JJ to the fire station. Earl was still sore and hurting as he got out of the car. He turned to JJ and said, "You know that I don't agree with you. You should have let the judge put them away."

"Why didn't you say something?"

"I spoke my peace while on the stand. If all you guys are willing to give them a break, I'm willing to go along with it. But they better keep their asses away from this fire station."

"I don't think that you have to worry about that. I don't think that we will ever see them in Beachwood again! Thanks, Mr. Robbie. I'm heading home."

As JJ was walking home, he began to reflect on what had just happened. *Boy, was I scared. I thought that judge was going to eat me alive. And the guys stuck with me even though they didn't agree. And the captain could have killed the whole idea, but he didn't. I guess I'll have to stop calling him 'Jerk Face.' And Earl, they nearly killed him, and he's willing to give them another chance. I'm not certain that they deserve it, but it's worth a try.*

"Mom, I'm home!"

"How did court go?"

"It was amazing. The judge went along with my proposal."

"What proposal? Robbie called and said that you should be a politician, that you had everyone agreeing with you."

"It's no big deal. I'll tell you about it a little later. I want to call Justin."

"Oh, Justin called here. He said that his mother doesn't let him make phone calls on school nights, but he told her that this was very important, so she said he could talk for fifteen minutes, so don't get him in trouble."

"I wonder what he wants. He never calls me. Hi, Mrs. Casey. This is JJ. Can I speak with Justin?"

"You mean 'May I speak with Justin?' Hold on, I'll get him. Don't talk too long. Justin, JJ is on the phone."

"Hi, what's up?"

"I saw Tommy in school and he told me that you arranged for me to take his sister to the prom?"

"Well, yeah, kinda. I got a picture of her for you, and I was going to talk to you at school today. I forgot about this court case."

"I just want to thank you and find out exactly what you told her and what she expects. You know that I think she is really cute."

"Oh, so you remember her?"

"Yeah, she's the one that told me that she thought that my red hair was beautiful and that she loves red hair. I didn't know what to say to her."

"Yeah, well she remembers you. That's what she said to me: 'You mean that good-looking guy with the red hair?' She's all excited about it. She wants me to tell her as soon as I know your answer."

"I think she already knows. I told Tommy that I would love to take her to the prom. You know, he said something strange to me. He said, 'Oh, you date girls?' What did he mean by that?"

"I don't know, but I know that I'm going to kill him when I see him in school."

"Why?"

"He could have messed the whole thing up and made both of you mad at me."

"How?"

"Never mind, Justin. The answer is yes, and I'll talk to you in school tomorrow."

"Wait, I want to know more about the conversation."

"No, I don't want to make your mother mad at me. I'll see you tomorrow."

*Now I have to call Connie and explain what happened*, he thought.

"Hi, Mrs. Dunn. This is JJ."

"Hi, JJ. I understand he said yes."

"Mrs. Dunn, do you mind if I kill your son? He could have messed this whole thing up and had both of them mad at me."

"JJ, it's okay. Connie is in seventh heaven. She's floating around the house singing songs. And Tommy is enjoying tormenting her. I'm making arrangements to get her a gown and to get her hair done. I'll tell you the color of the dress when I know."

"Why?"

"In case he wants to try to match the flowers."

"Are you supposed to do that?"

"You don't have to. You can always buy white. But if you can match them, it really looks nice."

"Do you think that I should talk to Connie?"

"If you want to talk on the phone all night, 'cause she will have a million questions. And since she already knows the answer, I don't think it matters if it waits until tomorrow. Do you want to talk to Tommy?"

"Hell no. I mean, heck no. I told you that I'm ready to kill him."

"Okay, JJ. I'll tell him to avoid you tomorrow."

"Thanks, Mrs. Dunn. This has been a very busy day, and I'm going to bed."

"Yes, I heard that you are a hero again."

"What?"

"Yeah, it's on the local news about the six guys from Sunrise

Beach. The news said that you were better than their lawyers and that you convinced him to give them a second chance."

"Oh crap. I better stay up until my father gets home. If he hears that, he's going to think I've gone soft in the head."

"Not according to the news. They said that you should go to law school."

"Mrs. Dunn I'm going to bed. I hope that my father doesn't turn on the news. Good night, Mrs. Dunn."

# Chapter 14

IT'S FRIDAY, AND SCHOOL IS about to let out. Tommy sees JJ in the hallway.

"Are we still meeting Mr. Wierdo at five thirty?"

"Yeah, assuming that the boat engine will start."

"Are we doing anything? Are you going to race him?"

"No, no race. My boat, *Julie*, is a little slow. Not like the real Julie—fast and *hot*!"

"Boy, she is *hot*! Have you got the key to her bra yet?"

"That's none of your business. And if I did, I sure wouldn't tell you. You're like an old gossip. You told Justin about Connie before I had a chance to talk to him."

"Lighten up, JJ. It gave me a chance to talk to Mr. Weirdo. You know he doesn't talk to anybody unless they talk directly to him."

"So, what do you think about Mr. Weirdo?"

"He's okay, but he's a little thick. I told him a couple jokes and he didn't get any of them, and when I told him that my sister has big tits for a thirteen-year-old, he looked at me like I was crazy."

"You are crazy. Why would say anything to him about your sister's tits?"

"I told him that he better not mess with them."

"Tommy, you are crazy. Does she?"

"Does she what?"

"Have big tits?"

"Yeah, I'll bet they are as big as Julie's. And I've seen them with no bra."

"Oh, yeah. What did they look like?"

"They look like mountain peaks with a dark top instead of snow. What are you supposed to do with them?"

"*I'll* let you know after I get the keys. I see all these men playing with them, so they must be fun."

"Why do girls have big ones and ours are flat?"

"I do know the answer to that. I learned that in health class. When women have babies, their tits fill with milk so they can feed the baby."

"How do they do that?"

"Come on, Tommy. Haven't you ever heard someone say, 'Go suck your mother's tit'?"

"No, I don't remember sucking on my mother's tit."

"God, Tommy, for all the bullshit that you talk, you sure don't know much."

"Well, where are you supposed to learn all this stuff?"

"First, you listen to what the older men say, and second, you pay attention in health class. Then you put them together and at least you have some idea. Didn't you ever talk about the birds and the bees with your father?"

"Yeah, but he didn't give a lot of details. When he finished, I knew why we wear jock straps and they don't need one."

"Well, you knew that anyway from seeing your sister naked. Don't you ever hear your father saying something to your mother?"

"Yeah, and she smiles and laughs, so she must like it."

"Yeah, girls like sex as much as guys. They just don't talk about it as much as we do."

"Yeah, I'd like to be a fly on the wall when some of those girls are together talking. What do you think they say about us?"

"I don't know, but I hope that it's good. Okay, I'll see you at five. Keep your mouth shut about Justin. Let them decide for themselves if they like each other."

"Oh, so I'm not supposed to tell my own sister that the guy that she is going to the prom with is a weirdo!"

"God, Tommy, you've already said that a dozen times. Give it a rest!"

JJ goes home and takes the tarp off the boat. He starts the motor. No problems. *Good, we're all set to go.*

"Mom, I'm going to meet Justin in a little while, around five thirty."

"Okay, but remember that there aren't any street light on the water, so start heading back as the sun starts to set. Allow yourself enough time to get back, 'cause when it gets dark on the water, you can't see anything, and you don't know your way around."

"Okay. Here comes Tommy. He's going with me."

"That's nice. That will be the blind leading the blind!"

"Don't worry, Mom. Justin knows his way around. He'll make sure that we get back all right."

"Come on, Tommy, get in the boat. Let's go."

JJ starts the motor and starts out of the cove. It takes only a few minutes to get to the pier. As they leave the mouth of the cove and turn around the bend, they see this boat way off in the distance. It's moving very fast. Within a minute, the boat passes them, circles around them, and then circles around them again. It's Justin. He slows down and yells to them, "I'll meet you at the pier!"

As they pull up to the pier, Tommy says to JJ, "This guy's a show-off. I told you he was weird, circling around you like that. He just wanted to show you how fast his boat is. I'm going to give him a piece of my mind."

"Tommy, he's just proud of his boat. He didn't mean anything bad."

"Bullshit. He's a show-off!"

"Hi, guys. Tommy is that pretty sister of yours getting ready for the prom?"

"Yeah, I think so. It sure has her and my mother talking a lot of girl talk. I know that she's excited about going out with you, and that I don't understand. What's so exciting about you?"

Justin didn't know if Tommy was serious or just kidding, and neither did JJ.

"Well, I don't think that it's me. I think she just excited about the prom."

"Whatever. I know that her and my mom went and bought a gown."

"They did? Do you know what color it is?"

"No, I just heard them talking about not having any straps. They think that's a big deal. But my mom told JJ that she would tell him the color after they bought it, so I guess you will know by the weekend."

"Justin, where did you get the money to buy a boat like this?"

"Oh, I didn't buy it, Tommy. My father gave it to me for my twelfth birthday."

"You're kidding. He gave this to you when you turned twelve? This must have cost a lot of money."

"I don't know. Of course he didn't tell me. But later on, I heard him talking to my brother, David, and he said he paid over $5000 for it."

"Go to hell! Five thousand dollars?"

"Yeah, he brought David his boat five years ago when he turned twenty-one, and he paid over $30,000 for that one. Of course, it has an onboard motor and all that speed equipment."

"Geez, I spent over $400 to get *Julie* in the water, and I thought that was a lot."

"You did a good job fixing up this old plank-style boat. I've never seen one of these except at the fisherman's pier, where they use them as workboats."

"Yeah, well, you know that this washed up into my yard, and I went down there to see if anyone lost it. But no one claimed it, so I had a boat."

"Yeah it was so old and in such bad shape, I guess no one wanted it back." Justin could tell by the expression on JJ's face that he had said the wrong thing and that he had hurt JJ's feelings, so in an attempt to recover, he said, "You picked a good color combination."

"All the paint was donated. Julie's dad gave me the bottom paint, and my father got the gray paint from the PX."

"Well, they blend well together."

"Well, it's starting to get dark. I promised my mother that I would allow enough time to get back before dark. So, I guess that I'll head back."

"How about tomorrow? I'll pick up guys up here and take you for a ride out to the Big Rocks."

"No thanks," said Tommy. "I'd rather walk!"

Justin, attempting to make a joke, said, "Oh, you can walk on water?"

"No, but apparently you think that you can!"

"How about you, JJ?"

"I don't know, Justin. I'll have to check to see if my father has anything that he is expecting me to do, or if I've gotten any calls for odd jobs. I'll call you if I can do it."

Justin could sense that he had upset JJ, but he didn't know what to say or do. "Okay, if I don't see you over the weekend, I'll see you in school. Only a few days left."

They both departed and went in separate directions. As they pulled away, Tommy couldn't hold it back.

"JJ, I told you that this guy was weird. Now I'm going to add *asshole* to the title. Some friend he is. He knows how hard you worked to get this boat into the water, and he refers to it as an 'old workboat.' It probably came from fisherman's pier. So what? He's a first-class snobby asshole. I'm going to go home and tell my mother that she shouldn't let Connie go out with him."

"*No*, don't do that. What he said wasn't nice, but most of it was true. It is an old boat. And it may have come from the fisherman's pier. It is so old and in bad condition that no one wanted to do the work, so they didn't claim it. But to me it was a project, and I could get a boat for free."

"JJ, why do you always defend people who say and do stupid things?"

"I don't always defend people, but think about it. He has no friends. He shares a room with his brother, Andy, who has no friends and doesn't want any. His mother will not him to leave the property on school nights. She doesn't allow him to make phone calls on school nights. So all he does all week is come home and do school homework and listen to records. So, the only thing that he has are those material things that they buy him, so he thinks that they make him important and that people will like him because he has them."

"So what? I don't give a damn about his boat."

"I know that, but he thinks that offering you a ride in his expensive speedboat will make you like him."

"Yeah, I'd like to punch a hole in its bottom."

"Tommy, I don't like what he said, but it didn't hurt me. Do see any bruises on me? I still have my boat, I still have my girlfriend, I can still play baseball, and I still have you as my friend! Life's pretty good."

"Here throw that rope over that pole and tie her up. I told my mother that I would be home before dark, and we just made it. I'll see you tomorrow. Go home, and don't say anything to your mother or sister about Justin."

"Why not? They should know what an asshole he is."

"Tommy, for Pete's sake. What do you think your life would be like if your mother wouldn't let you out of the house all week, or if you had to ask your mother's permission every time that you wanted to call me on the phone?"

"So what? I can't help what his mother does."

"No, but you could be his friend. It won't hurt you. It won't put any bruises on you. And who knows? You might actually like the guy."

"JJ, you are a nutcase! This guy insults you and makes fun about your boat, and here you are defending his dumb-ass behavior."

"Tommy, I would do the same for you."

"Yeah, but I really am your friend."

"Yes, you are, but Justin is also a friend. He just has learn how to be one. I'll eventually say something to him. Maybe I tell him that boat needs some paint—that it's too plain, it needs some color, that we need to paint a yellow border all around the perimeter."

"JJ, you really are crazy. I'm going home, and I promise that I won't say a word to my mother or sister."

Justin is nearly home, and he realizes that he really said some stupid things. But he doesn't think that a simple "I'm sorry" will fix everything. He would like some other suggestions, but he doesn't have any friends to talk to, and he knows that Tommy is mad at him. Maybe he could talk to his older brother? As he walked in the door, he said, "Mother, I'm home."

"I see that you are, my dear. What's the matter? You don't look very happy."

"Oh, Mother, I said something very stupid, and I don't know what to do."

"Tell me about it. Maybe I can help."

"Justin tells his mother all about the conversation and his mother thought about it for a few minutes."

"Justin, I don't see where you said anything improper. You simply told him the truth, and it never hurts to tell the truth. You told him that the boat was very old. It's made of wood. It's painted and probably came from the fisherman's pier, where it was once used as a work boat. That's all true."

"Yes, mother, but stupid Tommy asked me how much I paid for my boat. I told them that Dad gave it to me for my twelfth birthday and that it was worth $5000. They couldn't believe me. JJ told me that he had spent about $400 to fix up his boat, and he thought that was a lot of money."

"Well, for a poor boy from Beachwood, that is a lot of money. But you shouldn't have told them about your boat. That was none of their business."

"Mother, you've missed the whole point. Five thousand dollars is probably more than his father makes all year. And it sounded like I was bragging because my boat was better than his."

"Well, it is?"

"Mother, please! To JJ, this is his baby, and he is thrilled to have a boat, and he loves it. JJ is the kind of guy who is happy for me. I'm sure that he doesn't care that my boat is newer, faster, and prettier. What I said was terrible. I sounded like a little spoiled brat, and frankly I feel like one. I really like JJ, and I don't want to lose him as a friend."

"You're not a spoiled brat. I told you not to get involved with those boys from Beachwood. Now they have you feeling that you've done something wrong. You haven't done anything wrong."

"Yes I have, Mother. I've hurt the feeling of my only real friend, and there was no reason to do so. He wasn't being mean to me, and he was actually excited to see my boat. He said that it was beautiful and that he loved the natural wood. Why couldn't I just say something nice, like, 'I really like the paint colors of your boat.' No I have to tell him that it's old and was probably a work boat that nobody wanted. What a terrible thing to say to your friend. I just want to go to my room and hide! Mother, I have to be able to use the phone!"

"Justin, it'll be all right. You go ahead and make all the calls you need to, dear."

"Mother, please stay off the extension. You don't seem to understand the issue anyway. If I can fix this, I'll explain everything to you later."

Justin went to the phone and called Connie.

"Hello, Mrs. Dunn. This is Justin. May I speak with Connie?"

"Yes, Justin. I'll call her."

"Hi, Connie, can you help me with something."

"You want me to help you? With what?"

"I need you to call JJ for me and tell him that you and I were talking and that I told you what a terrible thing that I said to him and that I feel so bad but I don't know what to say to him."

"You want me to call JJ? I don't talk to JJ that often. I don't think that he will listen to me."

"Do you think that you can get Tommy to do it? I know that he is mad with me."

"*No*, I wouldn't ask my brother. He would just screw it up! How about if I call Julie. I could talk to her, and she could tell him that she and I were talking and that you and I were talking and that you told me this story—and how bad you feel but don't know how to fix it."

"Wow! When you say it that way, it really sounds complex. But yeah, that sounds like it will work. Will you do that for me?"

"Yes, I'll call her tomorrow. I don't want to call while Tommy is in the house. He'll listen in on the conversation and tell JJ that we planned all this. If I get a chance, I'll call you back. But you can be sure that I'll do it. I hope that it works. I know that you and JJ are friends, so let's see if we can mend the friendship."

"Thanks, Connie. Now I think that I can sleep tonight. See ya."

# Chapter 15

It's prom night and everyone is excited. They were supposed to have Buddy Dean as a DJ for the prom, but the Teacher Committee overruled the Teen Committee. They didn't think that Rock and Roll was appropriate for a Prom, so they had a live band called The Walkers, and apparently the teachers didn't do their homework because The Walkers were one of the best local rock and roll bands in the entire area. They were really great, but no one knew that before the start of the prom. Everyone was complaining that the teachers had no right to change the format for the night. By the end of the night the complaints changed to praise, and the teachers, who knew nothing about the band, were now thought to be brilliant.

JJ had taken the money that the police officers gave him to replace his Elvis jacket, and instead he bought a white sportcoat and a new satin shirt, dark blue to match his blue pegged pants. Now he really looked like Elvis. A white sport coat, a blue satin shirt, blue pegged pants, and Cuban heeled shoes, and of course he bought a pink carnation for the lapel. Wow! Did he look sharp.

Julie had a cream/almost white, strapless gown, and beautiful red patten leather shoes with three-inch high heels. JJ bought her beautiful red roses for her gown, which ended up on her waist, because there was no place to pin it up higher on the dress! Besides, she was wearing a push-up bra, and JJ was enjoying the show. Her hair was some flowing style that her and her grandmother had done, slightly past her shoulders. JJ thought that he was taking Cinderella to the ball.

Julie's mother was driving them to the prom and told them that she would take them where ever they wanted to go after the prom, but they had to be back by 1:00 a.m., because she had to go to work the next day. Besides, they were only fourteen, and that was late enough for them to stay out. JJ and Julie really didn't care; they were happy to be together and Julie's mother was fun to be around. Julie's mother was reliving the prom that she never got to go to when she was younger.

Justin and Connie were supposed to meet them at the prom. Justin's older brother, David, was taking them in his brand new car, and while the parents didn't set a time for them, it was understood that they would be expecting them before 2:00 a.m.

Justin was in a full formal black tuxedo with tails. He really did look handsome. Everything was perfectly in place. He looked like he just stepped out of a male fashion magazine. The perfect gentleman.

Connie, who was just thirteen, looked like a beautiful young woman, maybe eighteen to twenty-one years old. She had a beautiful emerald green gown, strapless with a pushup bra. And for thirteen, there was a lot to push up. Justin bought her beautiful yellow roses that went perfectly with the emerald gown.

The prom started at 8:00 p.m., and everyone was lined up at the door to get in. All the girls looked like beautiful young ladies. All the guys looked like movie stars. The night was perfect.

When Justin arrived, and they met up at one of the tables. Things were a little uncomfortable. Justin knew that he had damaged the friendship, but he didn't know what to do. JJ felt that his friend looked down on him because he was poor. That he thought that his material belongings made him better than other people, and JJ was right. But Justin couldn't help that; his mother and father had protected and spoiled him all his life. He had never met anyone like JJ. JJ wanted the material things, but if he didn't get them, it didn't matter; he was happy with life. He didn't know that he was poor, and until Justin pulled his little stunt, he didn't care about being poor. Justin had talked to his mother and his older brother, but they were no help. He told Connie some of the story, and got her to call Julie to help repair the damage. Julie talked to JJ and knew that JJ was okay with things. But Justin warned Connie that things could be a little cold in the relationship. Connie, like any thirteen-year-old, said to him, "You worry too much. Tell him that he looks like Elvis, and you'll break the ice."

"Holy smoke, JJ, you look just like Elvis. And Julie, you are prettier than Cinderella." Boy did that work.

"Justin, I don't want to sound insulting, but you look like a penguin with those tails on that tux. Why did you rent a tux?"

"I didn't. My parents bought this for me when my brother got married. Now, JJ, don't get mad about that. My parents buy me a lot of things. I can't help that."

"I'm not mad. And I don't care what your parents buy you. But it does bother me if you think that those things are more important than your friends."

"I really don't think that, but until now, I didn't have any friends. You, Julie, and Tommy, and now Connie, are the only people who wanted to be friends with me. So all I've ever had are those things that you talk about!"

Connie and Julie had tears in their eyes, and for the first time ever, JJ was speechless.

The girls both said at the same time, "Well now you got us, so like it or not, we are more important than that tux."

"Oh, I think he looks great in that tux. Come on, let's dance."

"That's a fast dance, and I don't know how to do that."

"That's okay. You get out there on that floor with me, jump around a little bit, and I'll show you how to pick up the beat. Nobody will be watching you and nobody cares. You look at me and I'll have you dancing before the night is over!"

Justin was all smiles as he and Connie walked onto the dance area.

"Julie looked at JJ, who still had not said a word. Well, what happened to you? Did the cat get your tongue?"

JJ was trying to gather his composure, his voice could barely speak. "Did you hear what he said? He's fifteen years old, and we're his first real friends."

"Looks like he has a new one now. Look at him and Connie. They're having a great time. And here we are sitting like two bumps on a log."

"I'm sorry, Julie. Do you mind waiting a little while before we dance?"

"Wow, he really got to you, didn't he?"

"Yeah, I don't know what to think. I've got a whole school and a whole community full of friends, and I've never thought about it. And I wouldn't trade any of my friends for his fancy boat, his tux, his record collection, or his money!"

"I know that you wouldn't, JJ. That's what makes you special. Come on. Let's go get a soda. This conversation is getting too deep."

"Hey, do you know, I think I love you."

"Wow, now this conversation is really getting deep."

"So what? I think that I love you."

"I think that I love you too, JJ, but I think that we're too young to be in real love."

"Why? Can't young people be in love?"

"Yes, I think that they can, but how do they know if they are?"

"I don't know, but I do know that the way I feel about you. I've never felt that way about anybody else."

"I feel the same way, but can we just keep this to ourselves?"

"I'll try."

"Can we get that soda now?"

They walked out to the entrance where they had some soda and cupcakes.

"Hey, JJ."

"Tommy, what are you doing here?"

"I was walking down to Pop's Place when I saw Kathy all dressed up for the prom. She was sitting on her porch crying. Her date didn't show up. He didn't call or nothing. She told me what happened, and I asked her if she would like me to take her. She said yes, and here we are. I don't know what we are going to do after it's over. I don't have any way to take her anywhere."

"Justin's brother is taking them somewhere in his new car.

Maybe you can double up with them? Boy, he and your sister are getting along great: Tommy, let me tell you something before you go in there. Justin considers you a real friend, and he doesn't have many friends. So you are kinda special to him, and now that he and your sister are becoming a number, could you work a little harder to develop the friendship?"

"Yeah, we'll become great friends—if he lets me and Kathy go with him!"

"Tommy, I swear, you are hopeless."

"I'm just kidding. I'm actually starting to like the weirdo."

"Julie and I are going back inside. I'll talk to you later."

"Julie, they are playing a slow dance, let's dance and forget about all this deep stuff."

"Hey, JJ, I just saw Tommy. He's here with Kathy."

"I know, Justin, and he going to ask you if they can go with you at the end of the prom."

"He already did. Connie didn't want him to tag along, but I convinced her that we should do it. Right. That's what friends are for. I told Connie that I would take her to Teen Club next week. I can join your Teen Club, can't I?"

"Yeah, you can join. You don't have to live in Beachwood to be a member. But is your mother going to allow you to be in Beachwood?"

"I don't know. I'm going to ask David if he will talk to Mom and tell her that."

"You guys are okay, and that the fire hall has adults there all the time. If she thinks that I have a date with Connie, I think she will say okay."

"Sounds like you and Connie are doing well."

"Yes we are. She is great. You would never know that she is only thirteen. She acts like she's seventeen. I really like her. Thanks, JJ, for hooking us up. And thanks for being my friend. And I'm really sorry about what I said about your boat. Will you take me out in it and teach me how to crab from a boat?"

"Sure, Justin, that's what friends are for."

By now they both are nearly crying, and Julie had tears running down her face, but she mustered up enough voice to say, "Justin, I sure am glad that you and Connie could double up with us tonight." This gives them enough time to clear their throats and begin talking in a normal voice.

"Yeah, and now that Tommy is here with Kathy, we have a threesome. Julie, do you know Kathy?"

"Oh yes, she's part of the girl group. I think that she is the same age as Connie, but because she has an older sister, she hangs out with us."

"Did you know that this band does a show?"

"No, what kind of a show?"

"They have a guy who does Jerry Lee Lewis's 'Great Balls of Fire' on the piano. Hey they are getting ready to start now. Let's move up close to the stage."

This guy was really good. He had the whole place rocking. The next guy was a Buddy Holly look-alike—black horn-rimmed glasses and all—and he got the place jumping. The third guy was Johnny Cash, and he slowed it down a little by singing "I Walk the Line," but everyone was dancing.

Then they had two women. Brenda Lee and Connie Francis. This was a great show, and of course they closed it out with the "King," Elvis the Pelvis Presley. The teachers weren't certain that they should let this go on, but everyone was yelling and screaming, "Let him sing," so they decided to let him go on. This guy was great. He started with "Hound Dog," which got everyone laughing, even the teachers. Then he sang "Blue Moon." Followed by "A Hunk, A Hunk of Burning Love." Even the teachers were dancing and singing. He closed it out by singing "Loving You." How perfect could it be?

JJ and Julie couldn't take their eyes off of each other. If this wasn't love, it was the next best thing. When the song was over, the singer did the Elvis closing "Thank you, thank you very much" and Julie looked at JJ and said, "I think you were a better Elvis."

"I love doing Elvis, but I really just want to be myself. I don't know where life will take me, but so far it's been pretty good."

The next song played was "White Sport Coat." The leader of

the band saw JJ and Julie leaving the floor and he called to them, "Hey, you over there. Yeah, you in the white sport coat, you can't leave the floor. This is your song. Come on up here next to the stage." The music stopped. "Stagehands, shine that spotlight on this lovely couple." JJ and Julie didn't know what to do. The spotlight was turned on and the music started playing. The entire prom crowd formed a circle around JJ and Julie. They started dancing, and the crowd started singing the words to the song. JJ thought the song would never end. About halfway into the song, all the others began to dance, but they never took the spotlight off of our couple. The song ended, and JJ thought, *Thank God it's over.* But the band leader piped in, "Let's hear it for our lovely couple. Come on up here; I have something for you." As they walked to the stage, the band leader jumped down onto the dance floor.

With the microphone in his hand he said, "Here's six new records for you and your lady. What's your name?" Before JJ could answer, several people in the crowd shouted, "Elvis," and the band leader laughed. "He does look like Elvis. We should have had him sing with our Elvis. Do you sing?"

"Yes, sir, but I couldn't compete with that guy. He was great!"

"What did you say your name is?"

"JJ Kapok."

"Well JJ, in addition to the records, I have a gift certificate for two to the new Sea Side Restaurant. You can take your lovely lady out to dinner tonight after the prom."

"Thank you. I know where it is, but it's so new that we haven't been there yet."

As they walked back to their table, everyone was cheering for them.

"That's one hell of a prize, JJ."

"Yes it is, and I'd like to give it to you."

"What?"

"Yeah, I know that you weren't planning on taking Kathy to the prom. I assume that you're broke; you always are. You and Justin can split the bill."

"I'll take care of me and Connie, and they can have the gift certificate."

"That's great. Thanks, JJ." With that Kathy reaches up and kissed JJ on the cheek. "You really are a great guy."

"Hey, that's what friends are for, right, Justin?"

"Yes, sir. That's what friends are for."

"Well, mister, why did you give my ticket away without asking me?"

"Julie, you and I think so much alike that I knew that you wouldn't mind. Besides, we're going to the Hot Dog Place. I'll buy you and your mother a foot-long hot dog and a Pepsi."

"That sounds like a great plan. You know, you really are something special. My Grannie says that you're going to have a star in your crown."

"I don't know exactly what that means, but if your Grannie says it, it must be true, and it must be something good. She is really something special!"

It was about 11:30 p.m. and almost everyone had left. Justin, Connie, Tommy, and Kathy were walking toward David's car.

"Do you want us to wait until Mrs. Connors gets here?"

"No, you can bet that she will be here in a few minute. It's a nice night. We can wait. You all go ahead. Have a great time."

"We already have."

"Me too. Could not have been any better. See ya. Here she comes now."

Mrs. Connors pulled the car next to where Julie was standing.

"Where do you two want to go?"

"We decided to go to Billy's Burger Palace and get a couple of foot-long hot dogs."

"What? You're going to a burger joint on prom night?"

"Yeah, we thought about going to Johnny's Bar, but he stops serving food at 12:00 p.m., and there are a couple of adults there that would be watching us like hawks. It would be like sitting under the light at the end of the pier. So Billy's sounds good."

# Chapter 16

SCHOOL HAS LET OUT FOR the summer. The days are getting longer and the teenagers of Beachwood are beginning their summer vacation. The Parks and Recs director has delivered the topsoil and the grass seed to the baseball field. Julie's brother, Roy, has put his boat in the water. It's a 15-foot no name with a fiberglass bottom. Much lighter in weight than JJ's, and he has a 30-horsepower outboard motor. This boat is fast enough to pull people on water skies. And that's what the two brothers do all summer. They do use the boat to go fishing and crabbing. It's a pretty boat, but it is used for everything. Their boat is fast enough to run circles around JJ's boat. And, yes, they do tease JJ whenever possible.

JJ has picked up all kinds of work and still works at the golf course. He is making over $100 a week and is putting most of it in the bank. He wants to buy a car before the end of next summer. That allows him enough time to get it ready for December, when he turns sixteen. Justin's mother is allowing him to use the phone now that school is out. And she does let him go out in his boat. He's allowed to go to Beachwood for Teen Club, and he and Connie are really very close friends. It would be more but neither of their parents will let them "go steady." She's too young, and his mother doesn't think that he should go with one girl. Since he doesn't have any other girlfriends, it really doesn't matter.

JJ is still trying to get the keys to Julie's bra, but she's keeping it locked up tight. Other girls have offered him their keys, but his is a Boy Scout, and he's staying loyal to Julie. However, it is summer, and all the guys and girls do go swimming at the pier. And many of the girls there like to show off what they have, so some of the boys are getting lessons in sex education. Some of the older men come down to the pier and pick up some of the older teenage girls. By the start of school, some of the girls won't be going back to school because they will be expecting babies. Most of them will get married, and some of them will go on to have a nice family and a good life. That is a normal life situation in Beachwood, and there is very little conversation about it; it is simply accepted.

JJ and Tommy were going up to the baseball field to see how much work had been done. When they got there, the boys from Sunrise Beach were still working. As they approached the field, Bow, the driver of the car, the one who hit Martin with the club, stopped working and came over to JJ.

"Hi, I just wanted to let you know that I'm going into the navy in six weeks. My dad loaned me $1000, and I've paid my part of the damage. All the other guys are on track to pay what they owe. You really saved our asses. Without you, we'd be in jail. My father suggested that when I leave, I should give you my car! And I'd like to do that."

"That's nice of you, but I really can't take your car."

"Why not?"

"Well, I didn't do that so that I would get something for it."

"I know. Why did you do it?"

"I don't know. It just seemed like the right thing to do. And it looks like I was right. In a few weeks, you'll be in the navy, and your buddy will be in the army. And these guys will be going back to school. So it turned out good for everybody."

"Well, not everybody. Whatever happened to your black friend from Freetown?"

"Bow, you really hurt Martin. He had to get thirty stitches in his head, and he has a scar that will never go away. You're lucky that he didn't show up in court that day, or I think that judge might not have listened to me. His mom tells me he's okay. He still gets some sharp pains in his head, but is doing okay."

"JJ, I gotta do something for him."

"Bow, his family is very poor, but I don't think that they

will take any money. You're going to be working and making some money. Maybe you could do something for them around the holidays. You know, Thanksgiving or Christmas."

"That's a great idea. I won't be here, but I can get my father to take them something. I'll do it. You can count on it."

"Now I know why I did it! Bow, you are already a better person. Thank you."

"No, man, you're the one that should be thanked."

"Tommy, you've got a great friend!"

"Mr. Bow, you're absolutely right. JJ is a special friend. His granny says that he has a 'star in his crown,' and now I know what she means."

"Bow, when the hell are you going to get our field done?"

"It'll be done tomorrow, but you guys won't be able to play on it yet. You gotta give the grass a couple of weeks to grow in."

"Shit, man, we'll give that grass ten days, and then baseball season starts."

"Okay, Bow, we're going to head home. Don't forget Martin. And send us a card to the fire hall when you get out to sea. Don't forget us!"

"I'll never forget you. See ya, Tommy."

Tommy and JJ are feeling a little too old to be riding bikes, but it beats walking, so they head back home.

"JJ, how you think of all that shit?"

"What do you mean?"

"Suggesting that Bow send something to Martin's family. I would have told him to send money."

"I think that he probably will, but they wouldn't accept it. They may be poor, but they work for everything that they have. They don't take handouts. Too much pride. But you give them a turkey with a Merry Christmas card, and God tells them to accept it. It'll make everyone happy. I'm going to go down to Julie's house."

"You're always there. What do you do there?"

"Well, when she's not there, I go over to Grannie's Place. She's always making cookies or pies. And she thinks little fat boys like me should eat them, so I never disagree with Grannie, and I help her out. Sometimes I horse around with her brothers or walk down to the pier. They treat me like family. Mr. Roy is always bringing home steaks and telling me that they are extras, and he needs someone to eat them so that they don't go to waste. I love it there."

"I don't blame you. They treat you like a king! I'll see you later."

As JJ approaches Julie's house, he doesn't see Mr. Roy's car. The brothers are not in the yard. He can smell the cookies baking at Grannie's place. Julie's aunt is just coming home from work. She got off early today. Damn, she is *hot*! In her business suit with a tight top that is low cut so that you can see her cleavage. Those short legs look great coming out of the businesslike skirt. It's hard to walk down the stone driveway with high-heeled shoes, so she leans over to take the shoes off. Wow, all you could see was those perfect breasts! She knew that JJ was looking at her, so she took her time removing the shoes. While she was very classy, she was still a woman and liked having men look at her. They both started walking toward Grannie's front door. JJ held the door open for her and enjoyed the view as she passed by. Boy, did she smell nice! As he walked in the door, Grannie said, "I saw you coming, so I poured you a glass of milk, and there are cookies at the end of the table."

"That's why I love you, Grannie. Do you know where everybody is?"

"They're out on the creek water skiing. You can go on down. Those cookies will still be there when you get back."

"I'm going to change into some shorts," quipped Auntie!

JJ was thinking, *Boy, I'd like to help her.* As he walked down to the pier, he could see the brothers in the boat with one of their friends. Julie was in the water with her hands on the skies rope. She was waiting for her brother to get the boat moving fast enough for her to ski.

They were about forty feet away. Roy Jr. gave the motor some gas, and they started moving fast. As they began moving toward him, Julie came up out of the water and waved to JJ, and JJ finally saw the lovely breasts that he had been attempting to get the keys to the bra for over a year. The three boys in the boat couldn't believe their eyes. They were laughing hard. They swung the boat around to give JJ another look. They were laughing so hard that Julie couldn't figure out what was so funny. She didn't know that when she came up out of the water that the force of the water pushed her two-piece bathing suit top over the top of her breasts. She couldn't tell that it was up that high. As they were about to pass JJ again, Roy Jr. was laughing so hard he couldn't keep a straight face. He was yelling to Julie, trying to tell her about her problem, but she couldn't hear him over the noise of the motor. He was now laughing so hard that he nearly fell out of the boat.

Julie still can't figure out what was so funny. Roy continues to yell to her, and now he is pounding his chest. Just as she waves to JJ again, she looks down and sees her breasts are exposed and she is really embarrassed. She lets go of the ski rope and sinks into the water while trying to pull her top down to cover her breasts, but her problems are not over. You see, Julie doesn't know how to swim! She can dog paddle well enough to stay afloat, but she can't swim back to shore. JJ doesn't have any way to get her, and she doesn't want to get back into the boat with those young boys. Roy brings the boat around and pulls up close to her.

"What do you want to do?" he yells, while laughing so hard he can hardly get the words out. "Do you want to get back into the boat?"

"*No.* I don't think you guys are funny."

"Why not," yells Chuck, her other brother. "We were just enjoying the show."

"Very funny, wise guy. Wait until I tell Dad what you guys did."

"We didn't do anything. We can't help it if your clothes come off."

"Very funny. Throw me that rope and pull me in slowly toward the shore. Don't go near him. I don't want to see him."

"What did he do?"

"Never mind! Just pull me in."

"Roy did as he was told. When Julie got to where she could walk out of the water, she literally ran to shore and up the hill to her house. JJ was calling to her, but she refused to answer him. By now, JJ is also laughing at the way she is acting. The brothers are pulling up to the pier and tying the boat up for the night.

"What's the matter with her?"

"Why ask us? She's your girlfriend. Haven't you seen her boobs before?"

"No, we don't do those kinds of things."

"Well, as mad as she is with you, you may never see them again."

"*Me*, what did I do? I was just standing on the end of the pier. I'm going to see what's going on."

As JJ got to the top of the hill and was heading to the house, Auntie was coming out of Grannie's house. Looking at JJ, she said, "I don't think you should go over there right now."

"Why not? What did I do?"

"You looked at her exposed top!"

"Well, yeah, but I didn't do it. How could I look at her and not see her boobs?"

"You shouldn't have looked. When a girl wants to show you her boobs, she decides, not you. Go talked to Grannie and finish your cookies. Grannie doesn't know what happened, so don't tell her, okay?"

"Okay."

"I'll let you know something later, but I think that you can pack up some cookies and head on home."

JJ goes over to Grannie's, drinks some milk, eats some cookies, and starts toward home, thinking to himself as he's walking, *Geez, what's the big deal? She's going to show them to me or some other guy as she grows up. And those dance outfits that she wears shows most of them anyway. And that bathing suit that she was wearing—how is that any different from wearing panties and a bra in public? Boy, this started out as a good day. I didn't do anything wrong, and I'm still in trouble.*

"Hi, Mom. I'm home."

"Come to the phone. It's for you. Julie's calling."

"What? Well … hi."

"If you think for one minute that just because you saw my boobs today you now have the keys to my bra, you are sadly mistaken. In fact, nothing really changes. I'm not going to strip naked just because you want me to. It's my body, and I control what happens to it. And I intend to keep it covered up for a long time. So you can put your dirty mind in your pocket."

"I love you."

"What did you say?"

JJ, speaking in a low voice because he knows that his mother is trying to hear the conversation, repeats, "I love you."

"Stop that. You aren't going to soften me up!"

"I said that I love you, and yes, I am going to soften you up. I didn't do anything wrong. I still respect you, even if you do have lovely breasts."

"See, you're getting smart already."

"No, I'm not. I just don't know what to say to you. I'm sorry that you are embarrassed, but it doesn't make any difference between us."

"It does to other people. As soon as my father came in the door, my brothers told him what happened. They told him that they were big, and where the tan line stopped, they were pure white with these dark spots on them. They all laughed. My aunt went out there and told them to shut up. 'Your daughter is too embarrassed to look at you,' she said to my dad. They walked into the other room, and my father said, 'Why does that bother her? I watched her grow up. I've seen her nude before. Hell, I've seen you nude before!' My aunt said, 'Yes, but she just heard her brothers describe her breasts to you in great detail.' My dad says, 'So what? I'll go up to Johnny's so that she doesn't have to face me. I'll have her mother talk to her when she gets home, and I'll tell the boys that they *must* keep their mouths shut.' My aunt told him, 'That's a good start,' and he left. And so did she."

"So what's the problem? Everything is okay."

"I don't know if it is or not. I don't know what I think."

"Julie, we all come into the world naked. It's our society that puts clothes on us. I do think that the United States makes a big deal out of nudity and sex. In France, their TV has men and women having sex totally nude on there all the time. In Africa, the women don't wear any tops. In some of those Mideast countries, the men have several wives, and they run around the house all day with no clothes on. I'm not saying that they are right and we are wrong. I'm just saying that you control your life the way you want it. Your friends' opinions are important, but they don't rule over you. You live the way that you feel comfortable. And if that means showing me your boobs, I think that's great!"

"I knew that you couldn't keep it serious. You're a nutcase. I'm sorry that I got mad at you. It wasn't your fault. Guess what."

"What?"

"I love you too! Are you coming back around?"

"I sure want to."

"Well. Come on back. Grannie made a dozen cookies for each of us, and you know that I can't eat a dozen cookies. I'll eat three and give the rest to you and my brothers."

"I've already eaten a dozen."

"That's okay. That's why Grand Pap calls you the fat boy."

# Chapter 17

WE'RE BACK IN SCHOOL, AND this is JJ's first year at Glen Brook High School. He's in the tenth grade, and everything seems new and different. When you are in high school, it won't be long until you will be going out into the world on your own, getting a job and doing something. *But what?* JJ began thinking. In less than three years, he'd be expected to take care of myself. He wondered if my parents would let me stay at home for a few years until he figured out what he was going to do. And what about Julie? They were the same age, but she was a year behind me. *I wonder what she'll be doing. What will we be doing? Will we still be together? It's been almost a year now. We've never had an argument. We really do get along well together and I like her family.*

He liked his new classes. He had an English teacher that made that boring subject fun. All the guys hated English, but she had all of them reading books, and they had to do book reports. But the difference was they could pick any book, any subject that they wanted. Nobody wanted to do it, but she told the boys that if they read more books than the girls, she would make the girls bake them cookies. She told the girls that if they read more books than the guys, the boys would have to carry their books to class for one week. Now, the boys didn't care about the cookies. But they couldn't let the girls beat them. JJ started to read a book about a basketball star that seemed easy. Miss Monroe saw what he was reading and said to him, "You're going to spend all that time reading. Wouldn't you like to learn something? You already know how to play basketball."

"I don't know, Miss Monroe. I didn't give it much thought. What do you think I should read?"

"Didn't you say that your father was in the navy?"

"Yes, he was. He fought against the Germans, and his ship got damaged so they brought him back to Norfolk. He was home for about a month when they sent him to fight the Japs."

"Maybe you could find something about that."

"I don't know; he doesn't talk much about the war."

"It doesn't have to be about the war, but maybe something that took place during the war. Let me give you a book to read that I think you will find interesting."

"You're trying to trick me. You're going to give me something hard."

"Yes, I am, but I'll make a deal with you. If you read the entire book, I'll give you an A no matter what your book report says. But you must finish the entire book."

"I get an A no matter what?"

"That's right."

"Okay, I'll take the deal. What do I have to read?"

"Let me find something here. Okay, here you are: *From Here to Eternity.*

"That looks like a love story."

"You made a deal!"

"But it's a love story. What can I learn from that? How to make love?"

"No, I don't think so. Read the book as you promised, and tell me what you think."

"But this book has over two hundred pages."

"Yes, I know. Set a goal for yourself that you will read ten pages a night before you go to bed, and you'll be done before Thanksgiving."

Now Miss Monroe was a smart lady. Without them knowing, she made the same bet with every boy in the class, giving them all difficult books to read, but each had good subject matter. She knew that the girls were going to slaughter the boys, but she wanted those boys to read a book, something worth reading.

Mr. Smith was the US history teacher, and Miss Monroe told him what she had done. He didn't think that he could match that, but he was teaching about our forefathers and their thinking as they developed the Constitution. He thought, *I know that most of these guys hate to read, so how do I get them involved?*

He decided that he would read one chapter each day to the class. They had to take notes, and the next class they were going to debate and enact what they thought each founder was thinking and why. He broke them up into groups of four, each representing someone—Jefferson, Adams, Franklin. The results were amazing. Every day, the boys couldn't wait to get to history class.

These guys were loving school, and they didn't know why. This happened in several of the classes. These teachers had found a way to make learning interesting and fun. In the school music class, Miss Royal, who loved her students and her work, established a Boys' Glee Club. She had talked to Mr. Smith, and he told her how excited that the boys were to come to class each day. They loved what they were learning.

She decided to get the boys to sing all the patriotic songs from history. She never had a problem getting the girls to sing, but the boys were always a problem. Within days, the boys were making suggestions for songs to sing. They were on time to class and ready to sing. And the talent was great.

She taught them four songs, then made arrangements for them to sing at the Glen Brook Rotary Club for their lunch meeting, in front of all the local businessmen. When the boys finished, the men were standing and applauding and begging Miss Royal to bring them back again. The boys were so proud that they walked through the halls, singing their songs. The principal had to come out of his office and calm them down. This really had become an exciting school year. Everyone, Tommy, Jimmy, JJ, and others, were still talking about baseball, but most of the conversation was about Miss Monroe, Mr. Smith, and Miss Royal. These teachers had captured the hearts and minds of these students, and the results were exciting.

Cold weather was coming early this year. It wasn't Thanksgiving yet, and already there had been three snowfalls. The days were getting shorter, and there wasn't much to do.

Tommy, Jimmy, and JJ would meet after school each day at Jimmy's house to play some cards. Then they would go home to do their homework, watch some TV, and go to sleep. JJ was going around Julie's house most night, but he wasn't staying long. Julie was still teaching her dance classes twice a week and taking her own lessons on Saturday. She has become a very good dancer and has appeared on some local TV talent shows. Some of the people from the TV station told her that she should apply to become a New York Rockette at Radio City Music Hall. They sent tapes to New York, and they seemed interested.

Now you had talent and beauty in this very young girl. She had beautiful legs and was the perfect height for a dancer. This could be her future, but JJ didn't know what he wanted to do.

The next morning, everyone woke up to twelve feet of snow on the ground. The schools were closed, and most businesses closed. The banks closed. Everything had come to a standstill.

Mr. Kapok owned a 1932 Case tractor with a snow blade on the back. This thing was all steel, including the wheels. You had to crank it with a spin bar to start it. And if you weren't careful, this thing would snap back and could break your arm. This thing only had a four-cylinder engine, but it was so powerful that it took all of JJ's strength to spin the engine. He generally could get it started.

JJ wasn't prepared for a snow storm like this. He didn't have any snow boots, and his winter coat could not handle zero-degree weather. His father wanted him to go out and start the tractor. So his mother wrapped plastic grocery bags around his shoes and tied them to his legs. He took a snow shovel and made a clear path to the tractor. He tried spinning the crank several times. He couldn't get it started. It was minus 3 degrees, and his feet were freezing. He came back into the house. By now, his father was up and fully dressed for winter. He had on a heavy sweater, his navy peacoat, a scarf around his neck, a skull cap with earmuffs, heavy-duty pants with long johns under them, and a beautiful pair of insulated rubber boots. He was ready for the snow.

"Come on, boy. You get on top of the tractor, and when I spin it, you pull the choke. It's cold, and the choke has to be almost completely closed to start." JJ was so cold that he could hardly move, but he was following his father's orders. They proceeded as planned. The tractor started without a problem. His father cleared their driveway without a problem.

Mr. Kapok yelled to JJ, "You walk behind me, and we will head around to Roy's house and clear his driveway. We'll catch a few others on the way." It was two long blocks to Julie's house. The snow was up past JJ's knees. His plastic bags were no match for the weather conditions. Mr. Kapok did about five other driveways before he got to Roy's place.

Roy owned two cars and a four-wheel drive pickup truck. He really didn't need John's help. But he did have a long driveway, and so did Grannie. John completed the driveways and started back. I don't know why he wasn't letting JJ ride on the tractor. But Roy saw that JJ was frozen and had no boots. So he yelled to him, "Hey, come here," and he waved John off. "Thanks a lot."

"JJ, come in the house. Mrs. Connors has made some hot tea for you." JJ was so cold he couldn't respond. His father went on home, and JJ went into Julie's house. At first the brother began teasing him because he was covered with snow and clearly frozen. Julie saw him and went to her room to get some blankets. Roy Jr. began taking his shoes off.

"Where are your boots? What are these plastic bags?"

"Mrs. Connors brought him some hot tea."

"Dad, he doesn't have any boots!"

"Yeah, I know I don't have anything large enough to fit him. I've got some dry insulated socks."

"Let's dry his shoes and get some new plastic bags. Put these warm socks on him and wrap him up tight for a little while."

"JJ fell asleep and began to warm up now that he had dry socks and a blanket."

Roy looked at his wife and quietly said, "What the hell's the matter with that guy? I appreciate the help, but no one is going anywhere today. The snow plows will be here in a few hours, and if they aren't, what the hell difference does it make? I'm certain that I can get out with my truck. We'll wait a couple of hours and I'll take him home."

JJ slept for a few hours, when he woke up, he hardly knew where he was.

"Are you all right?" Julie asked.

"Yeah, why?"

"Why? You nearly froze to death."

"Ah, it's cold out there, but I'm okay. Whose socks do I have on?"

"My father's."

"Boy, they feel good."

"You can keep them on. I'll get them back later. The snow plows have come through and most of the roads are clear. Mom has fixed you some soup and a sandwich. After you finish eating, my dad will take you home."

"Man, thanks, Mr. Roy. It's really cold out there."

"Yeah, it's warmed up about 20 degrees, but it still cold."

JJ ate the food and was ready to go home.

"You ready to go, boy?"

"Yes, sir."

"What size shoe do you wear? I'm going to look at the shop and see if we got anything that fits you. Sometimes when guys quit their job, they leave stuff at the shop."

As they were riding home, JJ asked Roy, "Now that the road is clear, do you think that we will have school tomorrow?"

"No, I don't think so. They still need to clear all the parking lots, and I doubt that all the teachers can get out of their communities. All right, you're home. Tell your father that I said thanks. Tell your mom that I think that I have some boots at work that will fit you."

"Okay, see you tomorrow."

As Roy was driving home, he knew that if he didn't have any boots at the shop for JJ, he was going to go to the surplus store and buy him a new pair.

Roy decided to drive around to Johnny's Bar. Since the roads have been cleared, he was sure that they would be open. As the night dragged on, a patron came into the bar with a box of snow shovels and a box of insulated boots that he had just stolen from the place where he worked. He tossed them up on a table and announced, "Three dollars for the snow shovels. Ten bucks for the boots."

Roy yelled over to him, "I'll take one of each if you have a size ten in those boots." He drank down his beer and started back home. As he entered the door to the house, Julie called to him.

"Is that you daddy?"

"Yeah, I took the fat boy home."

"Is he okay, Daddy. He looked pretty bad! I hope that he doesn't get sick."

"He's okay, and it'll be a miracle if he doesn't get sick! Here, give him these boots when he comes around tomorrow. Tell him he can keep the socks. I'm going to see if I have another pair to give him. Don't tell him that I bought them. Just tell him that I got them from work."

School remained closed for the week, and it was now Saturday before Thanksgiving Day. The phone rang and JJ answered it.

"JJ, this is Mr. Bowers. Bow's father."

"Hello, Mr. Bowers. How are you? How's Bow doing?"

"He's doing fine. He sent me a check for $50 and wants me to buy Thanksgiving dinner for Martin's family. So I need their address and phone number if you have it."

"Sure, hold on. I get it for you."

"JJ, how many people are in Martin's family?"

"It's him and his mother and two sisters. I don't know how old they are, and I don't know where the father is. I know that he doesn't live there. This is great, Mr. Bowers. I'm sure they can use it. So, old Bow really remembered!"

"Yeah, Bow will never forget what you did, and neither will I."

"It worked."

"What worked?"

"The judge gave him a second chance, and it worked. He's in the navy and is learning a trade. When he gets out, he'll be able to get a good job and get a new start in life."

"JJ, you know that Bow has his car up for sale? He really wanted you to have it, but he said that you wouldn't take it."

"No, Mr. Bowers. I'll be fifteen just before Christmas. I have one more year to save up enough money to buy a car."

"You know that it's a 1953 DeSoto Convertible. He just put a new top and new paint job on it."

"He wants $800 for it, but if you want it, I'll sell it to you for $400."

"Four hundred? That's a great deal, but why would you do that?"

"Bow said to tell you, 'That's what friends are for.' I guess that is some kind of inside joke with you guys?"

"Yes, sir, it sure is. Let me talk to my father and see if he will lend me $200. I already have $200."

"Just ask your father if it's okay. You can make payments to me to pay off the balance."

"I'm sure that it'll be okay. I'll talk to him when he gets up."

"Call me if it's okay and I'll bring it around to your house."

"You mean that I can have it before it's paid for?"

"Yeah, if it's okay with your father."

"Thanks, Mr. Bower. That's a great deal. Bye, now."

"Mom, I just bought a car—a 1953 DeSoto Convertible. You think Dad will let me buy it?"

"Well, yes, I don't see why not."

"And guess what, Mom? Bow sent money for Martin's family to have Thanksgiving dinner. I'm going to tell the captain so that he can tell the judge that it worked."

"Yes, it did, JJ. It really did work."

# Chapter 18

It's Pearl Harbor Day. Everyone in History Class is listening to the radio. They are replaying President Roosevelt's famous speech declaring war on Japan. There were no Japanese students in Glen Brook High, but Mr. Smith asked the class if they thought it was proper to place people who were Americans with Japanese backgrounds into separate housing camps. The discussion was lively. Nearly everyone agreed that it should be done. All except JJ. Mr. Smith was surprised, and he asked JJ why he thought that it was wrong.

"I'm not certain that it was wrong, but my dad, who is against everything and everyone, said that these were not the Japs that we were fighting, that many of them had never been to Japan and that the only country they knew was the United States and he didn't think they would do any harm to us."

"Well, what do you think JJ?"

"I don't know, Mr. Smith, but to say that they are bad just because they have Japanese parents or grandparents doesn't seem right. It's like my friend Martin, who is black and lives in Freetown. Why does he have to go all the way to Annapolis just to go to school? Why can't he come here to Glen Brook? Because of the color of his skin he's a problem in our school?"

"Isn't Martin the boy who got beat up by some white boys for being in Beachwood?"

"Yes, he is."

"Don't you think that Japanese kids would have the same problem during the war?"

"Yes, I guess they would. That's why I said that I was not certain that it was wrong. If we did it to protect them and their families, then I think we did the right thing. But was that really the reason?"

Mr. Smith said, "I don't know, JJ, but it seems to have worked."

"The class agreed and they went on to discuss other things."

JJ had just walked into his house when the phone rang. JJ answered it.

"JJ, this is Mr. Robbie. I have some bad news for you. There was an explosion on the ship that Bow is serving on, and Bow was killed. I don't know exactly what happened, but his father just called me and told me the bad news. His father could hardly speak. He doesn't have any of the details, and he doesn't know what the funeral arrangement will be. I'll let you know when I know more."

"God, Mr. Robbie. I don't know what to say."

"No, neither do I."

"Do you think that I should call Mr. Bowers?"

"No, not right now, maybe when we have more information."

"Does the captain know?"

"Yes, I spoke with him as soon as I knew about it. I also told Earl. I haven't told anybody else, yet, but you know that the word will spread quickly."

"Yeah, thanks, Mr. Robbie. Goodbye." JJ began to cry.

"What's the matter?" called his mother from the kitchen.

"Bow is dead!"

"What? What happened?"

JJ told his mother what he knew from the phone conversation and said that he was going to his room for a little while. Then he thought that he would go around Julie's house. All he could think about was that Bow had just turned eighteen years old. Why does God let some people live to be a hundred and others only eighteen? Why Bow? There were nine hundred men on that ship. Why Bow? He was turning his life around and was going to come back get a good job and maybe later open his own shop. Isn't that what God wanted him to do?

He tried to get his mind off of the bad news. Tomorrow the book report was due, and he didn't want to disappoint Miss Monroe. He had written most of the report, but he just can't concentrate on anything except Bow's death. He thought that he would just put a short ending to it and turn it in. He finished what he had to do and headed for Julie's house. As he walked up the driveway, Mr. Roy was cleaning the salt off his truck caused by the snowstorm.

"Hi, JJ. How you doing?"

JJ looked dejected, and really didn't want to respond. "Not so good, Mr. Roy. I just got news that one of my friends was killed in an accident."

"A car accident?"

"No. You remember my friend who joined the navy? Well, there was an explosion on his ship and he was killed."

"I'm sorry to hear that, JJ. That's terrible. There is nothing worse than having a close friend die. When I was in the war, I watched several of my buddies die and there was nothing I could do."

"What did you do? How did you get over it?"

"I thanked God that it wasn't me, and I never did get over it. I can still remember watching them die. And I asked myself, 'Why them?' What are we doing here? War is ugly, and I don't think that anybody wins. You won't get over it either, but life goes on, and so do you. If I can do anything to help, I'll try. Julie's in the house. I see that you have your boots on. How do you like them?"

"Man, they are great. But so are those socks. Thanks, I'll talk to you later."

Entering the house, Julie and her mother were sitting at the kitchen table. Mrs. Connors told JJ that there was hot tea on the stove. He fixed himself some before he sat down. Before he could move, Julie was up and pouring him a cup.

Mrs. Connors laughed. "Oh, I forgot that she was sitting there."

"Sit down, JJ. I have the tea ready for you. What's the matter? You look sad."

"I am. I just told your father that there was an accident on the ship that Bow was serving on, and Bow got killed."

"Oh, JJ, that's terrible."

"Thanks, Mrs. Connors. He wasn't one of my best friends, but it's still a shock."

"Do any of the other guys know?"

"No, Julie. I just found out about it before I left to come around here. I guess that I'll tell them tomorrow at school."

"What do you want to do tonight?"

"I was hoping that you could help me go over my book report. It's due tomorrow in class. Miss Monroe saw me in the hall today and asked me if I was ready. You know that song, 'Eternal Father Strong to Save' that we sing in the Christmas show at school this year?"

"Yeah, I've heard you singing it."

"I don't know how I'm going to sing those words and not think of Bow!"

"You'll do okay. And that's good. That's what songs are for. Now, whenever you here that song, you will think of Bow, and his life will live on forever in your heart. Bow would like that. You should tell Bow's father that. Maybe it will help him too."

"He's got to be heartbroken. Bow was his oldest son, and he was so happy when he joined the navy. I really don't know what to say to him."

"Isn't that the man that you bought your car from?"

"Yes, Mama, it was Bow's car. Bow asked him to talk me into buying it from him for way below what it is worth. I don't know how I'm going to drive it without thinking of Bow."

"What's wrong with that?"

"He's dead, Mrs. Connors!"

"No, he isn't. As Julie said, Bow lives forever in your heart. When people who mean something to us in our lives die, we have to continue to live, and the way we cope with it is by remembering all the good things that they meant to our lives. You can remember the bad things too, but it's the good things that will put a smile on your face and make you glad that you knew them."

"I'll always remember our conversation on the baseball field just before he left. He told me that he would never forget me for what I did for him in that courtroom. Tommy almost started to cry, and I didn't know what to say to him."

"You see, Bow's not dead. You already have fond memories of him, and those memories will stay with you forever."

"We've got to stop this talk. You two are going to make me cry! But I do thank you."

"That's okay, JJ. To use your favorite expression, 'That's what friends are for.'"

JJ and Julie worked on his book report, and he was ready for Miss Monroe the next day in English class.

"Miss Monroe started the class by announcing. The results of the contest were much closer than I expected, but boys, I must tell you that the girls did beat you. No cookies and a bunch of heavy books next week. Now, girls, no rocks in the backpacks, just the books that you need for class. The results were sixty-five books for the girls and thirty books for the boys."

"We girls slaughtered them."

"Yes, you did beat them. But for the first time in my class, every boy read at least one book, and they all turned in a book report."

"What's the big deal, Miss Monroe? You expect all of us girl to do that all the time."

"Yes, I do, but doesn't it make you feel good that you inspired all these boys to do something that they have never done before?"

"I guess so."

"Well, we are going to hear some of their book reports. Now, don't laugh, girls. You don't like it when they laugh at you on the softball field."

"JJ, we are going to start with you."

"Now, Miss Monroe, how did I know that you were going to start with me?"

"Because your book is a love story, and girls like love stories."

"It's more than a love story. It's about people's lives and all the difficult things that they face. But no matter what happens to them, their love will go on for eternity."

"And is that all."

"No, it points out that there are different kinds of love."

"What do you mean?"

"Well, I don't think that the book says it directly, but I had a long conversation with Julie, my girlfriend, and her mother, and some talk with her father. I told them that one of my friends died this week in an explosion on the navy ship that he was severing on."

"JJ, we're sorry to hear that."

"Thank you, but I don't want to lose my train of thought. I told them that I was sad, my friend was dead. They told me, 'No he's not dead; he will always live on with the love in your heart.' So that's one kind of love. Then I told them that this song that we are singing this year in the Christmas show will always remind me of my friend Bow and the navy. Julie pointed out that we all have songs that we love and cause us to think about people that we love. So my love of music and songs is another kind of love. Her father told me about watching his buddies die in war, and he could never forget that. That's painful love, but it is a type of love. And the people in this book have the same type of life experiences, and that made me think that the things that happened to them back then are repeating themselves again now in your generation and I guess in our generation, and while that may not be the intention for the name of the book, it is eternity. So it gave new meaning to the words in the book. So I'm going to read it again to make sure that I didn't miss anything."

When JJ stopped, he looked around the room. It was completely silent. All the girls had tears in their eyes and tissues to dry them. The boys had totally blank expressions on their faces. Miss Monroe was recovering from the emotion in the classroom.

"That's the end of my report."

Gathering her composure, Miss Monroe replied, "And a good report it is, JJ. I think we will have some more reports tomorrow. I don't think any of you want to follow that one."

The bell rings for the change of class. Everyone was up and moving. Not a word was spoken.

JJ looked at Miss Monroe and asked, "Did I do something wrong?"

"No, JJ, that was a very good report. You earned your A. I've very sorry for the loss of your friend. I'll see you tomorrow in class."

# Chapter 19

It is a few days before Christmas, and the school Christmas program is scheduled for tonight. During the day, at noontime, the school and the community held a memorial service for Bow. The navy had already given the family the American flag that was draped over his casket at the funeral service. The Color Guard fired the twenty-one-gun salute, and they played "Taps." This service was going to be similar, but it truly was for the students, teachers, and community. The school felt as if they had to do something, and this seemed to be appropriate. The Naval Academy in Annapolis provided the naval detail. Everyone knew that this was difficult for Mr. and Mrs. Bowers, but they seemed honored that everyone wanted to do this.

After the service was over, the school allowed everyone to go home for the balance of the day. Most of the community would be coming back that evening for the Christmas program. This program was a major event for everyone. It was done every year just before school let out for the Christmas break. Students wouldn't be returning to school until January 3 of the New Year.

Last night, Julie's parents had a birthday cake with candles, soda, and some ice cream for JJ's fifteenth birthday. Everyone was trying to move on with their lives, and JJ was excited that in six months he could apply for his learner's permit to drive. He had paid off the balance of what he owed Mr. Bowers, and the car belonged to him. He had to have the title in his father's name, but it was his.

It's 7:00 p.m., and the people are gathering for the start of the show. Miss Monroe had the program split so that the boys and girls sang mostly Christmas songs together. The middle of the show was songs from Broadway shows, and the end was going to be the boys with their patriotic songs. Of course, the show opened with everyone standing and singing the "Star Spangled Banner." All the traditional Christmas songs were done perfectly. This group of students sang very well together. When they sang the Broadway songs, you felt as if you were in the theaters in New York. Now, at the closing, all the girls moved to the back of the stage and all the boys moved forward. They were impressive looking, with their red sasses around their waist, their red bow ties, and black patten leather shoes. They started with "Eternal Father Strong to Save."

By the time they finished the song, there wasn't dry eye in the place. Someone from the audience yelled, "We love *you* Bow." JJ choked up and had to stop singing for a few verses, but the show moved on without him. They moved directly to the "Battle Hymn of the Republic." The boys had modified it somewhat and reviewed it with Miss Monroe. Several Boys had parts where the singing would stop, and they would call out their parts. One stated, "We hold these truths to be self-evident," next, "that all men are created equal," next, "that they are endowed by their creator," next, "with certain unalienable rights," next, "that among these rights are life, liberty, and the pursuit of happiness."

By now the entire audience was on their feet, cheering and shouting. The boys were stunned by the reaction. But they kept their composure and began singing, "Glory, glory, hallelujah." The crowd joined in. They came to the last song, in which the girls joined in: "God bless America, land that I love." By now, everyone is singing. They sang "God Bless American" three times. The crowd simply didn't want to stop. Finally, Miss Monroe walked onto the stage and thanked everyone. The boys presented her with an arm full of roses. The crowd began to disperse and things were calming down. The boys and girls of the Glee Club were emotionally spent. They didn't know what to say to each other. They looked at Miss Monroe and said, "What just happened?"

Miss Monroe, with her voice cracking, said to them, "You just did something that is rarely ever achieved. You won the hearts of your audience, and they responded. Let's go home."

# Chapter 20

THE SECOND HALF OF THE school year is over. Nothing eventful happened, but the boys of the tenth-grade class had really matured in a short period of time. They gave credit to the three teachers that inspired them to do more than they thought they could do. All the boys had read five books or more, when most of them had never read a complete book in their lifetime. Mr. Smith stated that this was the best class that he had ever taught and that he truly enjoyed watching them grow both mind and body. Miss Monroe won the statewide award for "Teacher of the Year," and everyone felt that she truly deserved it. She loved her students, and it showed in everything that she did. She was asked to accept a position in the state Board of Education as an administrator. Many in the class were crying at the thought of her leaving. The boys felt the same way but didn't want to show their emotions. On the last day of school, the principal announced over the PA System that Miss Monroe had decided not to accept the job. She wanted to return next year and teach young people how to enjoy music and to enjoy life. You could hear the cheers of approval throughout the entire school. These teachers had had a very fulfilling year for themselves, and their students would never realize what a great year it was for them.

JJ was working long hours at the golf course and saving most of his money towards customizing his car. It was a beautiful dark blue, almost the color of his pegged pants. The car and the person matched very well.

Julie was teaching her dance classes and planned on making a couple of trips to New York to see if they were interested in her and if she was interested in New York. Her aunt volunteered to travel with her for a few long weekends. JJ truly wanted the best for her. But he was certain that if she got a job in New York, they would fade apart and go their separate ways.

Justin was planning on working the summer at his father's business and spending a lot of time in his boat with Connie. They have really become a couple, and were doing everything together.

Tommy had gotten a job with a local construction company and was working from sunup until sundown. He was making a lot of money, and he loved the work. Jimmy had gotten a job at the local grocery store, and the owners treated him like the son that they never had.

Everybody was busy, and they were finding it difficult to spend time together. They would see each other at Teen Club on Friday nights, and they all committed to their ten baseball games a year with the boys from Freetown. Martin seems to have grown up overnight. He's now 5' 9" tall and weighs about 180 lbs. Other than the scar in his scape, he has become a handsome young man. He is active in his community and his church. He is the leader in his Boy Scouts troupe and is working on his Eagle Scouts badge.

Overall, the boys find their lives and their time just flying by. Everything seems to be "fast paced," and they're not certain that they like it. They are beginning to realize that they soon will be out of school and have adult lives like their parents.

Julie's father and brothers have finished 90 percent of the work building the house, and they are moving everything inside and will begin living there. JJ will be the first male from his family to graduate from high school. He has an older female cousin who is very bright and has won a full scholarship to college. She has been encouraging him to go to the University of Maryland. JJ had not given college much thought. He didn't think that his grades would get him in. He knew that he could not win a scholarship like his cousin, and he couldn't afford to live at the university, so college was not something that he could accomplish. But he talked to some of the teachers at school, and they all thought that he should try. They told him that with his car he could commute (30 miles one way), and probably find a few other students to ride with him and split the cost. He knew that he could save the money for the tuition, and his mother said that she would pay for the books and help where ever possible. The Kapoks were not what you would consider poor, but they didn't have any extra cash. JJ's father had a good job that paid over $10,000 a year, and he had a navy pension of about $160 per month.

So by blue-collar standards, he was earning a good living. They received free medical care from the navy, so it was possible to make a loan for part of the education and pay cash for the balance. Now the decision seems to be, does JJ want to do it? He had plenty of time to think about it, as it would be about one year before he would begin applying to schools for acceptance. In the meantime, the golf course offered him a project to make some extra money. They wanted him to recruit three other boys to dig some drainage ditches, three feet deep, two hundred feet long, by two feet wide. They had nine of them that they wanted done, and they wanted them completed within thirty days.

They were paying JJ $2 per hour and the others boys $1 per hour. JJ estimated that it would take two days each, or $32 per ditch, for him. He didn't understand why the golf committee simply didn't hire a contractor with equipment to do these ditches, but he was happy. That was a lot of money to him. After they were dug, they had to be filled with 18" inches of stone and then backfilled. But the golf course had a tractor with a small grading blade on the back that they could use to do the backfilling.

The first three went fairly easy. It took them two and a half days to do each of them, but then JJ began to lose his helpers. Every day, at least one of them didn't show up for work, so it slowed them down. It took them four days each to do the next three ditches. By the time that he began the last three ditches, two of his helpers had quit. The remaining two were not happy. They said that the work was too hard for $1 per hour. JJ told them that he would talk to the golf committee, and he asked them to pay an extra $0.25 per hour and said that he would give them $0.20 per hour out of his money. They agreed to keep working, and they finished the job on time. When JJ told the golf committee what he had to do to keep the helpers, they decided to pay the total increase, and JJ got to keep his money. JJ asked the Committee why they hadn't hired a contractor to do that work. The Committee Chairman said, "The contractor doesn't need to go to college. You do."

Back in Beachwood, as the boys were getting older, they began doing things that they shouldn't do. Jimmy, who was planning on quitting school in September, had developed a bad drinking habit. He loved the feeling of being drunk. No one knew where he was getting the booze, but every Friday and Saturday night he would be so drunk that he could barely stand up. Several times they had to take him home for fear that he would walk into traffic or fall flat on his face. Jimmy was older than the group. He was sixteen, almost seventeen. He was planning on buying a car soon and was looking for a better job. He didn't seem to realize that quitting school made it difficult to find a better job and that he had a good arrangement with the store owner that he was working for.

Jimmy's father was a much older man and was about five years away from retirement. He decided to buy a new car while he was still working and give his car to Jimmy. He did not know about Jimmy's drinking problem. Jimmy's mother covered up his Friday and Saturday problems and would tell the father that he was sick or simply not feeling well. Now Jimmy has a 1949 Chevrolet, a four-door sedan. It was in good condition and had low mileage on the engine. Jimmy had no knowledge of automobiles. He knew how to turn the key and start it. His father showed him how to check the oil and the water, and that was the limit of his ability to work on cars. Everyone who knows him is concerned about him drinking and driving, and sure enough, the first Friday after receiving his car, he stopped by Teen Club. It was about 10:30 p.m., and he was drunker than a skunk.

JJ and Tommy both attempted to take his keys away from him, but he refused to give them up. The next day, the car was parked at the store where he works. The entire passenger side of the car was damaged. Front fender, both side doors, and the rear fender.

JJ was about to enter the store when the police pulled up and asked him if he was Jimmy.

"No, sir, I'm not, but he does work at this store."

"Yes, we know that. Hello, are you James Button?"

"Jimmy knew why they were there. Yes, sir, that's me. What can I do for you?"

"Is that your car parked outside?"

"Yes, sir."

"Will you explain all the body damage to the passenger side?"

"Last night I was driving home when the car coming at me with his high-beam lights and forced me over to the right-hand curb. I hit a row of mailboxes that were all together on some 2 x 4 post. I managed to avoid hitting him, but I wiped out all those mailboxes. They flew into one of the yards. It was very late, maybe 1:00 a.m., so I didn't stop. I thought that I would go back today and talk to the owners."

"Mr. Button, we have a citizen who tells us a different version of this accident. Are you sure that you don't want to revise your accounting of what happened?"

"No, that's what happened. What did they say happened?"

"She said that she was sitting on her porch when you came down the street, swerving all over the place. She thinks that you may have fallen asleep. You hit the mailboxes and kept on going. Had you been drinking, Mr. Button?"

"No, sir. I was at Pop's Place talking to some friends. I did drink a Pepsi. I said goodbye to them and headed home."

"Well, I can't prove that you were drinking, but I am going to issue you a ticket for the property damage. You'll receive a notice of a court date for your case. I would suggest that you go make arrangements with the property owners to fix the mailboxes and any other damage that you may have done. Maybe the judge will go easy on you. I'd also suggest that you stop drinking while you are driving. This time you only damaged mailboxes. The next time it may be a person or yourself!"

The police officer left the store.

JJ looked at Jimmy and said, "You were lying through your

teeth! I saw you at 10:30 p.m. and you were already drunk! What the hell happened?"

"The woman on the porch had it right. I fell asleep and didn't wake up until after I took out all of those mailboxes. I tore the hell out of my car. My father hasn't seen it yet. I don't know what he is going to say."

"Jimmy, what the hell is the matter with you? You could have hit a tree instead of those mailboxes! You gotta stop that drinking. All the guys are concerned about you! And you gave me and Tommy a blast of shit for trying to get your keys. We're your friends. We don't want to see anything happen to you."

"Oh, you guys worry too much, I'll be okay."

"Yeah, that's what Denny Apple said last month when he ran off the road and killed himself. He wasn't drunk, but they said that he was doing over 90 mph when he lost control, hit that ditch and flipped over on the roof. The guys from the fire department said it was a mess. They couldn't identify him. Is that how you want to go?"

"Okay, JJ, give me a break. I told you that I'll be okay."

"Yeah, well, I'll tell you what I'm going to do: if I catch you behind the wheel drunk, I'm going to punch you in your mouth and take your keys away from you. Then I'm going to take them to your house and give them to your father! And your ass can walk home."

"JJ, mind your own business. I'm old enough to take care of myself."

"Maybe so, but I don't want to be the one to tell your mother that we tried to stop you but you told us to mind our own business! Your life is our business. We've been friends since third grade, and I'm not going to stop being your friend just because you are mad at me. You're acting like an asshole. You know that you shouldn't drink while driving. What if you kill one of our friends?"

"Before JJ could finish what he was saying, Jimmy walked away from him and went into the storage room. JJ couldn't go in there, so he walked back to Julie's house, which was only about half-mile away. When he got there he told Julie about his conversation with Jimmy. Both of them were distressed but didn't know what else could be done. Julie told JJ, "You've done the best that you can do as a friend. Let's hope that nothing happens to him."

"Maybe I should tell his father. You know he comes into Johnny's bar every now and then. I've seen him talking to your father. Maybe I could get your father to say something."

"Don't get my father involved. He doesn't know Mr. Button, and it might make things worse. He might not like being told that his son is a drunk, particularly by someone that he doesn't really know! I think that you should leave it alone for now. Let Jimmy work it out."

"You're right, but I don't like it. You know, he seems to be very lonely. Since Tommy started taking it up with Kathy and you and I started going together, we don't see each other very often. We're not interested in playing cards at his house on Friday night, and he is shy and backward with girls, so he doesn't come to Teen Club. I wonder if we could find him a girlfriend."

"Now, who do you know that would want to date Jimmy?"

"I don't know, but look at Tommy and Kathy. Who would have thought that they would get together? There has to be someone who would like to be with him."

"Who?"

"I don't know. Aren't any of your girlfriends lonely and would like to have a boyfriend?"

"Who?"

"I don't know. Why do you keep asking me that?"

"Because I can't think of anybody who would wants to date a drunk."

"But that's the point; maybe if he had a girlfriend that cared about him, he would stop drinking. What about that big girl, Margret? Or your friend Mary?"

"Mary has a couple of boys that she really likes, and she's expecting one of them to start taking her seriously. Margret is possible, but you know that she likes to drink also, so I'm not certain that would be a good match."

"Maybe not, but maybe it would solve both their problems. Besides I'm told that Margret like to do more than drink. You know—sex! Don't look so surprised. Just because you don't have sex on your mind doesn't mean that other girls don't think about it."

"How do you know that she has sex?"

"Guys talk about those things. I don't believe everything I hear, but I'm told that after she has a few drinks, she starts taking off her clothes. One of the guys has a pair of panties that he claims are hers. He says that she loves it and really doesn't need the drinks to get her started. He said that he went to her house after school, but they didn't want to do it in the house. They were afraid that they would get caught. So they went out back to her shed. She took all of her clothes off and most of his. I believe him because he told us details about her large breasts and that she had a mole on one of them."

"Okay, that's more information than I need. Let's talk about something else."

"Talking about sex doesn't hurt you. I need your help here. We may be onto something. Do you have anything that you can think of that would get them together?"

"No. and I don't want to get involved in this little scheme of yours."

"Julie, this might save his life."

"Yeah. Sex and booze is going to save his life!"

"No, but maybe they both will find other things to do rather than drink."

"Maybe they will go on real dates. Go out with us in the boat. Maybe he'll start coming to Teen Club again?"

"JJ you know that Jimmy thinks that he's too old for Teen Club. You know that he's more than a year older than us. He doesn't like school. They held him back one year, so he's older than everyone else in his class. He's going to get his father's car next week. It'll be totally his. Things are different for him. Julie, I can't just sit by and watch him drink himself to death. Even if he doesn't hurt himself or somebody else, what kind of life is that?"

"Why do you think that it's your responsibility to solve everybody's problems? And what if she isn't interested in him? What next?"

"I don't know, but I have to try."

"Fine. You do whatever you want, but leave me out of it! I don't know her that well, and I don't think that I want to. If all she thinks about is sex and booze, she doesn't sound like someone that I want to be friends with."

"You're already friends with her."

"No, I'm not. She hangs with the girls, but I don't really have a friendship with her."

"Well, who do you think would work?"

"I told you that I don't want to be involved. Jimmy is not my responsibility, and he's not yours either. Stay out of it."

"I can't! And what's with you and sex? Every time the subject comes up, you clam up and won't talk about it."

"I don't think that you talk about sex. Sex is something that you do to make babies, and I'm not ready for babies right now."

"What, do you think every time your parents have sex they want to create another baby? That's crazy. They do it because they like it."

"Maybe so, but they are married. If she gets pregnant, nothing changes except they have another child. If I get pregnant, it could and would change all my plans for life."

"I understand that. But you don't have to get pregnant. And how do you know that your plans won't change a thousand times in the next few years? I'm not even certain that I know what my future plans are."

"I'm not certain either, but I do have goals set, and I want to achieve them."

"Okay, but does that mean we can't have sex?"

"Yes, I just told you why."

"But you can have sex and not get pregnant. Would you mind if I had sex with other girls?"

"What are you crazy? Of course I would mind. You and I are supposed to be going steady, just me and you. What if you got some other girl pregnant? What would happen to us?"

"I just told you, there are things that you can do that don't involve getting pregnant."

"Like what? Never mind I don't want to hear it! What other girl would you want to have sex with?"

"I didn't say that I wanted sex with another girl. I want it with you."

"So, if I don't give you what you want, you're going to get from some other girl?"

"Well, you wouldn't have to worry about getting pregnant!"

"You're crazy. Why is sex so important to you?"

"I don't know if it's the sex or the fact that you won't do it with me. People who are in love like having sex together."

"So does that mean if you go have sex with another girl that you are in love with her?"

"No, I didn't say that. I said that people who are in love like having sex together."

"Oh, so you would have sex with her but you wouldn't like it?"

"Good grief, this is a difficult conversation. Can't you and I play with each other's bodies and enjoy it? Just taking your clothes off of you would be fun. Playing with your breasts and nipples would be nice. Don't you think that you would like that? There's no harm done. You simply put your bra back on, put your sweater on, and we watch TV. Don't you ever think about that?"

"Yes, I do, and yes I would like that, but if we start doing that, it'll lead to the next step, and then the next step, and the next thing you know we're in trouble. Neither one of us will want to stop."

"You mean that you would like to do it?"

"Yes, I'm sixteen years old. My body is nearly developed as a full woman. And I do love you. And I do think that we would enjoy it, but you know that it will get out of control. And it is against my values."

"Playing with you is against your values?"

"Yes, I've never taken my clothes off for anyone other than a doctor."

"Do you want to play doctor and nurse?"

"No, silly, I haven't done that since I was a little kid, and we were learning about our bodies."

"We're not little kids now, and I want to learn about your body."

"I want to learn about yours, too."

"What size are your breasts?"

"I'm a 36C, and while I don't complexly fill a C cup, I can't wear a B cup because it's too tight and smashes me down. What are you doing?"

"I'm getting that bra out of the way so I can play with your tits."

"You know that I don't want you to do that."

"That's not true. You told me that you wanted but you're afraid that we can't control it. So let's do a little at a time. At the rate that I'm going, you'll be eighteen before I get your panties off you."

"You promise to stay away from my panties and I'll take the bra off."

"Okay, but what am I supposed to do next?"

"I don't know, you're the one with all the sex on your mind. What are you doing now?"

"I'm licking and sucking on your nipples. Why? Does it hurt?"

"No, not at all. But I don't think that's the way a baby sucks."

"No, I'm no baby, and it's not supposed to feel like a baby. It's supposed to feel good and cause you to get excited."

"Well, it's working. I don't know how, but it feels good all the way down to my toes. Don't stop."

"Are you kidding? It has taken me years to get this far. I'm not stopping until your nipples are sore."

"Well, that's working too. My nipples are sore. Lets' stop for now. This was a nice first-time thing. I sure with practice you'll get better and my nipples won't hurt. Now you can brag to all your buddies that you got into my bra. That ought to make them happy."

"I don't know about them, but it sure has made me happy. You have perfect breasts. You can throw your bras away. They only get in my way. I love it."

"Oh, so now you think that this is going to be a regular thing?"

"Yes, I do, and I think that you want it to be."

"I do like it, because I love you, but promise me that we will keep it under control."

"I can't promise that, but I will promise to try."

# Chapter 21

IT'S THE DAY BEFORE THANKSGIVING, and JJ is at Julie's house when her father comes home from work carrying a huge turkey.

"JJ, I just got this turkey from work. Do you think that your friend Martin and his family would like to have it? Our turkey is in the oven. I gather that Julie's been working on it most of the day."

"Yeah, Mr. Roy. Martin has a part-time job, and it really helps the family, but I'd bet they would welcome that turkey."

"I've also got a ten-pound bag of potatoes in the back of my truck. We can stop at Pop's store and pick up some extra things and take this over to them so they can get started. It takes several hours to roast a turkey this size."

"That's really nice of you."

"Well, when they gave me this turkey, I thought, I already have one. What am I going to do with this one? And I remembered last year that Bow sent money to his father to buy Thanksgiving dinner for Martin's family, so I thought that we could replace Bow this year and this turkey won't go to waste. Do you want to call him and make sure that he is home?"

"Will do! He's not there, but his mother said he will be there in about a half hour, so that works well. By the time we stop at the store and drive to his house, he should be there."

"Let's go. You carry the bird."

As they arrived at the house, Martin was walking in the door. His mother handed him two pumpkin pies that she had made from scratch.

"Here. Take these to JJ before they get out of the car."

"Hey, JJ, what are doing here? Mooching pie off my mom?"

"No, actually Mr. Roy has a large turkey that was given to him at work, and he already has his turkey in the oven, so he thought that you and your family would like to have."

"Mr. Roy, that is very thoughtful of you. I just got my paycheck, and I was going to get someone to take up to that ACME store so that I could buy something for tomorrow. This is wonderful. My mother is a great cook, and we love turkey. Can you stay awhile?"

"No, Julie and her mother had dinner almost ready when we left, so I think that we will head back."

"Thank you again. You know that Thanksgiving is about counting your blessings and being thankful for what God has given us. And I'm very thankful for my friend JJ, even if I did get my skull split making friends with him!"

As they are returning to the house, JJ become a little emotional, "God, it feels great when I see that smile on Martin's face. He really does appreciate everything that we do for him and his family."

"Yeah, helping others is always rewarding, but don't get sobby on me, and make sure that I get some of that pumpkin pie."

Thanksgiving was a great day. JJ's father had to work, so he had dinner at Julie's house. They had a crowd of family, aunts, uncles, cousins, and Grannie and Grandpa insisted that they come over to their place for dessert.

Several days passed, and Julie and her family were having a birthday party for JJ. This was his big one, sixteen and soon to be able to drive his own car. He has his learners permit, and he already knows how to drive. Now he has to get his father to take him to the Department of Motor Vehicles to take the test.

His father agrees to take him in two days. When the day comes, it snowed the night before, and they weren't certain that the test were going to be given. But by the time they got there, the DMV had everything clear and ready. JJ was one of the first to be tested. He passed the written test, missing only one question. Then he had to take the road test. He immediately screwed up by pulling out without giving a hand signal. That cost him points. Then he comes to his first stop sign, and he doesn't come to a complete stop, and that cost him points. The driving tester looks at him and says, “Kid, I know that you know how to drive, so just relax.” He completes the balance of the road test and receives a 79. You need a 70 to pass, so he now is a legal driver in the state of Maryland.

Several of his friends had driver’s licenses, but JJ had his own car, so all the guys wanted to go for their first ride in the Blue Desoto, but he was taking Julie to the movie in Glen Brook, she was his number-one person, and she was going to get the first ride. The guys would have to wait their turn.

It was a 60-degree day in December, and JJ wanted to put the top down. Julie told him he was crazy, but he put the top down anyway. They drove two blocks, and JJ stopped and put the top back up. Sixty degrees in December is too cold to have the top down. Besides, the wind was blowing Julie’s hair and making a mess of it. That wasn’t something that JJ wanted to do on their first ride together. He wanted her to have fond memories of this ride to the movies. Neither one of them remembers what the movie was about. They just remembered their first freedom together. They stopped at Billy’ Burger Place and remembered Mrs. Connors taking them there prom night. By the time they got back, it was late, and he knew that Julie had enjoyed their first real free, independent time together and Julie’s parents realized that their little girl was about to spread her wings and fly on cloud nine. They were both sad and happy for her. It also let JJ and Julie know that her parents trusted them together. Mr. Roy knew that JJ was a solid young man and that he could trust his driving. JJ never even thought about her parents being concerned about his driving. He knew that he was a good driver and he thought everybody knew how good he was. He walked Julie to the door, kissed her, and heard Mrs. Connors clear her throat, since was just on the other side of the door waiting for her daughter to return from her first *real* date. So his first day as a driver was eventful and fun. For two sixteen-year-old kids, it was wonderful and the beginning of a bonding process that would live for a lifetime.

The next day, JJ was going to an interview for a new part-time job. He was doing okay, making money during the summer at the golf course and picking up odd jobs. But he now had a girlfriend and a car to support, so his cost of living had increased. One of his friends at school told him about a job at the local animal hospital. They needed a kennel boy to work from 4:00 p.m. to 8:00 p.m., three nights a week and every other Saturday, all day, and every other Sunday, all day. It paid $4 per hour, and the work schedule was perfect. He didn't know what the job entailed, but he was interested.

The owner said, "Fill out this application, young man. When you have it completed we'll discussed the job. Do you go to school at Glen Brook?"

"Yes, sir."

"Good. Let's look at this. You just turned sixteen? You're a big boy for sixteen. Do you have a way to get to work?"

"Yes, sir. I have my own car. I drive to school."

"You know what the hours are? And you are dependable?"

"Yes, sir. Actually, if you need me to work more hours, I can."

"Well, we say that the nighttime hours end at 8:00 p.m., but we work until we have completed all the patients in the waiting room—sometimes that may be 10:00 p.m.—and sometimes we have accident cases that need to be taken care of before we close. Is that a problem?"

"No, sir. As I said, I have my own car, so I'm not dependant on catching a bus. You do surgery? What kind of surgery do you do?"

"Sometimes we have animals, mostly dogs, that have broken legs that need to be set, or they have gotten into fights and need to have cuts sowed close. Does the sight of blood bother you?"

"No, sir, I don't think so. This job really sounds interesting."

"It can be, but it also has its bad parts. You have to clean all the kennels when you come in. Mop the floors. Put the dogs out in the outdoor runs to do their business. Clean the runs. Straight out the waiting room and the office and do whatever needs to be done to get ready for the nighttime customers. Do you think that you can do that?"

"Yes, sir. I don't see why not? If somebody else can do it, then I can do it!"

"Pretty sure of yourself."

"Yes, sir. I work hard at any job that I do. If you hire me, you won't be sorry."

"Somehow I think that you're right. One other thing: The other kennel boy who works here—you know, the one who told you about the job. He has a problem getting here on time after school. He has to walk that distance. Do you think that you could drop him off here? His dad picks him up at the end of the shift."

"Yes, sir, as long as he is ready when school lets out. It's only about a mile out of my way. I don't see any problem with that."

"I'll pay you for it each week."

"That's not necessary. I'll take care of it."

"Can you start the Monday after New Year's?"

"You mean I'm hired? Yes, sir, I'll be here. Thank you, sir."

"Do you have any questions for me?"

"No, sir. I'm sure that I can pick up on my duties quickly."

"Danny, your friend will work with you the first night to teach you what needs to be done. And you will meet Charles, our full-time groomer/assistant. He's a little strange, but he's okay. He's about fifty years old, and sometimes he drinks when he shouldn't, but he been working here for ten years, so we overlook some of his shortcomings. One other thing: paydays are Thursday, and we pay you cash."

On New Year's Eve, JJ and Julie sat in the living room and watch the ball fall at Times Square. Her parents were at some party at Johnny's, and her two brothers were allowed to stay up and welcome the New Year. JJ was excited about starting his new job in three days. Plus it was the first day back to school after the Christmas break.

It was Monday the third, and it had snowed hard the night before, so they closed school. JJ wasn't certain if the animal hospital would be open, so he called.

"Yes, of course we're open. Hospitals don't close. In fact, Charles couldn't get into work today. Do you think that the road is clear enough for you to come in right now?"

"Yes, sir. But I won't know what I'm doing!"

"That's okay, I'm here by myself and we do have some customers, so I need some help. You come in. By the way, my name is Dr. Erick. I work every day. Dr. Syman works Tuesdays and every other Sunday. He's the one who hired you. Okay, I'll see you as soon as you can get here."

JJ told his mother that he was going to work and headed for the animal hospital. As he pulled into the parking lot, a customer pulled in next to him.

"Please, can you help me? called the lady. My dog has been hit by a car and he is hurt. I can't carry him in there. Can you help?"

"Please wait at your car. I'll go get the doctor." Dr. Erick saw JJ rushing towards the door and he met him there. The sidewalks had not been cleared because Charles didn't make it to work. The dog was a large boxer, about 65 lbs. JJ knew that he could carry him, but he didn't know if he should move him. Dr. Erick just ran out the door directly to the car. It was freezing cold. He quickly looked at the dog and decided that they had no choice. They had to get him inside. He told JJ that they had to move the dog, and before doctor could move, JJ had the dog in his arms and was heading for the door. He called back to the doctor.

"Get the door for me. This dog is heavy."

Doctor Erick cleared the doorways and they put the dog on the examining table. He threw a blanket to JJ and said, "Cover him up. He's in shock, and I think that he is bleeding internally."

"Is he going to make it?" asked the owner.

"I don't know. I don't know exactly where he is injured. I'm going to give him an injection to help stop the bleeding, and we will take some X-rays to see if we can find the damage. JJ, you stay with the dog. I'm going to prepare the X-ray room."

The owner was now crying and clearly distressed. She began to tell JJ what happened, but she was sobbing so badly he could hardly understand what she was saying. Dr. Erick returned and handed JJ this very large apron that covered all of his chest and ended at his knees. The thing weighed about 30 lbs.

"What the heck is in this thing, lead?"

"Exactly, I need you to put it on. I need you to hold the dog quietly and still. He will try and jump when the X-ray buzzes, so you have to gently but firmly hold him in place."

JJ put the apron on and carried the dog to the X-ray room. You could see that the dog was quickly fading away. Dr. E. quickly placed the film plates under the dog where he thought he was injured. He took the picture, and two more. He then injected the dog with something that put him in a partial sleep. JJ moved him back to the examining table, and Dr. E. tried to calm the owner. He convinced her to go home. That he had more work to do and he would call her. The owner left and the waiting room was clear. Dr. E. turned to JJ and said, "How did you like that training?""

"I hope that was the hard part! I'm already exhausted, and it's only noontime."

"You did well, JJ, and it's nice to meet you. I have to read these X-rays. Do you mind getting the snow shovel and clearing the sidewalk before someone slips and breaks a leg?"

"Yes, sir. It was a little hard carrying that dog with eight inches of snow under me."

It didn't take JJ long to clear the walkway. It was only about 75 feet long. As he returned to the building, Dr. E. was looking at the X-ray film.

"Come here, JJ, and I'll show you what's wrong with our dog friend. See these three rib bones? They are fractured, and this one punctured the lung, causing blood to fill the lung. That's why he was having trouble breathing. Actually, the lung will heal itself fairly quick. The injection has slowed or stopped the bleeding. The ribs are more difficult because of the way dogs are built. We need to shave the hair off, down to the skin. Then I'll tape the individual ribs. And then we will wrap his entire ribcage. You'll have to keep an eye on him every time you go by his cage. As he begins to wake up he will try to remove the tape. We may need to put a mussel on him, but I don't want to do that unless we have too.

"It's past 1:00 p.m. Our morning hours are over. I'm going to go across the street and get some lunch. You can clean this mess up. There is a bucket and a mop in the back. Apparently the sight of blood doesn't bother you?"

"I don't know. Everything was happening so fast that I didn't notice that he was bleeding that badly."

"She."

"What?"

"He's a she. I hope you know the difference between a male and a female."

"Well, I didn't notice that either, but yes, I know the difference."

"Okay, I'm leaving. If anyone comes in while I'm gone, simply tell them that we open at 4:00 p.m., and if you have another accident case, you can handle it. After all, you've had two hours of training."

# Chapter 22

"Hi, JJ."

"Hi, Margret."

"Please, call me Margie. Where is Julie?"

"This is one of the nights when she teaches dance class."

"You know, JJ, all the girls think that you're *hot*! Why do you go with just one girl?"

"When you have so many things that you both like, or both agree with, it just makes it easy to be together. Julie and I think alike about everything. We like the same music, same movies. You know."

"Yeah, but that doesn't give other girls a chance to get to know you. I'd like to know you better. Wouldn't you like to know more about me?"

"Speaking about getting to know someone better, do you know Jimmy?"

"Yes, I know Jimmy. He works at the store."

"Yeah, that's him. Let me ask you something? Do you have a boyfriend?"

"No, but if you become available, I sure would try to change that!"

"Margie, I'm not talking about me. I'm talking about Jimmy. You know, he works so many hours at the store that he doesn't get to meet many girls. And you know that he's a little shy."

"Yeah, I'm a little shy too, but I know you from knowing Julie, so I feel comfortable with you."

"What do you think about Jimmy?"

"I don't know. I really don't know him that well."

"Did you know that he has his own car?"

"No, that's nice. But you have your own car."

"Margie, do you know how Julie and I started going together?"

"No, I don't."

"All of our friends thought that we were a perfect match, so they kept trying to set us up together. After a while we kinda liked the idea. We were already friends, so we kinda tried being better friends. We started by hanging together at Teen Club. I knew her Grannie and her aunt, and I was always looking for reasons to go around to her house. I got to know her parents and her brothers, and I just fit in. It got so I didn't need a reason to go around her house. If I didn't show up, somebody would say, 'Where's JJ?' and now we do everything together."

"Wow, that's great, but what does that have to do with me?"

"Wouldn't you like to have a relationship like that?"

"JJ, are you asking me to sneak around with you?"

"No, no, I'm doing with you what our friends did with us. I'm trying to match you up with Jimmy. I asked Julie to talk to you about it, but she said she didn't want to get involved with other people's relationships. But I think that you both might like getting to know each other better."

"So you want me to date your friend?"

"Yeah, I'd like to try hooking you two up and see if it works."

"How do you know that he wants to be with me?"

"Well, I don't, but I didn't want to talk to him until I was certain that you were interested."

"You know that I really want you, and I was willing to give you whatever you wanted to end it with Julie." She unbuttons the front of her blouse, exposing most of her very large breasts. "I'll bet that Julie hasn't offered you these? I don't think that she likes sex. All the other girls talk about it all the time. Some of them are having it every chance they get. Julie doesn't even talk about it. I think she's a prude."

"Margie, that's no way to talk about your friend. She really likes you. Button your blouse. I've seen tits before."

"Not mine!"

"Margie, stay focused. Don't you think that this could be good for both of you?"

"Yeah. If you think he's interested, I wouldn't mind trying. When do you want to make this hook-up?"

"I'm going to see if I can talk him into coming to Teen Club. He's a little mad at me at the moment, and he thinks that he's getting too old to go to Teen Club. He's seventeen, and I think that he turns eighteen in June."

"Does he know that I just turned sixteen?"

"No, I don't think that your age matters."

"What does he know about me?"

"Not much. He knows that you have big tits because he told me that about a month ago. I'll give him some information—at least enough to get you started talking."

"Great! So the only thing that he's interested in is my tits? That's a great start."

"I didn't say that. I said that he noticed them. Come on, give me a break. I've never done this before. Give it a try. Who knows? You might find that you were meant for each other."

"Okay, I'm going to do it. Maybe it'll be fun. Do you think that I can trust him in his car?"

"No! If you unbutton your blouse for him, you'll join the ranks of your other girlfriends who like sex. Then I know that you will become a couple."

"That ain't all bad. I'll remember that. Do you think that he'll take me out in his car after Teen Club?"

"Yeah, I'm sure that he will."

"Good, I'm starting to like this already. Set it up!"

"Okay, I'll call you. Is it okay to give him your phone number?"

"Yeah, I just hope my mother doesn't try to steal him away from me!"

"God, Margie, you don't even have him yet. What makes you think that your mother would go after him?"

"My mother is only seventeen years older than me. The place that we lived at before coming to Beachwood, I met this guy who was nineteen. I was only fifteen. My mother objected because he was much older than me. He kept coming over, and I wouldn't have sex with him. My mother's objection stopped. I came home early one day from school because I was sick. And there they were, naked in the living room, going at it. He blamed me because I wouldn't have sex with him, and she told me that I should take better care of my man. Needless to say, he became her man. They just recently broke up. So I don't trust her around my boyfriends."

"He's not your boyfriend yet. And you'll have to deal with your mother problems. God, one half of the world doesn't know how the other half lives!"

"Well, I have to plan ahead. You know she's made comments about you. She said—"

"*Don't tell me!* I don't want to know. I won't feel comfortable coming near your house."

"Okay, let me know when you have it set up. I'll take care of the other issues. See you later."

JJ pulled away from the curb. His mind was totally exhausted. He couldn't believe the conversation he just had. He thought to himself, *How much of that do I tell Julie? I have to tell her that I talked to her. She's going to ask what I said to her. I'll tell her that I told her that Jimmy said some nice things about her and that he was too shy to ask her out. I'm certainly not going to tell her about Margie's mother. Holy cow, what a messed-up family. Now I think I'll see if Jimmy's at work.* As he drove by Jimmy's house he saw his car. *Good, he's at home. I'll stop there.*

"Hi Momma Button." JJ loved Jimmy's mother. He referred to her as his second mom, and she liked him calling her Mom. "Is Jimmy in his room? He didn't wait for an answer and proceeded to Jimmy's room."

"Hey, I know that you're mad at me, but you'll simply have to get over it! We've been friends too long not to talk to each other."

"Go to hell, you asshole. And don't talk about my drinking in this house."

"No, the more I think about it, what do I care if you want to get drunk and kill yourself? My life will go on, and I won't have to worry about you anymore!"

"*Oh*, so now you don't care if I kill myself?"

"It's your life, buddy, but I'm going to remain your friend until you do it."

"Oh, shut up! What the hell did you come here for?"

"You remember that girl Margret? You know, the one with the big tits?"

"Yeah, I know who you mean."

"She told me that she likes you. She thinks that you're cute."

"Oh, *bullshit*! Girls don't pay any attention to me."

"They do now. You've got your own car, and they love guys who have a car. Some of them like the backseat."

"It does have a big back seat. Do you think that I could get her back there?"

"Hold on a minute. You have to meet her first. Talk some sweet talk. Dance with her, real close, close enough that you can feel those big tits. Then maybe take her to Billy's Burger Place and see where it goes from there."

"How do you think that I can do that?"

"Well, I've got a plan. When you get off work Friday night, come up to Teen Club. Don't stop at a bar! She'll be hanging with Julie and me at our table. I'll introduce you. You stand or sit next to her. When the music plays, you ask her to dance."

"You know I can't dance."

"Good. I tell her that you need someone to teach you how to dance. Girls love to teach guys how to dance. Wait for a slow dance to play. That'll give you a chance to talk to her while your dancing."

"What do I say to her?"

"I don't know. Tell her you like the way she did her hair tonight, or that you like her dress. Tell that you've always wanted to meet her but never had the right opportunity. Make up some bullshit. It won't matter. You are both going to be nervous, and you won't remember what you said."

"You think this will work?"

"Yeah, of course it will. Don't come there drunk or with booze on your breath! Girls don't like that."

"I won't. I get off at 7:00 p.m. on Friday, so I'll come home, clean up, and come right over."

"Put some of that aftershave lotion on, but don't overdo it. You don't have to wear a suit, but if you have a nice sportcoat, that'll work. Hey, I'm sorry about last week. We still friends?"

"Yeah, asshole. You know that I can't stay mad at you! Now you're going to help with this, aren't you?"

"Yeah, I'll be there, and Julie will help too. I'll see you Friday at Teen Club."

"Bye, Mom. See you soon!"

"You two friends again?"

"Yes, Mama, everything's okay."

It's been a long afternoon and early evening. JJ is mentally worn out. Julie's classes will be over in about two hours. He doesn't normally go around to house on work nights, but he's got to fill her in on the day's events. He'll call Mrs. Connors and ask if he can pick Julie up from work. She likes it when he does that, because it gives her a little break from all that driving. JJ drives to the Restaurant next to the dance studio. He buys a milkshake and takes it to the car. He falls asleep, and the next thing he hears is Julie tapping on the window. Good grief, she's wearing an all-black dance leotard. Those things are form fitting, and all he can see is this beautiful body. He's guessing 34-20-35, and he's dying to know if he's correct.

"Hi, how come you're picking me up? Where's my mom?"

"I gave her the night off. Do you want a milkshake or something before we leave?"

"No." She reaches across the seat and kisses him. "Take me home, driver."

As they begin the ride home, JJ tells the story of the day's events.

"How did you begin the conversation with her?"

"I told her that Jimmy asked me if I knew her and that he would like to meet her. She was flattered that he had noticed her. I told her that I would introduce her at Teen Club Friday night. She asked a few questions about him. She got excited when I told her that he had his own car."

"Somehow I think there is more to this story. What did you tell him?"

"I simply reversed the story and told him that she thought that he was cute and that he had his own car. He asked some questions about her, and I didn't know the answers so I told him that what he could talk to her about."

"What did he ask you? Maybe I know the answers."

"Her age—I did answer that—sixteen? Her bra size? Do I think she will kiss on the first date? Do I think that she's into sex?"

"JJ, why would he ask you those kinds of questions?"

"Julie, that's the kind of things guys talk about."

"Why would he think that you would know the answers?"

"Because other guys know Maggie—and they talk. For example, I know that she is a 40D and she loves to kiss. I know that she had sex with Paul from Sunrise Beach, but I'm not going to tell him that. Let him find out for himself. If she wants him to know that, she'll tell him."

"I can't get over what you guys talk about."

"You girls have the same kind of conversations. I know that you know about her sex because you all talk about sex. I don't know if you talk about bra sizes or not, but I'm sure that you talk about kissing."

"Well, what kind of information do you have about me?"

"You're 34-20-35, and they think that you are beautiful."

"I am not, my waist is only 18 inches, but now I guess everyone will know that."

"They won't hear from me, but if you tell any of the girls, it won't be long before it becomes common knowledge. And if you tell them that we have sex, I'll know it the next day!"

"Why would I tell them that? We don't have sex."

"Not yet."

# Chapter 23

It's Thursday, and JJ is at work at the Animal Hospital when Dr. Erick asks him, "What are your plans for the future?"

"I don't really know right now. I'm still thinking about it. My father would like me to go into the navy and follow his footsteps, but the navy has no appeal to me. I like the Naval Academy, but I don't think my grades would make it, and you have to be appointed by a congressman. My family has no political connections. I've thought about becoming a state trooper. I think that I would like police work. I was thinking that I could go to college for a few years and study criminal law. Then apply to become an FBI agent."

"Those are all good things. So you have given it some thought."

"Yes, but scholarships are not really scholarships anymore; they are given to people with low incomes, or if you are black. My father's income is just high enough to make me *not* qualify, and you can see that I'm not black. I heard at school last week that the state and county are going to start a different type college. They offer two-year degrees and special job skill training. They call it community college. And that sounds great to me. I hope they do it. It's supposed to cost much less than the University of Maryland, and they're planning on putting it somewhere near Annapolis. That would make it affordable, and maybe they will offer the classes that I need to join the FBI."

"Yes, we have a community college–type system back home in New York. I don't know if it would be the same, but they do offer classes like you're thinking about. What about becoming a lawyer or a doctor?"

"First of all, I don't think that I'm smart enough to do that. Second, there is no way that I could afford it."

"I don't know what your school grades are, but you certainly seem intelligent enough to be either. There are student loans programs to help with the financial issue."

"Yeah, but don't you have to go for eight years to become a doctor, and four to six years to become a lawyer?"

"Yes, you do."

"How would I live while I'm trying to do all that?"

"Many students work part-time jobs during school and full time between semesters."

"Dr. E., I don't think that I could do all that and do all the studying that needs to be done."

"It is very difficult, but it's worth it. And it prepares you for life."

"I'm going to do something, but I don't know what. I'm saving money for the University of Maryland, and I'm looking for a carpool of guys who are willing to do the traveling. The university makes you take all these classes that are not needed, and you have to pay for them. It just runs up the cost."

"What kind of classes?"

"They make you take four years of English. Now, I know that speaking correct English is important, but can't they teach you communication skills for life. I'm communicating with you, and you understand what I'm saying, and the intent of the conversation."

"They do that to make you a well-rounded person."

"Okay, but do you really need four years of that? How about all these people who are self-made millionaires, how did they make it? Apparently, they aren't well rounded, and they can buy and sell those college professors."

"Do you feel that money makes you successful?"

"Yes. I realize that there are people who have done great things in their lives and they aren't rich. But having enough money to do whatever you want to do doesn't hurt! You're a doctor, and I guess that you make a lot of money, at least by most people's standards.

Can you go out tomorrow and buy a new house for $500,000 and pay cash for it?"

"No, but that doesn't mean that I'm not successful. There are degrees of success. I live a fairly comfortable lifestyle. I support my wife and children. I drive a respectable car, and I have enough money in my pocket to take my wife to dinner. That, to some degree, is success."

"Okay, but I have a friend, whose father owns an auto repair shop. He didn't go eight years to college to become a doctor. He owns ten acres of land on the waterfront, with two beautiful houses. All of his cars are brand new. He has a 65-foot yacht, a 21-foot speedboat, and lots of other things. He didn't have to take four years of college English and a bunch of other crap to accomplish that!"

"How old is he?"

"I guess he's in his midfifties."

"Well, by the time I'm his age, I may have all those things, if I want them. And frankly, JJ, that's what makes America great. No one says that you have to do these things to become successful. They simply say that you have a better chance if you do get an education."

"I agree, but while they tell you that, they don't have any solutions as to how you accomplish it."

"They have some suggestions, but they can't do it for you. Once you determine what you think you want to do, you have to develop a reasonable plan as to how you are going to do it. Your plan may take you ten years. Someone else's plan might take them twenty years. But at least you have set some goals for yourself. You may not reach those goals, and you may change them several times, but you will be going in the right direction."

"Thanks, Doc. I'm starting on that plan now. As I develop some more ideas, can I run them by you?"

"Of course, JJ I'll offer whatever advice that I can. But that's all that it is—advice!"

"Doc, did I tell you why I switched days with Danny?" JJ begins to tell Dr. E. all about his efforts to hook up Jimmy and

Margie and that it was on for tomorrow night. He is excited that it is going to work and that they may be going on to be the best of friends. Dr. E. tells him that he met his wife that way, that some of his buddies in college introduced him to his wife. She was in the same college but a year behind him. She was studying to become a nurse. She only had one more year to go, and he still had three years to go. When she graduated, she got a job and an apartment. They decided to live together, and she helped him with expenses to finish college. Then they got married.

"How long did you live together?"

"A little over three years. I know that people don't think that you should live together until after you are married, but we both wanted to make sure that we could live with each other and get along. If the answer is yes, then we get married. And we did. We've been married for ten years."

"She sure is a pretty woman. Does she still do nursing?"

"No, we have two children, and she stays at home and takes care of them."

"When you were living together, did you do everything?"

"Well, that's pretty personal, but I assume you are asking if we had sex? Well you figure it out. We used the same bathroom. We undressed in front of each other. We slept together in the same bed. Could you be living under those conditions and not enjoy each other?"

"I'm sorry, I didn't mean to be that personal, but living together before you got married seems like a good idea. Maybe if more people did that, we wouldn't have so many divorces."

"Well, it worked for us. That doesn't mean that it works for everybody. I know that you are young and trying to understand sex. I don't know if you and your girlfriend have sex, but you should understand that sex is just one part of living together or marriage. And it is important that you both want it. But planning a family, buying a house, and enjoying doing things together are very important. Sex is an expression of your love for each other and not just physical fun. Think about this. She and I will talk for hours, maybe weeks, about buying a new car or buying furniture for the house. But we don't sit around talking about how we are going to have sex! It simply comes naturally form being with each other. So while I know that you are interested in sex, remember, there are a lot of other things in life that are more important."

"Yeah, and I want to find out about all of them, including sex!"

"That will happen soon enough."

It's Friday night at Teen Club, and it is "Poodle Skirt Night." All the girls were wearing a poodle skirt. That was a big deal with the girls. Buddy Dean would do the same thing on his show. These young ladies looked great. Many of them wore saddle Oxford shoes with bobby socks. With their poodle skirts, tight sweaters, and very little makeup (they didn't need it), they were developing into young women.

Julie and JJ had their table near the corner. Some of the guys were off to the right. Some of the girls were on the left side of the hall. Margie was next to Julie and constantly asking JJ, "Do you think that he's going to show up?"

"Yes, Margie, he'll be here. I talked to him today and he said that he would be here around 8:00 p.m."

"It's 8:00 p.m. now!"

"I know. Give him a chance. He'll be here!"

With that the door opened and in came Jimmy. He looked great. He had a crew neck sweater with a sport coat. He smelled like aftershave lotion, and he was as nervous as a cat on a hot tin roof. He stopped and talked to a couple of the guys for few minutes and then came to the table. You could tell by the expression on Margie's face that she was very pleased and happy to see him there.

"Hi, JJ."

"Hi, Julie. Good to see you. I haven't been here for a while, but when JJ told me that I would have a chance to meet Margie, I really wanted to come!"

"Jimmy, this is Margie. Margie, this is Jimmy. I know that you know each other from school, but you have never met formally. So this is your formal introduction. Jimmy, tonight is Poole Skirt Night."

"Hi, Margie, it's nice to meet you. I like your poodle skirt. I think that's a fun thing to do, have all the girls wear poodle skirts. Look at all the different colors! Julie, I like yours too."

"Margie, you have a job to do tonight. Jimmy doesn't dance too well, and he needs a beautiful young lady to help him learn. Do you think that you could be that beautiful young lady?"

"Oh, yeah, I'd be delighted. Do you want to do the next dance?"

"Yeah, that'll be great." Margie was wearing that button down the front blouse, and she left several buttons undone. All you could see were her big breasts, and Jimmy was having difficulty taking his eyes off of them. It was clear that Margie noticed him looking at them, and she seemed to like it.

A slow dance started playing, and Jimmy took her hand. He didn't seem to know what to do next, so Margie took over. She took his other arm and put it around her neck and shoulders. She pulled him close. Those big breasts looked like they were going to pop out of the blouse. By the expression on his face, you could tell that he liked her and she liked him. They made some small talk while they danced, and when they came back to the table, they never separated. When the club took a short break and all the girls went to the ladies room, Jimmy came to JJ."

"She wants me to take her somewhere when Teen Club is over."

"So?"

"So, where do you think I should take her?"

"Wherever she wants to go. She looks like she has a plan for you, so let it play out."

"Did you see those big tits? She was pressing them against me the whole time we were dancing."

"Yeah, well stop staring at them. I got a feeling that you are going to see more of them before the night is over!"

"Do you think so? I hope that you are right."

"Well, you can tell me all the details tomorrow. You know that you don't have to wait until closing. You could dance a few more dances and then suggest that you would like to leave and take her where ever she wants to go."

"Good idea. That's what I'm going to do. Thanks, JJ. I think that she is great, and I think that she likes me."

"All right, you can give me all the details tomorrow. Bring back her panties or bra."

"I don't think that I'll get that far."

"I just wish good things for you. Here they come. The music should start soon. I'm going to take Julie to Bobby's Burger Place at about 11:30, so I don't know if we will see you again."

"Maybe Margie would like to go there?"

"Maybe Margie would like to go park somewhere and make love? Which would you rather have, big tits or a burger?"

"You know the answer to that."

"Look, when you leave here, suggest to her that you would like to go get a milkshake and ask if she would like one."

"I'd rather get a beer or a bottle of wine. Do you think that she would be interested?"

"Yeah, she might be. Suggest the milkshake first. Then add, 'If you would like something stronger, like wine or beer, we can do that.' See what she says. I know that she does drink some, 'cause she told me that after a few drinks, she loosens up! Maybe you'll get lucky. For God's sake, Jimmy, don't get drunk on your first date, or it may be your last! Let it play itself out. See what she wants to do? Relax, take it easy."

"You want me to get you some booze?"

"Jimmy, how long have you known me? You know that I don't drink. I don't like the taste of beer. That Thunderbird wine that you buy is okay, but every time I drink that stuff, it give me the shits! So why would I want to do that to myself?"

"Hello, girls. Nice to have you back." As the music starts to play again, Jimmy and Margie go to the dance floor, and JJ takes Julie to the floor also. While they are dancing, Tommy comes in with Kathy. Tommy has been working evenings, loading trucks for his contractor boss and working weekend days. Nobody has seen either one of them for over a month. They looked fairly normal and seemed to be getting along well together. The dance music ended, and everyone was heading to the table. Julie and Margie began talking to Kathy. Tommy says hello to Jimmy and asks JJ, "How are you doing?"

"Things are pretty much the same. I'm working at the animal hospital and going around to Julie's as much as I can. How you doing?"

"I don't know, man. I think that I may have a problem."

"What's the matter?"

"I think she's knocked up."

"What?"

"You know, pregnant. All we do is make out on her porch. When we know that her mother is asleep, we drop our pants and go to it. We both love it, but maybe we've gone too far."

"Are you sure that she's pregnant?"

"No, but I think so."

"Does your sister know? How old is Kathy?"

"No, Connie doesn't know. If she did, she would tell my mother. Kathy just turned sixteen. Her mother got pregnant when she was sixteen. This is history repeating itself."

"What are you going to do?"

"If she is pregnant, I guess that I'll quit school and go to work full time. I know that the boss would hire me."

"Then what?"

"I guess we'll get married and move in with her mother. Her mother could use some help with the expenses since that drunken boyfriend left her."

Jimmy butts into the conversation. "How many times?"

"What do you mean, how many times?"

"You know. How many times did you do it before she got pregnant?"

"Hell, I don't know. We do it almost every night, and we've been doing it since prom night. She was so happy that night. When Justin dropped us off at her house, it was late. We sat on the porch and were kissing. She had that strapless gown on, so I just pulled the top down and started playing with her tits. She didn't object, and we just kept on going. She unzipped my pants and put her hand in there. And the rest is history. She called me the next day and asked me if I liked it. I told her that it was great. She said that her mother falls asleep around ten and wanted to know if I could meet her on the porch. And we've been doing it ever since. I'm telling you, this girl loves sex. But she seems to be worried about me being alone with her mother."

JJ speaks up, "I bet I know why? I just was told a story by one of the girls here tonight about her mother stealing her nineteen-year-old boyfriend. The guy took up with the mother and they stayed together almost a year. Then they moved here. So she doesn't want her mother meeting her boyfriends. I'll bet Kathy has had the same problem. You figure her mother was only sixteen when she had Kathy, so she's only thirty-two or thirty-three now. And other than her drinking problem, she's a nice-looking woman. Hell, Tommy, you may be taking care of two women. Do you think you can handle it?"

"Hell, yes. Do you think they can?"

"Hell, no. Two women in the same house, after the same man. That's a formula for disaster!"

Jimmy pipes in, "You guys are scaring the hell out of me."

"What, do you have something working, Jimmy?"

"Yeah, Tommy, and I was looking forward to it until you told me all that shit. I don't want any pregnant woman on my hands. I just want a little sex."

"Well, you have to be careful."

"Careful! I don't even know what I'm doing. And who are you to tell me to be careful? Were you careful?"

Jimmy turns to the three girls talking and says, "Ladies, let me interrupt here. I'm going to dance with Margie, and then I think we are going to leave."

As they begin dancing, Margie tells Jimmy, "I can't wait to tell you what Kathy just told us."

The song ends, and they say goodnight to everyone. They get into Jimmy's car. Margie slid all the way over to the driver side of the car.

"Where would you like to go? Do you want to go get a milkshake?"

"Yeah, let's do that for starters."

Jimmy brings the milkshakes to the car, and as he's getting

in he asks Margie, "What do you mean, for starters?" Margie unbuttons another button. "Well if you can pick up some wine, I know a place that we can park. And after a couple of glasses of wine, I talk a lot. Maybe we can get to know each other better."

Jimmy tosses the milkshake out. "I'm not going to put good wine on top of a milkshake!"

Margie tosses her milkshake out. "I want the full effect of the booze."

Jimmy drives to the local bar, where he has an adult friend who buys his booze for him. He buys his bottle of Thunderbird wine and a half-pint of sloe gin. She directs him to a dark spot at the end of a dead end road. As they stop, she asks him if he wants to get in the back seat. She slides out on the passenger's side and opens the back door. She slide across the seat on her stomach as Jimmy opens the back door on the driver's side. She grabs his zipper, pulls it down, and pulls out his very large penis. Instantly she is performing oral sex on him. Since he had had never had this before, he wanted to give it a try. It didn't take long, and he was feeling strange. He pulls his penis from her mouth and pushes her back into the car. She looks a little surprised.

"What do you want to do?"

He responds, "I want you to take your clothes off." He begins to unbutton the balance of the blouse, and as soon as it is off, she disconnects her bra, and out come these huge breasts. She takes off her skirt and removes her panties.

"Are you ready to do me already?"

"No, not yet. I want to enjoy every minute. Here have some of this sloe gin."

"I don't need that. I'm ready whenever you are. Let me finish with your dick."

"What do you mean by finish?"

"You know, take it all the way." And she did.

"Now Jimmy needs a rest." He played with her breasts the entire time that she was working on him. They sat back for a few seconds and looked at each other. They were both very pleased with each other.

"What do you want to do now? I didn't know that you were that big. Do you want to put it in me now?"

All Jimmy could think about was Tommy telling him to *be careful*!

"After all that, I don't think that I can get it up again. Maybe next time."

"How about your finger or tongue?"

Jimmy thought, the finger has to be safe. *What does she want me to do with my tongue?*

"Come on over here and show me what you would like the finger to do."

They played for a while longer. Jimmy kept giving her sloe gin. She wasn't drunk, but she was very close.

"Jimmy, let me put my clothes on and take me home or I'm going to jump on that big dick of yours."

"Okay, but I want to keep the panties."

"Why, so you can tell the guys that you did me?"

"Yes, how else would I have your panties?"

"Well, I'll tell them myself if you want me to. I'll tell them how great you are. You know that I did Paul—you know, the guy from Sunrise Beach—and he told all those guys all the details. So those guys were all trying to get me to do it with them, and I wasn't interested in any of them. So, if you're going to tell them, I want to tell them first—and tell them that they are *not* invited. I'm only interested in you, if you want it to be that way?"

"Yeah, I think that sounds good. So how often do you want to meet?"

"As often as you want, but you have to make me a promise."

"What?"

"If my mother tries to get you to do her, you have to turn her down. She can't have you."

"Your *mother*?"

"Yeah, she's still young, and she like young men. Where we lived before, I had a nineteen-year-old boyfriend, I was only fifteen, and I wouldn't have sex with him. So she did, and they became girlfriend and boyfriend for about a year. He finally left her. So I know that she would love to have you. Promise. No *mother*!"

"I promise. That's crazy."

"Here's your panties. Be sure to tell JJ what he could have had. Can we meet tomorrow night?"

"Yes, I'll call you."

"No. I'll call you. I don't want you coming in contact with my mother."

"Okay, I'll wait to hear from you."

# Chapter 24

EVERYBODY IS INTO SEX LATELY. Some good, some interesting, and some strange mothers. And all JJ is getting is rejections from Julie. Sometimes it bothers him, and other times he thinks about what Dr. E. told him about it only being a part of a relationship. That there are many other important things for him and Julie to enjoy. But right now, sex seems to be the most important. He respects Julie's wishes to wait. That there will be plenty of time for sex in their lives. Maybe Margie was right; he shouldn't be tied to just one girl. Look at all the girls he could have, and they are all willing to do it. *What's the matter with her that she doesn't want to do it? Dr. E. said that it is an expression of love. Doesn't she love me?*

JJ's mind is going crazy. All he can think about is sex. Yet he really didn't think about it that much until he heard about Tommy and Kathy. And now he's getting a play-by-play account about Jimmy and Margie. And they seem to be enjoying it all the time. And to think that she threw herself at him. He could be doing it with her every night if he wanted too. The only ones that seem to have a normal relationship, similar to him and Julie, are Justin and Connie. They seem to be having fun, and they are not having sex. So that proves that it can be done.

JJ is starting his shift at the animal hospital. He has just arrived when Dr. E. asked, "Can you go over to my house and see if you can get my wife's car started? I think that the battery is dead, and I have jumper cables on the car port. I got several things I have to do here before I can leave. Tell her that I don't think that I'll be home between office hours."

"Sure, Doc. I know how to do that, and if it's not that, I'll try to fix whatever it is."

"Hi, JJ. My name is Sherry," she said when she saw him. "I've seen you at the office, but haven't had a chance to talk to you. I told E. that I thought that you looked like Elvis."

"Yes, Mama, I'm told that a lot."

"Please don't Mama me. You make me feel old. Call me Sherry. Do you think that I look old?"

"Oh no, Mama ... I mean, Sherry. I think you're a very attractive mother."

"Speaking of mother, both the kids are asleep in their rooms, so we have to be quiet, very quiet," she whispered in his ear.

"Okay, I'm going to see if I can get your car started."

"Okay, I'm going to assume that you can, so I'm going to change my clothes."

As JJ works on the car, Sherry removes all her clothes except her panties and bra. She leaves the door partway open so that she can talk to him as he attempts to start the car." Be careful. The wiring is messed up on that car."

Just as she said that, the battery sparked back and burned JJ's hand. Not thinking, Sherry came running out to help him. He was pretty badly burned, so Nurse Sherry took him into the bathroom and put some type of cream and a bandage on his hand. As she finished, she said to him, "Have you ever seen a woman in her parties and bra?" Sherry was about forty years old and slightly overweight after having given birth to two children, but she had beautiful skin, with perfect 38C breasts.

JJ couldn't help but think, *I simply can't get away from this sex stuff.*

"Well, yes, Sherry, I've seen women before."

"Well, what do you think? Don't be shy. How do you think I look for a forty-year-old woman with two kids?"

"I think you look great—"

Before he could finish his words, she took his other hand and put it in her bra.

"What do you think of them? They're still in great shape."

JJ removes his hand. "Yes, they feel great."

"Don't look so embarrassed. Haven't you ever felt a breast before?"

"Not yours. Sherry, I have to get back to the hospital. I got the car started, so you can go where ever you are going. Dr. E. said that he won't be back between hours."

"That's great! Now, how am I supposed to go anywhere with two kids sleeping in the other room. Well, that means that you can stay a little longer, and I don't need to get dressed." She took JJ's hand and put it between her legs.

This startled him. He jumped up and started for the door. "I have to go."

"JJ, close the door and I'll teach you a little about life."

JJ began to open the door.

"Where you going? I want something from you. If you leave, I'll tell Dr. E. that you got smart with me. Now, you don't want that, do you?"

At this point, JJ doesn't know what to do. She comes over to him and unzips his pants. He is in total panic mode. She put her hand in his pants and grabs his private parts. Just then, one of the kids wakes up and starts to cry.

"Damn, I can't seem to have any fun. Go on, you're saved by a crying brat. But I'll expect you to come back soon and give me what I want."

JJ dashed out the door, jumped into his car and was gone in a flash. *What the hell am I going to do now? If I avoid her, she's going to tell him that I went after her. I could be accused of rape or something like that. I would surely be fired. I don't know what the hell to do now. God, as much as I wanted some sex, I wasn't expecting that.* He had to calm down and act like nothing had happened. *I think that the whole world is sex crazy. My friends and their girls' mothers, and now Dr. E.'s wife. No wonder Julie doesn't want to mess around. It makes life too complicated.*

When he returned to the hospital, he couldn't look Dr. E. directly in the eye. He really hadn't done anything wrong, but he still felt guilty.

"Hi, I'm back. It was the battery."

"What happened to your hand?"

"The battery sparked and burned it. Your wife fixed it for me."

"Remind me to give you some burn cream to put on it."

"We have a full waiting room, and none of your work got done, so it's going to be a long night. By the way, your buddy Jimmy called. He wants you to stop by his house on your way home tonight. He said that he has some things he needs to tell you. So we better get started or it'll be midnight by the time we finish."

They had way too many people in the waiting room. Dr. E. went to talk to them. "As you can see we have a full house tonight. I know that we will be here past midnight. If any of you can't wait that long, let me take your name and I'll come in an hour early tomorrow and you will be first on the list. If you're here for routine checkups or shots and it's not a problem for you, you will save a lot of waiting time."

About four of the people said that would work for them. JJ took their names and phone numbers and set them up on the schedule for the next day. They worked steadily for four straight hours, and they had only a few more waiting in the outside waiting room. It was a little past 10:30 p.m. when Sherry came into the side office. She had brought food for both of them and was laying it out on the desk. She opened the inside door and motioned to JJ to come in.

"What did you tell him?"

"Nothing, I swear."

"Okay, I'll tell him myself when you are done."

"What? What do you mean that you will tell him?"

"Go on back out there. You'll understand later."

JJ and Dr. E. ate a little bit of food between taking care of the last patients. "Okay, JJ you can lock up. Good job. We got them all done." JJ locks the outside door and returns. Dr. E. and Sherry are in the outside office laughing and smiling. JJ has no idea what she has told him, and he is scared to death.

"Well, JJ, what did you think of my house?"

"It's very nice, Doc. Nice car too."

"What do you think of my wife?"

"Oh, she's a very pretty lady."

"No, I mean, what did you think of her behavior?"

"I don't know what you mean."

"Yes, you do. Do you think that she's *hot*? Did like her panties and bra? How did you like her breasts? Sherry, look at him. He doesn't know what to say."

"Oh, I could tell he liked my breasts. And when I put his hand between my legs, I thought that he was going to faint!" They both laughed. JJ doesn't understand what is going on.

"It's okay, JJ. You remember the other night when we were talking about sex?"

"Yes."

"Sherry told me the day before that she would like to get you alone in our bedroom and strip you naked. You see, Sherry and I have what's called an 'open marriage.' That means that we both still like having sex with other people and it doesn't affect our time together in bed. Remember when I told you about us living together in an apartment while in college. Well, Sherry would invite her girlfriends over, and I'd invite my buddies. We all take our clothes off and begin making love with whomever we wanted. Sometimes we'd do it together as couples; sometimes we'd go in separate rooms. It didn't make any difference because we were all consenting adults and we knew what we were there for. We did that for the entire time that we lived there. Some of the others got married and decided that they didn't want to do that anymore; others we still meet whenever possible and have what's called 'swingers' parties.'"

"You mean that you still do it, with your children in the house?"

"No, no, we switch sites. Next weekend, we will have a babysitter come over for the weekend to watch the kids, and Sherry and I are going to New York to swing with about six other couples that we know. Sherry has a couple of guys that she really likes—they have bigger peckers than me—and I have a couple of women who I favor. So when Sherry told me that she wanted to give you a little sex education, I thought that you would love it."

"If you had told me the plan, I might have been prepared for it, but ..."

"That would have taken all of the fun out of it. I sure would have liked to see the expression on your face when she put your hand in her bra."

"She does have nice soft tits. But I wasn't ready for that."

"Are you ready now? Sherry, take your clothes off." Within seconds, Sherry was standing there totally naked, no panties or bra this time.

"Dr. E., I don't think that I can do this. I know that you two do it all the time, but I've never done it before."

"Tell you what, JJ. I'll let you slide this time. Sherry and I will show you how we do it. But the next time that I send you over to the house, I'll expect you to take care of her. Do we have a deal?"

"Yeah, Doc. What do you want me to do now?"

"Clear the top of the desk off. I'm going to do her right there. You watch and learn. Maybe join in."

With that Sherry, lies flat on top of the desk, and the Doc starts doing her. She is moaning with pleasure when she tells JJ to come over next to her. At this point, JJ is scared to death. He doesn't know what to expect, but his desire to have some kind of sex is raging. He walks over next to the desk, and she grabs his belt buckle and pulls his pants down. He is totally exposed. She begins the motions on his penis, and within seconds he ejaculates. She laughs and says, "Good job."

He can't speak. He pulls away from her and runs to the bathroom. He washes himself off, pulls his pants up, and reenters the room. By now, Dr. E. and Sherry have completed their sex and are getting dressed.

"JJ, what did you think of that?"

"Doc, it would be nice if you would give me some warning about what going to happen."

"You mean what Sherry did to you? I didn't know that she was going to do that. That's what makes sex so enjoyable—you just do what comes natural to you. Didn't you like it?"

"I've never had someone else do that for me."

"Oh, she didn't do it *for* you. She did it because she likes it. When you go over to the house, you better be prepared for more than that. She's going to eat you alive!"

"Dr. E., I'm not certain that I can keep that deal. I really need to think about it. She's way too experienced for me."

"Okay, how about another deal? When we go to New York next weekend, we have this eighteen-year-old babysitter coming over. Her parents are going with us, so she knows a little about sex. Her parents took her with us the last time. She didn't do anything but watch. She told us that she has done it a couple of times but didn't give us any details. She's a little skinny. But how about if I make arrangements for you two to do it? You'll have the whole house to yourselves, and nobody needs to know. Maybe you will like her."

"I don't know Dr. E. This is all too fast for me. I've never heard of this swinger stuff. And while you and Sherry like it, I'm not certain that I want to do it. I like the idea of just having Julie."

"Yeah, I know, but Julie isn't giving you anything. Maybe you'll end up marrying Julie, and she may be a virgin, but you can have some of your own pleasures before you get married."

"You don't have to be a virgin just because she wants to be. What she doesn't know won't hurt her."

Sherry pulls up her skirt and points. "JJ, when I get you down there, I'll teach you everything that you need to know. When you get Julie in your honeymoon bed, you'll make her wish that she never stayed a virgin."

"Okay, you two are ganging up on me now, and I can't handle all this. Sherry, what you did was great, and I liked it, but I need to think about this."

"JJ, you should ask Julie to do what I did. She can't get pregnant that way, and she remains a virgin. When you come over to the house, I'll give you some oral lessons. You'll love it. And she can do that too and still remain a virgin. From what you tell me, she's a hot little chick. How can you stand being around her and not doing anything? Besides, I'll bet that she wants to do something but she doesn't know what."

"Sherry, please, give me a break. Think about how much you two have dumped on me tonight. Up until now, I thought that you were just a normal married couple with a nice house and a couple of kids. I didn't know that you are sex addicts. I'm not being judgmental. I just need some time to think about it. Please, let me go home."

"Okay, don't forget to stop by Jimmy's house."

"Hell, no. It's too late. And frankly I've heard enough sex talk for one night." As JJ leaves, his head is spinning. *What the hell just happened? I just watched two good looking, intelligent adults have sex on a desktop while she plays with my pecker and laughs at me when I couldn't hold back. And all the while he's giving her what looks like a 9" dick. And they are so open and free about it. And he wants me to take care of his wife. When I don't even know what I'm doing. And when he realizes that I feel uncomfortable doing that, he wants to hook me up with the babysitter. And Sherry tells me that she's going to teach me oral and that I should suggest to Julie that we should do that.*

*Actually, I like that idea, if I can convince Julie to do it. Sometimes I think that I can get Julie to give in. She seems to be getting hot and bothered, but she has amazing self-control. I think that she would like to play around, but she's afraid that it will go too far, and so am I. Sherry would be a great teacher, and it would be safe. Her husband wants me to do it, and she would be wild fun. I don't know about this babysitter. I don't trust that idea, and she may know some of our friends. I think that I'll stay away from that house while they are away. What the hell are her parents doing taking her to a swinger party? I realize that she's eighteen and can do what she wants, but I don't get her parents teaching her that way of life. Good God, I can't believe all the things going through my mind. Hey, there's Jimmy's house, and his light is still on. I'm certainly not going to get any sleep, so I guess I'll find out what he wants.*

JJ taps on the outside of his bedroom window. Jimmy points to the front door and goes to let JJ in.

"Hey, Doc told me that you wanted me to stop by."

"Damn, you worked late tonight."

"Yeah, we didn't lock the doors until 11:30 p.m. What's up?"

"Remember all the details about Margie and me in the back seat?"

"Yeah, most of them."

"Well, I didn't want to admit that I didn't know what she wanted me to do with my tongue."

"That's what you wanted me to stop by about? I don't know. Ask her what she means. There are lots of things that you can do with your tongue."

"I feel stupid asking her what she wants me to do."

"It hasn't bothered you so far. And she seems happy. Hey, you know what? I know someone that I can ask who is trying to teach me a little about sex. I'll find out for you and let you know. Now I'm going home."

# Chapter 25

IT'S THE END OF BASEBALL season. This will be the last time that the boys will ever play together as two teams. Everybody knew that they would part ways, start their separate lives, and in some cases never see each other again. There was a mood of happiness for the end of another great season and a degree of sadness because of the reality that some good friendships might be lost. It is the black community's turn to host the banquet, and the community hall was set up and ready to go. There was so much food there that you could have fed an army. They had the church choir singing gospel songs, and when they weren't singing, they were playing rock and roll records, and the teenagers were dancing.

These people had become great friends, but the feeling of segregation still prevailed. The black boy knew not to ask the white girls to dance with them, and white boys would have liked to dance with some of those beautiful black girls, but none of them would ask for a dance. The adults felt the uncomfortable feeling, but no one had the courage to do anything, except our hero, JJ. He knew what everybody was thinking, but no one would speak up.

The choir had just finished singing, and they were about to start the records again when JJ went over to the record player and put on a slow dance. Then he turned and walked directly to Martin's mother and said, "This is something I've been wanting to do for years. May I put my arm around you and dance you to the floor?"

Mrs. Martin was a homely woman who showed the strains

of life on her face and body, but she had a beautiful smile and a beautiful personality.

"Well, honey, I've never had the chance to dance with Elvis before. I would be delighted."

As they began dancing, the crowd began applauding. There were tears of joy on nearly everyone's face, and while no one else joined in, everyone knew what it meant and what it was intended to do. The tenseness in the room disappeared. Smiles and laughter prevailed, and peace, love, and friendship took over the room for the balance of the evening. Once again, a sixteen-year-old boy made a statement that it's not the color of your skin but the content of your character. That matters, and that his generation was going to change the racial barriers without knowing that they were doing it. JJ had never met Martin Luther King, but he could have climbed to the top of the mountain with him that day.

The banquet was coming to an end, and JJ was about to perform another great moment. JJ began tapping his glass as you would at a wedding reception, and he stood up.

"Can I have your attention, please?" Everyone in the hall became very quiet. "Four years ago, when many of us met for the first time, we had no idea that such wonderful friendships would develop. We were just some kids who wanted to play baseball. And from that wonderful game, our families got to know each other. Adults who might not have spoken to each other in a lifetime have become lifelong friends. And I now feel a sense of sadness in the room, because those kids have grown up. They are about to start their own adult lives. And many of us fear that those friendships will be lost Can I ask the baseball players to stand up? Please join me in this pledge: No matter where we are or what we are doing in our lives, on the fifteenth of August at, 9:00 p.m., we will rise to our feet, hold our glasses high, and say, "Here is to the greatest friendships of our lives. May they live in our hearts forever."

"Hear, hear" was shouted. Grown men had tears running down their faces. Women were actually crying as you would see them do at a wedding. Julie, who was sitting next to JJ at the banquet table, dashed to the ladies' room because the tears were causing streaks in her makeup. Mr. Roy, a World War Two veteran, could barely contain himself. He walked up to JJ and said, "You really should be a politician. Those words will live in these people forever. And to these baseball players, August 15 will be remembered like I remember Pearl Harbor." He turned and walked away, and it was good that he did, because JJ had such a lump in his throat that he couldn't speak.

As the crowd was leaving, Martin and his mother and a beautiful young woman came over to JJ and Julie.

"JJ, we would like you to meet someone very special to us," Mrs. Martin says while turning to Martin. "Well, go ahead and tell him."

"JJ, this is my Julie. Her name is Delores. We plan to get married the first week in December."

"Married? Congratulations!"

"Yes, I'm joining the navy. I couldn't get into the Naval Academy, but I have been accepted into officers' training school."

"Good grief, man, I didn't know that you were that smart. Congratulations again! Hello, Delores, I don't know how he hid you from me."

"Martin and I have been friends since we were little children. We've gone to all the same schools, and I'm going to the University of Maryland, I think. I want to study law and work in the civil rights movement."

"Congratulations to you also. Boy, I feel like I'm being bombarded with all this good news."

"There is one more thing. I'd like you to be my best man at the wedding."

With that, JJ began to cry, and so did Julie.

"I will understand if you say no, but you truly are my best friend."

"You gotta to be kidding. There's no way that I could turn down that request. I will be extremely honored. Wow, Momma Martin, looks like I'll get to dance with you again. What a day this has been. I really will remember August 15."

"Well, don't forget December 5."

"Don't worry, I'll be there. Now, let me get out of here. I can't handle anymore. I'm running on overload now."

"Julie, do you want to take a little ride?"

"I'm with you. Wherever you go, I go."

"What a great day it has been. And isn't it great about Martin and Delores? And how about that guy getting himself into officers' training school."

"Martin really is a smart guy. I think that he will do well in the navy."

"Yeah, here he is, eighteen years old, and he knows what he wants to do. He has his woman and his life is all planned. I don't even know what I want to do—except make love to you."

"JJ, do you realize that Martin and Delores have known each other longer than you and I? They have gone all the way through school together. She is really beautiful, and I know that you noticed her big butt and those perfect boobs!"

"Yes, yes, and yes. We didn't meet until we were ten years old, so they have a few extra years. They had to go to the same schools, 'cause in this stupid county, all the black kids go to the same school, even if they have to ride a bus twenty miles. And yes, guys have eyes that are trained to notice big butts and perfect breasts. She probably asked him the same thing about you?

"I don't have a butt that big, and her boobs must be twice the size of mine."

"They are getting married very young, but I bet that it works for them. I'll bet that he could have made it into the Naval Academy but they don't allow you to be married until your last year. So he chose the officers' training class instead, and I think that's just a two-year plan and they pay you while you train. That guy has thought of everything."

"Don't worry. You have plenty of time to figure out what you want to do. You already know that you want to marry me, so you only have a few more details to work out. You already have the most difficult one done."

"Yeah, you certainly are the most difficult one!"

"Thanks a lot! At least I'm the one that you are most certain about. College, career, where to live—those are all easy ones to make."

"Yeah, that's why I don't have them worked out! They're easy. Come over here and make love to me."

"Let's find some place to park and put the top down and look at all the stars. You know that I love you."

"Yeah, let's go down to the swimming pier and park."

"No, we don't want to go down there. It's too close to my house, and you know that my father walks down there sometimes."

"Okay, let's go down to that dead-end street."

"That'll work. It's private, with clear view of the sky. It is a perfectly clear night with a half-moon, but it's bright."

They pull into their spot. JJ puts the top down and Julie snuggles up close to him. They are a beautiful couple. JJ puts his arm around her shoulder and his hand automatically falls directly on her right breast. Normally she would push it away, but she doesn't move at all. He's not certain what to do now. He's been trying for years to get this far, and he never thought about what to do next, so he just leaves it there as if that's where it belongs. She turns slightly and reaches up to kiss him. She pulls her sweater loose from her skirt and reaches up her back and unhooks her bra. She looks at him and says, "That'll make it a little easier for you." Bells and whistles go off in JJ's mind. She just gave him the keys to her bra. She lies back against him, and he slides his hand up under the sweater. When his hand touches her breast, they both give slight moans of pleasure. It's clear that she has wanted to do this for a long time, but she wants to make sure that she does it with the man she plans to marry. All that talk about marriage and future plans assured her that this was the guy and this was the right time.

JJ kept thinking about their conversation about not letting it get out of control. God knows that he really loves this girl, and he doesn't want to do anything stupid to ruin this relationship. They sit there quietly, watching the stars, while he caresses her beautiful breasts. He thinks, *This is a real commitment. I gotta figure out how I'm going to take care of this woman for the rest of our lives. We both have time to work on this, but this is real. She's telling me that she is mine forever. This girl would never let this happen unless she was absolutely sure that this was the real thing. I know that she would let me go all the way if I wanted too, and I do. But I have to show some responsibility to our future plans. As she says, we will have plenty of time for sex, and I think that the fact that I know that she is mine mean I can wait. At least, I think that I can.*

"JJ, you are very quiet. I thought that once you got your hand on my nipples, I would hear you say, 'At last, at last. Thank God they are free at last.'"

"Where the hell did that come from?"

She laughs. "I've had a lot of time to think about this moment after all you've been trying for years. All women think about the first time that they allow a man to touch them—what will it be like and who they will do it with. I decided that night that we talked about it that it was going to be you. I just didn't know when or where. That part wasn't planned; it just has to happen naturally, and it did. And I'm glad that it did and I was certain that it would be you. I love you, I really do."

"I love you too. As I said before, this has been a great night."

Julie sits up with her back towards JJ. She pulls her sweater up, exposing her back. "Here, hook my bra for me. I'm going to start your training right away. I figure that you will be doing this often, so you need to learn how it's done!"

"I will enjoy your training sessions. By the way, your breasts are wonderful."

"How do you know? You only tried one."

"You are a crazy woman, and I really do love you."

"Okay, driver, put the top up and take me home. My emotions have worked overtime tonight."

# Chapter 26

IT'S BEEN A WEEK SINCE JJ had his encounter with Sherry and Dr. E., and while he still doesn't know how to handle it, he has decided that he is safe with Sherry. She doesn't know Julie or any of her friends. He's certain that Dr. E. and Sherry are not going to tell Danny what has happened, although he is not certain that Sherry hasn't had Danny over to the house. Danny has cut back on his work hours, which is good for JJ, but there might be a reason for the change. Either he is avoiding Sherry, or he is going over there on a regular basis. JJ truly wants Sherry to perform oral sex on him, but he doesn't want to do intercourse, and he thinks that he can control that situation. He's going to ask Sherry the question that Jimmy asked him. He is certain that she will know the answer. He has about three hours between when school lets out and when he has to be at work, and he has about a half-hour before Dr. E. gets home between hours, so he has enough time to go over to Sherry, let her do her thing, and still get to work. He decides to call her.

"Hi, Sherry, this is JJ."

"I know who it is. Are you ready for some fun?"

"Yeah, kinda. I want to talk to you about a couple of things."

"Okay, I only talk when I'm totally nude. Is that okay with you? Can you concentrate on what I'm saying?"

"No, but I want to come over. I'll be there in ten minutes." As JJ pulls his car into the carport, Sherry opens the side door, and yes, she is totally nude. God, she is a beautiful woman. She could get any man she wanted. What does she want with a sixteen-year-old boy? She motions to him to come in and be quiet. As soon as she closes the door, she pulls his pants down and begins performing oral sex. She knows that he is excited, and she wants to make him explode quickly, and she succeeds. JJ is weak in his knees. She sits him on a little makeup style stool, and she lies on the bed."

"Did you like that?"

"Good grief, that was even better than I thought."

"Wait 'til I put you in me."

"That's part of what I want to talk to you about. I'm really interested in the oral stuff, but I really don't want to do more than that. I really do want to save that for Julie on our wedding night. Maybe after that I can come back if you like." JJ knew that would never happen. Once he was married and had Julie doing whatever they wanted, he wasn't going anywhere near Sherry.

"Well, how can I teach you how to do her on your wedding night without doing the real thing?"

"I really don't want to do the real thing until it's with Julie. You understand, don't you? Wasn't Dr. E. your first man?"

Sherry laughs. "Are you kidding? The night that I did Dr. E., me and two of my girlfriend did him and two of his buddies. Dr. E. knew exactly what he was getting when he married me. In fact, I think that is why he married me. He loves this stuff. He's been doing two of my girlfriends for at least ten years, and I've been doing their husbands. We love that lifestyle. Okay, JJ, I'll let you save yourself for Julie, but don't tell Dr. E. As far as he is concerned, you're doing me every time you come over, okay?"

"Okay, but why?"

"'Cause I'm going to do the next-door neighbor when he thinks that I'm doing you. His daughter is the skinny eighteen-year-old baby sitter. She's in the other room right now. I'm going to bring her in so you can see what you are getting."

"No wait, I have something else to ask you. What does it mean when a woman tells a man, 'Finger or tongue?'"

Sherry, lies back on the bed and spreads her legs, showing her entrance to sexual delight. "Well you can enter either with your finger or with your tongue—which do you want?"

"Oh, now I understand."

"Which do you want?"

"Oh, I don't want either. I got what I wanted."

"Typical man, get what you want and leave me frustrated. Wait a minute. I want you to meet Bonnie, and I'll give you a little demonstration."

"I got to go. Dr. E. will be coming in soon."

"No, it's okay. If he shows up, he'll just join in. I want to show you that two women can enjoy sex together. We pay Bonnie a lot of money to baby sit and do other things. Bonnie, come in here and meet JJ."

"Hello, JJ, how are you? I understand that you and I will be seeing each other this weekend."

"Yeah, so I've been told."

"Bonnie, take your clothes off and make love to me. I want to show JJ a few things. Bonnie wasn't as skinny as they said; in fact, she was at least an eight on the ten scale. The two of them crawled into bed, Bonnie on the bottom and Sherry on top. "Now watch, JJ. Finger or tongue," she says as she performs both of the actions.

"I got it now, Sherry. I gotta go. I'll send Dr. E. back to take my place."

"JJ come over here and show Bonnie that you like her before you go."

"Bonnie, I think that you're great. We'll talk later, bye."

Since both the women were naked, JJ assumed that they wouldn't follow him out to the carport. He was wrong. They came to the opened door and laughed, "What's the matter, JJ. Are you afraid of two little women?"

In his car and on his way to work, again he begins talking to himself. *What the hell do I do now? And where is this all leading to? I've got to find another job. I can't be around these two sex addicts. They are making me afraid of sex. That's not possible. I gotta get away from this somehow.*

As he walks in the door of the animal hospital, Dr. E. says, "Hi, I understand that the girls took care of you."

"Yes, they did. They're waiting for you. Bonnie said that she wants you to do her! Go ahead and go. I got this place."

"Yeah, I've done her several time. She's a little young, but she is good. But you'll find that out for yourself soon. I'm leaving."

*Thank God, alone at last. I don't think that I have to worry about these cats and dogs. The worst that can happened is one of them bites me! I hope that we have a normal night. And if Sherry comes over, I'm leaving. I'm only sixteen, and I can't keep up with those sex nuts! How does Doc get his work done? All he thinks about is sex and their weekend away. Well, I need a weekend away from them. Boy, Julie really looks great to me now! She would like to have sex, but she won't, so I get a rest. I'll talk to Jimmy shortly and tell him the answer. I'm sure that we will see Tommy over the weekend and he'll have the test results on Kathy. I don't think that she is pregnant, and if she isn't, I hope that this scares the hell out of them.* Sex*—I never thought that I would say this, but, "Leave me alone." I have plenty of time in my life for sex. Julie is right—we can wait! At least for most of it! You know, it really is different when you love someone. Those two women and Margie have no appeal to me, but I sure would like to do Julie! There I go again, nothing but sex on my mind. I'm going to call Jimmy and feed the animals.*

Things have calmed down, and JJ is waiting for Dr. E. to return for evening hours. He hears a loud noise directly outside of animal hospital. He can tell that it came from the main road and that something bad has happened.

He looks outside and sees a five-car accident. Three of the cars were directly involved, and there are people injured. The other cars must have had some minor damage while trying to avoid the cars in front of them.

JJ grabbed some towels and ran to the scene. The paramedics were coming down the street. They ran to a woman who was lying in the street. She wasn't moving, and it looked very bad. JJ ran to the back car. It was a mess. The driver inside was in severe pain. There was blood all over the lower part of his right leg. JJ asked him if he was able to move. Did he think that his back was injured? The man, who appeared to be in his early thirties, begged JJ to pull him out of the car. JJ refused, stating, "Don't move! I'm going to ask if it's okay to move you." JJ ran to the paramedics and shouted his question. They didn't respond. They were having difficulties with the woman. She wasn't responding and appeared to be dead. He ran to their emergency kit and took a pair of scissors.

"I be over in a minute," stated the paramedic. "I don't think that we can do any good here!"

JJ ran back to the car and told the driver to sit still, that the paramedic would be there soon, and that he wanted to cut the pant leg away so that they could see the wound. After he removed the pants, they could see the leg bone sticking through the skin. He had a compound fracture, and it was bleeding badly. This scared JJ badly, but he knew that if they didn't stop the bleeding, this guy wasn't going to make it. As he turned to call the paramedic. The paramedic opened the passenger-side door and crawled in to see what he had to deal with. He looked at JJ and stated, "We gotta get him out of the car and onto the ground. I'll push from this side and you try to let him down. Easy. Don't touch the leg. I'll handle that." This guy was athletic, and in good shape, but as they started to move him, the leg moved and he screamed in pain. He passed out. They quickly got him to the ground.

"Here, apply this towel to the wound with pressure until I can do something better. I'm glad that he passed out, 'cause he couldn't stand the pain." By now, the other paramedic had appeared and was injecting him with something. They attempted to straighten the leg to get it back in place. They couldn't do it. The muscle of the upper leg was so strong that they were afraid that they would do more damage, so they got these long, flat boards and placed them under and on both sides of the leg and wrapped it to make it stable. They wanted to transport him quickly because of the blood loss, and they could not tell if he had a head injury. They placed him in the ambulance and took off. The woman was dead. They placed a tarp over her, and the fire department crew was about to transport her. The driver of the third car had minor injuries, but he was so drunk that he couldn't stand upright. It appeared that he had caused the accident. According to a witness, the drunk had just stopped suddenly, for no reason. The woman couldn't stop and ran into the back of his car. Her head hit the windshield and killed her. The guy with the broken leg had the same problem. When she stopped, he didn't have enough time or space to stop, and he slammed into her back.

"This is a 45 mph speed limit road, but everyone travels it much faster. I don't know if we will ever know what actually happened, but we do know that it was caused by a drunk driver. One person is dead and the other seriously injured."

JJ had never seen a dead person before, and he was clearly shaken by it. When Mr. E. arrived he tried to help, most of the work had been done. He asked JJ if he wanted to take the night off. JJ didn't respond, so the Doc told him to go home. JJ refused. He said that he would rather work, stay busy, and keep his mind off what had just happened. So he and Dr. E. worked the entire shift.

During the shift, JJ tells Dr. E. about Jimmy's drinking problem and how that could have been him that caused that woman's death. "That guy was so drunk that he doesn't even know what happened, and now somebody's wife or daughter or mother is dead because of that stupid *drinking*." Dr. E. tried to help JJ deal with the issue, but he knew there was nothing that could be said. JJ was right.

"I glad that we had a light night. You can lock up now, JJ. Remember that I leaving in the morning to go to New York. I actually won't be back until late Monday afternoon. So, I won't be back here until Tuesday morning."

"And you don't work Tuesday. I won't see you again until Wednesday night. You have a good weekend, and don't forget about Bonnie."

"You do the same. I'll take care of things here." As JJ starts driving home again, his mind begins thinking about that dead lady in the street and Jimmy's drinking. Then it switches to Bonnie. *If I wasn't committed to Julie, I think I would fall into the same trap as Dr. E. and Sherry. I think Bonnie has a nice body. I don't think that it's as nice Julie's, but I don't know; I've never seen Julie without clothes, and I have seen Bonnie. Bonnie's tits are bigger, but I don't think that matters. I wonder if I could hook her up with Tommy or Jimmy. Then maybe she would leave me alone, and neither one of them are in a committed relationship. Hell, I bet if we find out that Kathy isn't pregnant, I could have them together this weekend. You know that guy, Paul, the one who did Margie. He might be better. He's older, and I won't get Kathy or anybody else mad at me. Geez, it seems like I spend all my time setting other people up for sex, and my girl is not interested. What a crazy life!*

# Chapter 27

JJ IS TRYING TO GET his life back on track with some normal relationships, but right now everything he does seems to be getting him involved with strange events that involve strange sex. He hasn't seen Joe in over a year. Joe's father got an offer to go to Africa with the parent company that his subcontractor works for, and he would get paid $45,000 for one year, plus all travel expenses, and he could take his family. This was a lot of money to him, and he would be doing the same kind of work. It seemed that his father was an expert at drilling water wells in difficult places. The US government was going to African villages and digging wells and purifying systems to help the people have clean water and be able to irrigate their farm land areas.

Joe had been gone for a year and came back in time for the baseball banquet. He looked different. He had gained a little weight. Had a slight beard and was a little taller. Joe had not seen his girlfriend, Debbie, for over a year, and he asked JJ if they could double date with him and Julie and go to a drive-in movie. They planned on meeting Justin and Connie, who were double-dating with Tommy and Kathy. It was a Saturday night, and the weather was good. Nobody knew what movie was playing because this was a drive-in theater, and no one watched the movie. This was make-out time for everyone.

"Tommy, are you and Kathy still on for tonight?"

"Yeah, JJ, we'll meet you there. I don't know what time, 'cause I'm riding with Justin and Connie, and Connie is never ready on time, but we'll be there. Oh, by the way, good news—she's not pregnant. I dodged that bullet!"

"Thank God. Now keep your pecker in your pants."

"No way, man. I got more good news. Kathy told her mother that she thought she was pregnant. She thought her mother would be mad, but instead, her mother told her about these pills that women can take that prevent them from getting pregnant, so they went to the doctors together, and they put her on these pills. It's like getting a green light to heaven, and with her mother's blessing. Her mother said that she knew that she wasn't going to stop having sex, so she would rather that she took the pill. Her mother said that she didn't want any little babies around just yet. Her mother also told her that if I wanted to move in with them, I could, as long as I paid half of the expenses. I make plenty of money, so I think that I'm going to do it."

"Man, you sure have had a lot happen in ten days! You know, I have some friends who lived together for three years before they got married, and it worked for them. It gave them a chance to make sure that they could live together."

"Hey, they must have known about the pill."

"Yeah, I'm sure they did, and a lot more. You know that Joe and Debbie are coming with us, so we all should have a good time together."

"Yeah, I haven't seen Joe since before he left to go to Africa. I'll bet that he will have some stories to tell. What do you know about Debbie?"

"Not much, we met her twice before he left. She seems nice. She lives in Parkside West, which is a step above Beachwood but can't compare to Wellington. I don't know how he met her. She's in a totally different school district."

"What does she look like?"

"She's okay, she looks a little like your sister, Connie, except she is two years older."

"She built like Connie?"

"Yeah, they are about the same size."

"Sounds like Joe got himself a nice girl?"

"Yeah, I think so. This is the first time that we've gone out together. But you know. Julie and I get along well with everybody. So I think that it'll be okay."

"What if they start doing it in your back seat?"

"God, Tommy, only you would think of something like that."

"I don't know if he has known her that long, and they wouldn't do that with me and Julie in the front seat."

"Why not? You're not supposed to be watching what they are doing."

"Tommy, remind me never to double-date with you and Kathy! And you better not do that with Justin and your sister in the front seat."

"Oh, we can wait until we get home. With this new arrangement we have a nice soft bed if we want it."

"You need to keep that information to yourself. Your sister is a little young to be learning about the pill, and Justin is treating her with great respect. They make a very nice couple."

"Oh, I'm not going to say anything to them, but I am going to suggest to my mother that she tell her."

"Tommy, your mother may not know about the pill. It's fairly new on the market. I don't know if they have perfected it yet. I've heard that some women can't take them, and that they are not sure if it works 100 percent of the time. You may be teaching your mother something new."

"That's okay. I know that they don't want any more kids, so maybe Mom will start taking them. I know they need something. I hear them going at it all the time. Their bedroom is next to mine, and Mom really enjoys her sex."

"Tommy, you're terrible."

"What? There's nothing wrong with Mom liking it."

"No, but I don't think that she would like knowing that you are telling everybody."

"I'm not, I just told you. And I don't think that you are going to have sex with my mother."

"Shut up, Tommy. Of course I'm not going to have sex with your mother, but now every time I look at her, I'm going to have a hard time not thinking about what you just told me. Your mother is a hot momma, and she should enjoy her sex life, but she doesn't need a nosey son tell everyone her business."

"Okay, I won't tell anyone! Can I tell you about me and Kathy?"

"You already do."

"No, I just told you that we do it. I want to tell you the details. You might have some new ideas."

"Me? How the hell would I have any new ideas? I don't even do it. I'm learning things from you."

"Good. Then the details will help you in the future."

"You're hopeless. I'll see you tonight."

"I think that I'll call Joe. After that conversation, hopefully I will have a more productive conversation. Joe and I haven't talked in a long time. I am interested in hearing about his year in Africa."

"Hi, Joe. JJ here, how are you doing?"

"Hi, I can't wait to see you and Julie tonight. What time are you picking us up?"

"That's what I was calling about. Is Debbie going to be at your house, or do we have to pick her up?"

"We have to pick her up. Do you know where Parkside is?"

"Yes, but I'll need you to direct me to her house."

"I can do that. What time?"

"I think around seven thirty for you, and then whatever time it takes to get to her. It starts to get dark right around that time, so by the time we get to the drive-in, they will have played all their Previews, and the show will be starting."

"I was told that they are going to show the highlights of the 1958 NFL Championship Game, where the Colts beat the Giants with Ameache's great run over the goal line. I think they are going to do it at intermission. What a great team. Johnny Unitas has got to be the greatest quarterback ever."

"Yeah, I remember watching that. It was great. But you'll miss all that stuff when you're in Africa. Most of the places we were didn't have electricity. My father had a device that worked off the battery of the car, or he could crack it several times and we could use it like a phone or a two-way radio. When we were in the big cities it was the same as here, but we didn't stay in the city. His job was to go out into the outlands and dig these wells. The Army Corps of Engineers were building the generator plants and the purification systems. You wouldn't believe how these people live."

"I really want to hear about it, but I want you to tell me while Julie is there so she can hear too."

"You don't want me to tell you while the movie is playing?"

"No, it doesn't have to be tonight. I'm sure that you and Debbie want to talk and share time together."

"Yes, we do. We've been on the phone a lot, but that's not the same as being together, so it will be nice seeing her. My dad made a lot of money working there, and he's going to buy a new car. He told me that I can have his old car. It's only five years old and it's in good shape. My uncle used it for the year that we were away, and he took good care of it. So when he gets paid his bonus check, I think that he's going to buy a new Chevy, and I'll get the old one."

"That's great, Joe. Do you know what you are going to do next?"

"No, I would have graduated this year with you, but they are making me take some kind of test to make sure that I kept up with my lessons while I was away. Which I did, but it wasn't easy with those living conditions. If I pass the test, they will allow me to graduate with you guys."

"That would be great. Are you planning on going to college?"

"I don't think so. I think I'm going to go to trade school. While I was in Africa, the army guys taught me how to operate heavy equipment, bulldozer and front-end loaders. There is a big demand for that, and it pays big money. I think that's what I'm going to do."

"That sounds like a good plan. Do you think that you will marry Debbie?"

"I don't know. We haven't been going together long enough to know if we are meant for each other. Right now it certainly seems possible. We seem to like a lot of the same things. She has a nice personality, and we seem to get along well. Her dad owns an electric company, and he's talked to me about coming to work for him. I just don't know yet."

"Seems like you have several options."

"Yeah, I do, and I've got time to think it through. But I know that I'm not going to try college. That's too difficult. With my grades, I think that I would really struggle."

"Okay, I'll see you at seven thirty. I have to call Julie next, so I'll see you later."

"Okay, seven thirty."

*Geez, I finally had an intelligent conversation with someone. I was beginning to think that wasn't possible. Sure sounds like he has thought things through. I don't remember him being that intelligent or mature. That time with those army guys really helped him. And did you notice, not one word about sex with Debbie! He really likes her, but I think he wants the same feelings that Julie and I have for each other, and apparently that's hard to find.*

"Hi, Julie. Are you ready for tonight?"

"No, not really. It's way too early. Besides, you know that I have two classes to teach this afternoon."

"I forgot about your classes. You should be there by now."

"Yes, I'm waiting for my mother. She's running a little late."

"Do you want me to come get you?"

"No, she should be here in a few minutes, so I'll wait."

"Are you okay with this double-date thing?"

"Yeah, we talked about it. I don't know Debbie, but she's not my date. You are."

"I just had a great conversation with Joe. He really has matured by being over there in Africa. Being around those Army guys has helped him. Wait until you here some of the stuff that he told me. He really has thought about these things and has some good options."

"I'm sure that we will hear some of it tonight."

"I'll pick you up around seven. What are you going to wear?"

"You're not interested in what I'm going to wear. You're interested in what I'm not going to wear. But we are going to have other people with us, so I plan to wear my bra. You'll simply have to behave yourself for one night."

"We'll have to test my skills at unsnapping your bra without anyone knowing."

"No we won't. You keep your skills to yourself, or I'll put safety pins on the bra and your skills will be defeated."

"You have an evil mind, woman! I love you. See you at seven."

# Chapter 28

JJ IS NOW ENTERING HIS last year of high school, and his teachers this year are some of the same ones that he had when he came to Beachwood High in the tenth grade. He had Mr. Smith for US history debate class. He still belongs to the Boy's Glee Club and has Miss Monroe, in addition to Mr. Carr for physics, Mrs. Dempsey for chemistry, Mrs. Brownski for English ligature, and Miss Bonn for algebra. This is going to be a great final year.

Miss Monroe has started early, planning some appearances for the boys at the Rotary and Kiwanis Clubs. The mix Glee Club will do many of the songs from previous years, with a few new additions. Instead of the patriotic songs, the boys are going to sing four of the song representing the armed forces: army, navy, air force, and marines. The boys will be dressed in uniforms, and the members in the audience will be asked to stand when their service song is sung. The girls will present them with a small gift and a card of appreciation signed by the entire Glee Club. Miss Monroe always creates a great show.

Mrs. Brownski is also a unique English teacher. Her goal was to prepare you for life by teaching you how to express yourself in writing, only she added a touch of common sense. We had to write ads for things to sell in the newspaper, sport stories about our school teams, make-believe letters from wives to their husbands serving in the war, and vice versa for the guys writing back home to their families. And, yes, we learned how to do resumes for job applications. Yes, we read Shakespeare and parts of *Gone with the Wind*. But the fun of this class was the open discussions about what to expect when you left school and entered the real world—many discussions about college and what to expect.

There were stark differences between the boys, who expected to flunk out, and the girls, who felt that being a mother was important but that having a career was equally important. Many of them expected to become doctors or lawyers, while the boys were just hoping to make it through the first year. The discussions were amazing, to hear the dreams and goals of young people just starting their lives. Mrs. Brownski had a way of making everything exciting and possible. She inspires everyone.

Then there was Miss Dempsey. How do you make chemistry interesting?

JJ thought that he was going to hate this class until he learned how to preserve wood by using certain chemicals. He learned how to kill bugs and mosquitoes and how to treat your garden to make things grow. All those boring test tubes and microscopes were suddenly related to things that he enjoyed in life. Miss Dempsey also demonstrated that subjects that you give very little thought to often have a major impact on your life.

Every student began asking questions. What was done to create that? What chemicals fixed that problem? What did the chemical do that created the result? Every day, someone came to class with a new question. Some we had the answers to, while others we had to explore. She made our minds work, and our thought process became better. This improvement in our thought process helped us in all our classes. JJ didn't know how she did it, but he looked forward to that class.

It was the last class of the day, and no one wanted to leave for the day without talking to Miss Dempsey about something. She made chemistry class a magic show, and everyone enjoyed it. Then there was physics class with Mr. Carr. This was an elective class, so it had nineteen boys and one girl. This class was right after lunchtime. JJ was like a snake; after he ate his lunch, he wanted to take a nap. He was always falling asleep in class, and Mr. Carr was not happy about waking him up. This was the class that JJ grew to hate. He managed to pass with C, but no one knows how. The one girl won some kind of special scholarship to Germany to continue her education in physics. One of the boys was appointed to the Naval Academy based on his near-perfect scores on the physics questions on the SATs. JJ was glad to get his C grade and move on.

And last on this list for this year was Miss Bonn, who taught algebra. She was fresh out of college, and she was not prepared for the boys in high school. To begin with, she was absolutely beautiful—5' 6" and about 125 lbs., with blond hair and blue eyes. She had to be 38-23-36. She had a very nice personality and was intelligent. She was twenty-three years old and should have been a fashion model. The older boys (eighteen and nineteen) didn't care what she was teaching. They were only interested in one thing, her body. They were constantly making crude sexual remakes to her, and she was constantly throwing them out of class and taking them to the principal's office. Nothing worked. They expelled two different guys during the year, but it still didn't stop.

She liked JJ and he liked her and treated her with respect. They became respectful friends. JJ struggled with Algebra in the beginning. She asks him if he would like some private instruction at her house. With all the sexual stuff that was going on in life, he wasn't certain she wasn't making advances on him, but he needed the help or he was going to fail this class and he needed it to be accepted into the University Of Maryland. So she made a deal with him. She needed to drop off her car at the auto repair shop, so she wanted him to meet her there and then bring her to work. He would take her back after school, and they would go to her house for the lesson. This seemed like a good deal for him since he could not afford to pay her, and she needed some way to get the repair work done on her car and get to work. They made the deal. The next morning, he picked her up at the auto place. She gets in the car with a short skirt and a tight sweater. *This woman is beautiful.* She notices that JJ is looking at her rather strongly.

"Something wrong JJ?"

"No, Mama, but do you mind if I speak freely?"

"No, I don't mind, as long as you keep it clean and respectful."

"Oh yes, Mama. I've never been disrespectful to you. You do realize that you are beautiful and you have a beautiful body!"

"I've been told that."

"All the guys that you've had trouble with at school have made those comments to you. Do you think that it could be that short skirt and that sweater top that's causing that problem?"

"JJ, the girls at school tell me that you have a girlfriend that you have been going with for a long time. And she is beautiful and fully developed. Is that true?"

"Yes, Mama."

"Well, when she wears a short skirt and a nice sweater, does that give the other guys the right to say smart, dirty, crude things to her?"

"No, Mama. They know that I would punch them out if they did that."

"Why is it okay for them to say them to me?"

"Well, you're not seventeen years old. You're twenty-five. If you dress like that, you should expect that kind of talk."

"You're right, and I do expect guys to say things, but when I respond and tell them that I'm not interested, that should be the end of the conversation."

"Yeah, but it hasn't been the end of the conversation. They keep coming after you. And you keep dressing that way. Doesn't that make you part of the problem?"

"Yes and no. I could let them force me to dress like an old maid—that would reduce some of the talk—or I can retain my independence, be myself, and object to their rude behavior. You've noticed me, and you like what you see, but you've never been disrespectful."

"No, I haven't, but that doesn't mean that I haven't had the same thoughts."

"Exactly, you have had those thoughts, but you were respectful enough to keep your comments and thoughts to yourself. And so should they. Just because I'm an attractive young woman doesn't mean that they can treat me like a piece of meat. If I'm proud of my body and I want to show it off, I should be able to do that."

"Yes, I agree, but it hasn't worked well for you."

"No, it hasn't, but I don't think that I'm going to allow them to defeat me."

"Okay, we're here. Can we finish this conversation on the way home tonight? These guys are seeing you in my car, and we will hear things soon about you and me going together."

"That's okay, but you should tell your girlfriend first, before she hears it from someone else. I'll meet you here after school lets out."

"Okay, see you then."

The school day went by quickly, and JJ was waiting in the car for Miss Bonn. When she got into the car she was not wearing the sweater. Instead, she had a loose-fitting button-down-the-front blouse. Of course she had it unbuttoned well below her cleavage line. She wasn't wearing a bra, and most of her breasts were exposed. JJ thought, *Oh my gosh, I was right. She is going to make a play for me.*

"Well, I see you changed your top!"

"Yes. I spilled coffee on it during last period, so I went to the teacher's lounge and changed. Yes, I took the bra off too. It's the end of the day and I'm going home."

"Yeah, but you have to stop at the auto shop and pick up your car. You going to give the guys there a free show?"

"Yeah, if it will lower the cost of the repair bill, he can look all he wants. Women do those kinds of things. Guys are really stupid sometimes. I guess he thinks that if he lowers my bill. I'm going to jump in bed with him."

"Are you?"

"JJ, women control that kind of thing. If I want a man, it is very easy to get one."

"Frankly, Miss Bonn, that blouse with no bra makes it look like you are trying to get a man."

"I might be, but it's not the auto repair guy. Come on, can we go?"

"We are going. I can't just pull out into the traffic. I'm not a woman driver!"

"Very funny. I've been driving since I was fifteen and I've never had an accident. Not all women are bad drivers."

"What was wrong with your car?"

"I don't know it kept stalling out on me whenever I would stop at a light or a stop sign. It would start back up, but it wouldn't keep running unless I held my foot on the gas."

"That should be an easy fix. Unbutton another button and he won't charge you anything."

"I've already done that with him. Whenever I'm short on money, he offers to come over to my house and take it out in trade. He's not a bad looking guy, and I've been tempted a few times to accept his offer, but I never have."

"Wow, maybe I'll open up an auto repair shop. Sounds like a good business?"

"Yeah, but I know the guy's wife, and I know that she takes good care of him. She's pretty hot. They have two kids already, and they've only been married four years. So I think that he's pretty active in bed."

"How did we get into this conversation?"

"You've been looking at my breasts and thinking about sex! You're trying to be Mr. Cool and stay somewhat respectful. I appreciate that."

"Well, you certainly are different from what I expected. You send mixed messages. You come across as Miss Prude, but you dress like you're ready to go out on the street looking for something. And you certainly have been talking open and freely to me. Do you have a boyfriend?"

"Yes, he lives in York, Pennsylvania, and I think that we are going to get married soon."

"What do you mean? You think?"

"He asked me, and I said yes. But I'm not totally certain that I'm ready for that."

"One-man-forever deal. But I think that we are going to do it this summer."

"You mean that you like multiple men?"

"Not exactly, but I do like other men—sometimes."

"Have you ever heard of swingers?"

"JJ, I'm twenty-three years old, I've been to college, and even you can't take your eyes off my breasts. Do you really think that I've only had one man? At college on the weekends, we'd go over to one of the girls' house and start drinking. The guys all knew that we were going to be there, and they would come over by the carloads. Sometimes we'd be out back at the pool totally naked. We would party all night. I'd have sex multiple times in one night. I'd wake up the next morning with some guy sleeping with me, and we'd start over. I don't know how I got through college without getting pregnant or contracting VD."

"How in the hell did you become such a pain in the ass as a teacher? Nobody is supposed to look cross eyed at you or say anything sexual."

"I had to put up a wall at work. I didn't want to teach high school math, but it was the only job available. I wanted to teach elementary school. Even the woman who hired me told me that it was going to be difficult because some of these guys were only going to be a few years younger than me. She actually said, 'Honey, with a body like that, you're going to need body armor,' and she was right. I had to stop it early on, but as you can see, I haven't been too successful. So I said, to hell with it, I'm going to do my own thing. I'll get through this year and I'll go teach somewhere else next year."

"They must do that at all college dorms. These friends of mine did the exact same thing that you just described. They did it for three years. They got married and they still do it. That's where I learned about swingers."

"Oh, yeah, you might have to introduce me to your friends. I thought about talking to my future husband and see if he would like swinging. I know that I would. But some people can't handle it. I don't know why. It's only sex. After it's over, you still have each other to share the other things in life."

"I don't know if I can handle it. I'm almost certain that my girlfriend, Julie, couldn't handle it. She doesn't even want to have sex now—with just me. She's afraid she will get pregnant."

"I don't blame her for that, but there are all kinds of ways to play safe. Ha, listen to me, I never played it safe. I did everything, and I did it often. As I said, I don't know how I finished school."

"Now these friends of mine want me to do it with their eighteen-year-old babysitter, who is the daughter of a couple that they swing with. They have taught the daughter to take part, and she has, and she likes it. I'm supposed to hook up with her while they are away in New York. They told me that I can use their house."

"Really? Do you know if she likes girls? Maybe I'll join you."

"Oh, yeah, the wife introduced me to her. They started making love and they wanted me to join them, but I left."

"Why, don't you think that you would like it?"

"I don't know, I don't know anything about these things. I was shocked when I found out that my friends were swingers. My head is still spinning from all of this shit. I got all these people wanting to have sex with me, and I've got a girlfriend who doesn't want to have sex. It's crazy."

"Yeah, life is crazy. Let me know if you decide to go over there."

"Oh, I don't think that I'm going anywhere near there this weekend."

"I think that you will. Swingers aren't crazy. They've just found another way to live life that they enjoy. And you should make life enjoyable."

"Here we are. Are you going in to get the car, or do you want me to do it for you?"

"I'm going in. I don't think that he's interested in your tits! I'll see you at my house. You know how to get there?"

"Yes, Mama, I know the way."

JJ leaves and again he begins talking to himself, *I certainly didn't expect that conversation. Now I know another person who likes swinging. Maybe I should go over and do Bonnie. I might be able to take her with me, and I can just watch the two of them go at it. That way I don't get involved. This sure is complicated, but I'm enjoying it. So the teacher uses her tits to get her discounts—that's funny—but it does show how stupid we are as men and how they control us. I hope that I remember all this, but I would do the same thing. If I fixed her car and she stuck those tits in my face, I'd surely give her a discount. Here we are. I'll just pull over to the curb. After she pulls into the driveway, I'll pull in behind her. Here she comes. That didn't take long.*

"Hi, that didn't take long. He must have caved as soon as you unbuttoned the next button."

"That's funny, but he wasn't there. The guy who handles the bill could hardly concentrate on what he was doing. He was so busy looking down my blouse that I leaned over the desk and gave him a full view. He smiled and handed me my bill. Let's go in. Now listen to me. I know that my tits are distracting you, but we have to get your grades up. I could just pass you through class, but that wouldn't prepare you for college. So let's get it straight: you're here to learn Algebra. You already know about sex. Every time you pass a test with at least an 80, I'll let you choose what you want. But no slacking—you must get an honest 80. Here, sit at my desk. Here's a work booklet. This is like a teacher's guide to each lesson. This is called teaching to the test. It's not totally honest, but if you learn what's needed on the test and it sticks with you, it will prepare you for college life. Here's a pencil and paper and some light on the subject. You get started and I'll be back in a few minute. I'm going to fix us some hot tea."

JJ digs into the work. The teacher guide does help him to better understand the problems, and he is doing well when she returns. She has removed her skirt and shoes and is down to her panties and a loose-fitting bra-less blouse. Now how is he supposed to concentrate? She comes over to the desk and stands directly next to him.

"I know what you want, but we have a deal. You need to complete this first quiz. I really want you to learn this stuff. It's not that hard."

"It may not be, but I am," he says as he reaches up her backside and pulls down her panties.

She pulls them back up. "We have a deal. Now finish the lesson. We can take care of your hardness later. She walks away from him because she knows they will stop for a sex break if she stays there. She goes to her bathroom and takes off the blouse and puts on a bath robe. She comes back about a half-hour later. She can see that his hardness had faded away and his pants are back where they should be."

"Are you ready to take the first test?"

"Yeah, I think so. I have a few questions. Do you want them now or after the test."

"This is our first attempt, so let's do the test first, and maybe the results will answer some of the questions."

"Sounds good."

"Okay, here are the quiz questions. You have twenty minutes to answer them. Start now."

JJ begins the quiz and he is having difficulty. He completes the test and gives it to her. She grades it, and he only scored 65.

"Well, you didn't make it this time, so maybe we need to go over the questions and try again."

They spend some time reviewing his questions and going over his wrong answers. When they are finished, she asks him, "I can give you a retest now, or we can do it before your next lesson tomorrow. What do you want to do?"

"If I take the retest now and I score an 80, do I get my reward?"

"Yes. I'll try again."

"All right, you've got twenty minutes. Get started." She goes back to the bathroom and removes her panties. She knows what he is going to ask for if he passes.

She comes back and grades the test—75. "Sorry, JJ. I guess you'll have to come back tomorrow and try again. Here's another lesson. Take it home with you. Can you come back at noon tomorrow?"

"Yeah, but don't I get anything for today's effort?"

"We had a deal. You need to get 80 in order to get a treat. A deal is a deal."

JJ is absolutely dejected, and it shows.

"Tell you what. I'll give you a preview. Maybe that will make you study harder." She steps back and opens the robe. What a beautiful body. This woman could compete with any movie star or Miss America.

"Well?"

"Well what?"

"What do you think? Were all those boys right about me?"

"Oh, yes, but this is torture. How do you expect me to sit here looking at that and not want it."

"I don't. I know that you want it, but we made a deal, and I want to see you get into college. You will see plenty of bodies like this when you get there."

"I don't think so. There aren't many bodies like that around. How about if I come back later tonight and I score an 80."

"When you score an 80, you get your treat."

"I feel like you are training a puppy dog! Let me asks you something else? Were you serious about meeting Bonnie and the two of you letting me watch?"

"Training men is like training a puppy dog. And yeah—if you think Bonnie would like to do it."

"Bonnie will do whatever I ask of her. She has been given instruction to do whatever I want."

"Why would you give me away to someone else?"

"I'm not certain that I fit in to this swingers thing, and you clearly do, so I'm working all the angles. If you and Bonnie connect and my friends come back from New York, I assure you that they will want you to join them. In fact, I think that she will like you as much as he will. I know that you will be able to do a threesome, and I can keep my way of life with Julie."

"Really, maybe you should call Bonnie now? Julie is foolish. She should be getting as much of you as possible. I know that you can get it hard, and from the looks of that wet spot on the front of your pants, I know that it works."

"You want to go over there now?"

"Yes."

"I'm not sure that the others have left yet."

"We'll find out."

"Hi, Bonnie, you are there. That means that they have left?"

"Yes, they left about an hour ago. Why?"

"I want to come over, and I want to bring a friend."

"Oh, does he have a big one?"

"He's a she, and you'll love her."

"You're bringing your girlfriend? I thought that she didn't do sex?"

"No, this is somebody else, and she is beautiful—twenty-three years old with a great body."

"Do you think that I can handle her?"

"If you can handle Sherry, I think that you can handle anything. We'll be there in thirty minutes."

# Chapter 29

It's nearing the 1960 Presidential Elections. It's Nixon vs. Kennedy, and Mr. Smith has his debate class gearing up for the high school mock election. This will be an interesting debate, since the area is five to one Dems to Reps, but the area has a strong anti-Catholic sentiment. Mr. Smith knows who he wants to be the debaters for each side, but he doesn't want to pick them. He wants the class to pick sides, and pick their leaders. The school is allowing all students to vote. They feel certain that the students will reflect the views of their parents. While Eisenhower is still popular, his VP Richard Nixon is not well liked. John Kennedy is a young man, a US Senator from Massachusetts and a Catholic. People of other religions believe that if you elect a Catholic president, the pope will direct our policies. Others believe that Nixon is too conservative and has very poor understanding of the needs of the country. He is a Mormon by faith, and most people don't know much about the Mormon religion. They just know that they do not want a Catholic president.

JJ assumed that because Kennedy was a Democrat, his parents would be for Kennedy. And Charles, who was the smartest guy in the class, would be for the Republican, Nixon. Charles was attempting to win a scholarship into college that would allow him to enter the US Foreign Service. Apparently his father worked for the State Department, and Charles could already speak French. He wanted to go to Russia and work at our embassy.

Mr. Smith thought that he would start a classroom conversation. He split the class in half, with Charles on one side and JJ on the other. He told the class that they were each to go home and prepare talking points for the candidate of their choice. At the next class, they were going to present their positions, and they would be allowed to join the side that represented their person. When Mr. Smith made his announcement, Charles spoke up. "I already know who I am supporting. I backing Kennedy." This caught Mr. Smith off guard. Some others spoke up and took sides. JJ and many others said nothing. They were content to wait until the next class and introduce their talking points.

JJ had been following the newspaper and TV reporting, but he had not decided who he was going to support. He was disappointed that he would not be able to vote in the real election because he would not be eighteen until December and the election was held in November. Charles was already eighteen, and everyone knew who he planned to vote for. Many of the classmates had already turned eighteen, and this would be their first time to vote. They were excited about the debate because they wanted to know more about the candidates.

That night JJ was watching TV when the news came on. They showed Kennedy speaking on the floor of the US Senate. JJ's mother stood next to the TV and began shouting at it. "Yeah, you Mick son of a bitch. The pope probably told you to say that." JJ was shocked. To begin with, his mother knew nothing about national politics, and she had never shown an interest in it. She never went to church, and while she claimed to be Lutheran, she had never spoken about the Catholic Church, and he wondered what she knew about it, if anything. She apparently knew that the pope runs the church. Mr. Kapok wasn't home, but JJ thought that he would ask his mother who they were supporting.

"Mom, I never heard you yell political comments to the TV. Who are you expecting to answer you?"

"Ah, he makes me so mad. He's a spoiled little rich boy from up north. He even speaks funny. You can't understand some of his words. His father got rich smuggling illegal booze into this country while claiming to be such a good Catholic who doesn't believe in drinking."

"But, Mom, you and dad are Democrats. You mean that you're not voting for him because of his father's money and because he's Catholic."

"No, I'm not voting for him. I've never voted for a Republican before, but I am this time."

"But you said that the Republican were for the rich?"

"Yeah, well look at who's rich now. They have so much money that they couldn't spend it in their life time. Your father can tell you more about him than I can."

"Some of his shipmates went to work for them, and while their business is legal now, they got in trouble for not having the tax labels on their bottles. They locked up the drivers. The old man is so rich and so corrupt that he bought off the judges and got them off scot free. Your dad will tell you more."

JJ knew that there was no purpose in discussing this anymore with her. She was clearly just repeating things either that she had heard his father say or some other type of gossip. But the things that she said were good talking points for school class. The newspaper had some comments about Nixon that were negative, basically saying that he was a "do-nothing" vice president and that Eisenhower didn't give him anything important to do. And while that was correct, the fact is none of the previous presidents had given their VPs any real responsibilities. But that was another talking point.

The nation's economy was in bad condition. US Steel was losing money. The cost of our steel was much higher than other countries, and US Steel was one our major employers. The labor unions were going on strikes, the auto industry was struggling, and the Eisenhower administration, and the Republicans did not seem to have any solutions. While many voters believed that Kennedy was too young to be elected, the country seemed ready for a change.

The next day in Debate Class, Charles told the class that Kennedy was rich and therefore could not be bought off by people making big contributions to his campaign. That he was a US Senator with a great education and a lot of business knowledge. He was considered a moderate to conservative Democrat. He did not mention that Kennedy was Catholic. Mr. Smith told him that those were all good, valid statements.

Everyone was expecting JJ to speak next, but JJ wasn't certain who he was supporting. So Howard, who was clearly for Nixon, spoke up. "Mr. Nixon has been vice present to President Eisenhower for eight years. As VP, he presides over the Senate and only votes in cases where there is a tie vote on an issue. He has held both national and state office. As VP, he has knowledge of all the issues and was presented by Congress and by the president. He has been involved in all new proposals made by the president and has represented the president at many Foreign Policy meetings, including a recent trip to Russia." Again, Mr. Smith stated that those were all good valid points.

"Now, who can tell me what negative thing will be said in the campaign?"

Charles spoke up. "VP Nixon has failed or flopped on several of his foreign policy trips; in fact, his trip to Russia was considered a disaster by many, and many feel that he has not been well informed on many issues before the Senate."

"Howard defends some of those claims by saying they are only opinions, not facts, and that no one has pointed out a specific issue that is was ill-informed. Senator Kennedy has one of the worse attendance records of all the US Senators. He has missed as many votes as he has made. In fact, he has missed votes that benefitted his own state."

"Anything else, ask Mr. Smith?"

JJ stands up. "I noticed that Charles has avoided one of the most volatile issues of this campaign. Senator Kennedy is a practicing Roman Catholic. And most of the remaining religions believe that the pope would have too much influence on US policy."

Charles jumps to his feet. "Religion has never been a factor in a presidential election!"

JJ answers, "To my knowledge, we have never elected a Catholic president, and it is a factor in this election, no matter what you say or whether you attempt to hide it. My parents have never voted for a Republican president in their lives, and they will not vote for

Kennedy. You also made a point about the Senator's wealth. Many believe that his wealth comes from illegal money from the import and sale of booze—I believe Scotch."

"Okay, class, we have two for Nixon and one for Kennedy. Are there other comments?"

"Wait, Mr. Smith. I didn't say that I was for Nixon."

"You just gave reasons why you shouldn't vote for Kennedy."

"Well can't I be like a lawyer and defend my client regardless of how I feel about him?"

"You can do that in a debate, but you can do that when you go to vote. Okay, class, those of you who are for Kennedy stand over here with Charles. Fifteen students, move over to Charles. Okay, that means that the balance of you are with Nixon, so move over here with Howard and JJ. Fourteen students moved. The class is evenly divided, exactly sixteen on each side. That is difficult to believe. But now you must pick your leaders. Everyone in Charles's group voted for him. In the other group, four voted for Howard and eleven for JJ."

JJ says, "Mr. Smith, this doesn't seem fair. Howard is clearly a Nixon supporter, and I'm like the lawyer. I'm kind of neutral."

"JJ, your classmates elected you. That's no reflection on Howard. They simply think that you are a better debater. The fact that you don't support Nixon is not important. Can you go before the student body and make your case for Nixon? Use Howard as your cocaptain. Maybe you can switch on the issues that you feel strong about, and Howard does the same for his issues. Charles can pick a cocaptain and do the same thing. You each will have ten minutes to make opening statements. We will have a panel of teachers asking you questions giving to them by the students. The person asking the question has two minutes to answer. The opponent has one minute to rebut. The panel may extend time to each of you if they feel that the question merits further explanation. This will last for forty minutes. Then you each will have seven minutes to make closing statements, and we will end the debate and have the voting by closed paper ballots. The panel will tally the votes.

"There will be more than six hundred students in the auditorium. The balance will be in their classrooms, and their teachers will collect and count their ballots. The principal will announce the results over the PA system. Class, this is a big deal. We will be the first high school to hold an election. The newspapers will be there, and we think that two of the local TV stations will cover the debate. Okay, we have two more classes before the debate. We will devote that time to your preparation. Each team should try to think of the kind of questions that will be asked; you need to throw those questions at your captains without them knowing what you are going to ask. Captains, you need to prepare your statements. Okay, see you all tomorrow."

This really was a big deal. The teams put up campaign signs in the hallways, lockers, and outside doors, and the entire school was buzzing about the debates. Both Charles and JJ were nervous about their roles. Howard was scared to death, as was Charles's cocaptain.

JJ has decided to have Howard do the opening statement while he does the closing. Charles and his cocaptain have decided that Charles will do both.

It was estimated that 1300 votes would be cast, maybe more.

The big day has arrived and the auditorium is filling up. They were testing the PA system and making sure that everything was working. The TV stations were there and setting up their equipment. The radio station had their microphones set up and ready.

Mr. Smith announces the panel and explains the rules of the debate. Charles and Howard take their positions, and the debate starts. This was as real as it gets. Everyone has done their preparations, and both young men have delivered a great opening statement.

JJ and Howard changed places, and the questions began. The teachers were very good at allowing the debaters to respond. They had some follow-up questions, and you would have thought that the real candidates were answering these questions. The teachers had attempted to group the questions by subject matter, but they were coming in so quickly that they had to skip around some. The quality of the questions was exceptional. The students were really prepared. The panel had to stop for a few minutes to get their thoughts together. The forty minutes just flew by. When the questions ended, the students called out, "More, more, more," but they were out of time, and Charles and JJ had to give their closing remarks. The roles should have been reversed. JJ looked like John Kennedy, and Charles looked like Richard Nixon, but as you know, it was exactly the opposite. The debaters did a great job. The students and the teachers stood and applauded, no one wanted to leave, except the two debaters, who were exhausted and glad that it was over.

Mr. Smith dismissed the students. They all wanted to come to the stage and congratulate the teams, but they couldn't. Classes had to continue. Everyone was anxious to hear the results of the election. Finally, it was lunchtime, and the principal came on the PA.

"I have the results of the Election: 621 votes for Kennedy, 702 votes for Nixon." Everyone was stunned. This area was so heavily Democrat that everyone believed that it would be a landslide for Kennedy.

The headlines on the newspaper read, "Nixon Defeats Kennedy at Glen Brook High."

# Chapter 30

Mr. Smith has arranged a bus trip to Washington, D.C., to watch President Kennedy take his oath of office. The entire debate class is invited, along with a few of the teachers from the school.

It's a cold day in January, but no one seems to notice. The excitement level is very high. Even the teachers are showing excitement and clearly indicating that they voted for Kennedy. He is a good-looking man with a beautiful wife, and he projects the image of a president. The news media refers to him as the "Camelot President," and he and his wife sure do look the part.

While JJ represented Nixon in the school debate, he really likes Kennedy. He can't believe that a man so young can be so smart. He thinks that Kennedy's vision for the future is inspiring. Kennedy's desire to get young people involved in government has everyone wondering what he is going to propose and whether Congress will approve it. After all, this was the closest election ever. He certainly wasn't given an overwhelming mandate. In fact, there are many who believe that if the election had been held a month later, Nixon would have won. Many in the Republican Party wanted Nixon to demand a recount. They knew that there was major voter fraud in Chicago, and some believed that Father Kennedy had bribed the mayor of Chicago to ensure the election. Apparently, in some of the voting districts, there were more votes cast than the number of people registered to vote. That where the expression "people voting from the grave" comes from. But Nixon refused to ask for a recount, and some say that he stated that even if Chicago votes were changed, it wouldn't give him enough Electoral College votes to change the outcome. There were others who believed that if he could have proven voter fraud, he could demand a new election. No one seemed to know the answer. Nixon took the position that he didn't want to put the country through all confusion and uncertainty.

Kennedy looked young, vibrant, and ready to take charge. His acceptance speech was magnificent, including the famous words "Ask not what your country can do for you. Ask what you can do for your country." The young people felt that this was aim directly at them.

That this was a call for them to get involved in government, to set goals to achieve things that they never dreamed possible.

JJ, Charles, and all the other classmates were so excited that they sang all the patriotic songs that they could think of as they traveled back home. Mr. Smith told them that over the next month they would hear and read about things that the new president would be proposing and that they should write down what they hear and cut out the newspaper articles. He said that by the end of the next month, they would be having open discussions on these proposals and would be voting on them in the same manner as Congress. So there would be plenty of debating and they would learn the "art of compromise," which is necessary to pass any kind of legislation. This had been another great day, and again Mr. Smith had found a way to stimulate these young minds and begin the process of understanding the government of the greatest nation in the world.

"Charles, have you heard anything about your scholarship?"

"Yes, I have been offered a government program that will pay my way to either the University of Maryland or to the University of Baltimore to take two years of Law. After that, I will be hired by the State Department to work in an intern program that prepares me to go to work in one of our embassies. And it's possible that some foreign country will hire me to represent them in Washington."

"Which would you prefer to do?"

"I don't know yet. I would really like to go to Russia. I think that is where the action is. Two superpowers going head to head."

"Charles, you've got to be a little crazy to want to go to Russia!"

"No, man. I've already started with the language stuff. I want to be able to speak their language without any type of accent. You never know—I might want to become a spy or secret agent."

"Now I know that you're crazy!"

"Why? Somebody has to do that kind of work. It's important to our country."

"Yeah, but why Russia?"

"It doesn't have to be Russia. It could be one of their associate countries, but I want to be where the action is."

"Well, I can't even decide what I want to do in the future, and you have your whole life planned."

"Not exactly, and remember that the grass always looks greener on the other side of the fence. You've got a great girlfriend, lots of community ties and friends. Because of my father's type of work, we keep moving around, and I don't have time to develop roots or make friends, so even if you don't realize it, you've got a lot going for you. You're even friends with your girlfriend's family, her mother, and father, her brothers. You even know her grandparents and her aunt. That has great value. I hope that you realize that."

"Geez, Charles, I didn't know that you knew that much about me, but I thank you for your insight."

"Yeah, you're a lucky guy, and I'm glad that my guy won the election. My father hates Eisenhower. He said that he is soft on Communism and that Kennedy will kick them in the ass."

"Well, I think that we are going to find out soon enough with all the bullshit that is going on with Cuba!"

"I hope that you are wrong, but I think that you are right. There is trouble brewing."

"Do you think that the election was rigged?"

"JJ, do you realize how difficult that is to do, how many people it would require to pull off? Somebody would screw up. I don't see how they could do it."

"Do you think that asshole in Chicago had dead people vote?"

"It sure looks that way, but how would he know in advance that the election was going to be that close? They were predicting that Kennedy was going to win by a mile. He may have messed with the ballot boxes, but not enough to swing the election."

"No matter now. We have a new president, and he sure sounds great."

"What, you're jumping ship that quickly? Nixon just got back home, and you've deserted him already."

"The election is over, and he's my president now. I just want him to do well."

"Me too, I'll see you in school tomorrow."

JJ is walking to his car when someone calls to him. As he turns to look, Joe taps him on his shoulder.

"Hey, I saw you getting off the bus. I've got good news. I passed all the tests, and they are going to let me graduate with you guys. Isn't that great?"

"Yeah, Joe, that is good news. Are you going to go to that trade school?"

"Yeah, I think so. Debbie's father wants me to become an electrician. And you know they pay well, and they seem to be in demand. But I'm not certain that I want to work for her father. I'm not certain that we are going to get married, but if we did, I don't think that I want to be dependent on my father-in-law."

"I certainly understand that, and the other option sounds pretty good."

"It is, and they guarantee you work as soon as you finish their training, so it's a sure thing."

"Let's get together again this weekend. The girls seem to hit it off well for having just met."

"Yeah, they never stopped talking."

"Yeah, and I wanted to hear about your stay in Africa. You know, the drive-in has a couple of tables and chairs over next to the concession stand. Maybe if the weather is good, we can all go over there for a little while, and you can tell us about it."

"I'd love to do that. I'll have to leave some parts out because you can't talk about it in front of the girls, but we can cover that stuff at another time."

"Okay, so you want me to set it up for Saturday?"

"Yeah, can we make the same arrangements?"

"Yeah, I'll pick you up at 7:30 p.m."

# Chapter 31

JJ IS BEGINNING TO BELIEVE that all the adults that he knows have some type of sex addiction. Most of his young friends think and talk about sex but basically have normal lives with normal interest. But now it's Wednesday, and he is on his way to work at the animal hospital. Dr. E. is back from his trip to New York, and Sherry has already called to thank him for bringing Miss Bonn over to meet Bonnie. He has no idea what to expect when he gets to work. He has convinced himself that he has to quit this job and get away from this mess.

"Hi, Doc. How was your weekend away?"

"It was great. I had forgotten how much fun we have with that group. How did your weekend go?"

"I think that you know the answer to that. It was crazy, somewhat interesting but not what I want to do in life."

"That's too bad, because I love it and can't get enough of it. That schoolteacher that you brought over to Bonnie is extremely *hot*! She, Sherry, and Bonnie did a threesome together. I had to come to work, but I'm supposed to do her tonight. She loves it too! She wants to come over every night, but we're packing up things. I got a great job offer to buy into an established animal hospital in the New York area, and we are going to move back there. We will be leaving in about two weeks if Dr. Casey can find a replacement for me. He had another guy talk to him about two weeks ago about coming to work here, so I think that he'll be okay."

"You mean you are moving, that quick?"

"Oh yeah, we've been talking about it for about three months now. We love our arrangement in New York, so I've been looking for a place to work. I actually got a better deal than I expected. There's a doc up there who just turned seventy, and he wants to retire. So, he is selling me a half interest in his hospital. I'm going to work there for two years and give him 25 percent of my income as additional payment. Then he is going to retire fully, and I'll give him 15 percent of the profits for ten years. After that, it becomes mine. It does a great volume of business, and I'm excited about the deal. I can own my own place for about half what it would cost to open up my own place at a new location. And this place is already established."

"That does sound like a great deal. Plus, you already have friends up there."

"Yeah, Sherry is excited, and so are our friends. We're trying to convince Bonnie to go with us. She doesn't have any ties to this area, and her parents will be coming up there every other weekend. So she could be a live-in babysitter who is very well paid. With the kind of income that I'll be making, I can pay her $150 a week. She won't be paying any taxes. She'll have her own room, doesn't have to buy food, doesn't have any utilities to pay, and has a car available whenever she needs one, so I think that she's going to do it."

"Man, sounds like you've got it all worked out."

"Yeah, do you want to come? You could live with Bonnie for a while."

"No, thanks. You know that I have my woman, and if I can get accepted, I'm going to try going to the University of Maryland for a while. I think that I'm going to take business law."

"How did you come up with that?"

"Martin's girlfriend—soon to be wife—is going there to take civil law. She wants to work in the civil rights movement. She tells me that the classes are small and that you get more help and attention in those courses. I'm still going to take some of the general classes, and they make you take English, but I think it is worth a try. I really wanted to go to the community college, but it doesn't look like they are going to get it open for another two years.

Miss Bonn is helping me with my Algebra, but I'm not required to take it if I go into law."

"What else is Miss Bonn teaching you?"

"I think that you're going to find that out tonight when you get together with her. You know that she has a man that she is going to marry?"

"Yeah, she told Sherry that she was going to talk to him about joining the lifestyle! Who knows, she might not marry him. That woman could take her pick of any man she wants!"

"She sure has a hot body. But she also has a very nice personality. Somebody is going to get a nice wife."

"Well, I think it's time for us to start seeing some patients. Let's get started."

They worked a normal night, and as soon as the last patient left, Doc was out the door and heading home. All JJ could think about was that his problems are over. His prayers have been answered, and he can concentrate on getting things back to normal. His relationship with Julie is great. Joey and Debbie seem to be normal, and Joey seems to have thought out his future. Justin and Connie are enjoying their relationship, and he thinks Justin will be going into the family business. Kathy's not pregnant, and while their arrangement seems a little strange, it certainly can work for them, and her mother seems satisfied with Tommy living there. Things seem to be improving quickly. Now all he has to do is manage this deal with Miss Bonn.

Martin's wedding will be here shortly. JJ saw Delores at the 7-11 store, and she told him that she had been accepted into U of M's early enrollment. Apparently, she has taken all advance-credit courses, and they are going to let her start in January. She'll come back in June and graduate with her high school class, but she doesn't have to wait to start her college courses. That works great for them. Martin has a similar situation. The navy is taking him right after they get married. He has all the credits needed for his high school diploma, so he doesn't need to go to school after the first of the year. So they going to take him the first week in January and send him to Pensacola, Florida, to begin flight training school.

When he finishes, he will be a pilot and an officer. He has no idea where they will send him, but it doesn't matter. It would be great if he got stationed at Pawtuxet Air Base, in southern Maryland. If everything goes well, Delores will finish two years at Maryland, and she will go wherever he goes. She'll get a job in a lawyer's office and finish her law degree at night school. All this stuff is hard work, but both of them are hard workers, and they will make it.

Martin wants to get married wearing his dress uniform. It's unknown if you are able to do that, since he isn't really in the navy yet, and no one knows if there are any laws that prevent him from doing it, so it's possible that he will be in dress navy blue!

Julie and JJ may be the only white people there, but they don't care. JJ is so proud to be the best man. They will know nearly everyone attending, and he'll be sitting with Momma Martin. They have never been in an all-black church before, but they don't think that it is any different from their church. God doesn't have any color. They saw a picture of a Black Jesus. It was strange to them, but then again was an all-white Jesus strange to blacks? Who knows? Maybe Jesus was black. What difference did it make? He's still Jesus.

JJ doesn't understand why adults are so hung up on race. His friendship with Martin hasn't been any different than his friendship with Tommy or Joey, or any of his other white friends. And these same adults got along just fine with all the blacks at the baseball banquets and all the backyard cookouts. Yet they called each other names. *Do my black friends blame me because their families were once slaves? I didn't have anything to do with that. But if you listen to the news media, you would think that we all had slaves and treated them badly. We will never solve this problem unless we clean the slate and begin treating each other on an equal basis. Martin's wedding isn't going to solve this issue, but at least some of us will be working toward that goal.*

Just as JJ was about to reach his house, the car radio announced that a seventeen-year-old black woman had been raped just outside of Freetown and the police are holding three white boys from

Sunrise Beach as suspects. All that JJ could think was that he hoped he didn't know any of them.

*This is terrible.*

As JJ entered his house, his mother is waiting for him.

"JJ, Martin just called. He seemed very upset. He wants you to call him as soon as you get in."

"Did he say what it's about?"

"No, he just asks that you call."

"Hi, Martin, this is JJ. My mother said that you wanted me to call. What's up?"

"Did you hear the news?"

"About what?"

"The rape!"

"Yeah, I just heard it as I was pulling into my yard."

"The girl was my next-door neighbor, and the whole community is about to explode."

"About what?"

"The three boys from Sunrise Beach. They're the guys who worked on the baseball field who were friends with Bow. The guys over here want to kill them! I don't know how to calm them down."

"Martin, these guys are only suspects right now. Nobody knows if they did it or not. Why are the guys jumping to the conclusion that they are guilty? We don't know any of the facts."

"You're right, but logic doesn't seem to matter right now. Everyone is angry. You know they beat this girl up pretty badly."

"Are the police there talking to them?"

"Yeah, they even sent a black officer, hoping that would help, but it didn't."

"God, Martin, I don't know what to say?"

"What would you say if it had been three black boys who raped a white girl?"

"Martin, that's not fair. You know that I don't condone this type behavior no matter who it is."

"Yeah, but you know if it were reverse, the police would be tar and feathering them!"

"Martin, that's the most racist thing that I've ever heard you say."

"Well, it's true, and you know it."

"Martin, this just happened a few hours ago. You gotta give the police a chance to do their job. They don't seem to be trying to cover up anything. They got these guys in custody. What more do you want from them?"

"I want a confession out of them."

"Martin, you don't know if they did it. For God's sake, you need to calm down. Man, if you are that upset, no wonder the community is explosive."

"I think that you need to come over here."

"Me! What the hell can I do?"

"These people know you, and they trust you."

"I can't even get you to calm down. How am I going to do that with people I don't know?"

"I don't know, but maybe if they see a white face that they trust. They will listen and maybe let the system work."

"God, Martin, that's expecting a lot from me. I don't know what to say to them."

"Yes, you do. You always seem to find the right words when needed."

"What if I come over there they may get mad at me and shoot me!"

"No, these people like and respect you. Please, come over and try."

"Okay, but my life is in your hands! I'll be there in twenty minutes. Can you keep a lid on things until I get there? Is the girl there? What's her name?"

"I'll try to keep them calm. No, her name is Pamela, but she's not here. Neither is her mother. I think that they are still at the hospital."

"Okay, I'll be there shortly."

JJ tells his mother what he is doing. She tries to discourage him from going. She doesn't think that it is safe. Neither does JJ, but he told Martin that he would try. As he gets into his car and heads for Martin's house, the radio announces the unrest in the Freetown Community. The residents feel that the police have not done enough at this point in time. Now JJ really has doubts about going there. But he made a commitment, so he is going. As JJ arrives at Martin's house, Momma Martin comes out to walk him into her house. There are about a dozen people in front of the neighbor's house. They are apparently waiting for the Mother and daughter to return home from the hospital. One of the young men spots JJ and yells, "What are you doing here, you honkie piece of trash?"

JJ stops and begins to walk toward the crowd, when another one yells, "Don't come over here, white boy, unless you want your ass kicked."

Momma Martin yells back, "That ain't no way to talk to JJ. You all know him. He's here as a friend."

JJ is frightened by the attitude, but he slowly continues to walk toward the crowd. "I'm sorry about what happened to Pamela. I wouldn't want that to happen to my Julie."

"Well, she's next," yells someone from the crowd.

"I really hope that you don't mean that. We've spent years building real friendships between our families. We can't allow this to destroy that. You and I didn't have anything to do with this terrible crime. I can't undo what these thugs have done. But please don't allow it to tear us apart. I love this community and all the friends that I've made here, and I hope that some of you feel the same way towards me and my friends. Can't we let the system work? You remember the police captain that I brought here to meet you. He loves this community too. I promise you that we will find the people who did this to Pamela, and we will prosecute them and send them away."

"We love you, JJ, but you know that's not going to happen. Those white boys will hire some fancy lawyer, and they won't even get a slap on the wrist."

"No, that's not so. This is rape. This is a serious crime. This isn't like busting a car windshield. These guys are going to do time! But don't you want to make sure that we convict the right guys?"

"Yeah, of course we do, but they got the right guys right now!"

"Oh, please. We don't know that. Let the police do their work. We'll get the right guys—I promise."

"If you were doing the investigation, I would believe that, JJ. But not all white people think like you do. This is some poor black girl. They aren't going to convict these white boys, particularly if they are rich or politically connected."

Just as JJ was about to respond, Pamela and her mother pulled up and got out of the car. Pamela did not want to be seen by anyone. Momma Martin rushed her into her house. Her mother stopped to address the crowd.

"Thank you for coming out to support us. Right now we simply need some time to think. Please go home and we will try to keep you posted as we have new facts. Please just go home for now. Thank you."

Pamela's mother turned to JJ. "I don't know what you are doing here, but I'd rather that you went home. I don't think that my daughter wants to see a white face at this time. Please, just go home.""

JJ chose not to respond. He simply turned to Martin and said, "Say goodnight to your mother. I'm going back to Beachwood."

As he drove home, he was very sad.

*I hope that this rape case doesn't ruin all the good things that exist between the two communities*, he thought, but somehow he knew that it would do some damage. *I hope that the captain can find these guys quickly and that those guys are wrong about them getting off with nothing but a slap on the wrist. I don't know Pamela, but her life is just as important as anybody else's. just because she is black doesn't mean that they can rape her and get away with it. I sure hope that it wasn't the boys from Sunrise Beach. They seemed to be getting their lives straight. They haven't been in any trouble since the Martin fight. I hope they find whoever did this, and I hope that they do it quickly, before this thing gets out of control.*

# Chapter 32

It's been two days since the rape of Pamela, and the police do not believe that the boys from Sunrise Beach are the guilty parties. The problem is that they don't have other suspects at this time. They are following other leads and have four boys from Baltimore City who they know were in the area at the time of the rape. JJ is fearful of the case going cold and the people of Freetown reacting badly. The police captain assured JJ that they are close to making an arrest, but he doesn't have enough evidence to hold the boys from Sunrise Beach. They both know that if they release the boys, the Freetown Community is going to protest and seek media coverage. JJ doesn't know how much longer they are going to remain calm.

Another part of JJ's life has become complicated as well: Dr. E. and Sherry have become close friends with teacher Bonn, and JJ is scheduled to go to Miss Bonn's house for another lesson. He is not certain that he wants to do the lesson. Now that he is considering taking business law in college, he knows that he doesn't need the algebra credits. But he's not 100 percent certain that if he changed his mind about what he should take in college, he might need the algebra. So he calls Miss Bonn.

"Hi, this is JJ. Are we still on for tomorrow afternoon?"

"Yes, we are. It may be a short lesson, as I plan to go over to Sherry's house a little later. You're welcome to come along!"

"No thanks. I can't handle all that swapping-around stuff. You know, we've had sex together and I don't know your first name?"

"It's Jennifer. They call me Jay."

"Are you going to introduce your future husband to them?"

"Yeah, but if he doesn't want to join the group, I may find someone else. I simply love swingers, and I'm certain that I will meet other men up there in New York. I've already begun checking about jobs in their school system, and I assure you that I won't teach high school classes."

"Well, I think that you now owe me a favor since I introduced you to them. I think that you should give me at least a B grade in your class and let me move on with my life."

"JJ most men would love to have the opportunity to be alone with me in my house, and if I opened that robe for them, they would go nuts!"

"Yeah, you're right, and I love that beautiful body of yours, but I've got to many issues going on in my life right now. Besides, you've got your new friends to take care of. I'll bet that they both simply can't get enough of you. And you have similar feelings towards them."

"Boy you're right. I don't know which one I like best, him or her! And if Bonnie goes up there, we're going to become bedmates. You know, I'm only four and a half years older than her, and she is great in bed."

"Well, how about letting me off the hook. I'm going to pass your class with at least a C grade anyway, so help me out a little."

"If you don't continue the lessons to improve your knowledge, how are you going to manage in college?"

"If I find that I need algebra, I'll take a college remedial course."

"Okay, you just passed with a B grade. Does that mean that you aren't interested in my oral sex? I thought that I was pretty damn good."

"You are great, and I love it, but for right now I want to get my life straight, and to do that I need to reduce my sexual activities with adults. Life has gotten too complicated."

"I understand. You know that I'm going to New York with them. Are you ever coming up for one of their parties?"

"No, I don't think so. I'll keep in touch by phone, but I have to pursue my goals in life, and becoming a swinger is not one of them."

"Are you coming over tomorrow afternoon?"

"No, Jennifer, you should go enjoy your relationship with Bonnie. I'm going to see if I can help the police captain with his rape case, and if I can help with the community. This is a very bad situation, and I'm going to ask Pamela's mother if I can talk to her. She may be willing to tell me something that she wouldn't tell her mother or the police."

"Okay, JJ. I'll see you in class tomorrow. Good luck."

"As JJ hangs up the phone, he can't help but think that he has just solved a big problem in his life, at least for now. He knows that it will not be permanent, but for now, the sex addict adults are busy with themselves and leaving him alone. They will be moving to New York and perhaps be gone forever.

But now he faces the problem with his friends at Freetown. The police department must release the boys from Sunrise Beach, and unless they make some other arrests, the families in Freetown will protest in the streets. JJ decides to visit Pamela and speak to her mother. As he pulls into Martin's driveway, he sees Momma Martin talking to Pamela's mother (Mrs. Scott) in their front yard.

"Hi, Momma Martin. How are you doing?"

"Not well, JJ. We just heard that they are releasing the boys from Sunrise Beach."

"Yeah, I know. That's why I came over. I was hoping that Mrs. Scott would let me talk to Pamela?"

"Why should I allow you to talk to my daughter? Who the hell do you think you are? You'll just upset her all over again."

"Please, Mrs. Scott, we have to try everything. This community could get out of control, and people could get hurt. Some of the boys here could end up doing something stupid and get themselves arrested. Please, let me try. Maybe Pamela remembers something very small that she forgot to tell the police that might help. Momma Martin, can't you help here?"

"JJ, Pamela's mother has every right to be upset and not trust the police."

"Why? Mrs. Scott, the police are doing everything possible. Pamela was very upset and hurt the other night. Maybe now that things have settled down some, she may remember some small detail that will help."

"I don't know what the hell you think that you can do that everyone hasn't already tried."

"Mrs. Scott, I really don't want to be here, but these are my friends, and I love this community. I don't want to see anything bad happen to them. And you know this thing can get out of hand very quickly. Please let me try."

"Okay, but I'm going to watch every word that you say."

"Mrs. Scott, I need to talk to her privately. There may be something that she would say to me as a teenager that she wouldn't want to say with her mother there."

"Too bad, boy. I'm not turning you loose on my daughter alone. I don't know you. How do I know that I can trust anything you say?"

"Mrs. Scott, I've been coming over to Martin's house for over five years. You met me when our Boy Scout troupe came here, and we've talked at all the bake sales and the baseball banquets. I wouldn't lie to you about anything. But Pamela may be willing to tell me something that she is too embarrassed to say in front of you."

"Sorry, boy. I'm going to let you talk to her, but not without me there."

"How about if Momma Martin was there? Would that make you feel better?"

"Martin, I don't want to do that. I've known Pamela since she was born."

"Exactly, and she trusts you. But you're not her mother. In fact, that would be better than me being alone with her. She will be more comfortable with you there. Please, Momma Martin. We're talking about saving this community and all the friendships that have been made here."

"Well, if her mother is okay with that, I'll reluctantly do it."

"No, I'm not okay with it, but if you are willing to do it, I'll go along with it. I don't think that Pamela is going to tell his little white ass anything that she hasn't told me or the police. I'll get her out to the living room, where you can talk to her while I stay in the Kitchen. Momma Martin, I'm depending on you to protect my child."

"Don't worry. JJ is a very good person. He would never do anything that would harm Pamela."

"Mrs. Scott returns to her house to get Pamela, while JJ and Momma Martin follow somewhat behind her."

"JJ, what are you going to ask her?" asks Momma Martin.

"I don't know."

"What? All this, and you don't know what you're going to ask her?"

"No, I don't, but we must try to hear the story as she tells it, not third-handed."

Momma Martin is really nervous now. "Hi, Pamela. Do you remember JJ, Martin's best friend."

"Yes, Mama, everyone knows JJ."

"Well, me and JJ want to talk to you about your attackers from the other night. Are you okay to discuss it with us?"

"I don't know what I could tell you that I haven't already said."

"Hi, Pamela. I know that you have told your story to everyone, but that was right after it happened. I'm sure that you were emotionally upset. It's possible that now that things have calmed down and you've had more time to think about it. You may remember something that didn't seem important at the time that may be helpful in catching these guys. Can you start from the beginning and tell us all that you remember?"

"You know that I work at the gas station up at the main intersection. Well, as my shift was ending, the three guys from Sunrise Beach came in to get gas. You know, the guy with the purple colored Ford. We all know each other, and they are always making smart remarks to me."

"Like what, Pam?"

"Momma Martin, please forgive the language. You know that I don't talk like this. But these boys always ask me about my tits or my butt. So one of them asks me if they could take my bra off and play with my breasts. I ignored them like I always do. Then they ask me if I wanted a ride home, and I told them no. As I was leaving and walking across the parking lot, the one with the blond hair came up and grabbed my butt. I pushed him away, and they laughed. Then they said some nasty things like have, 'You ever had sex with a man?' So I insulted them by telling them that there weren't any men in that car. That made them mad, and they drove off."

"They left?"

"Yes, they went down toward Sunrise Beach."

"But, I thought that you told the police that they assaulted you?"

"No, I never told the police that. I did tell the police all the nasty things that they said to me."

"But, you never said that they were the guys who assaulted you?"

"No, I told the police that they were the ones who found me along the side of the road with all my clothes torn off. They're the ones who called the police, but they were afraid to stay there because it was so close to Freetown. They thought the black boys would kill them."

"Did you tell the police that?"

"No, they never asked me that. They ask me if they were the last boys that I saw, and I said yes. The one guy took off his baseball jacket and put it around me, since I was totally bare. I found my blue jeans in the ditch and put them on just before the medical people got there. The guy with the jacket was going to stay with me until someone came, but the other guys convinced him that it wasn't safe for them. They went to the gas station to call the police. They came part way back, just far enough that they could see me. Once the Fire Department guys got there, they left."

"Why did the police pick them up?"

"I don't know. I thought that they wanted to ask them questions."

"Pam, did you tell your mother and others that the Sunrise boys didn't do this?"

"No, I didn't know that they thought that they did it. In fact,

I told the hospital people that I thought that it was only two guys, not three, but I really don't know. Whoever it was, they came up in back of me. No that's not right. It was just beginning to get dark, and their headlight were blinding me. One of them came running at me and knocked me to the ground and held me down. The other one must have been the driver. I heard the car pull up next to me and the lights went out. They had me face down in the ditch. The other guy—or guys, I don't know for sure how many there were—came to me. They flip me over and put a towel over my face. They pulled my jeans off and tossed them in the ditch. Someone ripped my shirt off and then tore my bra off. Someone pulled my panties off. Now I have nothing on except this towel. They pulled me over to the car and push me into the seat."

"Was it a front seat or a back seat?"

"It was a back seat. I wasn't certain at first, but you know how some of these cars have an ashtray in the center of the back of the front seat. Well, I was trying to fight these guys off, and I got my one hand free. I grabbed that ashtray and hit the one guy on the side of his head. That's when he hit me with his fist. Boy, did that hurt. I thought that he broke my cheekbone."

"What happened to the ashtray?"

"What do you mean?"

"Did you drop it? Did you throw it? What happened to it?"

"I don't know. He hit me so hard that I almost passed out."

Pam is now sobbing.

"By now he had finished his dirty work, and he pull me partway out of the car. The other guy climbed on top of me and had his way. The other guy was chocking me, and I don't remember much after that."

"Is there anything else that you remember about the car?"

"Like what? They had a towel over my face."

"Was it leather or vinyl seats?"

"Oh, I do remember that. They had those old cheap-type cloth slipcovers. I remember because as he drug me across the seat, I could feel the cloth on my skin."

"Do you remember anything else?"

"No, as I was waking up, the boy with the baseball jacket was covering me up and talking to me. But I don't know what he said. He didn't want to leave me, but they were really scared."

"Pam, did you tell the police all this stuff?"

"No, they didn't ask me all the questions that you have."

"What did they ask you?"

"They wanted to know if I knew the guys who did this to me. They wanted to know if I had a fight with my boyfriend. They did ask how many times I was actually raped. They said that they needed to know that to determine how many guys attacked me. They asked me if I was wearing underwear. Since they didn't find any there, they assumed that the guys took them with them."

"What else did they ask? Did they ask about the car? Or the size of the attackers?"

"No, they did ask if I could tell how big they were. At first I thought that they meant the size of their penis. I started crying, and the office explained that he meant the body size. By that time a female officer appeared, and her main concern seemed to be to get me to the hospital. The medical guys laid me on that nice soft mattress and I fell asleep. I don't remember anything until we got to the hospital and the female officer was talking to me. I don't know what she said."

"Pam. Have you told anyone this exact story that you just told me and Momma Martin?"

"No. They had some people come here a take a written statement that I had to sign. But no one asks the questions that you ask, so I didn't remember some of that stuff."

"Momma Martin, I have to go visit the police captain. Something is wrong here. You need to tell Mrs. Scott what we just heard. If any trouble begins to brew here, she is the only one who will be able to keep it under control."

"You don't need to tell me anything, Momma Martin. I heard most of the story from the kitchen. I didn't question Pamela like that because I didn't want to make her relive that attack. She is my child. Mr. Kapok, I'm sorry that I spoke to you the way I did. You seem to be the only one who really wanted to get to the truth. Why didn't the police investigators ask those questions?"

"I don't know, but I intend to find out. Can I count on you and Momma Martin to keep things cool here?"

"Everything will be all right for now."

"JJ, I do remember one other detail about the car that I think is correct."

"You know those little lights that are just below the headlights? I think they call them parking lights. On most cars, they are white. But on this car they were blue. At least, I think they were."

"Thank you, Pamela. Between the ashtray and the parking lights, the police should be able to find this car."

"Momma Martin, can I use you phone and steal a Pepsi from your refrigerator?"

"You can have two Pepsis if you want. You are an amazing young man."

As JJ opens his Pepsi and contemplates calling Captain Rogers, he begins to wonder, did the police fail to do a good job simply because it was a black girl, or did they simply fail to perform duties as expected?

"Captain Rogers, this is JJ Kapok. I really need to speak to you—in person."

"JJ, it's 7:00 p.m. and I'm just leaving the police station. Can it wait until tomorrow?"

"No, sir. I don't think that you would want this to wait."

"Well, can we meet at the Beachwood Restaurant? That way I can get something to eat while we talk."

"That sounds good. I'll meet you there."

JJ orders a milkshake and waits for the captain. His stomach is turning. The last bit of information that Pamela told JJ revealed the attacker's identity. JJ knows who the car belongs too. He didn't want to say anything to Mrs. Scott or Momma Martin because his knowledge makes the matter even worse than it was.

"JJ, what's so damned important that you couldn't wait until tomorrow?"

"I know who attacked Pamela Scott. And worse than that, I

think that your police investigators also know and are covering it up."

"That's a very serious charge, JJ. You better have some facts to back it up."

"I have the facts, but first I need to know if I can trust you."

"What? What the hell are you saying, boy?"

"I'm saying that when the heat gets turned on, are you going to stick by your oath to uphold the law?"

"Okay, boy, you've just pushed our friendship a little too far. You need to tell me what's going on in that little brain of yours."

"Not until you promise me that this is not going to be swept under the rug because this rape was a black girl."

"JJ, you are really making me mad. I'm a police captain. My father was a police captain. We have dedicated our lives to law enforcement. What makes you think that I would throw this all away for one case?"

"Because it's the county commissioner's son."

"What? What makes you think that?"

"Your investigators did not even ask Pamela Scott the most basic of questions. I'm not a police officer, and I had a one-hour conversation with her and got a reasonable description of the car, along with the fact that she struck one of her attackers alongside the head with a car ashtray. She may have hit him hard enough to require stitches, but no matter; if you send an officer there to examine his face or that of his sidekick Norman Masters, one of them will have an injury."

"How do you know it was him?"

"I wasn't certain until she gave me the last clue. First, she told me that the ashtray was in the center of back of the front seat. That tells me that it's a four-door sedan. There are only four makes that I know of that place the ashtray in the center of the front seat toward the back. So, I couldn't be certain that it was his car. Then she told me that the car has cloth slipcovers on the seats. His car has cloth seat covers. But then she gave me the final clue. She said that the car has blue lenses on the parking light in the front. Jack Benson installed them on his car on the school parking lot approximately one month ago. Several of us, including myself, watched him install them. It was a simple job. To my knowledge, no one in this area has those blue lenses. And this is basic investigating work. A rookie police officer would have asked the questions that I asked, much less an experienced investigator. You have one of two issues here. You have a racial issue that caused poor police work. Or you have a cover-up because they know that it was the commissioner's son."

"Wow, you've done a good job JJ. Now you have to trust me that I will do my job. I'm going to put an APB out for the car. When it is stopped, we will examine his face or that of his sidekick. If your information is correct, we will make an arrest."

"Captain, send someone to the scene of the rape to search for the ashtray. She thinks that he threw it out after she hit him with it. If you find it, you have found the smoking gun! One other thing. I think that a personal phone call to Mrs. Scott is in order. She is attempting to keep the community calm. They know that the Sunrise boys have been released."

"Better yet, JJ, I'm going to drive over there right now and assure them that we have new leads that should direct us to the attackers before the end of the week."

"Captain, please don't tell her that I knew who it was before I left her house. Just tell her that the information provided has greatly helped."

"I will do that, JJ. Can I buy you another milkshake?"

# Chapter 33

AFTER INVESTIGATING THE INFORMATION THAT JJ gave to Chief Rogers, the police are ready to make an arrest. However, because the commissioner's son is involved they need to be careful in the manner in which the arrest is made.

The police chief made a personal phone call to Commissioner Benson asking him to bring his son to the police station. His car will be towed, or they can bring it in. The commissioner's son, Jason, will be processed and released to his father. Norm Masters will also be processed and released to his mother (father is deceased). Efforts were made to keep the news media away, but it did not work. The front page of the local newspaper reads, "Commissioner's Son and Friend Arrested for Rape of Freetown Teenager."

Commissioner Benson tried every angle possible to have the charges either dropped or reduced, but both his son and Norm Master are eighteen years old and must be tried as adults. Benson has hired the best trial lawyer possible, while Master has applied for a public defender.

Motions were made to try them separately, but that was denied. Motions were also made to move the trial to another jurisdiction, but that was also denied.

Masters wanted to have a trial by jury, but Benson wanted a trial by judge. Because of the political position of his father, Benson decided to accept the trial by jury. He did not want anyone to imply that his father could apply pressure to the judge.

As the courtroom filled with reporters and the public, the

attorneys made all kinds of technical motions to suppress certain facts from the jury. They claimed that the evidence had not been handled properly and therefore could not be introduced. All the motions were rejected, and they were ready to select a jury. This was a difficult process, but after two days of effort, a jury of eight women and four men was selected.

In the opening statement from the district attorney, nearly all the facts that JJ had uncovered were explained in great detail. The defense attorneys stated that there were no witnesses to the actual rape and that all the facts were based on the victim's statements. They attempted to prevent the boys from Sunrise Beach from testifying based on the fact that they arrived after the rape occurred. They were overruled.

**The DA opened his case by putting the boys from Sunrise Beach on the stand to tell the jury what they saw when they found Pamela on the roadside.**

The first person called to the stand was Kenny Austin, who was the young man who put his baseball jacket over Pamela when he found her.

"Mr. Austin, in your own words, please tell the jury what you saw on the night of the rape."

"We were returning to the gas station to get some more gas when the headlights hit on what looked like a body on the side of the road. I yelled to Bobby, the driver, to stop and back up. We could barely see her. She is black and it was dark. But when we got alongside of her, I could hear her moaning. I got out of the car and walked in the ditch. I saw this woman, totally nude, lying face up in the ditch. I went to her and ask her if she was all right. Clearly, she was not. She knew that I was there, but she couldn't respond. We didn't know what to do. We didn't realize that it was Pamela from the gas station because she was covered in mud. There was a towel laying on the ground near her head, so I took the towel and wiped her face clean. Then I realized that it was Pamela. I yelled to Bobby to go to the gas station and call the police for help. I stayed with Pamela. I took my jacket off and covered her up. Again, she knew that I was there but couldn't respond. Within minutes, Bobby returned. He said that help was on the way and that we should get out of there. I ask why? And he said that we might get blamed for whatever happened. I didn't want to leave her there, but they kept yelling at me to get out of there. We waited until we heard the sirens and saw the lights. I jumped in the car and we went over to the gas station. We could see everything from there. When the police and fire department got there, they treated Pamela and transported her to the hospital.

The DA says, "What did you do then?"

"We left, we did not want to get involved."

DA: "What happened then?"

"The police came to Bobby's house and arrested us."

DA: "Why?"

"They said that my coat was found at the scene and that we were last seen there."

DA: "What happened?"

"They questioned us and kept us overnight in the lockup. Later they told us that we could go home. They didn't give us any reasons, just let us go."

DFA (Defense Attorney): "Mr. Austin, Did you see the actual rape take place?"

"No, I did not."

DFA: "And how long—or better yet, what time—did you find the young lady in the ditch?"

"I think that it was between 9:00 p.m. and 9:30 p.m."

DFA: "And what did you see?"

"As I stated, I saw a person lying in the ditch on the side of the road. At that point, I didn't know if it was a male or a female, so we stopped to help."

DFA: "You stopped to help, but none of you were involved in the attack?"

"No, when we realized that it was a person who had been attacked, we called for help and waited for a little while. She was totally naked, so I took my coat off and covered her up."

DFA: "Why did you leave?"

"We were afraid that we would be accused of attacking her."

DFA: "Why did the police arrest you and your friends?"

"I don't know. I guess because I left my coat there for her, and they traced it back to me. I really don't know."

DFA: "What did the police ask you?"

"They separated us into separate rooms and questioned us for hours. I was scared and ask to call my father, but they continued to question me. Finally, I told them that I wasn't going to answer any more of their questions until I spoke to my father. So they let me call him. My dad told me not to say anything else until he got there. He was there in about thirty minutes, but they never stopped questioning me. I simply stopped responding to them."

DFA: "What happened after your father arrived?"

"My father told them that we were not going to answer any more questions until we had an attorney present."

DFA: "What did they do?"

"They locked us in a holding cell until my father was able to post bail."

DFA: "So, the police file charges against you and your friends?"

"Yes, I guess that is what they did. About three hours later, they told my father that they were holding us overnight until we could appear before a judge."

DFA: "So the next morning you appeared before a judge, and he released you on bail?"

"Yes. My father got an attorney, and he got the judge to allow us to go home."

DFA: "No more questions at this time."

The district attorney and the defense attorney continued to question the other two boys from Sunrise Beach, asking basically the same questions of each of them. The trial was continued to the next day.

DA: "The state calls Miss Pamela Scott to the stand." After swearing her in under oath, the DA proceed with questions. "Miss Scott, I know that this is difficult for you, but I must ask you some very personal and unpleasant questions. The defense attorney will be equally unpleasant, but we must get the story correct. First let me ask, how old are you?"

"I'm sixteen, soon to be seventeen."

DA: "Prior to this attack, had you ever had sexual intercourse with a man?"

Tears fill Pamela's eyes as she begins to answer.

"Yes, I have a boyfriend, and we have had sex together."

DA: "So, you know the difference between consenting to have sex and being forced to have sex against your will?"

"Yes, I do."

DA: "On the night of the attack on you, had you seen the defendants earlier in the evening or day?"

"Yes, they came into the gas station and bought some gas."

DA: "Did you speak to them or they to you?"

"Yes, they always make some crude remarks when paying for the gas."

DA: "Like what? Give me some examples."

Pamela is nearly sobbing now, tears running down her face.

"Well, they would say things like, 'I'll give you a couple extra dollars if you let me play with your tits' or 'How about if I give you an extra ten bucks and you let me fuck you?' and many other comments."

DA: "So these guys have been vulgar and unpleasant many times prior to the attack?"

"Yes, many times. I simply ignore them or tell them that I'm not interested. That one' pointing to Benson 'ask me how big is my boyfriend's dick? And went on to tell me how big he was. The other one, Masters, has grabbed my breasts many times, so much so that I now keep a police Billy stick behind the counter. The last time he grabbed me, I smashed the back of his hand with the stick. I thought that I broke his hand."

DA: "What did he say?"

"He called me a black bitch and told me that I would pay for that!"

DA: "What did he mean?"

"I don't know, but he was very mad. Lucky for me, there was a police car sitting in the station, or I think he would have hit me."

DA: "Did Mr. Benson ever touch you?"

"Only once. He grabbed my butt and told me he wanted me to play with his big dick. He didn't know that my boyfriend and some of his friends were sitting in their car and saw him. When they got out of their car, he ran, got in his car, and left. My boyfriend was going to go after him, but I told him not to do it, that he was the commissioner's son and he would cause them trouble."

DA: "So you have had problems with the defendants in the past, but you overlooked them or ignored them because you knew who Mr. Benson was?"

"Well, yes and no. I've had problems with them both in the past, but I ignored it because they were customers of the station. I didn't want the owner to think that I was chasing his customers away. I thought that Commissioner Benson would cause me problems simply because I'm a black person from Freetown."

DA: "Now, Miss Scott, tell me in your own words, what happened on the night of the attack?"

"I left work and was walking home when this car past me and yelled something at me. The car went up the road and made a U-turn. Now it was coming back towards me. The headlights were in my face. The car stopped about twenty feet in front of me. Someone got out of the passenger side and ran straight at me. He hit me hard like a football tackle and knocked me to the ground. I was stunned. The car pulled off to the side of the road next to me and turned off his lights. Within seconds, the guy who tackled me was tearing my blouse and bra off. I told him to stop, but he took the back of his hand and slapped me very hard. The driver came over and put a towel over my face and held my arms above my head. The other guy pulled my blue jeans off and ripped my panties away. Within a second he had his penis inside me. He pounded me for what seemed like forever. Finally, he ejaculated inside me and said, 'How'd you like that, you black bitch.' He pulled me up and dragged me to the back seat of the car. I tried to fight him off. I grabbed an ashtray that was in the middle of the back of the front seat. I hit him hard with the ashtray. I knew that I hurt him. He jumps back. He was mad. He grabbed my legs and flipped me over. Now I was face down on the back seat. I heard him tell the driver,

'It's your turn now,' and he came around the car, open the door, and put the towel over my face again and slammed the door shut. The driver pulled my body toward the open door and inserted his penis from the rear. This guy had a very large penis, and he hurt me badly. He kept pumping hard, and I was crying in pain, and he said, 'I told you that I had a big dick. What's the matter, you can't handle it?' It was so painful that I prayed for him to finish. Finally, he did. He said to the other one, 'We're done. The bitch can't handle anymore.' The other guy pulled me out of the car and said one more thing, and he hit me so hard that I thought that he broke my cheekbone. He knocked me out. The next thing that I remember was Mr. Austin putting his cost over me and saying, 'Everything is all right. We've called for help.' I couldn't respond. Then I remember being put on that soft stretcher and taken to the hospital."

DA: "Wow. That's some story, and you seem to remember a lot of detail. Did you see the faces of your attackers?"

"I saw the face of that one" pointing to Masters "when he opened the door to the back seat the light came on and I saw his face and I hit him with the ashtray. The other one I only know by his voice and what he said to me. It was exactly what he had said once before."

DA: "Do you remember anything else about the second attacker?"

"Well, this isn't very pleasant, but he said that he had a big dick. And it is. He is huge. So large that it hurt badly, and he knew it and enjoyed hurting me."

DA: "I submit the hospital report stating that Miss Scott was severely torn and damaged inside her vagina. No more questions at this time."

DFA: "Miss Scott. You seem to remember a lot of detail. Why did you not tell all of this to the police when they questioned you?"

"They questioned me right after the attack, at the hospital. I had just been knocked out. I was in extreme internal pain. And they had given me medicine for the pain. In fact, it wasn't until JJ came to my house and ask me a lot of questions that I started thinking about exactly what had happened. After all, this is not something that you want to remember. It is very hard to relive that night. I don't know why these guys wanted to hurt me, but they did."

DFA: "You state that you saw Mr. Masters' face. Why didn't you tell the police?"

"I couldn't remember his name. I told the police that I was certain that it was not the boys from Sunrise Beach, and I didn't remember their names either. I think that it took a few days for my brain to get back to normal. Once I had a few days' rest, I started remembering things, but the police didn't come back to question me until after JJ told Captain Rogers what he had discovered after talking to me."

DFA: "Miss Scott, have you ever been in Mr. Benson's car before?"

"No, sir, I haven't."

DFA: "And you have never performed oral sex on the defendants in return for money?"

"No, sir. I've never had sex with those guys until they raped me. They were always coming into the station and saying, 'I'll give you ten bucks to give me a BJ, either in the car or behind the building.' They even suggested that I go into the bathroom stall with them. They are disgusting guys."

DFA: "And you identify Mr. Benson by the size of his penis?"

"No, I know his voice. He used the same exact words that he had said to me several times before. No one else has ever used those words to me. And if you examine the size of his penis, I would bet that it is much larger than most men. My boyfriend has a nice-size penis, and we have had normal sex together, but this guy felt like he was pushing on my stomach and could go further. When I said that he was huge, I mean huge."

DFA: "Okay, I get the picture. So it's his voice and the words that he used?"

"Yes, that should be enough. And it was his car."

DFA: "We'll let the jury decide if that's enough. Now, tell me about your clothes? You stated that they ripped off you blouse and your bra, and pulled off your jeans and tore off your panties?"

"Yes, that's true."

DFA: "Miss Scott, have you ever gone to work with no bra and no panties? And the blouse that you were wearing—would it allow someone to see your breasts? If you did not use all the buttons, perhaps?"

"No, I never go to work without a bra, and I button my blouse very high. I may not always wear panties, but you can't tell that when I'm wearing jeans."

DFA: "Miss Scott, how is it that the police never did find your panties or bra?"

"I don't know the answer to that question."

DFA: "You are sixteen, soon to be seventeen? With how many people have you had any kind of sexual relationship?"

"I don't know exactly. This is my second real boyfriend."

DFA: "So it's at least two? Does that include oral sex?"

Pamela is now sobbing.

"Yes, I would say at least two. And, yes, in my younger years, at parties, the girls would often give the boys blowjobs. That stopped them from pressuring you for intercourse."

DFA: "So, Miss Scott, is it fair to say that you are very knowledgeable about sex? And that you enjoy it?"

"Yes, Mr. Attorney. I am knowledgeable, and I do like it. But sex by consent and mutual agreement is not the same as being knocked down, having your clothes torn off you, and being forced to have intercourse with people that you do not know. And I hope that this jury understands the difference."

DFA: "We will see if they believe that you were raped or gave consent, many times. No more questions at this time."

DA: "At this time I would like to call Mr. JJ Kapock to the stand." After swearing in under oath, the DA began his questions.

"Mr. Kapock, Please explain your relationship or involvement to this case."

"I am friends with Miss Scott's neighbors, the Martins, and I know the defendants because we attend the same school."

DA: "Shortly after the attack took place, did you go to Miss Scott's house and question her about the details of the attack?"

"Yes, sir. The next day, I went to the Martins' house to calm down some of the guys there who were upset and angry with the manner that they thought the police were handling the case. They felt that because it was a black girl, no one cared and nothing would be done."

DA: "Why you? And what were you supposed to do?"

"Well I helped establish the Boy Scout troupe in Freetown, and we also established a Baseball Rivalry between Freetown and Beachwood communities, so I knew most of the guys. I guess that I was supposed to talk to them to calm them down."

DA: "Did it work?"

"Some. The guys were mad. Some of them didn't want to talk to me."

DA: "What happened next?"

"Well, I saw Mrs. Scott in her yard and I asked her if I could ask Pamela some questions. She was hostile toward me and said no. So I asked, what if Mrs. Martin was with me? Would it be okay? At first Mrs. Martin didn't want to do it. I explained to Mrs. Martin and Mrs. Scott that I thought that Pamela might tell me, another teenager, something that she would not want to tell her mother. Mrs. Martin agreed, and she convinced Mrs. Scott that it was worth a try."

DA: "So did it work?"

"Yes, more than I thought it would. When the police talked to Pamela, she was still shocked and confused. But now some time had passed; her mind was clearer and her emotions were under control. It was through my questioning that we found out that Pamela had hit one of the attackers with the ashtray. The location of the ashtray also told us that it was a four-door sedan. She also told us that it had cloth slipcovers over the seat. But the real piece of news was that the car had purple/blue lenses on the parking lights. I knew that it was Jack Benson's car, 'cause I saw him install them on the parking lot at school."

DA: "Did you tell them that you knew who it was?"

"Hell no. I was scared. I wanted to talk to Captain Rogers, but I was even afraid to tell him."

DA: "Why?"

"This was the county commissioner's son! I wasn't certain what to do. I trusted Captain Rogers, but I knew this would be a 'political issue' for him. But I had to tell someone. Captain Rogers was the right one."

DA: "What did Captain Rogers say?"

"He said that no one is above the law, and that no matter who it was, he would find them and lock them up. And he did. He found the car. He found the ashtray, and he arrested the defendants."

DA: "No more questions at this time."

DFA: "So, Mr. Kapock, you saw Mr. Benson install blue lenses on his car?"

"Yes, I did. And so did several other people."

DFA: "Mr. Kapock, do you believe that Mr. Benson's car is the only car in this county that has blue lenses for its parking lights?"

"No, sir, I don't. But it may be the only four-door sedan with an ashtray missing that has blue lenses."

DFA: "Isn't that up to the police department to prove?"

"Yes, it is. And I hope that they can. But if they can't, I hope that the jury can come to its own conclusions, and I hope that the cut on Mr. Masters' head came from that ashtray, and I hope that they can prove it!"

DFA: "Did you see either of the defendants attack Miss Scott?"

"No, I did not."

DFA: "No more questions."

DA: "Call Captain Rogers to the stand."

"Captain Rogers, you have heard the testimony. In your own words, do you have anything to add?"

"No, sir. Things happened pretty much as described. When Mr. Kapock gave us the information, we confirmed it with Miss Scott and put an APB out to find the car. We found it in Mr. Benson's driveway. We found the ashtray at the scene of the attack. It had both Mr. Masters' and Miss Scott's fingerprints on it, and of course Mr. Benson's, and it fits into the space in the car. We know that it is a match. Mr. Benson does have cloth slipcovers on his back seat, as described by Miss Scott. The car does have blue lenses on the parking lights."

DA: "Did you question the defendants?"

"Jack Benson was home, and we asked him basic questions. When his father realized what the charges might be, he stopped the questions and said that he was obtaining a lawyer for his son. We picked Mr. Masters up from his part-time job and took him to the police station. We questioned him until his father came with a lawyer to represent him. Both men are eighteen years of age, and both denied any involvement in the attack."

DA: "Do you feel that you have arrested the correct persons involved in this issue?"

"Yes, we have ended our investigation, because everything stated by the victim has proven to be true and factual. Mr. Masters had a cut on his forehead where he was struck by something. We assume it was the ashtray."

DA: "No more questions at this time."

DFA: "You concluded that Mr. Masters was there because of the cut to his forehead?"

"There was blood on the ashtray that matched Mr. Masters' blood, and there were fingerprints on the ashtray that matched Mr. Masters', and Miss Scott clearly saw his face."

DFA: "But the ashtray could have been there prior to the attack? Mr. Masters could have been injured by the ashtray prior to the attack?"

"All that is possible, except that Miss Scott clearly identified Mr. Masters as one of her attackers."

DFA: "Miss Scott knew Mr. Masters prior to the attack, and she could be identifying him because she is mad at him for things that he has said to her in the past."

"I think that I'll leave that conclusion to the jury to decide."

DFA: "Let's talk about the car. How can you be certain that it was Mr. Benson's car that was involved?"

"We ran checks with the DMV (Department of Motor Vehicles) and there are no other cars of that make and model within a

50-mile radius of the area, and none that we know of with the blue lenses on the parking lights."

DFA: "But it is possible that another car could look like Mr. Benson's?"

"Yes, it is possible."

DFA: "Other than the car, do you have any proof that Mr. Benson was present at the time of the attack."

"Miss Scott identified his voice and the size of his penis."

DFA: "The size of his penis?"

"Yes, according to hospital research, the average male penis is between 4" and 6" in length. Mr. Benson's penis is 13½". If you recall Miss Scott's testimony, her attacker was very large and caused her pain."

DFA: "So you are depending on the voice and the size of the penis to implicate Mr. Benson in the attack?"

"Yes, along with the car."

DFA: "But he could have loaned his car to a friend, who also has a large penis?"

"Yes, that's possible. But he can't loan his voice!"

DFA: "No more questions at this time."

DA: "The state rests. We are ready for closing statements."

DFA: "The defense calls Commissioner John Benson."

"Commissioner Benson, where were you on the night of the attack?"

"I was home for part of the night and at a community meeting for the balance."

DFA: "Can you provide more details about the time frames?"

"I left my house around 7:00 p.m. and returned around 11:00 p.m."

DFA: "Do you know where you son was during that time frame?"

"When I left the house, he was home watching the baseball game on TV. And he was still watching TV when I returned."

DFA: "Commissioner, the attack took place around 8:45 to 9:00 p.m. Isn't it possible that your son left the house while you were away?"

"Not unless he walked. He didn't have his car. He loaned the car to Mr. Masters, who brought the car back just about the time that I was arriving home."

DFA: "You spoke to Mr. Masters?"

"Yes. He came into the house, and Jack, my son, was cleaning and taping a cut on his head."

DFA: "Did he explain how he got the cut?"

"No, and I didn't ask. I was tired and I went to bed."

DFA: "Where was your wife during this time?"

"She is visiting her sister in Florida."

DFA: "No more questions."

DA: "Commissioner Benson, you are testifying that your son was at home and that your son loaned his car to Mr. Masters?"

"Yes, that's correct."

DA: "Is it possible that Mr. Masters came back to your house and picked up your son?"

"I guess that's possible."

DA: "So you can't really say that your son was in the house while you were away?"

"He was there when I left, and he was there when I returned."

DA: "And you saw the cut on Mr. Masters' forehead?"

"Yes, I did."

DA: "Thank you, no more questions."

DFA: "Defense calls Jack Benson. Mr. Benson, in your own words, please tell the court where you were on the night of attack?"

"I was home watching baseball on TV. Baltimore was playing New York."

DFA: "Did you leave the house?"

"No, sir."

DFA: "Did you loan your car to Mr. Masters?"

"Yes, I did. He said that he wanted to do some shopping."

DFA: "What time did he bring the car back to you?"

"He got there just a few minutes before my father got home. So it must have been around 10:30 p.m. He was bleeding from a cut on his forehead, so we went to the bathroom to fix it up."

DFA: "Did he say how he got the cut?"

"He said that he walked into a display at the store."

DFA: "What time did he leave your house?"

"I'm not certain, but I would guess that it was about 11:30 or 11:45 p.m. I took him home and then came back to the house."

DFA: "No more questions. Defense calls Mr. Norman Masters."

DFA: "Mr. Masters, you've heard the testimony regarding the night in question. Please tell us your version of that night's events."

"I don't know what's going on here, but both Jack and his father are lying."

"I did not borrow the car, and Jack and I were together all night. But we didn't rape that girl. I know Pamela, and I'd like to have sex with her, but I didn't rape her. Jack and I went to Bobby's Burger Place, hung there for a few hours, and went back to his house. We were only there for a little while when his father came home."

DFA: "How did you get the cut on your head?"

"I walked into a low hanging tree branch near Jack's driveway."

DFA: "So, you never saw or spoke to Miss Scott that night?"

"No, I saw her early during the day at the gas station."

DFA: "No more questions."

DA: "Mr. Masters, you see what your buddy Jack is doing to you. He's going to claim that he loaned you his car, and you and someone else went out and raped Miss Scott. Now we have enough evidence to prove that you were one of the rapists. You are going to jail for a long time. But do you want to give your pal Jack a free ride? Do you want to let him off the hook completely? I think that I have enough to convince the jury that Jack was the other guy. But you never know. Should he get a free ride just because his father is a big shot? Should they be able to dump all this on you?"

"No, but we didn't do it."

DA: "Come on, Norman. Miss Scott identified you. You have the cut on your head as described. We have your fingerprints and blood on the ashtray. And you can't account for your time. And your buddy, who was supposed to back you up, just turned the tables on you and is leaving you to take all the blame. Give it up,

Norm. Do you really think that this jury doesn't see what really happened that night?"

"We didn't do it."

DA: "Yes, you did. And I've provided enough proof to put you away."

By now, Norm is sobbing and is an emotional wreck.

DA: "Norm, change your plea to guilty and tell the truth. Maybe this jury will show you some mercy! You are guilty, and they are going to convict you."

"Okay, okay. I admit it. We did it. Pamela, I'm truly sorry. We were both drinking and were near drunk. I didn't want to hurt you, but when you hit me with that ashtray, you hurt me and made me mad. So I hit you. But Jack is just as guilty as me, and he shouldn't walk away scot-free just because his father is a commissioner. His father is lying. He knows that Jack didn't lend me his car. He doesn't know if Jack was home. They made that story up to pin this all on me. I agree with the DA. This jury can see what really happened, and they need to find us both guilty. I'm truly sorry."

DA: "Your Honor, we have an admission of guilt. I move that we allow the jury to retire and bring back a verdict."

DFA: "Your honor, we can accept the confession of Mr. Masters, but we want to continue with the case against Mr. Benson."

Judge: "Really? After the case that's been presented here, do you really think that this jury would not find your client guilty?"

DFA: "Yes, I do."

Judge: "You know that I can dismiss the jury and render a verdict. I'm going to prosed this trial until tomorrow at 10:00 a.m., at which time I will listen to your arguments as to why we should continue."

The DFA asked the DA for a meeting. It was granted. The DFA attempted to get the DA to reduce the charges against Mr. Benson. The DA refused.

The next morning, the DFA entered a guilty plea for Mr. Benson.

"The judge will allow the jury to bring in a guilty verdict, and sentencing is scheduled for thirty days."

# Chapter 34

THE NEW PRESIDENT HAS BEEN sworn in, and the people of Beachwood and other communities are beginning to settle down to their normal lives. JJ's parents are not happy that Kennedy won but Julie's parents seem to be quite satisfied.

Joe's father is expected to give him his car this weekend. A 1954 Chevy, two-toned red and white. It is a very nice car, and he is suggesting that they use it for the double-date on Saturday night. Everything is set up, and they plan to meet Justin, Connie, Tommy, and Kathy at the drive-in theater.

"Hi, guys. How are you doing?"

"We're doing great. That's a nice looking car, Joey. Where did you get it?"

"My dad gave it to me. He just bought a brand new '61 Chevy, cold black. It's a beauty. That's a beautiful car that you have, Justin. It looks brand new."

"No, this is one of my father's cars. It's a '52 Hudson. He bought it when it was new, but he hardly ever drives it. He keeps it in the garage almost all the time. I think that I use it more than he does, but he won't give it to me."

"I love the color states, Connie. It's actually a three-tone. It's a beautiful two-tone brown with a white top."

"It looks brand new?"

"No, as I said, it's a '52, but it's only got 15,000 miles on it. He really babies this thing. You would think that it is gold plated, the way he treats it."

"Yeah, you guys put my poor Desoto to shame."

"Yeah, but you got a ragtop. You're Mr. *Cool*, riding around with your top down and that hot chick Julie hanging on your arm. You got life going in the right direction!"

"Debbie, how are you enjoying having your boyfriend back from Africa?"

"It's great. That year seemed like forever. We had just met and were getting to know each other when he left. Boy, it really was lonely, and he doesn't like writing letters. And even if he did, the mail service there was very bad. If it wasn't for the army guys sending their mail by the government, I don't think that I would have heard from him at all."

"Sometimes we were in the middle of nowhere. We'd be 100 to 200 miles from any town, and we'd be there drilling a well for a village of about 150 people. They lived in the sand or clay huts that had grass roofs. Some of them just slept in the bushes. They would get up in the morning and walk to the river to wash off. Every now and then they would take their clothes off and wash them in the river. They would hang them over the bushes and let them dry. They totally lived off the land. They would catch fish in the river and eat them raw. They thought that it was funny when we would cook them. But that river was so dirty that I didn't want to eat those fish, but when you don't have anything else, you eat fish.

"We were lucky. Between the army and my dad's company, we received a supply of food and water every two weeks. Sometimes it would come by truck, and other times they would fly over and drop it out of an airplane. The food was bad, but it was better than those fish!

"But they would eat anything. Desert rats. Insides of tree branches. Anything. They would find and eat things that you would never dream could be eaten. But you know what? They were happy and they didn't expect much. When we started pumping clean water, they were thrilled. They couldn't believe that we could find water that far down in the ground, but they weren't dumb. By the time we left, those army guys had taught them how to operate that generator, and it was solar powered. They knew how to get and bottle the water. They knew what was needed to make the purifier work, and it mostly consisted of simple sand filters. And sand they had plenty of. Frankly, I still don't understand how those filter systems work, but I know that the water was cleaner than that river. The first couple of time that I drank it, I got sick from it, but I guess that your body adjusts to it, because I got to the point where I could drink it if I had too. I generally only drank from our supply shed."

"Didn't you have problems with lions and tigers and other animals?"

"Not, really, those animals stayed away from people, and people didn't go near them. Sometimes the men would go steal the leftover of something that a lion killed. They would eat that meat raw! It made me sick to watch them. The army CBs taught some of them how to cook the meat, and they did like it better. They would cook some and give it to their women and children, but they thought that it was manly to eat the meat raw! They were quick to learn things, and we taught them how to create farm fields and direct the water to the crops. The problem was that they didn't have much that would grow there. And every time that they would get a crop growing. The wild animals would come along and eat whatever they grew. They really were nice people, but even the poorest of the poor here in the US live better than they live. The difference is that they don't know that they are poor. They are enjoying life."

"What did they do for entertainment?"

"Not a whole lot. As long as it was daylight they taught others how to do different things, like weave a thatched roof. Or make sandals for their feet. Most of them didn't have any kind of shoes. Sometimes they would build a fire and do crazy dances, but really not that often. They did enjoy sitting around and talking to each other. They were always laughing. I learned some of their words, but we mostly communicated by making hand motions and pointing to things, but we really did do well with that."

"Sounds like you had a great experience with them."

"Yeah, I did, but I'm glad to be home. I now enjoy turning on a light bulb or getting a glass of milk from the refrigerator, simple things that we take for granted here at home, being able to sleep in a nice clean bed with no bugs!"

"Would you like to go back?"

"No, I don't think so. My dad is going back in three months for a six-month stay. He said that he's not taking the family this time, and I'm glad that he doesn't want me to go. I think that I want to get my life started, see what Debbie wants to do and help my mother while he is away. He really makes a lot of money doing this, so I assume that he is going to do this on a regular basis."

"Hey, what about you guys? I've been doing all the talking. JJ, what did you think about seeing the President getting sworn in?"

"Man, that was exciting! I think this guy is going to be a great president. Did you guys listen to his speech?"

"They played it over the PA system at school, so everyone got to hear it. And the TV replayed most of it all night. And yes, I agree with you, he sure sounds good. What did you girls do this week?"

"Mostly girl stuff. Clean the house, cook some meals, and wait for you guys."

"Yeah, I taught some dance classes and read some books. But this has been the most interesting part of the week. Joey, your trip to Africa is something that you will remember for your entire lifetime."

"I sure will, but JJ tells me that you may go to New York for your dancing?"

"I think that I'm going to go and see what it is all about. But I don't think that I could leave my family and friends and live there by myself. If I could get JJ to go with me that might make it interesting."

"You mean that you're ready to get married?"

"We've been ready, but neither of us knows if that's what we want to do with our lives. We are pretty certain that whatever we do, we want to do it together. We just don't know when."

"Hey, does anybody know what the movie is about?"

"Heck, I didn't even know that it started."

"I was told that they may sell this drive-in theater to some developer. He's proposing to build a shopping center. Apparently, the theater is making money, but the land has become so valuable that they are going to sell it."

"Heck, where are we going to go?"

"I know that there is another one over near Laurel, but it isn't as nice as this one. And sometimes if they don't have enough customers, they simple close up for the night. So you never know if they're going to be open."

"I guess they are dying off. That's a shame."

"What are you guys doing tomorrow? I've got an outside grill down next to our pier. Connie and I have gone down there a couple of times and cooked some hot dogs. Do you want to come over for the afternoon—if it isn't too cold?"

"Sounds good to me. Julie and I will be there."

"Tomorrow is Sunday. Kathy and I are going to be on the sofa, under a blanket watching the football game. It's the last game of the season. I think that the Colts are playing Green Bay. You know that is going to be a great game."

"I'm available if Debbie can do it. We'll be there."

"Let's shoot for two o'clock. You can park over next to my brother's house and walk down the steps to the beach. I'll bring the food. How about you guys pick up something to drink?"

"Okay, we'll see you tomorrow. We're going to leave."

"I think that Julie and I are going to stay for a while longer, unless Joey and Debbie want to leave, 'cause we're with them in Joey's new car!"

"No, we're okay with staying. We'll see you tomorrow."

"JJ, Julie, Joey, and Debbie went back to the car. The drive-in has electric heaters that attach to the speakers, but it was still cold in the car. Both couples had blankets to crawl under, and they had their love to keep them warm."

"The next day the sun was out and the temperature was about 55, so it was a good day for a cookout. Justin's father told them if it got too cold that they could go into the yacht. And you know that they wanted to do that. The yacht was like a luxury house on the water. It had a main suite that had a dining area and a heating system just like your home. Suddenly the outside grill wasn't so appealing. They started the grill up and tossed some hot dogs on it. As soon as they were ready, they gathered them up and headed for the yacht. The yacht even had a TV so they could watch the football game if they wanted, but the girls weren't interested in the TV. They wanted to see the rest of the yacht. This thing had three staterooms and two small baths. It had a small galley and a small sleeping area for the crew in the forward compartment. This certainly was the lifestyle of the rich and famous.

After the boat tour, they sat around the main suite and talked about school, cars, and the future. It was really a nice day for all of them, and Justin finally felt as if he had some real friends. Justin's mother, who was a real snob, was actually thrilled to have the young people there, and she invited them into the house, where she had made some cookies and tea. The group loved it; even Mr. Casey came into the room and talk to them for a while. This was a big deal for them to have guest in their house. All that wealth and no one to share it with. They instantly fell in love with the young adults. The bonding was amazing. It was nearly 6:00 p.m. and the cook had dinner ready. The kids began gathering up their things when the Caseys insisted that they stay for dinner. The kids were excited.

The dining room table must have been fourteen feet long. It could seat at least sixteen people. Beautiful mahogany finishes, with a white-laced tablecloth. The guest had never seen so much silver in one place. Beautiful hand-painted china and crystal water glasses. The girls thought that they were at Cinderella's ball."

The Caseys were so happy to show off all their things. There was a grandfather clock in the entranceway that was over a hundred and fifty years old. Its history dated back to Philadelphia, and it was believed to have belonged to Ben Franklin. It was the pride of the house. This had turned out to be a wonderful day for everyone. As they were leaving, Mr. Casey invited them to come back when the weather was better, and he would take them for a cruise down the Chesapeake Bay. They were excited by the invitation. Everyone was smiling and laughing. This had been a perfect day.

Justin was pleased that his parents had been so nice to his

friends. His brother, Andrew, came down for dinner. He didn't talk to anyone except his mother before returning to his room. Justin was leaving to take Connie home when they heard a strange noise from upstairs. When they went to investigate, they found Andrew past out on the bathroom floor. Mr. Casey ran to the bathroom to examine Andrew. He immediately turned on the cold water in the shower, picked Andrew off the floor, and held him under the spray of cold water. The shock of the cold water woke Andrew up. He didn't know where he was for a minute or two. He attempted to make up some stupid story that he slipped and fell, but it was clear that he had been drinking. Apparently, he mixed some kind of drugs with the alcohol, and it caused him to pass out. The Caseys were embarrassed because they knew what was wrong. This had happened before, several times. It seems that Andrew has a drinking and drug problem that no one except the family members knew about. Since he had no friends, it was easy to keep it a secret. But now Connie has seen it. However, Connie didn't really understand what was going on. She asked several times, "Is he all right? Is he alright?"

Justin turns to his mother and says, "We're going to leave now!"

"Go ahead, dear. We can take care of things here."

As they get in the car, Connie continues to ask, "Is he all right? What's the matter with him?"

"Justin attempts to ignore her question, but he knows that he has to tell her something."

"For Pete's sake, Connie, haven't you ever seen anyone drunk before?"

Connie was shocked. This family was so prim and proper that she never expected something like that. She certainly didn't think that it would take place in their house with the parents present.

"Well, yeah, I've seen plenty of drunks before, but I didn't expect it of your brother—in your house. Has he had this problem before?"

Clearly upset Justin snaps back, "Yes, he's a damn drunk. My parents can't keep alcohol in the house or he'll drink it up and they will find him passed out somewhere in the house. He bribes the household help to buy him vodka because you can't smell it on his breath."

"I've never noticed it before. He seems so normal. How long has he been like that?"

"He was thirteen when I first picked him up off the bathroom floor. We're eighteen now! They've had him to all kinds of doctors and specialist and nothing seems to help. He'll sit in bed at night drinking booze. He has fallen asleep and spilled vodka or gin all over the bedding. We've had to wash the bedclothes and shampoo the mattress. The bedroom stinks. We need to open the windows and let the fresh air in. It's a mess. I'm sorry that you had to see it. Please don't say anything to JJ and Julie or any of our friends."

"No, of course not. I wouldn't say anything, but I don't think that it would make any difference to them. They're your friends. You're real friends. They care about *you*!"

"I know, but I know that my parents are going to be upset."

"Justin, every family has internal problems that they don't want the world to know about. Don't worry, honey. Everything will be all right."

"You called me honey!"

"Yes, you are my honey. Don't you know that I care about you?"

"Yeah, and you know that I care about you. And we've been a little frisky at times, but that honey sounded loving."

"It is loving. Don't you know that we are in love?"

"Yeah, I guess that we just haven't expressed it very often."

"I've left that up to you. You're so shy that I've just let it grow slowly. I figured that when you were ready, you would tell me that you love me."

"I love you."

"That certainly was romantic! How about waiting until you stop the car, kiss me good night, and try that again."

"Okay, but I still love you."

# Chapter 35

Martin and Delores postponed their wedding until after the national elections. It seems that the navy was concerned that the new president might reduce the size of the armed forces, so they didn't want to disrupt people's lives and then not move forward with their plans. However, it became clear that President Kennedy did not intend to address that issue until much later in his term. But they had already moved the date to February, and both were staying in school until the end of the school year. Martin is now talking about changing it again to the end of June, depending on what the navy decides to do. Delores stayed in school even though she didn't need any credit to graduate. The navy told Martin that he should take certain classes which will lighten his load of classes when he gets to Florida. All those things worked well for them, but now they must deal with this Rape issue in their community. They had planned to invite several of the white families to the reception that was being held at the community center. Now they are not certain that the racial tension will cause the white families not to attend. What a mess!

JJ had made the front page of the local newspaper: "High School Student Solves the Freetown Rape Case." Captain Rogers sent a crew of investigators to the crime scene and they found the car ashtray. It had Pamela Scott's fingerprints all over it, as well as Jack Benson's, the commissioner's son. That placed the car at the scene, but they still had to prove that he was driving and was there. It was Norman Masters that Pamela struck with the ashtray, not Jack Benson, but Police were certain that Masters would confess to the crime and that he would implicate Jack Benson. Since it was proven that it was Benson's car and he had been seen driving it earlier in the day, any jury could connect the dots and conclude that Benson was the other attacker.

Commissioner Benson was doing everything possible to slow down or impede the case. But he had to be careful, because Freetown was in the middle of his election district. In fact, his district had the highest number of black voters in the county, slightly higher than the Annapolis area. It would take six months or more to get this case to trial, and by the time it was resolved, they would be in the middle of the election campaigns for local offices. Commissioner Benson was in a no-win situation. This was his son who he was trying to protect, but no matter what he did, the black community was going to be angry with him and the behavior of his son. Commissioner Benson was a wealthy man, so he could afford the very best attorneys, but he couldn't buy off the anger of the Freetown voters. The residents of Freetown were trying to convince Momma Martin to run against Commissioner Benson. She is well liked, intelligent enough to do the job, and all but one of her children are grown up and about to complete school. She would be the perfect candidate. Meanwhile, Captain Rogers was considering running for the sheriff's job, which is the top law enforcement job in the county.

Life is really getting complicated for JJ. He was personal friends with Norn Masters and Jack Benson. They didn't travel together in the same group, but they knew each other very well. The other group of kids that Benson hung with were starting a rumor that Norm Masters and Pamela Scott had once been boyfriend and girlfriend and that they had sexual relations together. Everyone knew that this wasn't true, but they were attempting to discredit Pamela as a person. They were going to say that is was merely a fight between the couple. This further enraged the Freetown community. Everyone knew that Masters was a racist and that he referred to black people as "niggers." They also knew that he thought Pamela was beautiful and he was always going to her workplace trying to get her to have sex with him. Many of the co-workers had seen and heard his remarks. But that wasn't going to stop the rumors. This was ugly. Many of the boys were going into the gas station and making sexual remarks to Pamela. JJ and his friends tried to put a stop to the rumors, but it was nearly impossible. However, there was one person who took this issue on as a mission to correct the injustice toward Pamela: that person was Kenny Austin, the young man from Sunrise Beach who stopped and put his baseball jacket around her on the night of the attack.

He saw how badly beaten she was. Even if it was possible that this was an argument between a couple, that didn't give Masters the right to beat her and strip her of all her clothes and leave her in a ditch on the side of the road. Kenny couldn't believe the total indifference of people toward the facts in this case. Kenny begged the school principal to allow him to go onto the school PA system, a state-the-facts for everyone to hear, but Pamela went to a different school, and the principal didn't think that this was a proper issue for the entire school to hear. But Kenny didn't give up. He went to the local newspaper and requested that he be allowed to do a guest editorial about the issue. He complained about the lack of support from the principal and the public school system. He raised the issue about it being the commissioner's son. This was meaty, bloody stuff for a newspaper. They gave him the entire editorial page of the Sunday paper. He wrote an explosive editorial. It rocked the entire county like an atomic bomb. All the local TV stations carried it on Monday and continued throughout the week. Local elected officials were interviewed. The press demanded a statement from Commissioner Benson regarding his involvement. Overnight, Pamela became the victim, and Masters became the attacker, and the pressure was on to have an open and fair trial. Public opinion swayed quickly, and things were not looking good for the attackers. It seems that Kenny had never gotten his jacket back, and Mrs. Scott didn't know who it belonged to. Now she did.

Mrs. Scott invited Kenny to her house for dinner. She had taken the jacket to the cleaners and had it cleaned and pressed. It looked brand new. Kenny had not seen or spoken to Pamela since the night of the attack. He wanted to stop by the gas station and talk to her, but he felt that that was too public. Mrs. Scott invited JJ and Julie, and Martin and Delores. When Kenny arrived with his parents, Mrs. Scott began to cry. She embraced Kenny's mother and thanked her for raising such a wonderful young man. She looked at Mr. Austin, who was an ironworker at the steel plant, and with continuing tears, she embraced him also. She escorted them all to their seats at the table and insisted that Kenny sit directly across the table from Pamela. At first there was very little conversation, so JJ ask Kenny, "Well how do you think she looks now?"

Kenny stammered a little and responded, "She sure looks better than the last time I saw her. Her face was all bloody and swollen. You could barely see her eyes. And look at her now. She is beautiful and her eyes are sparkling. I'm so happy for you; I hope that you feel as good as you look.

Their looks were beaming at each other, and you could tell that there was love in the air. Kenny attempted to make a joke.

"Your dress is beautiful. You know, the last time I saw you didn't have a dress on. As a matter of fact, you didn't have anything on, and dummy me, all I noticed was your bloody face. I keep that up and my father's going to think that I'm gay."

"No, son, it takes a real man to do what you've done, both on the night of the attack and this past week. I'm damned proud of you."

"Hear, hear, the rest of us feel exactly the same."

Martin, with tears running down his face, said, "Kenny, I'm very proud to call you my friend. Your willingness to take on the school principal, the school system, and Commissioner Benson showed pure courage. You restored Pamela's reputation, and it didn't matter to you that she is a black girl."

"Is she black? I never noticed that. But I did notice that she is beautiful."

"Wow! That sounds like a man in love," replies JJ. "Please allow me to add mine and Julie's kudos. You are a great friend. I knew that day that I saved you from that judge that you were worth it, and now you've proven it. I'll bet that judge and Captain Rogers are busting their buttons with pride."

"Oh my gosh, JJ, I forgot to invite Captain Rogers. How could I do that?"

"That's okay, Mrs. Scott. Just remember to vote for him as sheriff; that'll make him happier than a free meal."

"I'll do more than that. I'll have all of Freetown vote for him. I'll never forget him making a personal visit here the night that released Kenny and his friends. I was sure that they were going to do nothing about my baby girl being raped. But he assured me that he wasn't going to rest until they found those guys. And he got them. We got to make him our new sheriff. And speaking of that, Martin, we have to get your mother to run for county commissioner."

"Mr. Austin, do you think that your union workers would vote for a black woman?"

"No, I don't, Martin. Some of them will because they are fed up with the current bunch that are running this county. It's hard to get blue-collar workers to vote for a black, just like it's hard to get blacks to vote for a Republican. But if you young people would get organized, you could make the difference. You take a solid black vote, along with a strong vote from the eighteen to twenty-five group, you could win it. It would be very close, but that's what elections are all about. Look at this Nixon/Kennedy election. Kennedy won by less than 600,000 votes nationwide. That's about one vote for each polling place, nationwide. Think about that. One vote either way could have made the difference in electing a president. I've never seen an election that close in my lifetime. So do I think that your mother can win, *yes*, but don't expect the vote to come from the steelyard; it could come from the schoolyard. Are you guys going to get involved in her campaign?"

"I'll work for Momma Martin," states JJ.

"So will I," states Kenny.

"You guys would work for my mom?"

"Yeah, damn right. She's a great lady."

"JJ, why are you and Kenny so different from the other white boys I've known?" asks Pamela.

"Well, I don't know about JJ, but you just heard my dad. He

thinks for himself, and he taught me and my sister that we should think for ourselves. You listen to what others say, but you decide on your own."

"I don't know why I feel so strongly about right and wrong. My mother and father would vote for a jackass if it has a Democrat label. Yet in this last election, they wouldn't vote for Kennedy because he is Catholic. They believe that the pope would be running our country. Now, how in the hell is the pope going to run this country from Italy with all the checks and balances that our forefathers put in place? I don't think that is possible. I love US history, and I've studied many of our leaders, and your dad is right. Our great leaders are free thinkers."

"Look at Jefferson. How could that man see so far into the future and predict how this government would function? Look at our Bill of Rights. Look at Lincoln and his wisdom. His simple speech at Gettysburg that says it all. Our rights are given by God, not by governments. We're all equal."

"JJ you sound like you are running for office."

"No, I'm not, but if Momma Martin wants to run, I'll go make speeches for her. I believe in her. All right, Martin. You've got to convince her to run. Tell her that you recruited two workers at dinner and that I'll put the top down on my Desoto, and Kenny and I will start putting up signs for her."

"Okay, I'll start working on her. Now, what else do we need to work on?"

"We need to get started on your wedding. You guys keep changing the date. Next thing you know you'll be coming to mine and Julie's wedding."

"No, I think we're going to do it the twenty-first of June."

"Now how did you come up with that date?"

"Well, school will be over. This trial should be over, and the navy is talking about taking me on the twenty-first of July."

"So is that a firm date?"

"I think so."

"That doesn't sound very firm to me."

"Well, when are you two going to get married?"

"I don't know. We've got lots of things to do before we get married."

"Can't you do them after you get married?"

"I guess most of them can be, but that isn't the way we planned it."

"Doesn't sound like you've planned it at all."

"Well, we've talked about it, but it's off in the future. We have plenty of time to plan it."

"Hello, guys, remember me? I'm Pam's mother, and I want to give Kenny his jacket. Kenny, I had no idea about the story behind this jacket. We brought it home from the hospital, and it sat in the corner of Pam's room all this time. When JJ finally got the truth out about that night, I kept thinking, 'Who was that nice young man who helped my daughter in her time of need?' I never dreamed that it was one of the boys that we were accused of the attack. In fact, we were ready to convict you and your friends, put you in jail, and throw away the key. Thanks to JJ, cooler heads prevailed, and the truth came out, but I still didn't know who this fine person was. Then I read the editorial in the newspaper, and I said, 'There he is. I've got to meet him and thank him.' And here we are. And what a wonderful night it has been. I never thought that a baseball jacket could be so beautiful. But I'm returning it to its rightful owner. Thank you, you wonderful young man. I will love you forever."

"I certainly hope so, because I plan on marrying your daughter. She just doesn't know it yet. In fact, if she will go out with me tomorrow night, I let her wear this jacket again, only under much nicer circumstances."

Pam is crying. "Yes, I would love to go out with you. Where are we going?"

"I plan like JJ. I don't really know where we are going. Does it matter?"

"No, I'll go wherever you take me."

"Good night, folks. Julie and I are going home. I can't handle any more of this emotion stuff."

"Yeah, I think that Delores and I are going to take that long walk next door."

"JJ, could you take me and Mrs. Austin home. I think that I'll leave the car for Kenny, in case he wants to take Pam to get a milkshake."

"Thanks, Dad. That's a great idea."

"Good night, Mrs. Scott. Looks like we are going to become family in the near future."

"Good night, Mr. Austin. I think that would be a wonderful union of families."

"Ready, Mr. Austin? Do you want me to put the top down?"

"JJ, are you crazy. It's only 30 degrees out here."

"Well, it's been a crazy night with a crazy ending. I just thought that I'd add to the craziness."

"I think we'll pass, JJ—just a nice, sane ride home with the top in place and the heater on. I'm glad it's only five miles."

# Chapter 36

We are closing in on the end of the school year. The weather is perfect, and most things are calm and normal. Graduation is soon, and Martin's wedding follows graduation. Joey and Debbie are now talking about marriage. Justin and Connie had their first sexual encounter on the yacht, and Mr. Casey caught them in the act. He actually was pretty calm about it. He seemed to enjoy seeing Connie totally naked. She had become a beautiful young woman. Mr. Casey had three sons, so he didn't know exactly what to say to her, so he handed her clothes to her, and simply said, "I'd prefer that Mrs. Casey didn't know about this." Connie and Justin got dressed and acted as if nothing had happened. Andrew, Justin's brother, has gotten worse with his drinking and drugs. They are putting him in a Rehab center as soon as he graduates.

Tommy and Kathy are living together in her mother's house, and the arrangement seems to be working very well. Her mother has a thirty-five-year-old boyfriend who is almost always drunk and is constantly trying to get them to swap partners. But Tommy isn't going to allow him to do Kathy, even though he wants to do her mother.

JJ is still working at the animal hospital. Dr. E. and Sherry have moved to New York, and Bonnie moved with them to become a "live-in babysitter." Miss Bonn goes up there every other weekend. She and Bonnie have become regulars at the swingers' parties. Teacher's future husband doesn't seem to like the arrangement, and it appears that the relationship will soon end.

JJ and Delores have both been accepted to the University of

Maryland. She has a full scholarship based on her minority status, and JJ won a $400 donation from the Rotary Club and a $100 grant from the YMCA if he makes the baseball team.

Mr. Casey has set a date to take the group down the Chesapeake Bay on the yacht. JJ asked if Martin and Delores could join them. Mr. and Mrs. Casey have never had black guests to their house. Their household servants are all black, but there are never black guests. At first, they told Justin *no*. Justin told them that if they said no, JJ and Julie would not come. And if JJ and Julie didn't come, he didn't think that the others would come. Justin pushed hard. These are all my friends, including Martin and Delores. The Caseys ask, "What will our hired help think?"

Justin responded, "Who cares? They work for you!"

"Well, what about our friends?" asks Mrs. Casey.

"What friends?" asks Justin. "You haven't had anyone to the house in five years. You only have social, cocktail friends that you see at parties. They don't care about you. These people will become your real friends, and you can do a lot to help them grow up by showing that you care about them!"

Mr. Casey speaks up. "He's right. We don't have any real friends! I like these kids better than most of the people that we know. Our servants will serve them just the same as they serve anyone who comes to our house. As far as I'm concerned, Martin and his girlfriend are welcome."

Justin is stunned. He never thought that his father would agree with him.

"Well, if you're okay with it, I'm okay with it," states Mrs. Casey.

"Okay, that's settled. Let's order some crab meat and ten pounds of shrimp. What do these kids drink? Beer?"

"Some of them drink beer, but most drink soda and ice tea!"

"Okay. We'll fill a couple of coolers and they can pick whatever they want."

Justin waits until him mother leaves the room. "Thanks, Dad. This is going to be wonderful."

"Yeah, I think that it is. Do you think that you and Connie can keep your clothes on? At least until everyone leaves?"

"Sorry, Dad!"

"No reason to be sorry. She's a hot little chick. Your mother was that hot when she was that young, and I tried damn hard to get her clothes off, but I never got more than her bra off. Do you think this is going to be your future wife?"

"Yes, I do. We are a perfect match. But marriage is a few years off. She wants to go to college, and I don't know what I'm going to do."

"Well, for now, let's concentrate on our trip down the Chesapeake."

Saturday arrives, and JJ calls Justin. "Hi, do you need any help getting things ready?"

"No, are you kidding. My father is more excited than I am. He had the cook prepare two hundred and fifty crab balls, ten pounds of shrimp, potato salad, and coleslaw. Both coolers are filled with drinks. He's on the yacht polishing the chrome and the brass. He can't wait to leave."

"It's only 9:00 a.m. We don't leave until noon."

"Yeah, I know, but he's like a little kid waiting for his birthday party!"

"I want to thank your dad for accepting Martin."

"I don't think that you need to say anything. I think that he is proud of himself for thinking outside the box."

"I think that Martin is excited. He's never been on a yacht before."

"Have any of our friends even been on a yacht before?"

"I don't know? I was on the governor's yacht with my school class, but I've never been on a personal yacht with two hundred and fifty crab balls and ten pounds of shrimp. I'll see you at noon. Wait 'til you see this outfit that Julie's wearing. Perfect fitting shorts to match her beautiful legs and a white halter top that fit her boobs perfectly. God, she is beautiful."

"Wait 'til you see Connie! I think that her boobs are bigger than Julie's, and she's wearing something like Julie's. This thing fits tight, and the material is thin. Her nipples look like headlights in the fog. I don't know what she is wearing on the bottom, my eyes never got off the headlights."

"Yeah, well you and I know that you can often get them to take the tops off, but to get the bottoms off is a different story. They close those legs like a locked safe, and they hide the keys!"

"Oh God, did I tell you that I got Connie to take everything off on the yacht, and we were going at it like two bunny rabbits when my father walked in. Connie was on top, so he got a full view. She tried to scramble to cover up, but those staterooms are so small, she really didn't have any place to hide."

"What the hell did your father say?"

"It was kind of funny. He didn't know what to say, but he took his time looking at Connie's body. He picked up Connie's clothes off the floor and handed them to her slowly. I think that he was enjoying it. The only thing that he said was, 'I'd rather that Mrs. Casey didn't know about this.' Then he left the room."

"Connie was embarrassed and upset. I tried to get her to finish what we were doing, and that made her mad."

"Do you think that I'm going to screw you while your father's outside the door?"

"I had to laugh, and I tried to convince her that he had left, but she didn't care. She got dressed and was up and out in the main cabin before I could get my pants on. When I got up there my father was gone, and she wanted to go home. I told her that by the time I got her home, it would be time to turn around and come back to the boat. I convinced her to calm down and just act normal. My father returned, and he could tell that she was embarrassed, so he asked her to go up to the house and get some napkins and paper towels. She was happy to do so, and she took plenty of time before she returned."

"Look, JJ. It's almost time for you to pick up Julie. I'll see you in about an hour. Don't tell Julie about me and Connie. She might say something to Connie, and I'll be in the dog house!"

"Okay, I won't say anything, and you can tell me all the details later."

JJ called Martin to see if he was ready. He was going to pick them up and then go.

"Pick up Julie."

"Hey, Martin. Are you guys ready?"

"Yeah, man. We've been ready and waiting for you."

"Okay, I'll be there in about twenty minutes." JJ then calls Julie and tells her the schedule. She's ready and waiting. Joey and Debbie are picking up Tommy and Kathy and they are on their way."

"Joey and his group arrived first, and Connie was so happy to see some other people. She couldn't look directly at Mr. Casey, and I think that Mr. Casey was enjoying her embarrassment."

"Hi, guys. Come aboard." Justin introduces Mr. Casey to everyone. They had met before, but he knew that his father wouldn't remember all the names. Just as he finished, Mrs. Casey arrives, and he begins the introductions again.

JJ has his passengers and is nearly there. Martin has asked him four times, "Are you sure that the Caseys are okay with us coming along?"

"Yes, Martin, everything is fine. Do you want me to give you some white cold cream, and you can do a reverse Al Jolson and sing 'Suwannee River'?"

"Shut up, JJ. That's not funny. I'm nervous. Not only are they white, but they are rich, and I'll bet that they don't have any black friends!"

"You're right. I'm sure they don't have any black friends. But according to Justin, they don't have many friends at all. They have their money and all their silver and gold but no real friends, and that's a shame because they are nice people. So you two turn on your charm and make them your new friends!"

"We'll try, but how do you know that they want to have black friends."

"Martin, you're not black! You're just Martin! I don't think of you as my black friends. I simply think of you both as my friends, and I love you both, and so will they. I'll bet that they are as nervous as you are!"

"Okay, we're here. Just relax and be yourselves."

"Hi, JJ. Welcome aboard. Mom, Dad, you know JJ and Julie. And this is Martin and Delores, our friends from Freetown."

"Hi, Martin and Delores. I'm Helen Casey, and this is my husband, Howard. We're the rich snobs that you have been nervous about meeting. And yes, we've never been to Freetown, and we don't have any black friends, but that's going to end right now. I truly hope that you will accept us as your friends. Just because we're white and live a high lifestyle doesn't mean that we can't come to love each other as God intended and be the best of friends."

"Thank you, Mrs. Casey. You're right. We were nervous about meeting you, and you accepting us for who we are. But right now I feel like I've known you all my life. With just a few kind words you have made me feel like I'm accepted. You are a wonderful, kind person, and I hope that you will become our friends. In two weeks, Delores and I are getting married and starting our lives together, and I hope that you will become a part of that new family."

"Wow! Martin, I never thought that I would hear those words come out of the mouth of my wife. And I am so proud of her. I'm so proud of my son, Justin, for looking beyond the color of your skin and creating a true friendship. You are all young, and the friends that you make at this stage of life will last forever. All of our money and the expensive things that we own, including this boat, have never made me feel as happy as I do right now. Thank you for accepting us snobs into your lives. Now let me start up this engine and let's enjoy the beautiful Chesapeake Bay!"

"Thank God, Mr. Casey. I was about ready to cry if I heard any more gushy statements."

"JJ you're the one who started all this when you stood up for a little black boy who had been hit in the head with a club and you developed a friendship that spread to Tommy, Justin, and Joey, and now to each of your girlfriends. Your baseball team has joined together two communities that might never have met. One small act of courage."

"Oh please, Mr. Casey. Start your engines or I'm going to start crying."

As they headed down the Chesapeake Bay, there were tears of joy and smiles of happiness on everyone's face.

"JJ, you were right about the Caseys, and Delores and I would like to invite them to our wedding. Do you think that they would come?"

"If you invite Justin and Connie, I'm sure that his father and mother would come. Why don't you ask them?"

"We did ask Justin and Connie, but they haven't responded."

"That was before today. I'll bet that if you ask Justin now, you will get a yes! And while you're at it, how about Tommy and Kathy, and Joey and Debbie. They are all your friends, and I'm sure that they are disappointed that they haven't been invited."

"I really didn't think that they would come."

"Oh, will you stop this *black* thing. They are your friends, and they love you. Ask them. I'll bet you will see big smiles and loud *yes*. Delores, you have a big job on your hands, making this guy realize that not everyone sees black when they are talking to him. Many see him as intelligent and bright with a great future ahead of him."

"JJ, not all white people think like you do."

"Delores, you and Martin need to face the world and change their opinions. You're a lovely, intelligent couple. When people meet you, they like you. If you could change one person a week, you would have a lasting impact on our community."

"We're going to test your beliefs. We're going to ask everyone here to come to our wedding."

"That's a good start."

"JJ, you should be a preacher. You never stop trying to improve the world."

"Julie, my love, I only say things that I think need to be said. If it helps someone, that's great. If not, at least I know that I tried."

"Justin, Delores and I sent you an invitation to our wedding, and we haven't heard back?"

"Martin, until today, I thought that my parents would object, but after hearing them both, I am so happy. And yes, if it's okay with Connie's parents, we will be there."

"Do you think that your parents would come?"

"If you ask them as you're leaving the boat, I'm sure that they will come."

"Thanks, I'll do that."

"Tommy, Joey, Delores and I would be honored if you would come to our wedding and bring your girlfriends."

"Damn, Martin, we didn't think that you wanted us there. You bet! We'll be there."

"The boat is almost back to the dock, all the crab balls, and all the shrimp and nearly everything else has been eaten. Everyone is tired and sleepy from all the fresh air and the emotions of the day. This has been a day that has changed lives forever, and no one knows what impact it will have on the future, but for now, it has changed the feelings and thinking towards each other."

As they are departing the boat, everyone is thanking the Caseys. As Martin and Delores approached the Caseys, Martin thanks them for a wonderful day.

"And may I ask one more thing of you? Delores and I would be honored if you would attend our wedding?"

"Mrs. Casey's eyes filled with tears as she looked at her husband. Mr. Casey looked at Martin with a huge smile and said, "Martin, it would be our honor to attend your wedding and watch two wonderful people become one, in God's eyes. Thank you for inviting us."

"As JJ, Julie, Martin, and Delores were heading back to Freetown, Delores began sobbing out of control. It so startled JJ that he pulled off the road."

"What's the matter?"

"Delores could barely speak. I've never had a day like this in my life. So many wonderful things happened that I simply can't control my emotion."

JJ looks at Martin. "Women. They cry when they are sad. They cry when they are happy. How the hell are you supposed to know which it is?"

Martin says, "I guess you have to ask them which it is."

"They all laughed, and JJ continued to drive."

# Chapter 37

THE BIG DAY HAS ARRIVED. Six hundred and six students are graduating. Fourteen will walk across the stage but will not receive their diploma until they complete some summer classes. Andrew, Justin's bother, is one of them. Justin made it by one point. He passed Algebra with a D, with a 61 on his final exam. Some believe that JJ used his friendship with Miss Bonn to make sure it was at least a D, but Justin doesn't plan to go to college, so it wasn't as important as JJ's B.

Mr. Casey plans to retire this year and his oldest son, Howard Jr., is going to take over the business. Justin will take the job that Howard has been doing for the past ten years. Justin doesn't think that he can work for his brother, but it is a good job that pays very well. No one knows what Andrew is going to do. He still has a drinking and drug problem that he hides very well.

Tommy has been offered a full-time job with the construction company, and his boss has been training him to do all the estimating for the jobs. This is a great job. He'll be making $15 per hour, plus benefits, with a great future. He and Kathy are planning a wedding between Christmas and New Year's. They were planning on moving into their own place, but her mother begged them to stay with her. Tommy's planning on buying the house and fixing it up with the leftover materials from the jobs. He has already talked to his boss about his idea, and the boss agrees. The boss is giving him $1000 for his wedding, and he has some money of his own for a down payment. What a great start in life.

Joey has the same type of start. His future father-in-law wants him to come to work for him, but he decided to go to the trade school that trains you for heavy equipment operations. He already knows how to run grading equipment, but the union boss at the Port of Baltimore told him that if he learned how to run the large cranes for loading ships, he would hire him at $21 per hour plus benefits, and they generally work forty plus hours with time and a half pay for anything over thirty-six hours. They work three days a week for twelve hours each, so he could work part-time for his father-in-law and decide which job he wanted. Joey and Debbie are also planning to get married. Debbie's parents want them to live with them. The house has six bedrooms and four bathrooms. The basement is a full-size apartment with its own entrance. But Joey wants his own place, so they haven't decided what they want to do. Joey's concerned that Debbie isn't going to be able to break the ties with her parents if they live there. He likes her parents, but he's afraid they will try to control their lives, and it's causing him to have "second thoughts" about the marriage.

JJ sees all his friends with their lives all planned, and he still doesn't know what he is going to do. He's going to the University of Maryland, but his heart really isn't committed to becoming a business major. Julie is going to New York in ten days to see if she has a dancing career. He's concerned that she will decide that she wants to dance at Radio City Music Hall or dance on Broadway in the various plays. Julie has one more year of school, so they have a little time to decide.

"The principal is giving instruction over the PA system. The program will start at 6:00 p.m. tonight, please arrive early, as we have a packed house. There are no extra seats. Anyone with extra tickets, please turn them in so that others may use them."

All week long, the students were having the teachers and their friends write something in their yearbook next to their picture. Most of the teachers wrote something nice about their future. The students generally wrote something silly or funny. Most of the girls wrote something *smart* about the boys, and most of the boys did the same, with comments about their short skirts or tight sweaters.

Good friends wrote something very thoughtful and nice; after all, this might be the last time that they see each other.

It's 6:00 p.m., as the principal steps to the microphone.

"Will everyone rise as the Glee Club sings the Star Spangle Banner, followed by the Pledge of Allegiance to the flag, followed by Pastor Jim Michaels from Christ Lutheran Church, who will bless this gathering. Please join in with the singing."

"We will start with the class president making his farewell speech to everyone."

"Next will be the class Valedictorian."

"We will proceed with many scholarships given by many local businesses, and community groups, as well as the colleges and universities. Altogether, ninety-seven awards are being given, ranging from $100 to $6,000. I congratulate all of you and hope that these awards will help you accomplish your future goals."

"We now will give five awards voted on by the student body."

"#1 Most likely to Succeed goes to Charles Woodside for his future in the State Department as an interpreter."

"#2 Best Nurse in the State to Nancy Grimes and her internship at University Hospital."

"#3 Future Farmer of America to Bill Sellers and the little garden that he created for the poor and homeless."

"#4 Future Businessman, Jim Boring, sponsored by the Rotary Club, which carries a $500 grant."

"#5 This award has never been given before, but the students felt that they had to create this one for a very special person. It is sponsored by the YMCA, the Association of Christian Churches, the Jaycees, and Sportsman Club of Glen Brook. Along with this award goes a grant for $1000. And the award goes to JJ Kapok, for his efforts in civil rights, his efforts through sports to treat everyone on an equal basis, and his ability to bring the Freetown Community and the Beachwood Community together to create lifelong friendships. Quite a feat for such an amazing young man."

# Chapter 38

It's the Fourth of June, and Martin and Delores have decided to proceed with their wedding plans. It seems that the navy has some silly rule that if you are single when you enter the flight training classes, you cannot date or marry until the class is complete (two years), but if you are already married and accepted in the program, they wave that rule. Delores's scholarship was increased by $500 if she is married; it is unclear why, but it simply increased. So both of them had reason to get it done quickly.

The group of friends got together and decorated the Freetown Hall and got it ready for the reception. It is beautiful. Sparkling white with red roses and blue tablecloths (red, white, and blue). Martin was granted permission to wear his navy white dress uniform. He looks like a movie star. Delores dress was a beautiful white with pearl beads. She stands 5' 9" tall with beautiful long hair—a very beautiful bride.

The church was very traditional, with a full gospel choir and an organ that extended to the top of the ceiling. It seated approximately 400 people, plus many more that could be placed in the basement recreation room. You knew that the music was going to be perfect and the entire community was going to attend.

The groomsmen were in light blue tuxedoes, except JJ, who was in a white tux, and Martin, in his white dress uniform.

The bridesmaids were in beautiful red rose dresses with white flowers. This looked like a wedding out of a Hollywood movie.

Now the guys were trying to plan a bachelor party for Martin. The problem was that ten out of twelve of them *did not drink*!

All of them had girlfriends or wives, and they did not want to do anything that would get Martin in trouble and mess up his entering the navy. They thought about the normal stuff, like a strip club or watching porn movies all night. But no matter what they did, they would have to explain it to their women. So, here's the plan. They called Danny's Restaurant and asked to rent their private room, for "dinner" (haha), no drinking. They hired three strippers, who would be totally nude for three hours, with sex toys, etc. As far as their women were concerned, this was only for men with gifts for Martin, like condoms, slave whips, and other sex toys.

*No women.*

They think that they can pull this off without any problems. Now they need to find out where they are going for their wedding night. They find out that they are going to Martin's cousin's house for the weekend. Martin's cousin is going to be in Florida, so they convince him to give them a set of keys, with the promise that they will not disturb them or damage the house. JJ and the group plan their dirty deeds.

Friday night after Danny's and the strippers, they go to the cousin's house. They lift the bed and tie a dozen small Christmas tree bells to the springs of the bed. Then they separate the mattress from the box spring and pour an entire box of Corn Flakes on the box spring and sew the box spring sheet closed. Then they sew the mattress sheet to the box spring sheet. Delores has left her nightgown hanging on the bathroom door, so they proceeded to sew the arms and the bottom closed. They replace the hard-boiled eggs with raw eggs! They remove all the knives, forks, and spoons from the kitchen. They put superglue on all the rolls of toilet paper. They thought of some other things, but they decided that they had done enough to spoil a very special night. They estimated that it would take them at least two hours to undo everything, while thinking, *What else have these* nuts *done?*

It's Saturday at noontime. The church is full. JJ and Martin are standing at the altar. The organ begins to play the wedding march, and the bridesmaids begin to enter on the arms of the handsome men. When the last person takes their place, the organ begins playing "Here Comes the Bride." Delores enters on the arm of her father. She is so beautiful that everyone gasps and the cameras begin clicking. As they reach the altar, the preacher asks, "Who giveth this woman to this man."

Delores's father, with his voice cracking, says, "I do."

The wedding goes off perfectly.

As the couple leaves the church, more pictures are taken and the guests begin to leave for the reception hall.

The entire wedding party looks at each other in disbelief. "Is it really over?" It's done? Let's go party!

Arriving at the Reception Hall, each couple is announced as they enter the room.

"And now appearing for the first time in public, Mr. and Mrs. Martin King."

As the new couple take their seats, spoons start clanking on the water glasses. Everyone knows that means public kissing and the official start of the party.

As the first song begins to play, the Champagne glasses are filled and the best man is ready to make his speech.

As JJ rises, someone yells, "Don't get long winded and gushy. We want to eat tonight." All kinds of thoughts are rushing through JJ's head. What do you say to a very special friend and his new bride? How do you express your feelings in a lighthearted manner without getting gushy and teary-eyed?

"Can we all fill our glasses and stand. Seven years ago, on a baseball diamond in Beachwood, a very special friendship was established most unusually. My friend Martin was struck in the head with a Billy club by some very bad dudes. It knocked him to the ground and split his skull. Several of us tried to help him, and some of our football friends came to the rescue. What a way to become friends. Some would say that he lost some of his brain cells, but it couldn't have been very many, because look at this very intelligent move here today—marrying the most beautiful and intelligent woman in Freetown, Delores! My girlfriend, Julie and I love them like they are part of our family. Martin is an amazing person, and he now has an amazing wife, so can we raise our glasses high for this toast.

"Martin and Delores, God has not provided me with the words to express our love for you, but as you now join as one, I want to wish you many days of happiness and sunshine. May you grow together and fulfill all your dreams and goals together. May you have at least nine children so you can have your own baseball team! And may you always remain our friends. Because we all love you!"

"Hear! Hear!" is shouted, and glasses begin clinking.

"Can we eat now?"

The reception was perfect. A few got drunk, but most danced and enjoyed each other.

Kathy caught the bride's bouquet of flowers, and Delores's brother caught the garter. And he doesn't have a girlfriend.

The newly married couple left in the Limo that JJ had rented for them. And all the guys sat around telling everybody all the silly things that they had done at Martin's cousin house. All they could do was laugh, thinking about the bells ringing, the cereal crunching, and the couple trying to cut the sheets free from the box spring. These will be memories that will last a lifetime, and they were already enjoying them.

Kathy looked at Tommy, who was so drunk that he could barely stand up. "I hope that our wedding is this perfect."

Tommy looks at Kathy and says, "I hope that I can remember this one so that I will have something to compare it to!"

Everyone laughs.

"Well, who's going to be next, you and Tommy or Joey and Debbie?"

"What about you and Julie?"

"Oh, I think that you guys will beat us, but we'll get there; besides, we already feel like we're married. We've known each other since we were ten years old. We've been going steady for four years. We do everything together. The only thing that we don't do is live together."

Tommy looks at Kathy and says, "Hell, that's the best part. When her mother isn't home, I grab everything that I can!"

"Okay, Tommy, it's time for us to go home before you tell everyone our personal life."

"As I said, I'm ready to go home."

"As drunk as you are, you'll fall asleep before we get there. Give me the keys. We'll see you all later."

"See you, Kathy. For your sake, I hope he falls asleep."

"Oh, he will. That's the beer you hear talking."

"Well, Joey, I guess that we are the last few couples to leave. This really was great."

"Yeah, and I'll be thinking about those bells all the way home. See ya."

As JJ and Julie are driving home, JJ says, "That really was a big wedding. There must have been five hundred people there."

"I don't think that ours will be that large."

"Hell, Julie, I don't think that I know five hundred people."

"Even if we do, I think close friends and family are enough."

"Weddings are for brides, so whatever you want to do is okay with me. Just one thing. We are *not* telling anyone where we are going on our wedding night!"

# Chapter 39

THE PACE OF LIFE HAS slowed down now that everyone has graduated and starting their lives and looking to the future.

JJ has been accepted into the University of Maryland and is working to save money for college expenses. No one from his family has ever attended college, so he doesn't know what to expect. He has a cousin, Pat Garman, who is very bright and about three years older than him. Pat won a scholarship to an all-girls college and is in her last year. He plans to meet with her and talk about college life. She is the first person in the entire family to go to college, and she has done very well. Pat moved out of her parents' house and has her own apartment, so he wants to talk to her about that and discuss with her if that is a good thing to do? Pat is a very beautiful woman. She's 5' 7" and 140 lbs, and it's all in the right places. Pat has a great personality and is very classy. She doesn't like the fact that she comes from a poor blue-collar family; after all, this college is very upper class, and that seems to have rubbed off on her. She doesn't have much contact with her family. She has a boyfriend that also is in his last year of college, and I think that they plan to get married. He is a tall, good-looking man who could be a football player, but he doesn't like sports. They make a perfect couple. They look like the Kennedys.

Julie is working and teaching her dance classes. She is saving money to help JJ when he starts college. Julie and her aunt are going to New York next week to visit Radio City Music Hall for her interview. They are both excited. Her aunt has been there before and has planned to see a couple of Broadway shows while they are there. *Oklahoma* and *The Sound of Music* are playing. The hotel got them tickets to both shows, and they were expensive.

JJ has decided to make the phone call to Pat to see if they can get together.

"Hi, Pat, this is your cousin JJ. How are you doing?"

"Things are good, JJ. Can you believe that I graduate next May!"

"Yeah, it seems like yesterday that you entered college, and now you are nearly finished. Hey, that's what I'm calling about. I've been accepted into the U of M, and I'm scared to death!"

"What are you scared about?"

"Everything. I don't know what to expect. Can we get together one night this week and talk about college life?"

"Sure, Phil, her boyfriend, comes over every night, but this Wednesday he is going to a birthday party for his younger sister. Can you make Wednesday night around 6:00 p.m., at my apartment? I'll make us some dinner."

"Yeah, that's perfect. I'll see you then. Do you want me to bring anything?"

"No, just you. It'll be great to see you again. It's been a long time."

JJ calls Julie to tell her about meeting with his cousin Pat.

"Hi, I just spoke with my cousin Pat, and we are getting together this Wednesday night to talk about college life."

"Well, that should be an interesting night. What are you going to ask her about?"

"I don't know, I thought that I'd let her do most of the talking."

"Well, that will be a first—you letting someone else do the talking!"

"Okay, smart ass, so I will ask a few questions, like how many classes does she take each day, and how many times during a week does she take the same subject?"

"Doesn't the college set the schedule?"

"Yeah, it depends on how many course credits that you take, but you can take several each day, or you can spread them out during the week. I want to see what Pat suggests that I do. Since I'm driving, I think that I want to take several each day, and have days off to study. That will give me time to rest and will reduce my cost."

"What about the college party life?"

"You know that I don't have time for that! Besides, that's a long drive over bad roads, and I'm not that good of a student. I know that I'm going to need free time to study and sleep."

"Well, that will work perfectly. You know that I'm leaving for New York that morning and won't be back until Saturday night."

"I had forgotten that was this coming week, but that does work well. I hope that you have a great time and enjoy the shows."

"I think that it will be fun, but I wish that you were going with us."

"Me too, but this is for you and you don't need any distractions. I think that I might stop and see Pat's sister, Jeannie, while I'm in the area and you are away."

"That's a good idea. Didn't she graduate from high school this year?"

"Yeah, she's the same age as us, and I'm sure that this is her last year of school. Is she going to college?"

"No, she took some kind of classes that gave her special training for the printing trade, and she has a good job waiting for her. She's going to start at $20 per hour and has a good chance to advance to high-level management. The company provides the training while you work. So I think that's what she is going to do."

It's Wednesday and JJ is driving Julie and her aunt to the train station for their trip to New York. The aunt is dressed like a movie star. She is so beautiful and so perfect that men stop just to look at her as she passes by them, and she is only 4' 10" tall. Julie looks like her little sister and is dressed much more casual. Respectable skirt and a damn perfect tight sweater that makes her perfect breasts look even better. A wide leather belt with a beautiful brass buckle makes that 19" waist looks even smaller. Wow, what a body for a seventeen-year-old woman. Perfection! There was a group of young navy sailors standing by the entrance when JJ pulled up to let them out. When he opened the door, and those beautiful legs appeared, the sailors went crazy. As hard as the women tried to avoid them, they couldn't help but smile. The sailors were funny and at the same time respectful. It looked like a scene from the show *South Pacific*, where the sailors are singing "There is nothing like a dame." They were having fun, and they even treated JJ with respect while at the same time teasing him about being too young to handle those beautiful women. Fortunately, the sailors were heading south to Washington, D.C., and the women were headed north to the Big Apple. JJ got the women and their baggage to the departure area, and within minutes the train arrived, and they were off. JJ returned to his car and was thinking about his meeting with Pat at 6:00 p.m. Getting out of Penn Station was difficult. Taxi cabs everywhere, blowing their horns and yelling at each other, transit buses letting people off at the entrance, and people simply lost and confused. JJ finally made it to the main street and was heading south out of the city.

It's 5:00 p.m. now, and JJ has to go to the Townson Area slightly northeast of Baltimore. It'll take him approximately one hour to get to Pat's apartment, but there is no strict time schedule. He decides to stop at a local store to buy her some flowers and pick up a bottle of wine. It feels like a date with an older cousin that he truly loves. He has never been to her apartment before, so he knows that he will get lost trying to find it. Pat gave him perfect directions, and he doesn't miss a single turn. As he gets to her door and is ready to ring the bell, she opens the door.

She had been watching for him and saw him coming up the stairs. She was more beautiful than he had remembered. Perfect baby pure skin, perfect white teeth, and smooth black hair, cut short and very stylish. She had a thin pink silk blouse on and no bra. All you could see were her perfect size-38 breasts and her perfect nipples. She had a black pair of shorts that fit tighter than a pair of gloves and displayed her bottom perfectly. As she hugged him, those perfect breasts pressed against him. They felt great. All he could think was *How am I going to get through dinner without staring at her nipples and having her notice?* God, she had a great body. They both were happy to see each other again.

"Come on in. I have some pasta ready, and I'm excited to hear about your future plans."

JJ hands her the flowers and the wine and pulls up a chair at the dining table.

As they sit down, Pats asks, "Do my breasts bother you? If you like, I'll go put on a bra. But when I'm home I try to be comfortable."

"Your breasts are beautiful, and yes they are distracting, but I like the distraction, so you can leave the bra in the bedroom."

"You sound just like Peter. He'd be taking the blouse off by now. He likes being nude."

"My kind of guy," JJ replies. JJ can't get over the change in Pat. She was an absolute *prude* before going to college. You couldn't say anything sexual to her without her getting offended.

"So you don't mind me enjoying your breasts?"

"Not at all. That's why God gave women breasts, so men could have some enjoyment in life. I'd take the blouse off now that I know that you don't mind, but Peter may stop by after the birthday party, and even though you are my cousin, he might get upset with me showing my bare tits to another man while he wasn't present."

"Are you swingers?"

"Not really, but all colleges have swinger parties, so we go, strip down, and enjoy the fun, but we don't have sex with other couples."

"I assume that you plan to get married?"

"Oh, yeah. As soon as we finish school and get jobs, we'll make all this nudity legal."

"So all colleges have swinger clubs? I thought yours was all prim and proper?"

"It is as far as the rules are concerned, but most of these girls come from rich families, and they don't play by the rules. The college looks the other way. These girls screw like rabbits. Some even go down to the block and prostitute for the thrill of it. Some are so stupid that they get pregnant or get VD. Abortion is a regular thing. They have so much money that they can solve any problem. In fact, it's so common that I can make a call and get you laid after you leave here."

"No, thanks. Maybe I'll take that offer someday, but right now I think I'll stay with what I know."

"So, enough about sex. We can get back to that later. What questions did you come here to ask me?"

"Well, I'm not a great student, and I'm going to be commuting every day. How many classes do you think I should take, and how would you do your schedule?"

"The college will allow you to take up to eighteen credits, but I wouldn't take more than twelve. In fact, for your freshman year, I'd take nine. There is no rush. As you adjust to the workload, you can always add more. But if you take an extra year, so what? And since you are carpooling, you want to find out what the last class of the day is for each of your drivers. Maybe do two or three classes a day, three days a week. Monday, Wednesday, and Thursdays. No Fridays. Classes are too big, and traffic is too bad at the end of the day. Besides, all the parties are on Friday and Saturday, and you should go to some of the parties. Just don't get involved in all of them. And stay away from the drugs, no matter what they tell you. They don't help you study better. Sleep does! What are you taking?"

"Business classes. I don't know what I want to do?"

"Why not get a job for a year or two. Look around to see what you like. Then enter college."

"I thought about that, but I'm afraid that I'll find a job that I like, get use to the money, and never go to college."

"So what? It's more important that you work at something that you enjoy than it is to have a degree. Many skilled jobs pay better than jobs with degrees, and if you decide that you need some formal education, you'll have the time, money, and experience to do something you like."

"I haven't thought about that option. But my problem is that I want to get married. Julie and I have been going together since we were fourteen years old, so we are reasonably certain that we are meant for each other and that it will work."

"You're very young to get married, but it sounds like you know each other very well. How about the sex?"

"We haven't had intercourse yet, but I'm certain that will not be a problem."

"You haven't had sex with her, and you want to marry her? Why haven't you had sex?"

"We wanted to finish school and see what we wanted to do in life. She has one more year of school. So I thought that I would go my first year of college. See if I like it and then decide. While I want to have sex with her, it can wait, and like you just said, if it takes me longer to decide what I want to do, so what? Here's a picture of Julie when she was fourteen years old."

"Gosh, she is beautiful, and she's only fourteen in this picture?"

"Yeah, she's into tap dancing and other stuff."

"She looks like a young woman nineteen to twenty years old."

"She'll be eighteen next month, and she looks even better now. All the guys in our group keep asking me about the size of her breasts and so on. They just assume that we are having wild sex together because they are all doing it with their girlfriends."

"At age eighteen, most guys and girls have had at least a few times in bed! But there's nothing wrong with what you have decided. It's just very difficult to be that close and not get involved."

"Yeah, tell me about it. Sometimes when we are kissing and making out, I think that my pecker is going to explode inside my pants!"

"Well, exploding in your pants is better than exploding inside Julie. Your pants don't produce babies!"

"How do you and Peter handle that problem?"

"That's a long, complicated story, but after my first semester at college, I started taking birth control pills. They still aren't perfected yet, but I don't want to get pregnant. The girls at this school thrive on the weekend sex parties, so if you want to fit in, you have to participate, and it's hard to go to those parties and not find someone or something sexual that you would like to do. I hadn't met Peter yet, and I don't like drinking until I'm drunk. When you have size 38Ds, all the guys at these parties are grabbing them. I was constantly fighting them off, and after a while I simply gave up. I didn't mind them playing with my breasts, but they would always want more. After all, this was a sex party! I never went to bed with any of them; I simply would find one of the girls who wanted to get laid, and I'd change places with them. The guys didn't care which girl they got, just as long as they got something, and I assure you that none of them ever left there without getting what they wanted. Then I met Peter, and I thought that I had found someone different. Peter wanted the same thing, but he had a smarter approach. When we were together, we would find a quiet corner and had long conversations about everything. Peter was trying to learn how to speak French, and I had mastered French before I completed high school, so I offered to help him. So we would have this conversation in French, and he would always ask me how to say all the dirty, sexy words, like penis, breasts, ass, intercourse, and so on, and as I would teach him the words he would say, 'How do you know that word? Do you like penis? Do you like intercourse?' Well, you know where that led to. Then we both decided that we would like to go to a swingers party. I swear, I've never seen so much open sex in my life. Everyone wanted us to join them, all offering to teach us something new and different. We decided to teach ourselves, and we've been enjoying the bedroom ever since that night. Peter technically doesn't live here, but he stays overnight more often than he goes home. We're in love, and we are sure of our relationship, so for us, it's been a good thing. I know that it's not for everyone, but for us, it has worked."

"Pat, I'm not judging you. If it worked for you, I think that it's great. My former boss and his wife met in college at a nude pool party. They had sex with everyone and later got married, and they still have sex with everyone. They do swinger parties every other weekend with the same people that they went to college with. They go up to New York, swap wives several times, and come back home happy. They have two children and are planning more. They love it, and I think that they are nice people. I just don't think that I can handle that."

"No, I don't think that Peter and I could do that. We do believe that sex involves love between two people. We like sex, but we are not in love with sexual acts. We are in love with each other."

"Pat, I came here to talk to you about college, and we have talked for an hour about *real life* issues. I'm so glad that you are my cousin and we talked all that time. I never once said anything about your beautiful breasts, and I do like your nipples."

"You really do sound like Peter. We will be having a great conversation and all of a sudden he will stop, look at me, and say, 'I need a nipple break.' Off comes my blouse, he plays around for a little while, and then we resume our conversation. It certainly makes life interesting, and it makes sex fun."

There was a knock at the door. It was Peter. Normally he would just let himself in, but he didn't know what Pat had told him about their relationship. JJ could tell that he was a little uncomfortable, so he thought that he would lighten things up a little.

"Peter, let me ask you something. How long have you been dating my cousin?"

"About two years."

"Two years and you don't have a key to the apartment yet? You're a slow worker!"

Peter looks at Pat, and she gives him a big grin.

"JJ, let me ask you a question. How long have you been here tonight?"

"About three hours."

"You've been here for three hours looking at those beautiful nipples, and your pants are still dry? Are you gay?"

Peter and JJ became instant friends.

"Peter, if she weren't my cousin, I would have had that blouse off within the first hour. Those nipples need to be worked on, and I think that you are just the guy to do it. I'm going to say good night, but I would really like to come back with Julie. She wouldn't like all the sex talk, but I know that she would like both of you."

"Let's do that. It'll be difficult, but I think that Pat and I can make it through a night without becoming sexual animals!"

"Great, I'll get some dates together and give you a call. Peter, it's nice meeting you, and I think that you and Pat make a great couple. I hope things work out well for both of you."

# Chapter 40

JJ HAS BEEN ACCEPTED INTO the University of Maryland and is working at the animal hospital and the golf course to earn money to pay for college.

His parents are coming up with the basic costs and books, but there will be all kinds of unexpected expenses, like lab fees, extra books, supplies, etc.

Julie is teaching her dance classes on the weekends and has taken a part-time job at a local retail store. She has been offered a job in New York at Radio City Music Hall as a Rockette in their dance line. The pay is very poor, and most of the girls live together to share expenses and survive. They work extreme long hours and are treated very poorly. She told them that she wanted to complete high school this coming year and could start next year. They accepted, but they want her to come up for three weekends to train and get established. Everyone is excited. Becoming a Rockette is a big deal. This could be the start of a Broadway career.

JJ and Julie are not certain what this will do to their relationship, but they vow to stay together forever. But both have doubts!

Auntie is dating a navy sailor, and JJ has caught them several times having sex in the back of her car. Auntie thinks that it is funny, and her boyfriend has asked JJ if he wants to join them. JJ doesn't know what to say, but he declines. Auntie enjoys showing JJ her breasts, and they are perfect. She tells him that Julie's are just as nice. She doesn't know that JJ has had the keys to Julie's bra for over a year now. Auntie and the sailor are talking about getting married, and he is scheduled to ship out to sea in about two months. Auntie is not as classy as JJ once thought her to be. In fact, with a few drinks in her, JJ is certain that he could take the sailor's place in the back seat of the car. Things are changing quickly.

Justin and Connie have been going steady ever since freshman prom night. They went to the senior prom together and went to an after-party where they both got drunk and had sexual intercourse all night. Connie is seventeen now and is a beautiful woman. She has cold black hair and looks like Elizabeth Taylor, the movie star. Justin tells JJ every detail of their sexual encounters. Their only concern is "not getting pregnant." They love the sex and are talking about marriage. Connie told her mother about her sexual activity, so Mom took her to the doctor for birth control pills. Mom knows that she will continue to have sex, and in fact she has asked her mother all kinds of questions. So the birth control pills seemed to be a reasonable solution. Justin will always have a well-paying job at his father's business, so he is not concerned about marriage and a family. In fact, he is looking forward to marriage and getting started.

Tommy and Kathy are living together in her mother's place, and it seems to be a good arrangement. He works a good job in construction and makes a very big income. He pays most of the bills at the house.

Kathy knows that her mother is a "drunk" and that when she is drinking heavily, she comes after Tommy for sex. She takes her clothes off and walks around the house totally nude. Tommy is a man, and Momma is a good looking woman. So Kathy has caught them in bed together many times. It causes problems, but Kathy likes all the sex, and she has had sex with Momma's boyfriend. She thought that Tommy would be mad, but instead, they began talking about it and actually have nights where they changed partners. This seems like a crazy way to live, but it seems to work for them!

Joe and Debbie just got married. Joe got a job with a union contractor, and he operates heavy equipment, bulldozers, and front-end loaders. He makes more money than most doctors. It didn't take him long to get Debbie pregnant, and they are expecting a baby in a few months. His father-in-law is still trying to get him to come to work for his electrical company, but he likes what he is doing, and he likes the money. He just bought a new car, and they have a rented house near her parents. Things seem to be working well for them.

The swingers, Dr. E., Sherry, and Bonnie, have moved to New York, and their sex parties are bigger and better. Non-stop, almost every night and all weekend. Teacher Bonn has dumped her boyfriend and moved in with Bonnie. They are together but independent. They make love to each other, have threesomes, and have their own little flings with others. Bonnie's parents go up to NY every other weekend. They have a threesome there with Sherry and others. Dr. E. is screwing teacher Bonn almost every night. Apparently, he has a very large penis, and she loves to ride it. They all swap around and do threesomes, foursomes, and more. It is one continuous sex party. They spend most of their time running around the house nude. Their clothes spend more time on the floor than they do on their bodies. Teacher Bonn has called JJ several times trying to talk him into coming up on the weekend to do her and Bonnie. So far, JJ has remained at home, but the temptation is weighing heavily, and he wants to go! All he can think about is the great oral sex.

Back to more sane people. Martin is at the navy flight training station and is doing well. He is competing for the Top Gun position in his class, but he is also dealing with the fact that he is the only black person in the class. Some of the classmates are from the Deep South, and they strongly dislike black people, and they make it known that they don't believe that he should be there! Martin has found notes on his bunk saying, "Black people are too dumb to fly jet planes!" But Martin outperforms the others, so he sets the pace for the class, and they cannot deny his abilities.

Meanwhile, Delores has begun her law classes and has joined a local civil rights group. She is new and "very green" to many of the issues, but she is a quick learner, and they are sending her to several of the so-called hot spots to train her as to what to expect. One of her first assignments was working with a group of lawyers who were trying to get Martin Luther King and a group of marchers out of jail. That was a real eye-opener for her, and she is truly hooked on the movement. She may become one of the marchers who is put in jail, but that's okay with her.

Mr. Roy has been promoted to supervisor at his work, and this means a 5000 dollar increase in his pay, so he is talking about buying a new car or another car for the family. Julie now has her driver's license and takes her bothers to all their events. Mrs. Connor now has a full-time job with the telephone company, which has also increased the family income. She and Mr. Roy still drink too much and are always fighting about something. The two brothers are always finding odd jobs to keep them in money.

JJ's world seems to be settling down, but he is still is uncertain about his future. He thinks that if Julie goes to New York to become a Rockette, their relationship will end, and he has never thought about life without Julie. So, while life seems to have improved, he certainly is not happy. What does life have in store for him?

Printed in the United States
By Bookmasters